I0822151

OUT OF THE FIRE

B. A. COLELLA

Out of the Fire

Written and Published by B.A. Colella

www.bacolella.com

First edition. November, 2023. Pittsburgh, Pennsylvania

Identifiers: ISBN 979-8-9877550-1-3 (Paperback).
ISBN 979-8-9877550-2-0 (Hardcover).
ISBN 979-8-9877550-3-7 (Ebook).
Library of Congress Control Number: 2023918059

Subjects: FICTION / Action & Adventure. FICTION / Thrillers. FICTION / Disaster

Editing by West of Mars
Cover design by TWL Studios
Interior design by Cissell Ink
Proofreading by Clio Editing Services

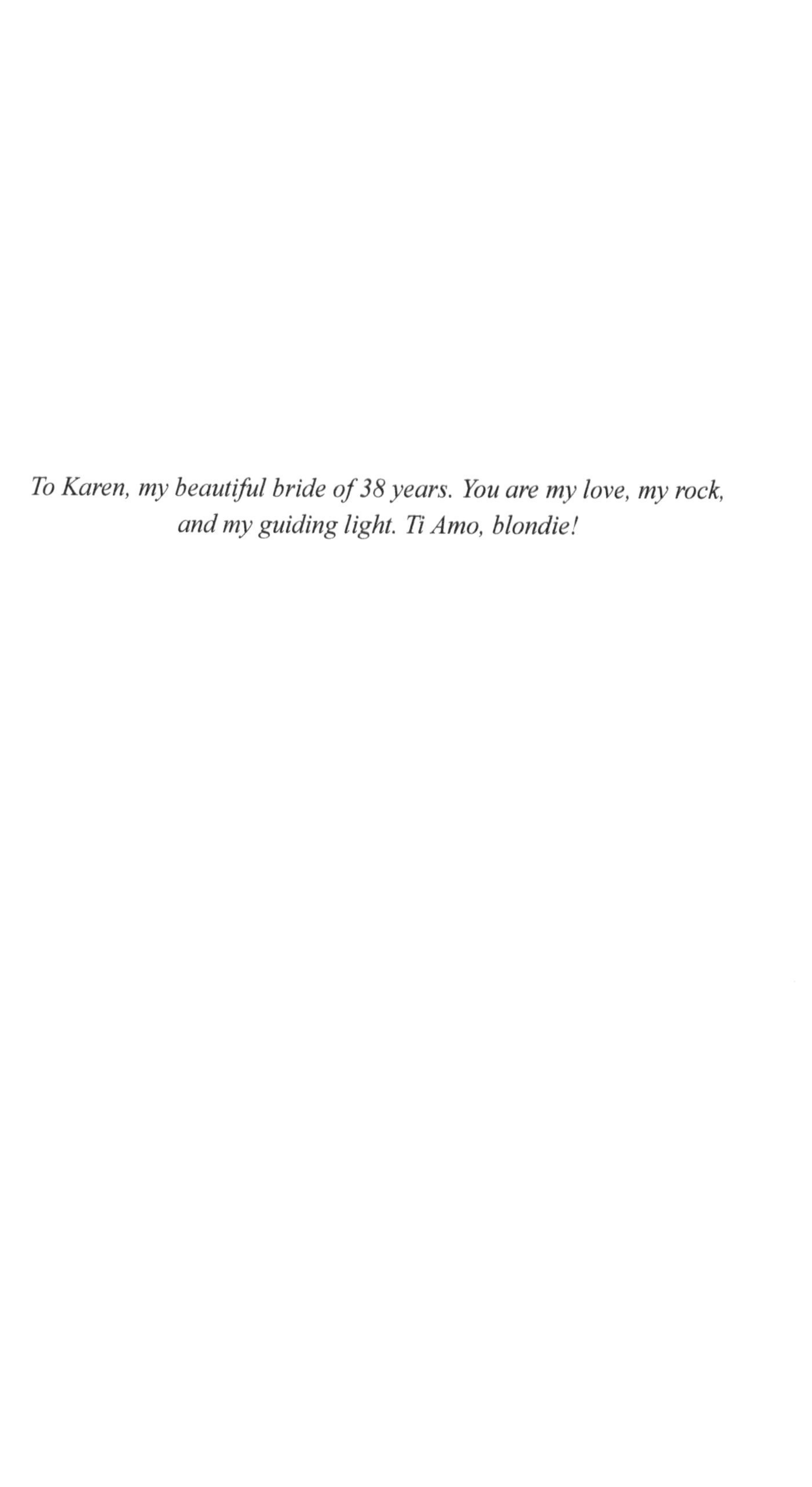

To Karen, my beautiful bride of 38 years. You are my love, my rock, and my guiding light. Ti Amo, blondie!

Part I

OPENING MOVES

ONE

Thursday, August 4

Thick plumes of black smoke billowed into a cloudless blue sky, fifty feet above the steaming fuselage.

Tony Moretti, in the lead position of the three-person hose team, gripped the nozzle against his chest as the afternoon's last training evolution commenced. The revving engines of two flanking crash trucks rose to a crescendo as hundreds of gallons of water from their roof turrets washed over his head, enveloping the aircraft simulator in mist and soaking his turnout gear with overspray. The edges of his facepiece bit into his skin, soot stung his eyes, and his shoulders sagged from the weight of the air cylinder. As the scene dissolved into an unfocused blur, he ran a gloved hand over his fogged-up visor, but it was futile.

He'd performed well in his other two training scenarios, but only in supporting roles. This was his chance to show what he could do, and much depended on his next actions. He needed the approval of the fire academy staff, and his colleagues, to gain admittance to the firefighting fraternity, perhaps his last shot at a stable career. And he didn't dare let Lisa down…not after what he'd put her through during the past fifteen years. His Personal Alert Safety System chirped a warning and he shook the chest gauge of his breathing apparatus to silence the high-pitched tones.

Tony's radio squawked. "Attack teams from command, get ready," Lieutenant Carl Abington ordered.

He inclined his head and keyed his lapel mic. "Attack-1 copies." He turned to his crew. "Go on air!"

Tony caught a whiff of propane as he removed the lung demand valve from his waistbelt, snapped it into the receptacle on his facepiece, and took a deep breath. Cool air washed across his face and he drew it deep into his lungs. His vision cleared. That was better.

"All units from command. Rescue-21 is shutting down," Abington radioed. "Attack-1, move in. Attack-2, back them up." Despite the background noise, the LT's baritone boomed over the airwaves. "Rescue-22, give them a wide covering fog."

That was the signal. Time for the ground teams to take over the fight. Tony tensed; trepidation roiled his stomach. Then doubt overtook him and he hesitated.

The radio crackled. "Get that line moving, Moretti!"

The spreading fire, given a reprieve when the turret from Rescue-21 shut down, rose in a solid wall of flame and licked the underside of the wing. How could he keep those flames away from the fuselage? *Focus*, he told himself. *I can do this.*

"Let's go, Tony!" urged Robbie Stegler, the hose team's backup.

Blistering heat penetrated Tony's gear as he waved an arm toward the plane and led the trio into the inferno. He grasped the bale of the nozzle; he wanted to move the metal handle to the open position, but not yet. *Wait for the order.*

"Attack-1 from command. Hit that fire. Narrow pattern."

Tony yanked back on the bale and staggered into Robbie as sudden pressure from the stream forced him backward. Grunting, he regained his footing and swung the hoseline left to right and back again. The water spray provided some protection from the heat, but not enough. He was standing in the middle of a blast furnace.

"Attack-2 from command. Move up and cover Attack-1."

"Hit the base of the fire, Tony! The base," Robbie shouted.

Tony aimed the nozzle down. The backs of his gloved hands began to tingle. Waves of radiant heat danced across the wing.

"Attack-1 from command. Get some water on that fuselage!"

Tony elevated the nozzle and swung it toward the plane. Clouds of steam formed as cold water collided with hot metal. He swept the stream fore and aft along the fuselage. The superheated skin sizzled while the flames rolled toward the hose team.

Robbie urged him forward. "It's blackened down. We can get through it. Move in."

Move in? A no-risk suggestion while Tony's six-foot-three, 210-pound frame shielded his partner from the heat. Before he could respond, a watery jet knocked him sideways. Firefighters from Attack-2 were moving up and directing their stream over and around their struggling colleagues.

"Knock that fire down, Moretti!" The lieutenant's command was personal. A direct challenge to Tony's competence.

"Let's move!" Tony said. He had the training; he could do this. *Stay calm.* He took a deep breath, leaned forward, and closed with the main body of the fire. Attack-2 drew even with Attack-1 and the flames sputtered as three hundred gallons per minute from two overlapping hoselines took effect. The heat subsided. He let out a breath. It was tolerable again.

Abington issued a fresh set of commands. "Attack-1, get that line into the plane. Use the overwing hatch. Search-1, ladder the wing and follow them. Attack-2, watch their backs." The orders were clear and concise, short phrases with no unnecessary words. The LT was a pro.

"Command from Search-1. We're moving in now."

Dave Jarvis, carrying a sixteen-foot ladder along the skin of the aircraft, led the two-person search team into the hot zone while Tony extinguished the spotty flames in their path.

Search-1 reached the leading edge of the wing, stuck the feet of the ladder into the gravel, pivoted ninety degrees, and lowered the beam against the steaming metal edge. Jarvis heeled the ladder and shouted to Tony, "You're good to go."

With Attack-2 covering their approach, Tony pushed the bale

forward to stop the water flow and strode to the ladder. Infused with energy and determined to get the job done, he clamped the hose in his armpit, climbed to the wing, stomped his right foot three times to test its viability, and stepped onto the leading edge. "It's solid," he shouted.

Robbie climbed up to join him, followed by the search team with their forcible entry tools and hand lights.

At the overwing hatch, Tony dropped the line and grabbed the exterior release lever. Heat shot through his gloves. "Damn! It's too hot; I can't get it open."

"Hold on." Robbie scooped the nozzle and doused the hatch with a burst of water. Steam rose from the hot metal. "Try it now."

Tony grabbed the handle again. Still too hot. No matter. He spun it clockwise. It moved halfway and stopped. He tried again. It wouldn't budge. "Come on!"

"Wait!" Jarvis came up with a raised Halligan tool and hammered the twenty-pound bar onto the lever. It moved. He hit it again. The lever spun free and the hatch fell onto the seats.

Tony reached through the open wing exit, grabbed it, and angled it out of the plane. He groaned as the hot metal reacted with his sweaty palms. The hatch slipped from his grasp, hit the wing, and slid off the slick trailing edge.

"Get in there, Moretti!" Jarvis said as black smoke found the opening and poured from the cabin. "Stop fucking around or I'll take that damn line myself."

Tony ignored him.

"Show them how it's done," Robbie said as he tossed the nozzle to Tony.

"Okay. Stay close." He crouched and stepped cautiously into the wing hatch, testing to make sure the floor was still intact. He glanced toward the cockpit and spotted a dull red glow. "The fire is forward." He was on his own. Robbie couldn't help him in the tight cabin.

"Command from Attack-1," Robbie reported. "We're entering the aircraft. Search-1 is right behind us."

Engulfed in darkness, Tony positioned the rigid hose in his outstretched arms and duck-walked his way toward the flight deck.

Airplane aisles weren't designed for firefighters in bulky turnout gear. His back spasmed but he gritted his teeth and moved on. He passed the first three rows but spotted no victims. Irrelevant. His job was the fire.

The orange glow intensified as he advanced. No one up front would have survived in such conditions, but passengers in the back might. Press the attack. Give the search team a fighting chance.

"Attack-1 from command. Status report."

Robbie answered the LT's query. "We have fire in the main cabin, forward of the wing hatch. Making our attack now."

Tony couldn't see Robbie through the smoke but knew his partner was feeding the hose forward. Flames migrated toward him and heat stung his ears. He hoped his Nomex hood was still tight against his facepiece. Going home with burns on his face would do little to reassure his wife that firefighting was the occupation for him. He dropped a knee to the floor and allowed his training to take over. He grabbed the rubber bumper, spun it clockwise to set a concentrated pattern, and opened the nozzle. One hundred fifty gallons per minute penetrated the gloom and met the approaching flames. It worked; the fire subsided and the cabin grew quiet.

Was the fire out? Calf muscles burning, he got to his feet.

Robbie came up behind him. "Sweet! Let's get into the cockpit and finish this thing."

Tony closed the bale halfway and stepped forward, then stopped as he spotted yellow flickers. A wall of flames erupted and swept into him. His mind raced. Use the line as a shield. He spun the bumper counterclockwise and the pattern spread wide. Confined by the cabin, thousands of tiny droplets converted to steam. The fire's thermal column became unbalanced, sending ferocious heat toward the floor.

"It's flashing over!" Robbie's words were barely audible over the crackle of the fire and the whoosh of the superheated air as the flames sought the aircraft's only exit, the wing hatch behind them.

The next seconds passed in a blur. A wall of flames tore through the aircraft. Searing heat sliced through Tony's turnout gear. A thousand bees stung his face and ears. The hoseline escaped his grip and he dropped to his stomach. "I lost it...can't reach it."

The uncontrolled hose, still discharging, whipped up and down. The nozzle struck Tony's back, then bounced off his helmet. Dizziness blurred his vision.

"Oooommph." A body fell on top of him. Robbie.

The blow knocked the wind out of Tony and dislodged his facepiece. Precious air hissed out and smoke entered through the broken seal. His PASS alarm chirped its warning, but he couldn't move his body to silence it.

"I've got you," Robbie said. "Oh, shit…can't grab the…aah."

His partner was taking a beating from the bucking nozzle, but Tony, with Robbie's weight pinning him to the floor, was helpless to intervene.

Robbie's weight pinned Tony to the floor. Body immobilized, he couldn't breathe. The PASS device leapt into a sustained, high-pitched warble. Panic gripped him.

A garbled transmission: "Rescue…thir…shut d…"

The flames petered out and the hose went limp.

"Command from Instructor-2. That was me on the emergency stop button. I've terminated the evolution and I'm venting now."

The floor vibrated as the roar of powerful fans filled the cabin. A stream of cool air replaced the steam. Robbie's weight was gone. Tony took a deep breath as sweat poured off his face. A hand reached down, reset his LDV, and silenced the screeching alarm.

"Hold on; I've got you," a voice said.

Tony strained to look up. Evan O'Brien stood over him. The fire academy instructor had operated the control pendant to cut off the gas-fed flames and bring the training scenario to an abrupt end. In less than a minute, the fuselage of the simulator cleared.

"You guys can get up," Evan said.

Tony rose to his knees and Evan hoisted him to his feet. His anxiety eased, but a new fear arose; repercussions were sure to follow. The last scenario of the day and he'd screwed it up. He wanted to crawl away.

"Nice work, Moretti. I'd say we'd all be dead just about now." Jarvis again.

Tony removed his dangling facepiece, reached back to close the cylinder handwheel, and headed for the forward door.

"Hey!" Jarvis called. "I'm talking to you. That nozzle could have killed someone."

Tony met the man's vindictive glare. Anger rose, but a deep shame tempered it and he had nothing to say.

"Do you hear me? I said you could've killed someone. Maybe me. I feel like a lobster because you couldn't put out the fucking fire." He spat into one of the metal seats.

"I'm…I'm really sorry, Dave. I thought I could—"

"You thought what, you dumbass? I've had it with your screwups. We all end up paying for them. I swear if you do anything like that again…"

"Okay, boys. That's enough," Evan said.

"Thanks, Instructor O'Brien," Tony said. "Sorry about the evolution."

"We'll talk about it later." O'Brien spoke in the cool, matter-of-fact tone of one who'd seen this situation a hundred times before. "How about you, Stegler? Going to live?"

"Yeah, Instructor O'Brien," Robbie said. "I'll be fine. My back is a little sore."

"I bet it is. Get over to the pavilion and let the EMTs take a look."

"What about *your* team, Jarvis? You guys both okay?"

"Oh, we're just fine. We couldn't finish our search, but we did rescue these two *professional* firefighters here."

Tony knew who the biting sarcasm was intended for, and his shame increased.

"Save the commentary for the hot wash," O'Brien said. "It's almost two-thirty and the after-action review with Lieutenant Abington starts promptly at four. I'm sure you guys want to get out of here on time."

"You got that right, Instructor O'Brien," Jarvis said. "You're the boss."

"I want all of you to hydrate before we clean up the field," O'Brien said. "You know the drill. Get yourselves and your equipment outside. Remove your gear; head to the garage or relax in the shade. Once you're out of rehab, roll up the hoselines, clean up the rest of your equipment, and wash your bunker clothes."

With that, the final training evolution of Reynolds International Airport's firefighter recruit class ended. Tony sat under a pin oak tree with his eyes closed during the half-hour rehab period. When his seven fellow students began to police the grounds, he worked alongside them without speaking. Nor did he make eye contact with anyone. An hour later, when Lieutenant Abington gathered everyone in the garage for a final debrief, he stood alone in the back.

After showering and changing into shorts and a t-shirt, he remained in the locker room after the other recruits departed. The place smelled of sweat and dirty socks. He hadn't moved from the hard wooden bench in twenty minutes. Or was it thirty? Who knew? He was so angry with himself, he couldn't think straight. Damn. He had thought he was ready. He knew what he had to do. He'd been determined to do it, and yet he'd failed. *What will Lisa think about today's fiasco?*

The longer he sat, the more frustrated he became. Firefighting came so easily to everyone else in his academy class. Almost like second nature. No one had his problems. His classmates were prototypical badass firefighters. And he knew they looked down on him.

"You still here?" Evan O'Brien asked.

Tony hadn't heard him enter the locker room.

"It's almost five-thirty and I'd like to vamoose."

"Sorry, Instructor O'Brien. I'll be out of here in five minutes."

"Call me Evan. Your academy days are over. And don't be so glum."

"Hard not to be. I seem to be the biggest screwup around."

"Oh no. I've seen far more impressive screwups." He laughed. "You're not even close."

Tony welcomed the show of empathy and forced a smile. Evan was a good guy. Tall and athletic, he was a pure Irishman with a shock of wavy red hair that was never under control. A fifteen-year firefighter and an instructor second only to Lieutenant Abington at the academy, Evan was also number one on the promotional list for lieutenant. He specialized in ARFF operations and tactics, and his enthusiasm for his work was infectious. He was, in Tony's opinion, the finest teacher in the department.

"This is a complex job. It'll take longer than four months for you to master it. Keep working and you'll get better. Now get going; I'm meeting the wife for dinner. She got a sitter for the kids and I'll be in big trouble if I don't get there on time. Besides, you have a graduation ceremony to get ready for. Make sure you're here *early* tomorrow. You guys are the setup crew."

"Sounds good. I've got to pick Lisa up from work. Her Civic is in the shop."

As he left the academy, Tony felt a little better. Maybe he *was* being too hard on himself, but while he hadn't yet processed the four months of training he'd endured, he knew he had to pick up his game, and fast.

TWO

Thursday, August 4

Tony arrived at the Western Maryland Medical Center after the forty-five-minute drive from the academy. Lisa's twelve-hour shift had ended at seven, but she never got out on time. Tonight was no exception.

As he exited the elevator to the third-floor oncology wing, the smell of disinfectant hit him. Tony hated hospitals and had ever since he was eleven, when his parents had taken him to say goodbye to his grandfather, who'd suffered a stroke three days prior. The pale, slack-jawed figure Tony saw that day bore little resemblance to the vibrant, fun-loving man who'd run, played, and roughhoused with him only weeks before.

Tony was proud of his wife but couldn't fathom her work world. Lisa, who had begun her career as an emergency room nurse, had switched to oncology five years ago. She said she needed an environment where she could get to know the patients and their families. She wanted to have a stake in the outcome of their long-term care, unlike in the ER, where the mantra was "treat 'em and street 'em, transfer them to other units, or pronounce them dead." Tony discovered she'd been right. Lisa was a natural at providing care to the cancer patients, many of whom returned for periodic treatment. And she was adept at providing support and comfort to their families. But there was also a cost, as she and her colleagues attended many funerals and shed buckets of tears for people with whom they'd become close.

Lisa stood alone at the nurses' station. She'd landed the job at the center shortly after the move from Pittsburgh in March, and she'd already been given supervisory responsibilities as an acting charge nurse.

Tony came up behind her, slid his arms around her waist, and gave her a hug. "How's my favorite nurse?"

She spun around. Her green eyes widened, and a big smile lit up her face. "Tony! Why didn't you call? I've been thinking about you all day." She paused and looked into his eyes. "Well? How did it go? Are you official?"

"I'm officially done with the academy, if that's what you mean. I won't be a full-fledged firefighter until my probation ends next April."

Lisa wasn't having it. "Four months of training over with. I'm so proud of you." Then a familiar look of worry crossed her face. "But you don't seem too happy about it."

"It wasn't a command performance."

She lowered her voice. "What happened?"

"I made a mess of the final evolution and I almost killed Robbie, but otherwise, no problems."

Lisa's features softened. "Oh, you're always so hard on yourself. I'm sure it wasn't that bad."

"It *was* that bad, and I was worse."

She smiled and stroked his shoulders. "Well, I'm not worried. This was all brand-new to you a few months ago. Look how far you've come. Give yourself a break, for goodness' sake, and some credit for what you've accomplished."

Lisa smiled, but her face held an expression he knew well, the one she'd used every time he'd started a new job. An expression of hope tinged with doubt. His stomach twisted as he recalled how he'd let her down so many times before. He had to assure her he could succeed this time, that everything would be okay.

"Yeah, I guess you're right," he said and kissed her on the

forehead. “Lieutenant Abington was a little harsh during our critique, but Evan O’Brien said I did very well. And I *am* graduating from the academy tomorrow, so I must’ve done something right.”

Lisa’s eyes brightened as she looked up at him. “I know you, Anthony Moretti, and I know you did a lot more right than wrong.”

He looked into those eyes. She was *willing* it to be so, and it tore at his psyche. “Anyway, that’s enough about my day. How are you doing, my girl?”

“One of my nurses called off ten minutes before her shift and I couldn’t find anyone to replace her, so guess who got her assignment.” She sighed. “I’m way behind on my paperwork and my feet are killing me.” On cue, a call bell rang. She sighed. “So, you know, just another day in paradise.”

“And you love every minute.” Even when she didn’t love it, she thrived on it. But this little unit was a far cry from the big oncology floor she had managed in Pittsburgh.

Her smile returned. “Give me ten minutes to check this out so we can get out of here and celebrate. I’ll worry about the paperwork later.” She gave him a quick kiss.

“Hey, none of that, you two. This is a respectable hospital.” Angela Morgan approached from the stairwell across the hall. One of the more experienced nurses, Angela had escorted Lisa around the Southern Pennsylvania–Northern Maryland area shortly after the move from home, and the two had become fast friends. With a booming voice, jet-black hair, and a frame that almost equaled Tony’s in height and weight, Angela presented a comical contrast to Lisa, a fair, smooth-skinned dirty blonde with a five-foot-three, 130-pound stature and quiet persona.

“Stuck with the overnight shift again?” he asked.

“Oh, I’m stuck all right. Stuck with sleeping patients, no obnoxious families, and no arrogant, pimple-faced residents.” She winked. “How’s our big strapping firefighter?”

“Still standing, Angie. The toughest part is over.”

Angry voices erupted from a room down the hall. A young girl in purple scrubs, one of the nurse aides, rushed out of the room.

"It's Frannie," the girl said with exasperation. "She's arguing with Mrs. Clawson again."

"Damn it," Angela said. "I'll deal with her. Why don't you guys go home?"

"Nope," Lisa said. "I've got it." She turned to Tony. "Sorry, hon. I won't be long."

Tony shared a knowing look with Angela as Lisa headed for the trouble.

"Your wife is really something," Angela said.

He knew it. *My wife is a rock star.*

* * *

The townhouse was a rental, but it was spacious, and they'd been lucky to find it. South central Pennsylvania wasn't exactly awash in modern rental units, and the new place featured two floors and accommodated all of their furniture. The price they'd received from the sale of their modest three-bedroom house in Pittsburgh's North Hills gave them enough cushion to afford a year's worth of rent while socking away a sizable nest egg in an S&P 500 index fund.

They'd kicked around the idea of taking their windfall and buying, but Tony's probationary salary was modest and Lisa's new job paid about half of what she had been making. Tony's radical change in occupations, along with his history of job changes, also gave them pause. They decided it best to rent for a year or two while they settled into their jobs and got a feel for the area. The townhouse was a twenty-minute drive to Lisa's job in Maryland and only ten minutes to the airport fire station. While the couple preferred an urban environment, the transition was more difficult for Lisa, a city girl, than for Tony, who was raised in rural northwest Pennsylvania.

A sofa and love seat, two wingback chairs, and a coffee table faced a corner fireplace in their cozy living room. Three Thomas Kinkade prints adorned the mint green walls. Lisa was partial to them, and Tony had surprised her with one on successive birthdays until she thanked him for being so sweet but suggested he find new gift ideas.

But the place was a mess. Four months after their hurried move, unopened boxes still lined the walls of the family room and filled one of the two upstairs bedrooms. Lisa had started her new job at the medical center two days after they'd moved in, and Tony's academy training had started three days later. Life had been a whirlwind since. Lisa came home exhausted after her three twelve-hour and one eight-hour weekly shifts, and Tony felt the same after his physically intensive days at the fire academy, which often stretched into the early evening.

Tonight, they set aside the stress and anxiety and sat down to pizza and vino. Unlike most of their friends, Tony and Lisa were explorers, not beach people. With so much to see, their wanderlust—aided by Tony's four-year marketing gig—took them far afield. Wine aficionados, they vacationed in the Napa Valley every couple of years, and now they enjoyed a bottle of their favorite red, Sattui Vineyards Russian River Zinfandel.

"Great wine choice, hon," Lisa said. "Goes really well with the cardboard stuck to my pizza."

"It's all about living the high life, my dear." He paused. "But I'm sorry we won't be able to take a real vacation until I'm off of this crappy probationary salary."

"Or mine," Lisa said with a hint of bitterness in her tone.

"But we might be able to get back home for Christmas."

"Might?" Now the bitterness morphed to disappointment.

"I'm sure we can. I just have to finagle a few schedule trades. I hear everybody does it."

Lisa looked doubtful but softened. "It's okay. The vineyards of Napa will still be there when we're ready, and if we can't get home for the holidays, our folks will visit us."

The tension eased and Tony's mood improved as the evening wore on. He felt relieved. He'd passed his first hurdle—the biggest one, he supposed. And for the first time since graduating with bachelor's and master's degrees, he was in an occupation that promised long-term stability, steady pay increases, and opportunities for advancement.

While he had never envisioned a blue-collar life, maybe this *was* the job he'd been searching for. At thirty-seven, he wouldn't have many more chances. It would be a godsend if firefighting worked out.

THREE

Friday, August 5

The graduation ceremony heralded the beginning of a less-structured on-the-job training program for the rookies. Their performance over the next eight months—under the close supervision of platoon officers—would determine if the rookies would survive their one-year probationary period and become full-fledged firefighters. Until then, none of their jobs were secure.

The newbies sweated through a steamy morning as they readied the grounds for inspection by family and friends. They spruced up the drill field, washed and waxed the academy's two crash trucks, and hosed out the aircraft simulator. The exterior was made of COR-TEN and therefore didn't need anything. The specialty steel resisted the corrosive effects of rain and snow by forming a protective layer of dark brown oxidation that gave it a perpetually rusty appearance. It reminded Tony of the US Steel Tower, where he had worked as a new college graduate. That building stood out as the best example of the product's durability.

After lunch, they moved inside, where they cleaned the reception area, conference room, simulator control center, classrooms, gear storage area, restrooms, and garage. The astringent smell of cleaning fluid stung Tony's nostrils as he wiped down every window in the building.

At three-thirty, Lieutenant Abington pronounced the facility ready, and the recruits showered and dressed in their new Class A uniforms.

By five o'clock, the sixty-odd chairs in the large classroom were full. Fire Chief Douglas Archer stepped to the podium and quieted the noisy crowd with a warm welcome to an event steeped in fire service tradition.

Visitors included the lieutenant governor, local elected officials, and representatives of regional emergency services agencies. Managers from each airport department stood along the walls, while family and friends of the graduating firefighters filled the seats. Although the air-conditioning was set to maximum, the overcrowded room stood at eighty-one degrees.

At 5:10, the distinct tones of a wall-mounted antique brass bell rang out eight times as the new firefighters marched in. Dressed in crisp white shirts, navy pants, black ties, gold name tags, airport lapel pins, and time-honored round firefighter's caps, they took their designated seats in the front row.

Chief Archer welcomed the recruits into the public safety fraternity, emphasized their significance to the safety of the airport, and thanked the gathered friends and family for the support they'd provided. Then he paused, beamed at the new firefighters, and said, "Each one of you should be proud of what you've accomplished. You rose to the challenge of a stressful and demanding curriculum that tested the limits of your physical and mental endurance. My officers and I look forward to seeing what you can do once you join your platoons. Congratulations and good luck."

Airport CEO Sterling Price, a graying fifty-something with a narrow face and chalky complexion, spoke next. Wearing a black pinstripe suit and wire-rimmed glasses, he spoke from prepared notes as he recounted the airport's history.

"Reynolds International is unique among airports anywhere in the United States. A creation of perceived necessity, blending a fortuitous set of circumstances and opportunistic risk-taking. It's the story of an old Cold War–era Air Force base that was slated for elimination by the Base Realignment and Closure Commission. Faced with a devastating economic loss to the region, Pennsylvania's congressional representatives, state legislators, and local leaders worked in concert to craft a plan to repurpose the facilities as a commercial airport."

Mr. Price explained the airport sat in the perfect geographical location to relieve regional airport congestion by absorbing some of the traffic from Reagan and Dulles, and other big airports like Philadelphia, Pittsburgh, and Baltimore-Washington, all of which were operating at or near capacity.

Tony sighed. The CEO lectured like his annoying World History 101 professor from freshman year at Pitt.

"Beyond merely reducing congestion, these forward-thinking officials and community leaders envisioned a true midsized airport that would serve as an attractive alternative for small and start-up airlines serving East Coast and mid-Atlantic routes." He paused and scanned the crowd. "A deal was brokered to take over the entire air base and operate it as an independent entity governed by an appointed board of directors, many of whom are present today."

Tony fidgeted. Enough pandering to the politicians. Wasn't this event about the recruits?

The CEO continued, "As a bonus, the Air Force agreed to keep their base open, converting it to a wing of the Pennsylvania Air National Guard. The Commonwealth and the authority offered to pay the lion's share of expenses for a decade of upkeep on key base facilities, including the hangars and maintenance plants." He smiled. "Those financial incentives turned out to be an offer the federal government couldn't refuse, and the newly christened South-Central Pennsylvania Airport Authority assumed control of the property."

The CEO glanced around the room again. "The three decades since have seen construction of new landside and airside terminals connected by an aboveground monorail, expansion and renovation of our aircraft hangars, and development of a modern cargo facility. The Federal Aviation Administration did their part by erecting a state-of-the-art control tower and providing the funds for this aircraft rescue training academy." Sweeping his arm in front of the seated recruits, he said, "And this is the airport these young firefighters are charged to protect." Mr. Price set his notes down. Audible sighs issued from the crowd.

Charged to protect? *Who talks like that?*

The Pennsylvania state fire commissioner delivered the keynote address. Unlike Mr. Price, she focused her comments on the new firefighters as she delivered a fiery oration about the challenges facing today's emergency responders as they carried out their critical role of protecting the public in the twenty-first century. "You've been trained to face dangers, overcome obstacles, and look out for one another." She paused and looked each firefighter in the eye. "But remember, your journey is just beginning." She exhorted them to learn something new every day, to put forth their best efforts to protect the traveling public, and to "uphold the rich traditions of the fire service." She ended with, "I wish you the very best in your new careers."

Tony smiled. *That* was an inspiring speech.

Chief Archer stood and summoned the recruits forward, where he administered the oath of office. Tony smiled when he spotted Lisa in the middle of the crowd. As Lieutenant Abington rang the bell, the chief moved across the line of recruits, pinning each with a silver fire department badge.

The chief turned to the assembly. "Ladies and gentlemen, please join me in congratulating our graduating class."

The room erupted in applause. Family and friends came forward to mob the graduates. Tony laughed as a plump woman rushed up to wiry, sandy-haired little Robbie, swallowed him in her arms, and kissed him smack on the lips. "Aww, Mom, you're embarrassing me," a red-faced Robbie protested as he tried to break free.

Lisa weaved her way through the crowd, put her arms on Tony's shoulders, and gave him a smile that lit up her face. "I'm so proud of you! I can't imagine what they put you through, but I knew you could do it."

"It'll take more than a shiny badge to make you a firefighter."

Tony turned and faced Dave Jarvis.

"You really think you'll make it through probation?" Jarvis

smirked. "You're no firefighter, and you ain't gonna be one in eight months. Why don't you do us all a favor and quit now, before you get fired…or get one of us killed."

Lisa scowled. Robbie's mouth dropped open.

Heat rose on Tony's face. Jarvis, a stocky thirty-eight-year-old with a weather-beaten face and a receding black hairline he tried to hide with an unconvincing combover, saved thirty-seven-year-old Tony from the distinction of being the oldest recruit in their class. The irascible Jarvis compensated by citing fifteen years of unspecified fire service experience ad nauseam, taking every opportunity to beat Tony over the head with it. He reminded Tony of the pint-sized kids in elementary school who tried to prove themselves by picking fights with their bigger classmates. Tony had never taken the bait back then, and he didn't oblige Jarvis now.

"Knock it off, Jarvis," Lieutenant Abington said as he joined the group. Lowering his voice, he said, "This is a big event for the airport. You're not going to ruin it."

"Yes, sir," Jarvis said and raised his hand in mock salute to the stocky LT.

"Sorry, folks," Abington said. "Ignore him."

"Come on," Robbie said. "Let's get something to eat, and then we can show our families around that torture chamber they call an aircraft simulator."

Tony escorted Lisa on an abbreviated tour but said little. Jarvis's words had crushed his spirit, as did the reality of what lay ahead.

FOUR

Monday, August 8

"Morning, Tony!" Robbie said as he leaned on the hood of his old Ford pickup in the airport fire station's parking lot. His turnout gear sat in a rumpled pile on the asphalt. "I thought we should go in together."

"Christ, Robbie. It's only ten after six; how long have you been here?" Tony asked as he pulled his gear bag out of his Jeep Cherokee.

"Been up since four-thirty; couldn't sleep. I've been waiting awhile."

Tony laughed. "You're something else. Do you know how many times I woke up that early…in my entire life? Maybe twice, and only because I hadn't gone to bed yet."

"Oh, right. This sucks," Robbie said. "I already miss our eight-thirty academy mornings."

"Bullshit. You can't wait to get in there, you swine." Tony shook his head. Youthful enthusiasm. Robbie was still on cloud nine from Friday's graduation ceremony. Hell, he'd been amped up since the first day of training in April. Every classroom session and practical evolution was an adventure for him. Even the last one, where Tony had almost gotten him maimed.

Tony envied his young friend's attitude, but he didn't share it. For

Robbie, a kid three years out of high school, this was a dream come true. The son of a volunteer fire chief, he'd joined his father's department as a junior member at sixteen. For Tony, firefighting was merely another in a long string of jobs. While his college friends were steadily progressing in their careers, Tony was starting at the bottom… again.

"A new day with a new challenge," Robbie said as the pair approached the entrance to the station.

"Where'd you get that one? On some motivational poster in high school?"

"Nope, my mom. Every morning when she got me up for school." Robbie pushed the intercom button.

A beep and a low static hiss issued from the speaker.

"Good morning. Stegler and Moretti, here for the A-platoon shift."

Tony grimaced. Why else would they be here at 6:15 a.m. in brand-new uniforms? Firefighters were no doubt standing at the monitor, laughing at the newbies.

"Hold up your IDs for the camera," a flat voice replied.

Tony pulled the department-issued ID from his pants pocket while Robbie unclipped his from the right epaulet of his cobalt-blue uniform shirt. They aimed them at the camera above the door.

"Stand by. The lieutenant will be out to get you."

A terse reply. Tony frowned. Good morning to you too.

"You know, this place doesn't look like a fire station at all," Robbie said. "It should have red bricks and a peaked roof and a hose tower. And a second floor with bunkrooms."

"Don't forget a shiny pole to slide down when the alarms come in, and a loft with some hay for the horses."

"Asswipe," Robbie replied and gave Tony a playful shove.

Tony laughed as he scanned the sterile one-story building. Gray cinderblock walls topped with a metal mansard-style roof, painted forest green.

"You're an American romantic, Robbie. I can see you in the middle of a Norman Rockwell painting."

"Huh?"

"Never mind. Here comes the LT."

Lieutenant Phil Wozniak, a short, muscular man with a friendly face, greeted them at the door and checked their IDs. He explained their day would begin with a visit to the platoon office for a meeting with the captain, followed by introductions to the other crew members.

During training, they had been given a series of glorified tours and a full twenty-four-hour shift—the first sleepover, they'd joked—so Tony and Robbie were somewhat acclimated to the daily routines of the fire department. But today's visit wasn't for a couple of hours, or a day. This was *it*. For the rest of their careers. Tony wondered how long his would last.

"Things are quiet now, but it'll get busy around here in about twenty minutes," the lieutenant said as he led them across the apparatus bays.

All ten drive-through garage doors were open on this warm and sunny morning, and the department's apparatus created a tight fit. Four airport crash trucks and the department's ladder tower fronted the bays, a mere two hundred feet from the taxiway, while a mix of structural equipment faced the back gate.

The serenity ended abruptly as an American Airlines A321 taxied past the station's front pad, its engines muting the conversation. A warm breeze blew the odor of jet fuel into the open garage.

"This is so cool," Robbie shouted over the noise of the airliner.

Tony agreed with his friend on this one. Very cool indeed.

The captain was on his phone when they arrived, so Tony and Robbie remained standing. A trim figure with an improbably full face, he looked to be in his mid to late forties, with bushy brown hair. He sported a deep tan that contrasted with his spotless white shirt. Fluorescent light beamed off his gold badge and name tag. Twin fire service horns on his right lapel denoted his rank.

The captain sat behind a tidy gray metal desk at the back of the rectangular office. The LT took a seat at an identical desk, this one littered with papers and Post-it notes, which faced and abutted the captain's position. Each featured a large computer monitor and keyboard.

A row of file cabinets and a large metal bookcase lined a side wall, and a microwave rested atop a mini refrigerator in a corner behind the captain's desk. Three bulletin boards, a midsized LED television, and a weather radar display hung from the walls. A hodgepodge of photos depicting fire department activities and airport events sat on a shelf which ran the length of the back wall. A, B, and C platoon officers shared the space, which explained the absence of family photos or other personal memorabilia.

The captain ended his call, stood, and introduced himself. He was shorter than Tony, about five foot nine.

"Good morning, gentlemen. I'm Peter Schrum," the captain said in a husky voice, which stood in contrast to his soft-spoken lieutenant. He surveyed his new charges and continued. "I don't believe I've had the pleasure of meeting either of you, but I'm very happy to welcome you to our platoon."

The introduction was formal. Probably a military vet.

"Lieutenant Wozniak and I believe we run the finest platoon in the department. You probably met some of the crew during your station tours, but I don't think you spent your twenty-four-hour overnight with us, correct?"

"No, sir," Robbie said. "They sent us to B-platoon for our sleepover."

The captain raised a hand. "Please, don't call me sir. We may have some quasimilitary ways around here, and we do have quite a few veterans, but we don't do sir or ma'am. You can call me Captain Schrum or simply Cap." He looked at Robbie. "Now then, do you prefer Robert?" he asked.

"No, sir—I mean, no, Captain. Some people call me Rob, but I prefer Robbie."

"And I go by Tony."

"All right. Robbie and Tony it is."

Schrum gave them a quick overview of the platoon—one of three that rotated every twenty-four hours. "As I said, A-platoon is the best, but that distinction doesn't come without hard work and serious dedication, so you both have a lot to live up to.

"Aircraft Rescue Firefighting is unique, much unlike a municipal fire department. Our city comprises landside and airside terminals, runways and taxiways, aircraft hangars, maintenance facilities, the fuel farm, the FAA tower, the Air National Guard base, and the FBO, our Fixed Base Operator that handles private aircraft. The airport's two biggest hazards are airplanes and the Jet A that fuels them.

"Our citizens are the people who work here and the thousands of travelers who pass through this airport every day." The captain leaned forward. "You're now part of the select and highly specialized fraternity that protects them, the aircraft rescue and firefighting service. You've got to be ready for anything and everything. Your academy experience was important, but you've still got a lot to learn. It will take hard work and dedication, but I have no doubt you're both up to the task." He shook their hands again and turned them over to Lieutenant Wozniak.

The LT escorted them to the dayroom for the seven o'clock morning briefing. "We have the best captain, too. He's a lock to be the next chief officer. By the way," he said as they entered the dayroom, "you can call me LT or just Phil. It doesn't matter either way."

The room, painted a nondescript shade of beige, was noisy and smelled of strong coffee. Tony counted sixteen firefighters, including himself. Each platoon was staffed with sixteen firefighters and two officers, for an authorized maximum strength of eighteen per shift, and a minimum of ten. With the captain and lieutenant on duty, today amounted to a full house, which Tony had heard was a rare occurrence. Some of the crew lounged in recliners, watching the morning news. Others sat at the tables. Steelers and Ravens fans debated which team would win the AFC North. Tony hadn't expected such a lively bunch at this hour.

A couple of derisive comments about "the new guys" came across clearly. "Is that kid old enough to drive?" and "The college boy is probably too good to empty the garbage." Tony bit back a bristle. The comment reminded him of the hazing that was still allowed during his fraternity days. But mostly, he and Robbie were ignored, as if invisible.

Everyone sat up, the TV was switched off, and the room quieted when the captain and lieutenant entered. Tony was impressed. The briefing itself was uneventful. Captain Schrum discussed items of importance regarding the airport at large—the big picture, as he put it. He introduced Robbie and Tony as the newest members of the platoon, said he was happy to have them, and left the room.

Lieutenant Wozniak took over and read a list of the day's driver and rider vehicle assignments, training activities, construction inspections, fire prevention visits, and other department activities. The LT assigned Tony to Rescue-15, the fire department's pumper, and to Rescue-11, a three-thousand-gallon crash truck. "Let's get those vehicles checked," he instructed as he ended the briefing.

The needling picked up as the crew headed for their trucks: remarks about which of the restrooms the new guys should clean first. Tony considered it juvenile. Weren't these people supposed to be professionals? *Am I going to fit in here?*

Drivers inspected the primary control systems of their assigned vehicles and checked fluid levels, tire pressures, and dry chemical extinguishing agents. Rescue-15's driver engaged the fire pump, Rescue-16's operator raised, extended, and rotated the 105-foot ladder tower, and the drivers of each crash truck tested their roof and bumper turrets by flowing them briefly onto the pad.

Firefighters in riding positions inspected or operated each rig's portable equipment, including hoselines and nozzles, hydraulic spreaders and cutters, electrically operated smoke ejectors, portable lighting, gasoline-powered saws and blowers, and self-contained breathing apparatus, or SCBA.

Tony checked Rescue-11's portable tools and moved over to help with Rescue-15, which carried three times the portable equipment of a crash truck. He knew the routine. Recruits had followed the same procedures each morning at the academy, where the department's entire rolling stock had rotated through at least twice.

After truck checks, everyone gathered in the dayroom for breakfast. Tony and Robbie sat together. Rosie Ramsey, a big man in his forties whose name was actually Roosevelt, was the day's cook, which excused him from other morning details. The smell of bacon, eggs, and burned toast filled the air.

The room itself was an open-concept design, bisected into lounge and kitchen areas. Twelve La-Z-Boy-style recliners, in three rows of four, faced a seventy-inch HDTV. Pretty fancy. Five square tables, made of institutional-grade wood and arrayed in a rectangular pattern, filled the space behind the recliners. A very comfortable arrangement.

The kitchen sat in an alcove and featured three large side-by-side refrigerator-freezers, a spacious modern range with stainless-steel hood, a dishwasher, and an ice maker. Generous counter space included a big center island with a deep wide-bowl sink. Three floor-to-ceiling cabinets sat along the back wall. Each refrigerator and cabinet carried an A, B, or C platoon designation and was locked. Could there be food pilfering amongst the troops?

Breakfast was delicious, and Tony went back for seconds, reminding himself as he did that he'd have to watch his weight if he kept eating so much. Small groups clustered in casual conversation, but Tony and Robbie sat alone at a back table, their cloak of invisibility intact.

Tony staffed the fourth, or hydrant hookup, position on Rescue-15 as Lieutenant Wozniak led them on a series of construction inspections. At nine o'clock, they issued a permit for ironworkers to use an oxyacetylene torch to remove old piping from a pump station. Moving to the airside terminal, the crew stood by as airport carpenters used circular saws to cut through some old paneling. Rescue-15 concluded the morning tour by inspecting a construction site where contractors were replacing a slab of concrete on taxiway Yankee, and the crew was back at the station by noon. An uneventful morning with no rah-rah fire stuff. Nothing like the nonstop activity at the academy, but Tony was okay with that.

At one o'clock, Wozniak brought Tony and Robbie to the boss's office, where they stood at attention as the chief spoke on his desk phone.

Tony noted a stark contrast between the platoon officer's space and the chief's office. Douglas Archer's desk and chairs were of a stylish dark oak. Matching bookshelves held works on management theory, leadership, emergency planning, and firefighting strategy. Memorabilia —fire helmets, nozzles, and an antique fire alarm box—decorated the office. Photos of the chief's wife and three teenage children took pride of place on his credenza. A mounted ceremonial axe and several plaques denoting outstanding service and leadership lined the walls. The space spoke to a long and distinguished career.

A Marine veteran in his midfifties with chiseled features, the chief sat erect with his shoulders back in a military posture. His salt-and-pepper hair was neatly trimmed, and his arms sported colorful but faded tattoos that Tony couldn't quite make out. Souvenirs of his days in the military? His crisp white short-sleeved shirt, creased along its edges and adorned with the accoutrements of rank, featured a polished gold badge, name tag, and collar bugles. It was a bit too much for a fire chief, Tony mused as Archer concluded his call. The chief had visited the academy a handful of times to observe and speak to the recruits, but Tony had yet to gauge his personality.

Archer greeted Tony and Robbie with firm handshakes, congratulated them on their graduation, and asked after their families. He made small talk, cracked a couple of jokes, and gave the new firefighters a brief history of the department. The man was affable, in contrast to the image in Tony's mind.

The chief's features took on a serious look. "I expect dedication and hard work from everyone, but as probationary firefighters you are under a microscope. My officers and I will be watching closely over the next eight months, and it's up to you to prove that you can do this job, that you belong."

The chief's phone rang and he excused himself with a smile, leaving Tony with the impression of a man who cared about his firefighters, was very much in charge, and should not be taken lightly.

Airport familiarization comprised the day's training and began at one-thirty. Crews rotated through the airside and landside terminals, where they identified fire protection equipment and emergency egress routes and noted the layout and specific hazards of each retail store, restaurant, and airline office. By the time they arrived back at the station for dinner, Tony was thinking he'd stumbled upon a cushy job, surely one he'd have no trouble measuring up to once he got a handle on it. And with two days off between every twenty-four-hour shift, he would have plenty of leisure time to do whatever else he pleased.

He spent the evening sitting outside with Robbie. Seventy-five degrees and humid, attenuated by a warm westerly breeze. They watched planes take off, land, and taxi past the pad. Robbie named each aircraft by manufacturer and model number. Whether a Boeing 737-700, an Airbus A320, or an Embraer E190, he knew the passenger capacity and fuel load of each.

By ten o'clock, Tony was under the covers in his private bunk room. His feet stretched to the edge of the single bed. It was weird to go to bed without Lisa beside him. Would this present another strain on their marriage? How would Lisa adapt to the new arrangements? He'd spoken to her after dinner, and now he fought the urge to pick up his cell and call her again. He'd have to get used to this.

FIVE

Tuesday, August 9

Allie Robinson arrived at the airport operations center five minutes late for her morning shift, and she wasn't happy with herself. She liked to set the example and hoped her tardiness didn't set the tone for the day.

Rotating off the midnight shift, she'd spend the next fourteen days getting acclimated to the time change before switching again, two weeks later, to the hated overnight eleven-to-seven shift. At thirty-one, she could still handle these bimonthly schedule changes, but it was getting more difficult every year. And it was playing hell with her desire to find a companion. Not that she considered herself drop-dead gorgeous. Her aunt had once told her she'd grown into a fine athletic young woman, a compliment she could have done without.

She'd lobbied Director Sharon Lambert to adopt a *monthly* rotation cycle, arguing it would give everyone more time to adjust, but her idea had fallen on deaf ears. She pushed the thought away. Aside from her boss, she loved this job and was determined not to develop the callous attitude of the senior ops staff, who seemed to despise everything about their work.

With a bachelor's degree in aeronautics, specializing in aviation management, Allie thrived as one of the airport's three operations shift managers, despite the minor annoyances. Unlike many of her friends from college who were now working at meaningless jobs in nondescript offices, Allie was on an adventure. Every day brought new challenges and opportunities to meet interesting people and solve new problems. She held on to that thought as she made her way to the conference room.

At seven-thirty, the daily airport-wide information session began, with the usual suspects in attendance. The director of airport operations, the director of field maintenance, a manager from engineering and construction, a deputy chief from the fire department, the duty lieutenant from the police department, the manager of security, the supervisor of customer relations, and the airport's public information officer.

Two of her ops specialists and the senior telecommunications operator from airport dispatch sat intermingled with officials from the Transportation Security Administration, the FAA, and two airline representatives from a rotating list of locally based station managers. Occasionally, someone from the airport's C-suite popped into these briefings, but only when something out of the ordinary was planned or expected.

Back when COVID-19 raged, the director had hosted the meetings via Zoom, but Allie much preferred attending in person. The best information—the inside scoop—was passed before or after the meeting, not within the structured agenda of the official discussions. And as a keen observer of human behavior, she gleaned much from what the participants didn't say. That dynamic had been lost during the pandemic, and she welcomed its return.

The ops conference room doubled as the airport's emergency operations center, with a rectangular table too large for the space provided. Late arrivals were forced to array themselves along the walls or against a row of desktop computer cubicles once the twenty seats filled up. Today's crowd was small, and everyone snagged a seat.

Allie tapped her foot rapidly as Ethan Majewski, one of the ops specialists, handed out the meeting agenda.

Sharon Lambert led off. "Good morning, everyone, and thank you for coming. As you can see by our limited agenda, we don't expect much in the way of excitement today."

Was excitement ever a good thing at an airport? Allie was already far away, planning her priorities and plotting to spend most of the day away from the office.

Director Lambert covered four routine points and queried the attendees for information that might be helpful to the group. Most replied with the standard *nothing new*, either because it was true or because they didn't want to share their secrets in an open forum. That was fine with the director, Allie knew. Sharon's happiest days were undisturbed until four-thirty, when she emerged from her office, uttered "Let's keep it quiet tonight" to no one in particular, and scooted through the door.

Allie was the first Black manager here at Reynolds International. A consummate professional respected by senior managers and laborers alike, she was a perfectionist in a world of people happy with *good enough for government work*, and she wasn't a fan of the director. Leaders must *lead*, but Sharon Lambert did not fit that job description.

Two items caught Allie's attention. Brian Murray, the director of field maintenance, announced that the annual snow-clearing drill, known officially as the winter operations exercise, was scheduled for Monday, September 26. His crews would stage a preparation day—a practice before the practice—on August 9. Christ, that was tomorrow. Why hadn't ops been involved in the planning? But it was no surprise. Sharon had ignored the strained relations between ops and field maintenance personnel for the last year and a half. Another example of her avoidance of controversy.

The second tidbit—from Deputy Fire Chief Scott Martone—was that eight new firefighters had completed their training and were assigned to their platoons. Allie had forgotten about that. Since ops and fire worked together every day, it was time to meet them.

"Well, I think we've covered everything from the authority side, so unless our friends from the airlines or the federal government have anything for us?" She paused. The TSA and FAA reps shook their heads. So did the station managers. "Okay, thanks again and let's have a safe and productive day."

Allie watched the crowd file out and fought the urge to scoot over to the fire station. She'd better stop at field maintenance first and try to interject ops into the winter drill. Misery before pleasure. "Welcome back to the day shift, Althea," she whispered to herself.

* * *

Allie parked Ops-2, the manager's Ford Explorer, in front of the nondescript field maintenance building, where she sat, thinking. How should she approach this? Winter ops was critical. Yet the long-running feud with maintenance showed no signs of abating. Maintenance supervisors wanted to run the show, which they regarded as part of their sacred domain. Heavy equipment drivers bristled at ops being on the field while blowers, brooms, and plows cleared the runways and taxiways. Allie had no patience for the bickering. Winter ops was all about keeping the airfield free of ice and snow, not winning a turf war.

Allie found Joe Shinsky, the lanky, grizzled daylight field maintenance supervisor, eating lunch with Greg Connor in the maintenance conference room. Connor, a heavy equipment operator, was the steward of Union Local 1733. She paused at the doorway. Time to be tactful.

"Hi, Allie. What a pleasant surprise," Shinsky said in his usual snarky tone. "Care for a donut? Greg brought them."

"Oh…no, but thanks anyway."

Connor leaned back and plopped his dirty work boots on the conference table. Shinsky, exercising the lack of control he had over his people, let him do it.

"So, what brings you to our neck of the woods this morning?" Shinsky asked. "We're not in trouble, are we?" Connor chuckled and folded his arms behind his head.

"You, Joe? Perish the thought. I wanted to go over the details of the winter operations exercise. I heard you're doing the practice run tomorrow."

"Yeah...we've completed our plans, but I'll be happy to show them to you. Got 'em on my desk. Or do you want me to email you a copy?" Shinsky smiled.

Connor eyed Allie. She offered no reaction.

"Couldn't we sit and go through it together? We're supposed to be planning it jointly, aren't we?"

"Yeah, technically we are, but—"

"You tryin' to do our job?" Connor asked. His tone was flat, but the pulsing vein on his forehead made his hostility clear.

Shinsky allowed the interruption without comment. Allie considered him a good supervisor but thought he was too buddy-buddy with the union.

Connor pulled his feet off the table and sat up. "And what the fuck do you know about moving snow? I never seen anybody from ops out plowing a runway."

Allie tensed. She was on the edge but she had to keep her cool. "Nobody's trying to do your job. It's your show. We just need to work together. We're supposed to be a team, after all."

"Team, my ass! You guys have no business on the field. All you do is get in our way."

Connor's outburst was uncalled for, yet Shinsky didn't intervene. He needed to grow a pair of balls. Who was the boss here?

"In your way?" Allie was incredulous. Her voice rose. "We follow *behind* your equipment and test the runway for braking characteristics. We don't interfere with you."

"You look over our shoulders to get some dirt on us and run to the front office. You make us look bad."

That was it. "What the hell are you talking about? Ops is out there every day, trying to keep everybody safe. I can't tell you how many times we've kept your guys out of trouble. If your head wasn't so far up your ass, you'd realize that."

Connor's face hardened into a scowl.

"And we appreciate everything the operations department does for us," Brian Murray said as he entered the room.

Connor sank back into his chair.

"It sounds like an all-out war in here," Murray said. "Two supervisors shouldn't talk to one another that way. What gives, Joe?"

It was Connor who answered. "We were just telling Miss Robinson here that we got everything figured out."

Murray glared at the union steward. "I wasn't asking you."

Connor closed his mouth and looked down.

"Well, Joe?" Murray asked.

Shinsky looked stunned. "I was just—"

"You were just what? Were you explaining to Greg that talking to an airport supervisor that way is grounds for suspension?"

"Ahh, no. We were going over the winter operations drill and it got a little heated, that's all."

"A little heated? How did you let it get to that point?"

Murray turned to Connor. "And why are you here? Are you holding a union meeting? Don't you have an assigned job to do?"

"Yeah, boss."

"Then hop to it." Murray pointed to the door.

Allie watched as the chastened steward got up and left. If only *her* boss had such chutzpah.

Murray took Connor's place next to Shinsky. "Sorry about that, Allie. Please have a seat so the three of us can discuss the winter drill."

Shinsky discovered his cooperative spirit as the trio leafed through the plan. Allie suggested an alternate timeline to avoid disrupting air traffic, but she agreed that her department would function purely in a support role. Field maintenance supervisors would determine the routes and procedures for the actual snow-clearing runs.

Ops personnel would communicate and coordinate the team's movements with ground control. After maintenance cleared a runway, the ops friction tester, a pickup that carried instrumentation to determine braking characteristics, would take readings and relay them to the tower. In all other aspects, field maintenance supervisors would be in charge.

Satisfied, Allie headed back to tell Sharon about the agreement she'd worked out. Her boss would take full credit, but so what? She was more concerned with how she'd been goaded into losing her temper.

Allie had been so angry that she didn't remember exactly what she'd said. *Did I call the union steward an asshole?* Her loss of control, exacerbated by sleep deprivation from changing shifts too often, troubled her. She'd get into hot water if Connor reported her, but she doubted he would. Whining that a girl yelled at him would mar his tough guy persona.

One of the marks of a professional is keeping cool, but she had her father's short fuse, a problem that had manifested itself in grade school, and she'd struggled to suppress it ever since. She recalled her mother's advice. *People are going to mess with you, and you'd better get used to it.* Her mother had warned Allie her temper would land her in big trouble someday, so she'd better learn to control it. "So true, Mom, but so hard to do," she said to herself.

SIX

Wednesday, August 10

Frank Barlow took in the scene as he trundled into the heavy equipment garage, his right knee clicking with every step. It wasn't going to be a good day.

Referred to as the shed, the storage garage was longer than a football field and twice as wide. At six-thirty in the morning it was already lousy with people. The smell of coffee mixed with a thick odor of grease and diesel fuel.

Drivers from all three shifts stood around in little groups of four or five, shooting the bull and filling their Styrofoam cups from three big urns. Frank knew them all, but he didn't stop to talk to anyone.

Frank kept his distance from his coworkers. He had eaten a lot of shit in the five years it had taken to get his cert as a qualified heavy equipment operator, and he didn't have to talk to anybody or do anything that wasn't written in the union contract. Some of the other dumbfucks would get out of their rigs and help the laborers with their jobs, but not Frank. He didn't give a shit and he wasn't going to pick up a shovel and help some idiot dig a hole or fill a pothole. Nope, he'd earned his position, and if they sent him to deliver a load of dirt, that's what he'd do. Unless he was called to make another run, he'd sit in his truck all day and nobody could stop him.

Today was prep day for September's snow-clearing drill. The muckety-mucks called it the winter operations exercise. The operators were here today to check out the rigs they'd be driving and get a little practice. Frank huffed. Everybody knew how to plow a runway. This was all a bunch of chickenshit, and it was happening on his regular shift, so he couldn't even get overtime pay for it. More crap.

Joe Shinsky, the maintenance supervisor on the seven-to-three shift, was acting the big cheese outside the shed's office. "This is an all-hands-on-deck event," he said to a bunch of seasonal employees who stood next to the donut table, munching the free goodies and nodding at every word he said. Who else would listen to his shit? Useless assholes.

"Hey, Frank, what are you driving?" Buddy Lynch asked as he rushed to catch up to Frank. Buddy was the closest thing Frank had to a friend, although that didn't mean much.

"I've got plowing duty on two-twenty-four."

"You mean that old piece of shit they should've auctioned off five years ago? I bet you won't make it halfway across the ramp before it breaks down," Buddy said. "Hell, I wouldn't be surprised if the damn blade fell off."

"Nah, our crack maintenance staff keeps the rolling stock in fine condition. Always ready to go."

"I'm getting my first crack at Yellow-217. Can't wait to see how the big new broom handles."

Frank turned away. Big deal.

Buddy continued his monologue. "I hate these stupid practice sessions. What a load of horseshit. All this, just to make the airport big shots look good at next month's drill. The CEO will be on camera, telling some bleach-blonde reporter in a short skirt how Reynolds International never closes."

Frank reached Yellow-224. Its faded paint job was flaking off and the plow blade was bent from years of abuse.

Buddy stopped and looked over the old plow truck. "Man, this thing's ready for the scrap heap. Hey, Frank, how many snowstorms do you figure this airport's seen in the last ten years? Three? Five? Big whoop."

Frank climbed into the cab. In the eleven years he'd worked at the airport, he didn't know how many storms there'd been, and he didn't care. Buddy was just trying to be friendly, but the shift was just starting and Frank had already had enough chitchat.

Buddy stood there, looking up at him with a stupid puppy dog face. What the fuck was he waiting for? Frank couldn't stand it any longer. "You just can't shut up, can you?"

"Easy, Frank. I'm in the same boat as you are."

"No, you aren't, you dumbass. Shinsky is fucking with *me*, not you. He's giving me a crap job in a piece of junk. He can't screw with me any other way, so this is how he does it without getting himself in the jackpot with the union."

"Sorry, Frank. I was just chewing the fat."

"I don't care what you were doing. Stay the fuck out of my business and stay the fuck out of my face." He regretted what he'd said, but people just couldn't shut their fucking mouths.

Buddy, his face bright red, stood there for a moment, looking like he was about to say something, but turned and walked away.

He shouldn't have let Buddy piss him off, but it was more than that. Frank had more than a decade of seniority, and by rights *he* should drive one of the new rigs—a plow, a broom, or even a blower. Instead, he was stuck with a clunker that nobody would send out in a real snowstorm. It was just a way for that prick Shinsky to get back at him for not being a *team player*. Fuck that. He should bring it up at the next meeting of Local 1733. Yeah, the operators' union should take a stand before management ate away at more of their rights. Bad enough they'd forced him to get a vaccine during that COVID-19 farce. Frank's hands shook. Damn, he'd let *them* get to him again.

After lunch, the drivers tested the specialized mechanical equipment on their plows, brooms, blowers, and deicer trucks. At two o'clock, they took the vehicles for test drives on the winding public access roadways at the rear entrance of the airport. Staying inside the perimeter fence, they drove past the fuel farm and the main hangar line. They turned around at the cargo apron, passing the field maintenance mechanical shop, and looped around to the shed.

By two-forty-five, the fleet was parked in the garage and Frank's anger had subsided. The long drive was easy duty and his knees felt okay for a change. But the whole thing was a waste and they'd returned just in time for him to punch out at three, missing the four hours of overtime he'd have gotten if they'd kept him ten minutes past the hour. Hot sweat broke out on his forehead. It was okay when Shinsky had racked up the OT in the years before he became a supervisor, but now he was a real company man. A real asshole. The rage had returned, and it followed him home.

SEVEN

Thursday, August 11

Tony kept to himself until all firefighters were called to the dayroom. He felt pretty good after two days off, and he didn't want to start his second day on the job as the target of new guy hazing. It worked. The morning briefing passed quickly and his upbeat mood remained. Lieutenant Wozniak read through a list of vehicle positions and Tony received his first dual assignment.

The LT assigned Tony to Rescue-11, one of the Oshkosh Striker 3000 crash trucks, and Rescue-15, the department's structural pumper, built by Pierce Manufacturing. Since the department didn't have the personnel to staff all the first-line equipment, crews cross-manned between the crash trucks and the vehicles slated for structural fires and other non-airfield responses. The only exceptions were the captain and his driver on Rescue-10, the rapid intervention vehicle, or RIV, and the two-person crew of Rescue-14, the department's modified F-450 pickup, which served as the medical response unit and all-around workhorse.

As usual, construction inspections followed truck checks and breakfast. A routine morning. Afternoon training—hose and ladder drills—was slated for one o'clock.

* * *

Allie flipped the visor down as she drove west on taxiway Sierra. The sky was clear and the summer sun sat high on the horizon. Eighty-two degrees with low humidity. What a perfect afternoon.

The airfield was quiet. A pair of vans from the electrical shop were the only signs of life, and the tower cleared her all the way to Station Bravo, where she planned to meet the last two firefighters from the recent recruit class. She pulled onto the front pad and keyed her mic. "Ground, Ops-2 is clear of the field."

"Ops-2, roger." The controller sounded bored.

The scene hummed with activity as A-platoon's crew, outfitted in their turnout gear, rushed back and forth around Rescue-15. Allie leaned against the hood of her SUV as a two-person team pulled a ladder from the top of the pumper and advanced it to the front of the station. They stopped ten feet from the wall, extended the top section, and leaned the ladder against the station's parapet. Concurrently, a second team pulled a hoseline from the pumper and advanced it to the ladder. The lead firefighter climbed to the parapet with a bundle of folded hose on his shoulder while his partner fed him from the ground.

A firefighter from the first team secured the ladder while the second firefighter climbed. Once over the parapet, the duo flaked out the hose and knelt at the edge of the roof. With an upraised arm, the nozzleman signaled Rescue-15's pump operator, who discharged water into the hose. Once the line became rigid, the team shot a thirty-second burst of water toward the parking lot.

Allie applauded. "Not bad. Not bad at all."

Lieutenant Wozniak turned and waved at her. As the teams returned the ladders to the pumper and repacked the hose, Allie walked over to the LT.

"Hi, Allie. Must be a slow day."

"Yeah, just like every day, Phil. It accounts for my gray hairs."

"You? Where? Now this is gray hair," he said, lifting his helmet and pointing to his receding salt-and-pepper hairline. "What can we do for the operations department today?"

"Where are you hiding your probies? I'm here to meet the latest additions to the world's finest ARFF department."

"You're in luck. They're the next up in the hose team hit parade. I'll introduce you after their evolution. I'll be right back."

As Wozniak walked into the station, Allie approached the pumper, where the two rookies were about to take their turn.

"Hey, Allie, why are you bothering with those noobs?" Jason Krigger asked. "You just saw the A-team in action."

Allie ignored him.

"Come on; can't a couple of the fire department's best get a *great job* from the best-looking girl in the operations department?"

Allie's heart rate shot up. Krigger fancied himself the great Casanova. She wanted to tell him where to shove his smart mouth, but she'd already let her temper get the best of her this week. But she couldn't leave it alone.

She'd heard the forty-something firefighter was having an affair with Monica Henderson, a twenty-seven-year-old ops specialist. It was also rumored that his wife had kicked him out and he was living above a friend's garage. Krigger had been quite the hunk when Allie started her job at the airport, but eight years had taken their toll. The fling was probably his way of denying the arrival of middle age.

Showing off for his buddies. Why were some guys such clowns? Allie couldn't resist the chance to put him in his place. She reined in her anger and shot him her best disarming smile. "Such a charmer," she said. "Your wife is one lucky girl. I bet she sits around, just waiting for her manly stud to come home."

Krigger dropped the leer. He looked puzzled.

Nathan Sawicki picked up the bait. "She *might be* waiting at home for a manly stud," he said, "but it's not Jason. She kicked his ass out three weeks ago." The crew roared with laughter.

"Score one for Allie," Manny Santos said.

"Don't worry," Nikki Leach, a short, muscled blonde, added. "If your wife doesn't want you, there's always Monica Henderson. Or did she drop you already?" She gave Allie a high five.

Krigger's face was a mask of hatred. "Funny" was all he said as he turned and stormed away.

Allie watched him go. She didn't like to stoop to his level, but she'd given him a dose of his own medicine while keeping her emotions in check. She just had to set the trap. Shaking her head, she turned her attention to the next evolution.

All four firefighters wore full gear and their breathing apparatus backpacks and tanks—BAs, as they were called—sans their facepieces. She recognized the firefighters carrying the ladder, and she scrutinized the two new guys on the hose team. The nozzleman was tall. A little old for a rookie, probably in his late thirties or early forties. His backup man sported a buzz cut and had the face of a kid barely old enough to shave.

The team donned their helmets and the older guy pulled a stack of hoseline from the pumper's side tray, placed the bundle on his right shoulder, advanced a few feet, and stopped. His backup did the same. "Let's get moving, boys," Lieutenant Wozniak said. "This isn't a dress parade."

"Go, Tony," Allie heard the younger guy say. With that, the nozzleman strode forward. He held tight to the bundle on his shoulder as one flake of hose after another played out from the top of the backup man's stack. So far, so good.

"Let's move faster," the lieutenant said.

The team was halfway to the building with another twenty-five feet to go when the nozzleman dropped his entire stack, causing his backup to do the same. The hose landed in a jumbled mess.

"Should we stop?" the nozzleman—Tony—asked.

"No!" the LT said. "Would you stop if it was a fire?"

Tony bent down, scooped up the nozzle and a few lengths of hose, and dashed for the ladder. He struggled to mount it while gripping the disordered armful. His backup grabbed the remaining sections and followed.

The rest of the crew gathered around the spectacle. The backup man deposited his line at the base of the ladder but stepped on it in the process, causing the nozzleman to jerk backward.

"Uh-oh," Allie whispered. This wasn't going to end well.

When Tony grabbed a rung to steady himself, the hoseline slipped from his grasp. He twisted sideways and leaned back to catch it, but he missed.

"Don't lose contact with the ladder. Keep one hand on the rail!" The LT's instructions were too late.

Five rungs up, Tony lost his balance. Then he fell backward and with a thud landed face up on the tangled pile of spaghetti.

"Oh, that's bad," Allie voiced as the crew rushed to the unfortunate firefighter's side. She started forward but stopped and stood back. This was fire department business and they were professionals. It was no place for her.

Santos and Wozniak checked Tony for injuries while the others huddled around the fallen man. Allie heard Tony say that he was okay. Apparently satisfied, Santos and the young kid lifted him to his feet, removed his BA, and helped him into the station. Poor guy. What a way to start his career.

Allie returned to her vehicle. She'd meet the unfortunate new guys another time.

* * *

Tony lay on his bunk with his hands behind his head, lost in his thoughts. In spite of the six ibuprofen he'd popped over the last eight hours, his back was killing him. It was a good thing he'd landed on the hoseline and not the pavement.

The lamp on the nightstand cast an eerie glow across the ceiling. He could hear aircraft engines as they revved for taxiing and takeoff. So much for soundproofing. It was past midnight and he'd been cloistered in his ten-by-twelve room since nine o'clock. He'd tried to read but couldn't concentrate and tossed the book into his overnight bag. He missed Lisa's company. It was past midnight, but he doubted he'd get much sleep.

His second shift had started out okay but ended in disaster. He'd followed the debacle at the academy with an even more embarrassing screwup today. He'd fallen off the damn ladder. In front of the whole crew. *It'll be a long time before I live down his performance.*

He'd been overconfident, but now his mind filled with doubts. Did he have the intestinal fortitude to put this latest episode behind him and move forward in a job that held little enthusiasm for him? The answers wouldn't come. But once he got home in the morning he'd have the next two days to get past it before his next work shift.

EIGHT

Friday, August 12

"Wear your gray suit with the blue pinstripes," Lisa said as she curled her hair in front of the bathroom mirror. "You look distinguished in it."

Tony came to the door and smiled at his wife's reflection.

"What a liar you are."

She returned the mirrored gaze. "No, I'm not." She had that playfulness in her voice that Tony loved. "You're a handsome man and I want to show you off."

A handsome man? Maybe, but Lisa was a gorgeous woman. In the sixteen years since they'd met as college juniors, she had blossomed. They'd both gained a few pounds, but unlike his paunch, the added weight only enhanced Lisa's looks. From a cute, skinny college girl into the enticing beauty she was today.

Standing there in her lacy black bra, thirty-six-year-old Lisa stirred him like none of the girls he'd dated in high school or college ever did. And he loved her, despite the ups and downs they'd endured.

"Stop staring at me, you hog. I'm not a piece of meat." She giggled.

"Stop standing half-naked in front of the mirror and I won't."

"I'm not half-naked and I'm trying to get dressed for dinner, you lech."

Moving in behind her, Tony kissed her neck and shoulders as he inhaled her perfume, the same vanilla scent she'd worn forever. He didn't remember what it was called, but the aroma brought him back to their carefree younger days. She wore the diamond heart earrings he'd given her on their fifth anniversary. "I love you, Leese."

"I love you too." She turned and gave him a playful shove. "Go get ready. I'm taking my newly graduated firefighter to dinner."

She seemed so happy and excited for him. And probably relieved that he'd made it this far. There had been times during training when he'd wanted to quit, head back to the 'Burgh, and resume his search for that elusive big business career. But he'd fought off those impulses. He wasn't a kid anymore. There were only so many chances, and he dared not let Lisa down again. She'd sacrificed too much, a lot more than he had. As they left the apartment, he wondered if Lisa's joy would be short-lived.

They listened to satellite radio during the thirty-five-minute trek north to Chambersburg. When they got to Carlino's, the family-owned Italian restaurant they had discovered, Lisa stumbled as they crossed the parking lot. Tony caught her arm, relieved his new firefighting reflexes had kicked in so easily and instinctively. "We haven't had anything to drink yet."

"I'm used to scrubs and Skechers, not dresses and heels."

"You're irresistible in either," he said, "but I prefer the dress."

"I know what you prefer," she said with a sly smile.

The hostess led the couple to a cozy corner table toward the rear of the dining room. With Tony decked out in his suit and tie and Lisa wearing a knee-length evening dress, they looked every bit the successful professional couple.

Lisa reached up and gave him a kiss.

"What was that for?"

"For my husband, who I'm very proud of."

Tony's troubled thoughts about the marriage disappeared as he recalled the unbridled passion they had experienced during their early years. God, they were something back then.

Lisa chose the veal romana, while Tony opted for the mostaccioli arrabbiata. The waiter suggested a bottle of imported Italian pinot noir, and it proved the perfect choice.

"Your meal is going to be very spicy," Lisa said. "I hope you can handle it."

"Don't worry about me, my girl. I like spicy things."

Lisa's cheeks flushed as she met his gaze. "We'll see about that."

The food was excellent, the subdued lighting lent an air of intimacy, and they had a fabulous time. With no one hurrying them along, they sipped their wine while they laughed and talked. The evening was going so well that Tony found himself to be happier and more relaxed than he'd been in months.

"I can't tell you how proud I am of you," she said.

"I don't know why. The academy was only the first hurdle. I still have another eight months of probation and on-the-job training before I'm official."

Lisa smiled. "It was hard for you to swallow your pride and start at the bottom, learn a whole new job. But I'm confident this is what you've been searching for. You can do *whatever* you set your mind to. Reynolds Airport just got the best firefighter it ever had."

Tony was moved by Lisa's words, but he knew it was time to tell her what he should have said months ago. "I realize how difficult it was for you to leave your family, your friends and a job you loved…to uproot your life and follow me here."

"Wait, Tony. You don't have to—"

"But I need to." He inhaled. "You had everything, and because of me, you had to give it all up."

She was looking directly into his eyes, her lips pursed.

"You moved here without a complaint. Not many women would have done that for their husbands, and I want you to know how much I appreciate it. How much I love you for it."

Tears welled in those rare and beautiful green eyes. As she dabbed them with a tissue, Tony raised his glass.

"Here's to you, Lisa Moretti, my best friend and the love of my life. I adore you, and I won't let you down again."

Back at their apartment, after they made love and Lisa was asleep, he lay awake, looking at the ceiling, desperately hoping the promise he'd made in the restaurant was one he could keep.

NINE

Sunday, August 14

Tony relished his new schedule, despite the downsides of being away from home—and Lisa—for twenty-four hours at a stretch. Where else could you find a job that featured two days off out of every three? And the bulk of the work occurred between seven in the morning and five in the afternoon, so if there were no evening alarms, he was on his own for the next fourteen hours. A pretty good deal.

He clocked in for his third day of work at 6:39 a.m. Department policy specified a ten-minute grace period for punching in and out, so he wouldn't get docked, but he was late just the same. After all the wine at dinner, he hadn't wanted to get up when the alarm went off at five. What an ungodly hour.

Lisa had to push him out of bed after he'd hit the snooze button twice, and two miles into his drive, he realized he'd forgotten his groceries and had to double back.

Jason Krigger stood in the hall as Tony walked to the kitchen with his groceries. "Nice of you to join us, rookie," he said. "Most new guys try to show up on time, at least while they're still on probation."

Tony shrugged.

"In fact, most guys get here a half hour early so they can relieve their brother firefighters on C-platoon. B-platoon does the same thing for us. I hope you ain't trying to fuck up our whole system. 'Cause I guarantee it'll fuck you up first."

"I get it," Tony said.

"Hope you do, rookie. Hope you do."

The day proved uneventful, despite its inauspicious start. Tony was assigned to Rescue-13, one of three first-line three-thousand-gallon crash trucks. He was cross-manned on Rescue-16, the department's aerial ladder tower. Neither vehicle turned a wheel all day.

Training was a breeze. Ignacio "Iggy" Rivas reviewed first aid procedures for fractures and serious bleeding. A slender man of about Tony's age, Iggy was a former combat medic who'd served in Iraq and was one of only a half dozen certified paramedics in the department. Tony had met him at the academy, where Iggy taught basic medical training.

Iggy divided the crew into two-person teams for the practical part of the lesson. Tony and Zach Worton—a tall twenty-something with a prematurely receding hairline—took turns applying splints and trauma dressings to each other's simulated injuries. Iggy released the crew at four o'clock. It was time for Tony to cook.

Elaborate dinners were a Sunday tradition at the fire station, and Tony and Robbie were now a part of the cooking rotation. No stranger to the kitchen—his mother had seen to that—Tony took the lead. He had chosen lasagna in a hearty meat sauce as the main dish and handled the cooking, while Robbie prepared what he was least likely to screw up, the salad and garlic bread.

Tony layered two large dishes with rows of cheese and lasagna noodles, spreading the sauce as he did so. He slid his creation into the preheated oven and set its timer for one hour. Certain the dish would please his colleagues, he was eager for some positive feedback, even if it wasn't firefighting related.

"This smells great," Robbie said. "At home, our idea of Italian food was a package of spaghetti with sauce from a jar. Can't wait to taste it."

After they served the meal, Tony sat with Robbie at one of the dayroom tables. The crew devoured the lasagna, going back for more until nothing remained. Yet they offered only a smattering of compliments, and one complaint about too much garlic. Most didn't say a word to the chefs, but Tony was okay with that. He had to earn respect for his cooking just as he did his firefighting skills.

After cleaning up, he plopped into a recliner and spent an hour pretending to watch some mindless reality show while he caught the latest world news on his phone. He smiled when he overheard a few of the guys talking about how delicious the meal had been.

Tony headed outside and watched a few planes take off and climb into the hazy early-evening sun. Zach Worton, who seemed like a nice guy, joined him and the two talked about the places they'd visited. Later he shared the news of his cooking success with Lisa and then opted for a paperback in the small quiet room. By ten-thirty, he was nestled in the bed, scrolling through his emails.

The overhead lights snapped on as a yelping alarm reverberated through Tony's room. He shot up in his bed. The squealing tones ceased and a voice came over the intercom.

"This is the tower with an Alert-2. We have an inbound KC-135 reporting one engine out. The aircraft will land on runway two-four-left in approximately twelve minutes. There are five souls on board and thirty-five thousand pounds of fuel. Repeat, this is an Alert-2 for a KC-135 landing on runway two-four-left in twelve minutes."

Tony sprang out of his bunk, put on his pants, and sprinted for the apparatus bay in his stocking feet. He focused. *Get to Rescue-13 with Robbie.* This was real.

"Moretti, jump on board Rescue-11," someone shouted. "Krigger went home sick."

Tony turned to see Captain Schrum. Huh? What was he talking about?

"Don't worry; 13 still has two guys," Schrum said. "Get your gear and take shotgun."

Tony felt another moment of confusion. Rescue-11...the new Oshkosh Striker crash truck in...bay number two. He met Robbie as his friend was climbing into Rescue-13. "I'm reassigned to 11," Tony said and didn't wait for a reply. He grabbed his gear and dashed to 11's bay and climbed to the cab's window seat. Hughes fired up the engine and did a quick check of the gauges. "Buckle up," he said.

Tony donned his headset, put his helmet on, and fumbled with the seat belt as Hughes followed Rescue-10 onto the station's front pad, bringing it to a halt twenty feet short of the taxiway and alongside the captain's truck. Rescue-12 and Rescue-13 moved into position on the right while Rescue-15 pulled up behind the four crash trucks. Flashing strobe lights cast a pulsating red glow over the taxiway.

Tony slid the bulky sleeves of his bunker coat into the straps of his SCBA and struggled with his seat belt as the ground control frequency came alive in his headset.

"Reynolds ground, Rescue-10." Captain Schrum's voice betrayed no emotion.

"Rescue-10, ground. Go ahead," the controller replied, equally calm. Their voices helped steady Tony's nerves.

"Rescue-10 and company on the pad at Fire Station Bravo. Request right turn on Bravo, cross the departure end of runway two-four-right, and take our Alert-2 positions on taxiway Tango."

"Rescue-10, that's approved. Proceed right on Bravo. You're cleared to cross runway two-four-right."

"Rescue-10, roger. Taxiway Bravo, cleared to cross two-four-right to Tango. Rescue-10 will have ARFF command."

Hughes followed the captain's RIV onto taxiway Bravo as Tony tugged at the seat belt, which was entangled in his SCBA.

"Ground, all vehicles are clear of two-four-right," Lieutenant Wozniak radioed from Rescue-15.

Hughes slowed as he approached taxiway Tango but then sped up into the left turn. Tony's right shoulder slammed against the passenger door and his helmeted head bounced off the window as he unsnagged the seat belt.

"Is that seat belt on?"

"It is...now," Tony said as he clicked it into place. "It was hung up on my pack."

Hughes hit the accelerator and the Striker's seven-hundred-horsepower engine, which could reach fifty miles per hour in twenty-five seconds, roared to life. Tony rocked back into the breathing apparatus bracket with relief as the vehicle picked up speed.

The five trucks spread out in a staggered safety formation as each driver headed for their designated Alert-2 positions along Tango.

"We're going long," Hughes said. "We'll set up at Tango-1. Make sure your BA is ready, but don't get too excited. We have these alerts all the time, especially with the Air National Guard tankers." Tony's headset added a static hiss to the driver's voice.

Taxiway edge lights merged into a blue blur as Rescue-11 sped toward the approach end of runway two-four-left. In front of them, Rescue-10 stopped at Tango-4, one of the high-speed turnoffs halfway across the runway. Tony tried to visualize every truck's position. Rescue-13—his original assignment—would stop at the opposite end of Tango, while Rescue-12 and Rescue-15 would join the captain at the center position at Tango-4.

"It's coming up," Hughes said as he decelerated for the turn onto taxiway Hotel.

Tony lurched forward into the seat belt harness. He clamped his hands onto the grab bar on the dash, but the rig came to a smooth stop after Hughes pulled onto Tango-1. With Rescue-11 facing the runway, Tony craned his neck and scanned the eastern sky. Nothing. He checked his gear. Jacket zipped, BA straps tight, facepiece hanging from its strap, Nomex hood in place, helmet snug. Scenarios of crash landings with aircraft on fire ran through his head. He tried to map out potential actions, but the fear of screwing up kept him from focusing.

"They're older than I am," Hughes said.

"Huh? Who is?"

"The KC-135s. They're old Boeing 707s built in the 1960s. They're not as old as the Air Force's B-52s, and they got new turbofan engines a few years ago, but still…"

Tony looked at his driver. Thin gray hair, a round, placid face. Probably nearing sixty. He seemed like a good guy.

"ARFF command from ground," the controller radioed. "The aircraft is on short final and will be the next to land."

"It's three in the morning, as if anyone else would be landing at this hour," Hughes said and chuckled.

Tony hadn't realized what time it was. A full moon bathed the airfield in a gloomy luminescence, while blue, red and white edge lights cast eerie patterns across the runway and taxiway surfaces.

"There it is. You can just make out the landing lights," Hughes said.

Tony spotted two tiny white dots, which quickly grew in size and brilliance. The tanker's hulking silhouette appeared; it was closing fast.

The captain's voice came over the air. "Ground, ARFF command. Request permission to follow the aircraft down the runway."

"ARFF command, that's approved," the controller responded.

"We'll be chasing him," Hughes said. "Let's get a head start." He backed Rescue-11 up and angled it toward the western end of the field.

The outline of the big Air National Guard tanker came into focus, its engine noise increasing as it approached. The plane descended and touched down in front of them. Beautiful. A perfect landing.

"Tell them," Hughes said, motioning toward the radio.

Tony thought for a second, then toggled the transmit switch to the tower frequency. "Ground, this is Rescue-11. The aircraft has landed without incident."

The KC-135's landing speed propelled it halfway across the runway. Hughes wheeled behind it in pursuit, but by the time Rescue-11 caught up, the jet had decelerated and was turning onto the taxiway.

"ARFF command, this is the tower. The pilot requests no further assistance. We are terminating the Alert-2."

"ARFF command copies," the captain replied. "Rescue-10 would like to follow the aircraft to the Air National Guard ramp. All other equipment will return to Fire Station Bravo."

Tony unclenched his jaw and let go of the grab bar. He took a breath and relaxed.

"Your first aircraft alert?" Hughes asked.

"Is it that obvious?"

"Well, you were breathing pretty hard and you had a death grip on that bar."

Tony laughed. "Yep, it's my first."

"You'll get used to it. After a while it'll be a routine thing."

The captain's RIV tailed the KC-135 as it headed east, while Hughes and Tony met up with 12, 13, and 15 at the western edge of Tango for the drive back to the fire station.

Hughes looped around the building and pulled 11 into its slot in the drive-through bay. He turned to Tony. "I'm Wayne, by the way."

"Yeah, I know. I saw you during my first shift but didn't get a chance to talk to you." Tony started to get out, but Wayne asked him to hang on a minute.

"This is the first time we've worked together, but I've been here a long time."

Tony plopped back into his seat. What was this about?

"All new firefighters have problems early in their careers." He paused. "It's not an easy job."

Tony considered. He'd feared a lecture, but now he wanted to hear what this man had to say.

"Don't get me wrong. It's a very satisfying job, but it takes a while to get the hang of it, like driving on the airfield at night. No one is born with the skills to do it. You've got to practice, over and over again."

Tony nodded.

"I'm not trying to get into your business, but I wanted to say what happened to you last Thursday was pretty typical of what new guys have been doing forever, especially when they come on this job without any firefighting experience."

Tony raised his eyebrows. He appreciated the kind words. Maybe his problems weren't so bad. He needed someone like Wayne to help him out.

"What I'm trying to say in my roundabout old man's way is this. Don't let it discourage you. A year from now, you'll be a seasoned vet and your mistakes will be distant memories."

"Thanks, Wayne. I really appreciate that." Hughes was indeed a good guy, and his encouragement was a welcome relief from the negativity he'd experienced and how it was affecting his performance.

"And by the way, your lasagna was delicious. I should have said so at dinner."

Back in his bunk, he thought about the older man's words, and about the long road ahead. A year's learning curve? *It might as well be a decade.*

TEN

Wednesday, August 17

Allie burned with frustration as she compiled, collated, and entered September's statistics into the monthly report. Friday's submission deadline coincided with her last daylight shift, and there was no way she was going to come in on the weekend before she switched to afternoon shift.

She was good at reports—timely and accurate, according to her last performance evaluation—so she got stuck with them. Reporting duties used to rotate among the three operations managers, but the director had tired of hearing Clint Slagle whine. God forbid the senior ops manager should enter the stats once in a while. "Computers just aren't my thing," Allie said aloud, mimicking Clint's voice. She had a bad habit of talking to herself when hyped up, and the door to the manager's office was open.

In fairness, Ellis Kim, the third-ranking ops supervisor in seniority, helped her by gathering the statistics on emergency incidents, foreign object debris found on the field, deer incursions into the inner perimeter, and bird strikes on aircraft. But the situation with Clint pissed her off. He was much better at loafing all day than he was at his job. In the past year, he'd been caught sleeping along the perimeter road, meandering through the airside terminal, giving unauthorized rides to airline employees, and eating lunch off airport property. The director was aware of each incident but did nothing. Hands-off management by Sharon "Avoid Problems at all Costs" Lambert.

"Everyone has their particular skill set," Allie said, parroting her boss's nasal tone.

"Did you say something?" Sharon asked as she stood at the door. She couldn't have missed the insult.

"Ah, no. Just talking to myself. These reports make me crazy."

"Uh-huh." Sharon frowned. "Anyway, we have ten new employees coming in for a tour. They'll be here at eleven. Can you handle that for me?"

Allie's anger flared. She shot a contemptuous look at her boss. "Well, I'd love to, but I've got at least two more hours of report writing to finish. How about I have Ethan take it?"

"He can't. I'm taking him landside to the construction meeting, and we won't be back until at least one. You can use Chrystal if you like."

"She's out and committed to inspections all morning." Chrystal, a nerdy twenty-seven-year-old ops specialist, had the personality of a wet blanket, and Sharon knew it. "I'll lead the tour."

"Great; thanks. This will be a wonderful experience for Ethan."

"No prob," Allie said without looking up.

The director closed the door and Allie voiced her thoughts to the empty office. "Eleven o'clock, huh? Well, thanks for all the notice, Sharon. By the way, why do you always take Ethan to meetings? It's not because he's a twenty-five-year-old good-looking single guy, is it? Oh no! Perish the thought." Allie picked up her stapler and hurled it at the door. It hit with a clang and rattled to the carpet. Clearly visible from the office window, the control tower radiated bright sunshine, beckoning her to the airfield. She leaned back, took a long breath, and sighed.

Twenty minutes later, the phone rang. It was Dean Rizzo, one of the telecommunications operators. "Hi, Allie. Jacqui Kline from HR is at the door. She has a bunch of new employees with her."

"Okay. Buzz them in." Allie sighed, shook her head, and walked out to the floor.

The HR rep led two administrative assistants, a marketing manager, an accountant from finance, three laborers, a customer service rep, and two of the new firefighters onto the ops floor. The taller one was the guy who had fallen off the ladder...Tony. He really needed a haircut.

Allie greeted the group, took them into the conference room, and seated them at the big table. She directed their attention to the seventy-inch display at the back of the room as she keyed up the official Reynolds International Airport orientation presentation. Yippee!

Allie began. "Reynolds International, or capital R-E-Y as it's known by its FAA three-letter designation, is a medium-sized non-hub airport, serving over one and a half million passengers a year." She brought a diagram of the airport up on the screen. "We have a landside and airside terminal, connected by an aboveground monorail, which you probably took here today." She pulled up a satellite view of the airside terminal. "The airport has thirty gates, split evenly between the A and B wings, as you can see in this photo."

Allie made eye contact with each new hire. They were fidgeting; most sat slumped in their seats. Bored. Who could blame them?

"The airfield itself comprises two parallel runways, oriented on an east-to-west line, and one crosswind runway." She explained how aircraft take off and land into the wind, and the particulars of aircraft approach and departure.

The two young administrative assistants started talking among themselves. Allie shot them a sharp glance.

"Our airport features a network of taxiways that act just like the on- and off-ramps of any interstate highway. This operations center sits at the heart of that network. From here, we monitor everything that moves. But that's only one part of it. Our ops team is out on the airfield day and night, making sure this interconnected web stays free of hazards."

The marketing guy was texting.

"We do this by conducting daily inspections." She paused.

A laborer's head bobbed back and forth as he nodded off.

Enough of this crap. Allie went off script.

Bam! She smacked her hand on the table. Everyone jumped. The laborer nearly fell backward in his chair. One of the admins let out a squeal. *Now I have their attention.*

"Something bad just happened." She paused and watched the crowd as they looked around, confusion etched on their faces.

"A crash, a fire, a terrorist attack." They stared up at her. Okay, now she was onstage. "Whatever it is, we swing into action. Our operations managers and supervisors drop what they're doing and enter crisis mode. Some remain here while others head straight for the scene. At the same time, our telecommunications operators dispatch the emergency responders.

"If the event is really big, we initiate the airport's emergency plan, with this conference room serving as the hub of what's known as the Incident Command System. Representatives from the airport authority and emergency services officials from the county and surrounding municipalities gather right here to direct and coordinate the entire operation. And don't forget, the region depends on this airport, so through it all, we've got to do our best to remain open. Each one of you plays a role in that effort."

That piqued their interest. Hands shot up and the visitors peppered Allie with questions about plane crashes, fires, and other calamities. She smiled at the crowd. What red-blooded American doesn't like to talk about disasters?

As Allie fielded their questions, she walked them to the ops pod, a thirty-foot oval arrangement of workstations where ten seating positions faced an array of radios, desktop computers, and video monitors. Two LED TVs hung from brackets in the ceiling: On one, a flight information display—known as FIDS—flashed up-to-date arrival and departure times. On the other, weather radar patterns for the Northeast and mid-Atlantic regions scrolled across the screen. Allie introduced ops specialist Ryan Parilla, who sat facing five closed-circuit monitors.

"We've got over a hundred CCTV cameras positioned inside the airside terminal and outside along the ramps and jetways," Ryan said.

"We have another forty cameras at the landside terminal and along the roadways approaching the airport. And there are a bunch more scattered around the fuel farm, hangars, and the FBO."

Ryan toggled through random views in and around the facility. "We can call up multiple views if necessary." The tour clustered around the monitors as he brought up a view of baggage claim and another showing activity in the airside concourse of Terminal-A. Even Jacqui Kline, the HR person, who had heard the orientation spiel many times before, was watching.

Allie nodded to Ryan. They were still interested. "Who'd like to try it?" she asked. Eager volunteers took turns moving the cameras and laughing as they zoomed in on unsuspecting travelers. Allie allowed the fun to continue for a few minutes and thanked Ryan for his help. It was time for the clincher.

Allie beckoned the group to the front of the ops floor, where a curved wall of glass jutted over the south ramp, facing the airfield. She stood back and watched as the group took in the view.

"From here, we have a three-sided two-hundred-seventy-degree view of the aircraft movement area. We see everything that moves on the ramp, the taxiways, and all three runways. We can spot aircraft several miles away and watch them as they land." On cue, a brightly colored Southwest Airlines 737 touched down on runway two-four-left, followed three minutes later by a Delta Airbus 320 on two-four-right.

"The floor above us houses ramp control, a service run by a collaboration among the airlines. They direct the movement of aircraft after they've left the runways and taxiways or when they're pushing back from the gates." A few bored looks again. Time to conclude. She opened the floor to questions.

"So where do you keep all the air traffic controllers?" one of the admins asked. Someone snickered and tried to cover it with a cough. Allie saw a few eyes roll.

"Oh no, they aren't located here. This space is reserved for the airport operations department. If you look to your right, you'll see the

FAA air traffic control tower." As if the girl could miss it. "The air traffic controllers are in that facility."

"Oh, I see. Sorry," the young girl said, her face flushing pink.

"Don't be. This is a world very few people ever experience." Seeing relief on the girl's face, she swept an arm across the ops floor. "We don't expect you to have any idea what we do or how aircraft operations are conducted. You were brave enough to ask the question that some of your colleagues were probably wondering about."

The girl nodded and flashed a shy smile. Allie felt guilty about what she'd thought of the young admin but was pleased she had saved the girl from her embarrassment. After a few more questions, she ended the tour. "Ryan will escort you back to the main terminal."

Allie pulled the two firefighters away from the departing group and led them to the manager's office. "Anthony and Robert, right?" she asked.

"I go by Robbie."

"And I'm plain old Tony."

"I'll remember. Robbie and plain old Tony. I haven't had the chance to stop and talk to you guys yet." No point mentioning the embarrassing exercise she had witnessed at the station a week ago. "I always try to meet the new firefighters as soon as I can. Ops and fire are a great team and we'll be working together a lot."

The two firefighters nodded.

"How about if we arrange a tour of the control tower? Unless you've been up there already."

"No, we haven't," Robbie said as his eyes lit up. "That would be great."

Tony smiled but said nothing. Maybe he was a quiet one, which was strange for a big guy. He had broad shoulders but was a little beefy around the middle. In his short-sleeve shirt, his arms were twice the diameter of skinny little Robbie's, but they were flabby. A former weight lifter or athlete who'd let himself go soft? Possibly.

"Okay, let me square it with Captain Schrum. I always ask as a courtesy, but he won't object."

Allie had to admit that after complaining about it, she enjoyed giving the tour. And she might even have infused the new employees with some enthusiasm. Once she'd entered the last of the statistics and sent the monthly report to Sharon, her thoughts drifted back to the two new firefighters. She was especially curious about Tony. He wasn't the stereotypical firefighter. *What's his story?*

ELEVEN

Saturday, August 20

If Tony *had* to work on the weekend, this was a good day for it: hot and humid with intermittent drizzle. Today was his fifth shift on A-platoon, and he'd arrived at the station promptly at six o'clock to relieve anyone from C-platoon who wanted to cut out a little early. He hadn't forgotten Krigger's snarky criticism. Early impressions were crucial, and he needed to rectify any negative opinions his workmates had about him.

The captain credited the miserable weather for the fact that all eighteen firefighters and officers were present. Who was going to burn vacation time on a day like this? The morning had been free of inspections, training ended early, and by two-thirty, raucous college football fans packed the dayroom as Penn State grappled with Maryland in a rare August opener for the Big Ten teams.

The evenly split fan base whooped and hurled insults at each other's home-state schools. Tony jumped up and shouted "Yes!" when a Terrapin defensive back ended the Nittany Lions' first drive by vaulting into the end zone on a pick-six.

At halftime, the room quieted as firefighters scattered or focused on their cell phones. Tony joined a group in the apparatus bays.

"Hey, Moretti, don't you own an iron?" Nate Sawicki asked. "This is A-platoon, not B or C. We have pride."

"That's right," Rosie added. "It looks like you got hit with a wrinkle grenade."

Much laughter accompanied the good-natured ribbing. Tony laughed along with his workmates, but there was no mistaking the message. Chastened and self-conscious, he scrutinized his colleagues' uniforms. Without exception, their pants and shirts were clean and pressed, most with well-defined creases along the legs and sleeves. The comments ended once the crew went back inside to watch the second half, but the message had been received. He'd let his appearance slip after graduation, and this was another aspect of his persona he'd have to tighten to cultivate the positive image he desired.

"Airport fire, structural response, Terminal-B." The prealert quieted the room and the TV was muted. The ear-piercing *ah-ooga* of the Klaxon broke the reverie entirely.

"I bet it's another burnt bagel," Nikki Leach said from the back of the room, where she sat picking at a bowl of yogurt and granola.

"We have a report of a kitchen fire at the Landing Zone restaurant in the B-Wing. Evacuation is in progress. Be advised our screens indicate a kitchen extinguishing system discharge and a sprinkler activation."

"That's no bagel," Manny Santos said.

Chairs scraped across the tile as the crews of Rescue-15 and Rescue-16 jumped from their seats and sprinted for their rigs.

Tony took a rear-facing seat in the crew cab of Rescue-16 and slid his arms into the straps of his breathing apparatus as the ladder tower pulled out of the station. As the designated can man, he was responsible for the two-and-a-half-gallon water extinguisher. Holy mother of God, he was on his way to his first actual fire.

"Hey, rookie, take it easy," Santos said from the opposite side of the crew cab. "You're gonna hyperventilate."

Tony realized he was gasping and took several slow, deep breaths. He had to calm his nerves or he'd be of no help to the crew.

Lieutenant Wozniak radioed the tower from his position in the pumper. "Ground, Rescue-15 and company on emergency to the airside terminal from Station Bravo. Request Bravo, Sierra, Delta to the south ramp."

"Rescue-15 and company, that's approved. There's an Airbus moving west on Sierra. I'll hold him in place for your transit."

"Rescue-15 received. The Airbus holds for us." The LT switched to the fire frequency. "Airport dispatch, do you have a view of the scene on your cameras?"

"Affirmative, 15. We see smoke entering the concourse area from the restaurant."

"15 copies," the LT replied. "Has the HVAC system switched to emergency mode?"

"It just kicked in. Six fans running. Two in exhaust, four in positive pressure."

Blue strobes flashed from the terminal's roof as the rigs pulled up in front of the jetway at Gate B-18. "Dispatch, Rescues 14, 15, and 16 are on scene. I'll have Terminal-B command," the LT reported.

"Dispatch receives. Be advised there are now two sprinkler head activations in the kitchen. Police are on the scene, reporting heavy smoke in the restaurant."

"Command copies. Get me another crew over here."

Eight firefighters in full bunker gear and SCBA exited their trucks and climbed the metal stairs of the jet bridge. Tony lugged the stainless-steel extinguisher while his partner, Manny Santos, carried a flathead axe and Halligan bar. Others toted standpipe hose packs, short pike poles, an A-frame ladder, and a portable thermal imaging camera, or TIC.

Rosie punched a four-digit code into the combination pad to unlock the jetway door. Lieutenant Wozniak yanked it open and led the crew into the jet bridge. The fire alarm grew louder as they approached the security door of Gate B-18.

Wozniak motioned for the crew to kneel. "Don your facepieces."

Taking care to do it right, Tony spread the Kevlar hair net, pulled his facepiece down, and tugged the two straps straight back until the facepiece was tight against his face.

"The standpipe is two gates down to the right," the LT said. "Engine crew, take your hose pack and hook up. Truck and squad crews, see what we have inside the restaurant. Can man, with me. Go on air and stay low."

Tony tried to focus as he struggled to pull his lung demand valve out of its belt-mounted holder. He steadied his hands and listened for the click that confirmed a secure connection to his facepiece. He inhaled. Nothing, no air. The plexiglass visor sucked in toward his face. The cylinder—he had forgotten to open it! Fighting a rising panic, he held his breath and reached back. When he found the handwheel at the bottom of his carbon fiber air cylinder he spun the knob. The BA emitted a pneumatic whistle followed by a high-pitched electronic tone as cool air flooded the facepiece. Had anyone seen his screwup?

"Open the door," the LT said to Rosie, who swiped his badge and punched his code into the card reader. The security door buzzed and the magnetic lock disengaged. Rosie pushed the door open. Thick black smoke rolled into the jetway. The fire alarm bellowed its penetrating warning: *wee-aah, wee-aah, wee-aah, wee-aah.*

"Let's go!" the LT shouted over the din. "Airport dispatch, silence this alarm," he called over his radio.

Tony struggled to hang on to the twenty-eight-pound water extinguisher as he duck-walked through the smoky haze. He lost his balance and stumbled forward onto the carpeted floor, and the water can fell from his grip. The rising crescendo of the fire alarm sent daggers through his head.

"Hey, Moretti. I said stay with me."

"Coming, LT." Tony followed at a crouch.

Smoke rolled over the restaurant's four-foot brick facade. Tony moved up and peered into the seating area. Lots of smoke, but no visible fire. The alarm cut off. Christ. Finally.

"Moretti, take this." Wozniak handed Tony his A-tool, an eighteen-inch bar with a fork at one end and a prying surface at the other. "Check the dining room. The entrance is on your left. Look for victims and fire. I'll keep an eye on you. Go!"

Four bodies jostled Tony as they hurried past him with axes, Halligan tools, pike poles, and the ladder. He followed them inside, veering off to the seating area as the others headed for the kitchen.

Tony left the extinguisher at the door and moved into the restaurant on his hands and knees. Using a right-handed search pattern, he slid the back of his gloved right hand along the smooth interior wall and swept the area with his left hand and the A-tool.

He got to his feet as the smoke lifted. No fire; no victims. His portable crackled with a garbled transmission. Something about fire in the wall. His ears rang from the now-silenced alarm. Light hit his facepiece and he turned to see the LT watching him from the low wall.

"Find anything in there?"

"Nothing, LT. It looks clear."

"Good deal. Let's join the rest of the crew."

Personnel and equipment crowded the kitchen. Santos and Krigger sliced into the smoldering back wall with their axes while Rosie used the thermal imaging camera to look for hidden hot spots. Nikki Leach, drenched with water, stood atop the A-frame ladder, hammering a rubber stopper into a sprinkler head. A second, already plugged sprinkler dripped slowly. The smoke was now a light haze.

Whistling air and an electronic warble signaled a low-air level on someone's SCBA.

"Moretti, that's you," the LT said. "You can come off of air now."

Damn. Tony grabbed his flashing chest gauge. He hadn't noticed he was the only one still breathing from his BA. Everyone else's facepieces were dangling from their neck straps. Worse, how had he missed the amber low-air warning lights of his heads-up display?

"Christ, Moretti," Nathan Sawicki said. "How did you go through a forty-five-minute air tank in twenty minutes? What'd they teach you at that academy?"

Tony burned, furious at himself. He unplugged his regulator, removed his helmet, and ripped off his facepiece. How could he be so stupid?

"Okay, gang," the LT said. "What've we got?"

"Looks like it started with a grease fire in the deep fryers," Santos said. "The cook must've tried to put it out before the range hood extinguishers dumped, but all he did was splash burning oil all over the place." He pointed at the scorched walls. "This paneling is made from some kind of plastic. That's why there was so much black smoke. The sprinklers put it out. We opened the walls on both sides of the fryers and scanned for heat with the TIC, but we haven't seen any extension."

"Nice work," Wozniak said and thumbed the mic of his portable radio. "Dispatch from Terminal-B command, this fire is under control. We're checking for extension and beginning salvage operations. Keep the exhaust fans running and return the extra help from Station Bravo. Notify the plumbers. We need the water shut off in this sector. And have someone from ops meet me here. This terminal is closed until further notice."

Tony and the rest of the crew remained on scene for another hour, removing pieces of the charred walls, sopping up water, and spreading salvage tarps to protect unaffected areas. The physical effort eased his anxiety, and he enjoyed working alongside his colleagues. After returning to the station, he was pulled aside by the LT.

"You did well today, Tony. I watched as you did your search. Your technique is sound. You just need to keep yourself calm. When you get too excited, you lose focus and your ability to think clearly. You're a smart guy. Slow down so you can use that brain of yours." Wozniak tapped Tony's helmet. "And try to control your breathing; concentrate on it. Breathe in through your nose and out through your mouth. It'll make you less anxious and you won't go through your air so fast."

Tony nodded but couldn't meet the LT's gaze. He was happy with what he'd done right but disgusted with what he'd done wrong.

"Listen, you're new to this and you haven't learned how we do things around here. You have more potential than most of the new guys I've seen. But you've gotta keep improving on what you've learned. It takes time, but you'll get it."

Tony was appreciative of the pep talk, but he needed to find someone to work with him if he was going to improve. He considered a few of his colleagues—maybe Iggy or Nikki—but he was too self-conscious to ask. It would be so much easier if Evan O'Brien was back on the platoon, but he was scheduled to be at the academy until November. *I don't think I can wait that long.*

TWELVE

Friday, August 26

"He should have been here by now," Robbie said. "We're supposed to be on the field at eleven-thirty."

Tony checked his phone: 11:27. Robbie had dragged him to Rescue-13 at ten after eleven to meet Steve Brooks for their first nighttime driver's training session. "Don't worry; he'll be here. What's the rush?"

"It's scheduled with the tower. They're gonna be pissed if we're late."

"Robbie, the airfield is dead. I don't think it will disrupt their schedule."

"This is the crap he always pulls."

"How can you say that?" Tony asked. "You barely know the guy."

"Zach told me all about him. Said he's the laziest guy in the platoon. Only does what he's told. Never pitches in to help anyone."

"*Zach* told you this? And you believe him?"

"He doesn't want to take us. He's probably asleep in his bunk." Robbie scowled. "We've been here a month. You ever see him do anything extra? Ever see him at all?"

Tony considered. "No, I guess I haven't, but that doesn't mean he's lazy."

"Zach said he hides. Has a chair in the hose room. He sits back there and sleeps."

"Who would sleep in that musty place?" Rumors circulated about Steve's lack of initiative, but Tony didn't take them at face value. He'd gotten to know Steve, and he seemed like a good guy. Quiet and solitary, but so what? He didn't run a side business or hold a part-time job, and he'd chosen the job because of the pay, benefits, and time off, but so had Tony. Steve was intelligent and Tony enjoyed talking to him.

Steve climbed into the cab at 11:35 p.m. Robbie's face brightened. "I'll drive first if Tony doesn't mind."

"Be my guest," Tony said. Better to get acclimated before taking the wheel. Operating a crash truck in the dark would be nothing like their daylight sessions.

Steve yawned. "Okay, boys. Let's make this as painless as possible so we can get back to bed. I don't think we'll need the whole two hours. A half hour for each of you should be sufficient."

"But we've never driven on the field at night," Robbie said. "We're gonna need a lot more than a half hour."

"Of course you are," Steve said. "But this is your first outing, right?"

Robbie nodded, but his smile was gone.

"If I expose you to too much too soon, you'll just get confused and forget most of it. It's better to learn it in small increments."

Tony doubted Steve's reasoning, but he didn't quibble.

Steve picked up his cell. "The LT sent me tonight's route." He scanned the email. "Yes…I see. We can make this a much more efficient drive." He laid out a simple route comprising two loops along the east–west taxiways.

Tony smirked. Robbie was right. Steve didn't want to conduct a meaningful training exercise. He just wanted to get it over with.

Robbie pulled Rescue-13 onto the pad and stopped short of taxiway Bravo. Steve told him to repeat the details of the drive, word for word. Satisfied, Steve let him use the radio.

"Reynolds ground, this is Rescue-13 on the pad at Station Bravo."

"Rescue-13, ground. What can we do for you?"

"Rescue-13 requests a driver's training route, as follows. Right on Bravo, left on Sierra, right on Hotel, and cross the approach end of runway two-four-right. Then right on Tango, right on Bravo, recross the runway, and drive back to Fire Station Bravo."

"Rescue-13, that's approved. Be advised we have no scheduled traffic during the next two hours. We'll advise if that changes. Use caution along Tango between Golf and Delta. Airport electricians are working on the taxiway edge lights."

Tony was awestruck by the shadowy grid of intersecting airfield lights. Low clouds blocked the moon, and the only illumination came from the blue post-mounted taxiway edge lights and the green in-ground center lights. White lights from the edges of the adjacent runways and flashing amber wigwags at runway approach points gave the field the same sort of effect a rock star paid thousands for. How could anyone navigate this alien world?

Robbie completed the drive in thirteen minutes. Steve told him to focus on the centerline but said little else. Not the best teaching method, that was certain.

Tony took the wheel next. Rescue-13, the department's newest crash truck, was a joy to drive. Nothing like the clanking old rigs at the academy. He soaked up the sights of the darkened airfield: the myriad of multicolored lights, the silhouetted hangars, the shadowy tree line to the south of the field, and the control tower, a hulking giant topped with its all-seeing illuminated eye in the sky. If he was going to master the intricacies of this surreal maze in darkness, rain, or snow, he'd have to use the tower as a wayfinding point. The thought eased his anxiety.

Tony made it back to Station Bravo in sixteen minutes. What a ludicrous route. There wasn't a lot of learning happening tonight. A-shift might be the best, as the captain said, but not *everyone* on the platoon rose to that level of performance.

Steve seemed wary of deviating from the planned route and ending the training too soon, so he gave Tony and Robbie additional practice by instructing them to drive around the ramp and past the jetways of Terminals A and B. Robbie remained unimpressed, and when they returned to the station, he grabbed his gear, jumped down, and slammed the door.

"You're welcome, Robert," Steve said as Robbie stormed away.

"He's just young and enthusiastic," Tony said. "He wants to learn."

"Yeah, but those types flame out. They want to fight fires and be heroes, but this isn't a big-city department. Guys like that lose their eagerness fast. They either leave for something different or spend their careers as malcontents. It's much better to be like us."

"Huh? Like us?"

"You know what I mean," Steve said. "I can tell you feel the same way. This is a great job, but there's no reason to get too excited about it. Not like your young friend does."

Tony considered.

"Don't get me wrong. I'm not saying you should shirk your duties or disobey orders."

Tony looked at Steve. Wasn't that what *he* had done tonight?

"Do your job, what's expected of you, but don't go overboard. Keep your head down and, for God's sake, don't volunteer for anything. That'll peg you as a worker bee and the officers will pound you with extra duties. And remember, once you're in the union, you're golden."

Afterward, Tony took a seat in front of the station. Everything was still. The night air was thick and warm, but the tranquility was a welcome contrast to the airport's daylight cacophony. Other than a single ops vehicle on a midnight inspection run across six-left/twenty-four-right, there were no aircraft or people to be seen. The only noises were the intermittent howls of a coyote and the hoot of an owl from the woods south of the runways. High above, the control tower loomed like a silent sentinel.

Tony reflected on his conversation with Steve as he gazed into the night sky, which was free of the light pollution that plagued big cities. Saturn and Jupiter were easy to spot, Polaris shone brightly, and the constellations of Ursa Major and Minor were remarkably clear. Imagine what he'd see if he set his telescope up on this pad.

Steve's reputation was spot-on after all; the man had confirmed the fact himself. But was he just like Steve? Tony had always been restless and driven, needing to move forward, to achieve. It was the reason he'd changed jobs so often. Could he discard those aspirations and perform to the minimum acceptable standard for twenty years. He didn't think so. If he was going to make a career of firefighting, he would do so the right way.

No, despite appearances, he wasn't a carbon copy of Steve. In many ways, he was like Robbie. But if he didn't want Steve's reputation, he would have to change his approach to the job, and soon.

THIRTEEN

Thursday, September 1

Tony stewed as he watched an Air National Guard tanker crawling past the station on taxiway Bravo. It was 3:37 p.m. His three-hour shift in the radio room should be over by now. Where the hell was his relief? He wanted to get back to *Team of Rivals*, his latest deep dive into Civil War history, but reading in the alarm room before six-thirty, the beginning of night shift, was a no-no. As if he'd miss the blaring radio or clanging phone because his nose was in a book.

The cramped workspace contained two office chairs, a desktop computer, and an array of radios. Room enough to stand and stretch your legs, but that was about it. Windows ran across the front wall, offering views of the apparatus bay and the concrete pad in front of the station. A fold-down bunk, recessed into the back wall, provided a place to sleep during the overnight watch.

Tony's primary duties entailed monitoring the airport's radio network, relaying important information to the officers, making announcements over the station's intercom system, entering details of each emergency dispatch into the fire reporting software, and answering the nonemergency telephone line. Radio room operators were also supposed to monitor regional fire, EMS, and police traffic, but the volume on those frequencies was set so low that they might as well be muted. So far, Tony had fielded six phone calls, notified the crews of three afternoon inspections, thought about his next two days off, and gazed outside. Robbie had stopped in for a chat at two o'clock, but now Tony sat alone, growing more irritated by the minute.

At 3:39, a prealert broke the silence. "Medical assist, airport fire." The Klaxon, mounted just outside the door, jolted Tony from his anger. "We have a construction accident at Hangar-2. First reports indicate a scaffold collapse with three injuries. South-Central EMS is responding, and they request rescue and medical backup."

"Airport fire copies," Tony replied and began logging the call as Rescue-18, the heavy rescue truck, responded with Rescue-14.

"Airport fire from dispatch, we're getting more phone calls on this incident."

Captain Schrum's voice came over the intercom. "Traynor and Moretti, take the squad. Meet 14 and 18 at the scene."

Robbie came to the door. "I'll cover the radios for you."

"Thanks," Tony said as he rushed past Schrum into the truck bay, grabbed his gear and met Kyle Traynor at Rescue-19, a Chevy Trailblazer used mostly to run errands.

"I'll drive," Kyle said.

"Should we grab a med bag?" Tony asked as he tossed his stuff into the back seat.

"They'll have what we need on 14, and the medics will be there in a minute."

They exited the rear gate and arrived at Hangar-5 just as a South-Central EMS paramedic supervisor pulled up in her Explorer.

Tony was thinking clearly now. He'd excelled during Iggy's fifty-two-hour Emergency Medical First Responder course at the academy, and he was eager to put his newly gained skills to use. And he wanted to demonstrate how motivated he was, unlike Steve Brooks. A chance to shine, finally.

The scene came into view as he and Kyle exited the rig. The front of the scaffolding was bowed out, and wooden planks were scattered about the ground.

Two injured workers sat slumped against the adjacent wall of the hangar. One grimaced and mumbled incoherently as he held his left arm while the other stared at a foot turned out at a grotesque ninety-degree angle. Nathan Sawicki and Keith Weston, who'd arrived on Rescue-14, tended to the victims. The medic supervisor, a petite blonde, raced over to them.

"Shit, those guys are messed up," Kyle said. "Let's see what we can do."

"Right, but weren't there supposed to be three victims?" Tony asked.

"Over here. Get the medics over here now!" It was Rolphe Hoffman, standing next to his partner on Rescue-18, Iggy Rivas, who knelt beside what appeared to be another victim. Kyle broke into a run and Tony followed him to the far end of the construction site, where a man lay atop a bed of metal grid work that had yet to be poured with concrete. A group of construction workers stood beside him, concern etched on their faces.

Tony recoiled. A bar protruded from the right side of the man's torso, below the rib cage, and the poor guy was conscious. His face was a mask of agony as his eyes darted right and left. Iggy placed dressings around the entry site as Rolphe checked for other injuries. Blood leaked from the wound.

The medic supervisor surveyed the scene. "What happened?"

"It just fell," one of the workers said. "No warning. We heard the crash and rushed over."

"What's his name?"

"It's Chuck. He's only been on this job a couple of weeks."

"Chuck. Hey, Chuck. My name's Teri. We're going to take good care of you."

Chuck, a young man in his late teens or early twenties, turned his head to her.

"We're going to get you out of here. You're going to be okay."

The victim closed his eyes.

"You've got to stay with me, Chuck. Do you hear me? Stay with me."

Chuck opened his eyes and stared into the sky.

"He's going into shock," Teri said. She grabbed two blankets from 14's bag and motioned to Tony. "Take these. Elevate his feet with one and cover his hips and legs with the other. We'll start an IV as soon as my first unit gets here." She lifted one of the bloody dressings and turned to Iggy. "Repack these and apply pressure."

Tony rolled up a blanket and placed it under the victim's feet while Iggy placed additional bandages along the edges of the bar and pressed down. Tony expected a scream, but the victim didn't react. His features were milky white.

Teri dropped to her belly and looked under the gridwork. "I can't see any other penetrating wounds." She got to her knees. "We've got a little access underneath him, so maybe we can cut the bar."

"We already checked," Nate said. "We have just enough space for a hacksaw."

"I'll get the toolbox from 18," Kyle said and dashed away.

"It'll take twenty minutes to cut through that rebar," one of the construction crew said.

"No choice," Teri said. "He needs a trauma center and we don't dare pull him off." She pursed her lips, looked at the victim, and inhaled. "Do it! Cut it as close as you can to his back. We'll leave it in place and get him out of here." Turning to Tony, she said, "Take over the wound. Put more dressings around the bar and maintain direct pressure. Got that?" Not waiting for a reply, she tossed him a pack of trauma dressings.

Tony knelt, ripped the bag open, donned a pair of nitrile gloves, and added another layer of bandages. Blood dripped onto the light gray gravel below the gridwork: the guy was losing a lot of it.

Kyle returned with two hacksaws and a handful of extra blades. Iggy took one, positioned himself next to the grid, and reached into the tight space.

Tony placed his gloved hands over the dressings and applied gentle pressure. Blood immediately soaked the new bandages. What was that odor? Tony began breathing through his mouth to avoid the coppery scent.

"I've got a good bite," Iggy said as he cut with short strokes. The blade squealed as it bit into the rebar. Chuck moaned.

The bar jerked sideways and the victim screeched as pain brought him out of his stupor. "Stop… please. It hurts."

Tony winced. Bright red fluid seeped through the dressing and oozed between his fingers. Bile rose in his throat. He swallowed hard to force it back.

"Keep that bar steady!" Teri said.

Tony clamped both hands around the protruding rod to clamp it in place.

Iggy picked up his pace. The hacksaw whistled as he pushed and pulled, digging deeper into the stubborn steel. The bar vibrated in Tony's hands with every stroke. He tightened his grip while envisioning the through-and-through wound and how it pinned Chuck in place.

Sirens announced the arrival of additional paramedics, who set to work. Kyle took over the cutting from Iggy. Tony focused on the job to push away a growing nausea.

Chuck mumbled incoherently, fading in and out of consciousness. Teri radioed a report to Chambersburg Hospital Medical Command. The medics started an IV.

Kyle called for another hacksaw and started in again. They didn't have much time.

The victim squirmed.

"Hold him still!" Teri commanded.

Iggy and Rolphe reached across the victim to steady him. The writhing movements stopped, but Chuck was fading fast.

Tony continued to apply pressure while holding the bar steady, but the victim's blood flow increased. Tony's head swam. The claret pool on the concrete widened, soaking through his uniform pants. He was kneeling in it. His skin grew cold.

"Hey, Chuck, we're almost done," Teri said. "We'll have you out of here soon."

Chuck closed his eyes. His head lolled sideways. It was a losing battle.

"I'm through!" Kyle said.

The bar jumped as it came apart. Tony imagined Chuck's guts spilling out.

Teri gripped Tony's shoulder. "Hey, are you okay?"

Before Tony could reply, or even turn his head away, he vomited all over the packed wound. He rocked back and sensed someone grabbing him. Everything went dark.

* * *

Tony looked up into a pair of big brown eyes.

"Good. You're back with us."

Tony focused. It was Teri, the paramedic supervisor. He was in an ambulance, on a stretcher. Teri sat next to him, checking his pulse. She gave him a sympathetic look.

"What's going on? Why am I…oh, no."

"You were unconscious for a few seconds, but you've been in a bit of a daze for about fifteen minutes."

"Oh, shit. I threw up all over the patient."

"Don't sweat it. Stuff like that happens. New EMTs do it all the time. I've even seen hospital interns toss their cookies at the sight of blood. Nothing to be ashamed of."

"But the victim?"

"On the way to the ER. He lost quite a bit of blood, but the wound didn't penetrate any vital organs. He'll recover. You didn't hurt him. In fact, you did a lot to help him."

He considered. "I don't think my crewmates will feel that way."

"It wasn't an easy scene to work." Teri gave him a quizzical look. "You're one of the new guys, right?"

He nodded.

"Don't worry; you'll get used to the blood." She handed him a bottle of water. "Hang out here for a few minutes before you try to get up."

"Thanks, I appreciate that." He meant it, but at that moment, he wished they'd taken him away, too.

FOURTEEN

Wednesday, September 7

Rescue-15's crew entered the dayroom as the local newscast ended. Manny Santos, Nate Sawicki, Kyle Traynor, and Nikki Leach had just returned from extinguishing a car fire in the long-term parking lot, carrying the smell of burnt rubber into the room with them. Tony sat in a recliner among a smattering of firefighters waiting for the *CBS Evening News* to begin.

"Save any dinner for us?" Nate asked.

"Chicken, mashed potatoes, and veggies are in the oven, staying warm for you guys," Rolphe Hoffman said as he pulled a casserole dish out of the range.

"And I thought you'd have eaten it all, Moretti," Kyle said as he pulled up a chair behind Tony.

"Nope. Saved you the burnt ends and the lumps in the mashed potatoes."

"I'm surprised you were able to eat after the day you had," Nate said as he joined Kyle at his table. "Did your ass move out of that La-Z-Boy in the last three hours?"

That was enough. "Go fuck yourself, Nate."

"Oooh, so sorry to offend you," Nate said.

Tony rose from his seat and made for the door.

"Don't leave on my account, probie," Nate said. "But if you go, why don't you mop the floor in the head? Bet you can do that without fainting."

Tony turned and faced Sawicki. "Why don't you take those three working brain cells and shove them up your ass? They'll be more useful there."

"Nasty," Santos said.

"Give the guy a break already," Nikki said.

"Yeah," Iggy added. "He's only been a firefighter on the platoon for a month."

"Why should I?" Nate asked. "He's a big boy. And who says he's a firefighter? Did I miss something? Last time I saw him, he was rolling on the floor of the B-wing, sucking his air cylinder dry."

"Or falling off a ladder onto his ass," Kyle added. More laughter and a few hoots.

"Don't forget the best one," Nate said. "Puking all over a patient." A couple of *oohs* broke out, but no laughter.

Tony bristled. "Just because I didn't quit community college after one semester, Kyle, or I'm not a grease monkey like you, Nate, doesn't make me incompetent at my job."

Kyle glared but said nothing. Angry red patches bloomed on Nate's cheeks. Tony's shots had hit their mark.

Nate slammed his fork on the table. "What the fuck does that mean?"

"Nothing," Tony said and turned again for the door. Maybe he'd gone too far.

Nate kicked his chair back and stood. "Wait a minute, asshole. Who the hell do you think you are? You haven't done a damn thing yet except fuck up, so just keep your mouth shut."

"That's enough, Nathan," Bruce Mihalik, seated at the back table, said.

Nate looked to Mihalik but remained standing.

Kyle chimed in. "He's a fuckin probie, Bruce. We can say anything we want."

"You can both shut up and eat your meals." Mihalik's voice was even but firm.

Nate grabbed his chair and sat. Kyle mumbled something unintelligible.

"Thanks," Tony said to Mihalik. "I was minding my own business."

"When you should've been trying to learn your job. Why don't you and I go to the quiet room for a bit?"

Tony crossed the hall to the quiet room and settled into a chair. Mihalik sat facing him and Tony braced himself. *Here it comes.*

"You know, Tony, we were all rookies once."

Tony looked at Mihalik, a man in his early fifties, judging by the lines on his face and thinning gray hair. Probably been here thirty years.

"This station is our home for twenty-four hours, and we work every third day. That's a lot of togetherness, and you can't avoid your coworkers all day."

"I wasn't avoiding anyone. I was sitting in the dayroom with—"

Mihalik raised a hand.

Tony averted his gaze and focused on a row of ragged old paperbacks in the corner bookshelf.

"If you can't take some ribbing, this job will be a miserable one for you."

"But I can't let them get away with that. It'll only get worse."

"This isn't middle school, and the guys you insulted aren't bullies who need to be put in their places. They are your colleagues."

They were, but Tony was sick of their hazing.

"We *all* had to earn our stripes around here. For some rookies, it's pretty easy. They learn fast, work hard, do their job, and keep their mouths shut until they're accepted by their platoon. A few others can't seem to do that. Maybe they lack a good work ethic. Or they don't put in the time and sweat to become good firefighters. Or they take every crack as a personal insult."

Tony looked at the floor. Mihalik's words were on the mark.

"Guys like that don't usually last long, and if they do, they become loners. And loners don't do too well in a place where everybody's locked up together all day."

Tony felt like a complete ass.

"You may not realize it yet, but your life could depend on one of those guys, and if it comes to that, they won't hesitate to protect you as if you were a member of their family." He paused and didn't continue until Tony looked up at him. "Because that's what we are. A family. We take care of each other, we help each other. And yes, we razz each other, sometimes without mercy. We get under each other's skin, just like siblings would."

Tony nodded.

"You're starting your second month on this platoon. You haven't *earned* the right to give anyone a hard time. How old are you, about forty?"

"I'm thirty-seven," Tony replied.

"Okay, thirty-seven. But not a spring chicken. You've been out in the world for a good while and you know how life works."

Tony, who'd been expecting a dressing-down, was surprised by Mihalik's tone. He was talking like a friend.

"Sure, I get it," Mihalik said. "This department has a lot of guys like you who've tried other things before getting here. Maybe they just couldn't find the right profession. For some of our people, it's their first full-time job. Those guys don't know anything else. Point is, I've seen it all."

He gave Tony a long, considering look. "The chief always asks me to review the job applications of the top-scoring candidates before the interviews begin. Give him my two cents. You've had your problems. Job-hopping isn't looked at the way it used to be, but it still sends up a red flag."

"I know it does," Tony said, surprising himself with his candor. "I've had trouble finding the right situation."

Mihalik nodded. "But after looking at your application, I gave it my okay."

Tony looked at him, puzzled. He might as well come clean. "To be honest, I didn't give some of those jobs a fair chance. Most times, I quit because it wasn't what I expected, or because there weren't any opportunities for advancement. I've always thought I could do better, no matter where I've been. So I'd look for reasons to leave."

"Go on."

"I never thought of myself as a quitter, but I'm questioning this job. Is it right for me? Do I have the ability to do it? Is it something I *want* to do? Those thoughts scare the shit out of me because I'm pushing forty and I moved my wife three hundred miles away from her home. If I screw this up, my life might go right down the tubes."

Mihalik paused for several seconds, placing a finger to the corner of his mouth. "You think you're out of place here, don't you? Like you have no business being a firefighter. Am I right?"

"I guess," Tony said. Mihalik was smart, and he could read people.

"What you have to remember is that over five hundred hopefuls took our last firefighter exam, and you're one of only *eight* who made it on the job. Five hundred men and women who would trade places with you in a heartbeat. Think about that before you decide to throw it all away."

"I hear you. The last thing I want to do is throw it away." And maybe Mihalik could help.

"As union president, I have responsibilities to everyone. The officers and the firefighters, the veterans and the new guys, the easygoing ones and the pains in the ass. Those responsibilities extend to the probies, but unofficially. The union doesn't represent you yet, but we do what we can to make sure you pass your probation and get your IAFF card. Once you do that, your coworkers will accept you. But you must *earn* that acceptance. Think of it as an apprenticeship."

Mihalik had Tony's full attention.

"You have what it takes to come through it, but if you don't change how you act—how you do your job and get along with your platoonmates—I'm not sure you *will* come through it."

Tony knew what he wanted to say, but he was waiting for the right moment.

"There's another thing I should tell you," Mihalik said. "Part of my unofficial responsibility includes rating the recruits for the chief. Tell him if they should pass their probation. I rely on my gut feelings for that assessment. How does each rookie fit in? Will he or she be an asset to the department, or a twenty-year problem child? He takes my recommendation *very* seriously.

"I think you have a great future here if you want it. I see your quality, your potential. It's raw, but it's there. You're super smart; that's obvious. You can be a top-notch firefighter, probably an officer someday." He smiled. "Who knows; maybe a chief, Lord help us."

The last comment stunned Tony.

"The next steps are up to you. This *is* a great job, but you've got to buckle down and take it seriously. And you need to grow a thicker skin or you won't last. And then you'll need another change of occupation."

"Thanks, Bruce. I've been an ass and I know it. But I'm not planning to fail. I've been trying to develop a plan of improvement, but I need some guidance. Can you help me find someone who can work with me?"

Mihalik nodded, smiling. "That's what I wanted to hear. Some guys are too stubborn to ask for help, and you just showed me something. And, yes, I can help you. Give me a little time to figure it out. I'm on vacation next week, but we'll pick it up when I get back. Can you survive that long?"

"Yes, I can," Tony said. He stood and stuck out his hand.

Mihalik took it. "Okay. I'm not into lectures, but I wanted you to know the score. Just keep your head low for a week and get along with your colleagues. That includes Sawicki and Traynor." He laughed. "I'm going to have a long talk with both of them. They won't be a problem for you anymore," he said as he turned to leave.

"Wait," Tony said. "Don't do that. I'd like to handle relations with my coworkers by myself. I can win them over."

"Fair enough, but in the meantime, don't let the needling get to you. Even if it does, don't let them see it. That'll only make it worse."

Tony smiled. "Got it."

FIFTEEN

Tuesday, September 13

"Moretti to Chief Archer's office."

Almost finished with the morning check of Rescue-14, Tony jerked up so suddenly that the oil dipstick fell from his hand and clattered to the floor. The chief's office? What for? A million negative thoughts ran through his head. Forgetting the dipstick, he slammed the hood shut, tucked his shirttails into his pants, smoothed his hair, and hurried to the chief's door.

Two officers huddled around the chief, who looked up and motioned Tony in.

"Good morning, Chief," he said, unable to prevent his voice from cracking.

"Take a seat."

Captain Schrum and Deputy Chief Scott Martone took flanking positions behind the chief.

Tony willed his racing pulse to slow. Deep breaths. Whatever this meeting held in store, he could deal with it.

Dispensing with pleasantries, Chief Archer asked, "How would you rate your performance on A-platoon in the five weeks since graduation?"

Tony forced himself to meet the chief's eyes. "Um…" was all he could muster.

"Well?"

Tony pressed his shaking hands into his lap, cleared his throat, and said, "I would give myself a C-plus. I've made some mistakes, but I think I'm starting to settle in now."

"Settle in. I see." The chief flipped through four stapled sheets. Tony glimpsed his own ID photo on the top page. "And what about relations with your coworkers, your brother and sister firefighters? How's that going?"

"I get along with almost everyone."

"Almost." The chief said it as a matter of fact and nodded slowly. He studied the papers again.

Tony shifted in his seat. He felt moisture at the nape of his neck, just below the hairline.

The chief looked Tony square in the eyes. "People take this job for many reasons. At one end of the spectrum, we have those who've dreamt of becoming firefighters since they were kids. Quite a few of them have generational ties to parents or grandparents in the fire service. Many of our people started out as volunteers. Did you know that?"

"Yes, I did. Robbie Stegler is from a firefighting family."

"That's right. Anyone can see the passion *those* individuals bring to this job. They live for it. They did it for free, after all, and many still fight fires with their local volunteer departments. They realize how lucky they are to be here, getting paid to do what they love."

Tony felt a knot in his stomach.

"But that doesn't describe everyone. Some of our best have no previous ties to firefighting. A lot of our folks were attracted by the steady nature of the job, the union card, the regular pay raises, and the chance at a traditional pension. Perks that aren't easy to find today."

Tony wasn't ready for this discussion. His plan wasn't in place yet, and Bruce Mihalik was still on vacation. For the first time, he noticed the deep creases in the chief's brow. Must be nearing retirement. *Will I make it that far? Will I even have a job after today?*

"As I said, there are many reasons people end up here." He set the papers down and steepled his fingers. "We've seen them all, and it doesn't matter *how* or *why* they got here. What *does* matter is how they perform once they *are* here."

Tony glanced up at the other two officers. Deputy Chief Martone maintained a stern countenance, while Captain Schrum tilted his head in what Tony took as a gesture of concern.

The chief continued. "I will not mince words. I'm not happy with your performance so far."

A drop of sweat trickled down Tony's cheek. He wiped it away. Soon it would spread, like it always did when he was caught unaware. Why did his body betray him like this?

"You said you're settling in. That troubles me. Do you know why?"

"No, sir," Tony replied in an unsteady voice.

"It troubles me because you should be doing anything *but* settling in. In fact, you should be very *unsettled* at this stage of your career."

Sweat dripped from Tony's forehead. Trapped, with no place to hide.

"You should have *questions* about everything we do and be working to get those questions answered. Have you spent your free time learning the job? Have you asked others for help?"

"Not yet, but I spoke with Bruce Mihalik about finding someone to work with me to get better at my job."

"I see." The chief seemed surprised. "That's a start."

Tony pulled out a tissue and wiped his perspiring face. He wished Bruce was here to back him up.

Martone spoke up. "We keep a close eye on all recruits once they leave the academy. We try to gauge their progress and their degree of effort." He looked up from the paper. "Your instructors raved about your ability to assimilate complex information, sort through the tactical options, and make a sound decision on the proper course of action. But those are skills we value in an officer or seasoned firefighter, not in a raw recruit. You're new to firefighting, but your basic skills should be sharper by now. Your proficiency level in hose handling, ladder techniques, ropes and knots, and search procedures are well below the standard for a firefighter of your experience level. Well below."

Tony dropped his head. The chief was right. He'd *wanted* to do something about his skills but hadn't figured out how, and so he'd never progressed beyond the planning stage. He wished Mihalik was here to back him up.

"These things are all correctable; you can learn what you need to know. But you aren't trying hard enough. The academy gave you a course in Firefighting 101, the introduction. You're quite intelligent. But so are a lot of your colleagues. You may think you can get by with your education and minimal effort, but you can't."

Tony sat perfectly still. What could he say? His back was clammy. He clenched the arms of the chair.

Chief Archer picked up the thread. "Reynolds International is designated as an Index C airport by the FAA. By those standards, we could get by with three crash trucks and six firefighters on duty. But those who came before us fought to have ARFF services classified as Index D, and that upped the number to eight. But airport management went further and established our strength at fifty-seven, with a minimum of *ten* firefighters per shift, which is why we have eighteen in a platoon."

Tony knew this but didn't dare interrupt.

"Unlike at other airports our size, we're not a part of a city fire department that can send reinforcements at a moment's notice. Reynolds is smack in the middle of a rural area with fire protection provided by small volunteer departments. Those outfits are well trained, motivated, and dedicated. But their rosters have been aging and shrinking for decades, just like everywhere else in Pennsylvania. Consequently, help has to be called from twenty or even thirty miles away. Our mutual aid departments don't have the people to send us, and they can't get to the airport fast enough to make a difference. Did your instructors explain this at the academy?"

"Yes, sir, a little."

"They should have gone into depth about it." Now the chief looked frustrated. He glanced back at Martone, who shrugged.

"The bottom line is this. For the first half hour to forty-five minutes, this department is on an island, and that's an eternity when it involves a terminal fire or aircraft crash. So we can only rely on ourselves, and that's why our personnel level is so high. But we don't have any slack, and we can't tolerate any deadwood. We need every firefighter to be at his or her best."

Tony bit his lower lip.

"So far, we haven't seen your best, have we?"

"No, sir." The sweating had stopped. Tony felt a fatalistic calm. The words no longer registered. He was about to be fired.

"I'm telling you now, if you don't buckle down and take this job seriously, you'll fail.

"I've asked Deputy Chief Martone to provide me with weekly assessments of your performance going forward. You have seven months left on your probation, but I will not wait that long. I'll give you three months. If I'm not satisfied with your progress by the end of the year, I *will* terminate your employment."

For a second, Tony's mind registered only the word *terminate*. Confusion followed as he interpreted the chief's meaning. He *wasn't* getting fired?

"Do you understand?"

"Yes, sir, I do." Tony willed his voice to sound strong and determined, but he didn't defend himself. "I will get better."

"Hmm. That's easy to say, but difficult to do. Questions?"

"No, sir."

"Very well. In the meantime, I suggest you decide if this is the right career for you, and if you have the wherewithal to commit to it. You're dismissed."

Tony spent the rest of the shift in a fog. He had started the day with enthusiasm, but by midmorning, his universe had changed. He hadn't been fired, but he might still lose his job, and with it, his marriage.

When Schrum pulled him aside that evening, Tony explained his plan to find a mentor. Schrum offered to help, but Tony was beginning to doubt if he'd ever be good enough at this job. Maybe it was time to look for something more suited to his talents.

SIXTEEN

Sunday, September 18

The weekend flew by in a torrent of activity. Tony and Lisa finally unpacked the rest of their boxes, hung their modest artwork, organized the kitchen cabinets, and arranged their family photos. What they didn't need, they boxed up for donation. The place finally felt cozy, and they ordered Mexican food to celebrate.

But Tony's mind was elsewhere. He'd been distracted since coming home Saturday morning. Lisa asked him about it, but he passed it off as exhaustion from a hectic day at work. He made no mention of his discussion with the chief, and by Sunday evening, his tenuous job situation was wearing on his psyche. He'd been so optimistic after his talk with Bruce Mihalik, but since meeting with the chief, his enthusiasm had waned.

"How about a bottle of chilled white merlot, Leese?"

"Perfect," she said as she plopped into her seat and pulled the cover from the aluminum takeout pan. "I'm beat, but the place looks great. Much better than coming home from work to all that clutter."

Lisa picked at her chicken burrito and fajita veggies, while Tony downed his three pulled pork enchiladas, pinto beans, and rice. He filled his glass for a third time as Lisa continued to sip her first.

"You put that away pretty fast, big fella. You sure everything's okay?"

Without thinking, he announced his news. "Chief Archer had a little talk with me."

She raised an eyebrow. Concern flashed across her face.

"He wanted to discuss my progress."

"Oh? What did he say?"

"He said I could do better."

Lisa put down her fork. "Better how?"

"He said my skill set wasn't where it should be. He…kind of… hinted that I have room for improvement."

Her eyes narrowed. He'd seen that look many times.

"The chief gave me a time frame to improve."

Lisa sat bolt upright. Her concerned look turned into a glare.

"Hinted at? Time frame? I know you so well. You're giving me bullshit. Tell me what he said. Exactly what he said." Anger tinged her voice.

He wanted to keep her from worrying, but he had to lay it out. "The chief said, in no uncertain terms, that my performance was not up to par. Then he accused me of not trying hard enough to learn my job. To top it off, he threatened to fire me if I didn't make big changes soon."

"Fire you? Are you kidding? How did it get to that point? I've *asked* you how things were going." She inhaled deeply and let it out slowly. "You haven't been honest with me."

"I've had problems, but I thought I'd get past them."

She slapped her hands on the table. Wine flew out of his glass. "Damn it, Tony."

"Sorry, Leese. I didn't want to worry you."

"*Worry* me?" She shot daggers at him.

What could he say? *I'm so screwed.*

"Whatever. It doesn't matter." She paused. "All that matters is what you're going to do about it."

He opened his mouth but hesitated.

"What? Spit it out."

"I had a talk with our union president, and he's going to recommend someone to help me…but."

"But?"

"It may be too late and I'm thinking about leaving the fire department."

Her features turned to ice.

He held up his hands. "Wait; I know what you're thinking. We won't have to move again. We can stay right here. I've been checking around online. There's some good stuff out there. I could land another marketing position, or a sales job."

She didn't move.

"With my experience, I'd move up fast, just like I did at Miller Safety Apparel. Remember how you traveled the country with me on business trips?"

"You quit Miller Safety Apparel." Her tone was now flat, matter-of-fact.

"Yeah, but, you know, it was the travel. Anyway, I'd move into management in no time."

"Of course. That big management job you've been talking about forever."

He let the comment pass. The hole was getting deeper. "Plus, with my master's degree, I could teach at one of the universities around here. Gettysburg College offers an international affairs major. Right up my alley. Who knows; I could end up doing both."

"I see. Work at some half-ass entry-level sales job all day, and then go out and teach at night." She nodded. "What's the going rate for adjunct professors these days? Especially if they don't have a PhD? Three thousand a semester?"

"Well, yeah, but with the money we've saved, we'd be okay. Hell, we might even be able to build a house."

"Build a house." She nodded. "That would be nice. One of your firefighter buddies must be a contractor. Let's have him draw up the plans right away. I'll start shopping for curtains."

"Leese," he said with all the conviction he could muster, "we could finally start a family."

“There we go. That’s the capper.”

Tony swallowed hard.

“Let’s start a family. Wonderful. You’re ready to have children. I’m so glad you can finally discuss it.”

He fell silent. There was no talking to her now.

Lisa grabbed her wineglass and the bottle, walked into the bedroom, and slammed the door. He thought about following her, telling her how he would make everything right, but she wouldn’t believe it. *He* didn’t believe it. He let her be.

Tony was sitting on the sofa with his feet propped on the coffee table, staring at a blank television screen, when Lisa emerged two hours later.

“Can we talk?” she asked.

“Sure.” He beckoned her to the sofa, but she sat at the table.

He joined her.

“What I’m about to say isn’t because of what you told me at dinner. It’s something I’ve been thinking about, even before we moved. I guess it started when you left your last job.”

His heart sank. What had he done?

“I agreed to leave my job—my career—and move here with you.”

“I know you did.”

“Please let me finish. I have to say this.”

He nodded.

“Back then, I made a decision. I would do this for you, and I wouldn’t complain. I’d give you my wholehearted support. But…”

Tony waited.

“But I also decided it would be the *last* time.”

He bit his lip, hard.

“You earned a master’s degree nine years ago, and you’re still looking for that perfect job. But there’s no such thing. You have a great opportunity here. You’ve got to grow up. Life is hard; work is hard. Nobody owes you anything and you can’t keep running away.”

That stung.

“I still love you, but you’ve put a tremendous strain on our relationship. I’m so mad at you right now, I can hardly think. I can’t live like this anymore, always wondering when the next predicament will slap me in the face." She was emotional but determined, which frightened Tony more than if she had screamed at him.

"You need to figure out what's important to you and what you're going to do next."

He was about to reiterate his plan but thought better of it.

"Just know that the next move I make will be back to Pittsburgh... *alone*." Her voice cracked on that last dreadful word.

"Leese, come on. You can't..."

"I think you should sleep in the spare bedroom tonight," she said as she rose. "We both need some time alone to think. We'll talk again in a couple days."

Tony sat, stunned. His world was collapsing around him, and it was all his fault. He stayed in the guest room, but there was no sleep.

SEVENTEEN

Tuesday, September 20

The workday crept along as ominous visions of the future clouded Tony's thoughts. He'd made a mess of his marriage, and he wasn't sure the damage could be repaired.

Once morning duties and afternoon training were over, he kept to himself. Firefighters weren't allowed in their bunk rooms before five o'clock, but that rule was seldom enforced, and at three-thirty, he retreated to the space he considered his inner sanctum. He tried digging into Stephen King's uncut edition of *The Stand* to take his mind off things but couldn't concentrate. Lisa filled his thoughts.

After a fitful night of sleep, he got up early, eschewed a shower, and punched out at 6:40. He wanted—needed—to talk to his wife, but not yet. He would wait, let her cool down, and talk to her in person.

But he couldn't bear to go back to the empty townhouse. Instead, he drove to nearby Interstate 81, headed north, and took the exit for US Route 30. Forty-five minutes later, he passed the Lutheran Theological Seminary, parked the Cherokee, and stepped into a world he knew well: the Gettysburg National Military Park. Tony had developed a lifelong passion for Civil War history during two visits to the park: one with his family when he was thirteen and another on a high school class trip.

A warm morning breeze wafted across West Confederate Avenue as he set out across the Rebel lines on Seminary Ridge. With tourist season over, a few walkers and joggers were the only people in sight. The sounds of families, cars, and tour buses were nonexistent. Eerily quiet. As he preferred it.

Sunlight bathed his face, and he allowed his mind to drift away.

Lisa had accompanied him to Gettysburg on a research trip the summer prior to their senior year in college. It was a memorable weekend. When they weren't making love in their cheap motel room, they walked the fields. Lisa soaked up the history and the natural beauty of the park while Tony fell head over heels for her. It was in Gettysburg that their young relationship had blossomed, and they'd returned many times over the years. Lisa often joked that she could give the tour herself.

During one of their visits, as he leafed through the *Gettysburg Times* at the Ragged Edge, a downtown coffee shop frequented by the college crowd, a notice for a civil service test caught his eye: the nearby John F. Reynolds Airport was recruiting firefighters. On a whim, Tony signed up for the exam. He scored third out of 516 applicants but heard nothing for almost three years. He'd forgotten all about it when, out of the blue, an HR rep called from the airport with a job offer.

For a sales rep at a business-to-business products firm—a position for which he had neither the skills nor the interest—the opportunity was fortuitous. It took a lot of convincing and a couple of trips to scout the area, but Lisa, a big-city girl through and through, agreed to uproot her life and move with him to rural south central Pennsylvania. How many spouses would do that?

He knew this battlefield intimately. He would drive Lisa crazy by stopping to read the inscriptions on every tablet and monument, pondering how the opposing generals positioned and shifted their forces and how they overcame the geographic obstacles of war. But today, as he walked past the rows of Confederate cannons, his own problems consumed him. After less than six months, he was in danger of losing his job, and with it, his wife.

Lisa was right about everything she had said on Sunday, but he hadn't suspected how close to the edge she was. Her words said it all: The marriage wouldn't survive another job change. And he knew his idea of finding another job in the region was a pipe dream.

Tony paused at the Virginia Memorial and looked over the field where ten thousand Confederate troops of the Army of Northern Virginia, massed together in rows and columns, had set out to break the Army of the Potomac. Tony followed their one-mile line of march across the late-summer grass toward the federal positions on Cemetery Ridge.

As he walked, he imagined the scene as union batteries rained cannonballs into the rows of approaching Confederates, swapping solid shot and explosive shells for double-canister, little steel balls that shredded the Southern troops.

Tony stopped in front of the little copse of trees that marked the Union center. From here, withering musket fire from a thousand blue-clad soldiers tore into the Confederate ranks. Yet the rebels marched on until the spear of their attack pierced the Northern lines and the fighting became hand-to-hand. They kept going until federal reinforcements flooded the breach. Until all was lost.

Tony visualized the carnage. A valiant, desperate charge, and a terrible slaughter. "Bad mistake, Bobbie Lee," he said to the open field. "You thought your soldiers were unbeatable, but Union troops, fighting on their home soil, and for a just cause, proved you wrong."

Compared to the suffering on this field, Tony's problems were infinitesimal. But there *was* a lesson for him in terms of the qualities the troops who crossed swords on this field possessed. In the third year of the war, most were hardened veterans with courage and a steely determination. And they were experts in their deadly trade.

Tony wasn't a firefighting veteran, but he had no qualms about his courage, and Lisa's words had fired his determination. He was confident he could whip himself into physical shape, but firefighting was a skilled profession, and that was the problem. He didn't have the background to master it on his own. He knew who could help him, and when Bruce Mihalik returned from his vacation, he'd enlist the union president's help to facilitate his plan.

Part II

GETTING BETTER ALL THE TIME

EIGHTEEN

Thursday, September 22

Tony checked his watch. The annual FAA inspection wrapped up in five hours and the timed response test was imminent. Staffing Rescue-12 with Evan O'Brien, Tony was caught up in the anticipation rippling through the station. Evan, who had run track in high school, likened the mood to the moments before the starting pistol was fired.

The challenge was simple. Once the tower initiated the test, the first crash truck had three minutes to reach the midpoint of the farthest runway and begin flowing water. At REY, that meant either runway eighteen-thirty-six or six-left/twenty-four-right. Subsequent crash trucks needed to reach the scene in four minutes.

The crash tones sounded at two o'clock. "This is the tower with a timed response drill to runway eighteen-thirty-six. Repeat. This is a timed response drill to runway eighteen-thirty-six."

Within a minute, four behemoths were speeding across taxiway Sierra. Captain Schrum led the charge in Rescue-10, and his fifteen-hundred-gallon Striker RIV quickly outpaced the heavier vehicles.

Evan steered into the tail-end position of the staggered line. Rescue-12 was the slowest vehicle because it featured a high-reach extendable turret, or HRET, commonly called by its trade name: Snozzle. The turret sat atop an articulating boom on the roof.

"Should I call out times for you?" Tony asked.

"No, let's make sure we get there safely. Time will take care of itself."

Tony watched as Evan focused on the vehicles in front of him while simultaneously scanning to his left and right.

"Okay, Tony, let's get that bumper turret ready."

Tony gripped the joystick with his left hand, moved the turret out of its nested position just below the windshield, and angled it toward the concrete. "Got it."

"Good, but let's aim the turret forty-five degrees to the left. That'll make it easier for the inspector to see the discharge from the tower. We only need to flow it for five seconds. You know the sequence?"

"Uh, yeah." Tony looked at the joystick controls. "Toggle the switch for water and low flow, then squeeze the trigger." He thought for a second. "It's low flow for the test, right?"

"Right. Make sure it's set for water only. We don't want a foamy mess on the runway. Set your pattern to a narrow fog. It's good practice for the real thing."

The radio came to life. "Rescue-10 is flowing."

"Cap's on it today," Evan said. He slowed the rig as they approached eighteen-thirty-six; 11 and 13 were already on the runway. "This truck is top-heavy. It's a real bitch in a turn."

"Rescue-11 is flowing."

"They got there fast, right behind the captain," Tony said.

Evan didn't respond. His face was a study in concentration as he eased the big vehicle into a smooth left turn. They trailed Rescue-13 by a hundred yards. Ten seconds later, Tony spotted a stream of water splashing onto the left edge of the runway.

"Rescue-13 flowing."

"Get ready. Center point coming up," Evan said as they passed Hotel-1.

Tony activated the water switch, initiating a flow from the tank and causing the pump's impeller to spin and build pressure.

"Wait…wait…wait…and…now. Hit it!"

Tony punched the discharge switch. A sideways shudder rocked the truck as five hundred gallons per minute shot across the runway.

"Rescue-12 is flowing," Evan reported. "Good job, Tony. Shut down."

Tony toggled the water switch off as Evan pulled up behind the other three vehicles.

"That's it," Evan said. "I'd say we're well under the required time."

"Nice," Tony said. "You're a pro."

"Hah, it's just a matter of practice. Let's get this big boy to the academy before the inspector arrives."

Twenty minutes later, the FAA inspector, a fiftyish former airline pilot, met Tony and Evan at the academy, where she set up a test stand in the shadow of the hulking simulator.

She used a computerized refractometer to test the foam proportioning system of Rescue-12, followed by each of the other three crash trucks from the timed response run. Rescue-10 was the last vehicle to cycle through, and before he returned to Station Bravo, Captain Schrum caught Tony's eye and nodded toward Evan. Shortly afterward, the inspector confirmed all foam systems were working properly, and she departed the academy.

"Okay, partner," Evan said. "I'll meet you in the lunchroom."

As Tony thought through the spiel he'd prepared, Evan came in with a big bag of chips and a jar of salsa. "I keep a stash in my locker," he said. He pulled two Diet Cokes from the fridge and sat with Tony. "Here you go. It's the best way to celebrate the end of a successful day. If you can't have a Sam Adams, that is."

"I shouldn't. I'm trying to get rid of this gut and get back in some kind of shape."

"A worthy goal, my friend, but this won't hurt you." He held up the bag. "See? They're baked. Besides, I thought our rigorous physical fitness program molded you recruits into Olympic athletes."

Tony laughed. "Yeah, it was *really* intense."

Evan raised his Coke. "Here's to a successful inspection."

"What's attached to that strap?" Tony asked, pointing to the black fiber cord around Evan's neck. "Is that a charm of some kind? I've never seen you without it."

Evan reached into his t-shirt and pulled out a silver amulet festooned with intertwining knots. "This, my Italian friend, is a Celtic protection talisman. It brings good luck and protects the wearer from harm."

"Really? Shouldn't you be wearing a four-leaf clover?"

"Very funny. Shouldn't you be wearing five gold chains?"

"Ha ha. Point taken. As long as you believe."

"I do," Evan said as the two made small talk. After a few minutes, he became serious. "So, Tony, I know we work on the same platoon, but between teaching here and using the comp days I built up during your academy class, I've hardly seen you since graduation. How are things going? Do you like the job so far?"

"Haven't you heard any gossip from the other guys? Rumors spread like wildfire around here." Evan had to know. There were no secrets at the fire station.

"I've heard a few things, but I like to get my information from the source."

Tony averted his eyes.

"It can't be that bad."

Tony met Evan's gaze. "It's worse."

Evan sipped his Diet Coke.

Tony looked out the window at the training field and simulator. "All this," he said, sweeping his arm. "All the classes we took, all the work we did on that field. The way we sweated in that damn rusty simulator. I thought it prepared me, but it didn't."

Evan narrowed his eyes.

Had he just insulted his friend? "I don't mean you or what you taught us. It wasn't the training. It was me. I did pretty well here, but it hasn't translated to the station."

"Really?" Evan said with a hint of doubt.

"Okay, I wasn't the best recruit. But I was competent, wasn't I?"

"You were competent in some things, way above average in a few, not so good in a lot of others. In short, you're just like all the other recruits I've met in the ten years I've been teaching."

Tony squirmed in his seat. He welcomed the objective opinion, but the comments stung.

"Hang on," Evan said. "I can see what you're thinking. You're *not* a lost cause."

Tony looked away.

"Look at me. And listen."

Tony complied.

"Yes, you've got some problems. But nothing that can't be fixed. If you buckle down and give it your all, you'll be fine." He placed a hand on Tony's shoulder. "You've got the physical raw materials and you're smart as a whip. Did you know you intimidated other instructors?"

Tony shot him a disbelieving glance.

"It's true. You picked up on the theoretical aspects of firefighting so fast that a couple of them had to brush up on what they were teaching."

"I enjoyed the theory, especially the strategy and tactics."

"Not just the theory. You blew your classmates away during the practical problem-solving exercises. You can take in complex information and make fast, intelligent decisions. That's a critical skill in our business, but very few of our colleagues possess it. Hell, I struggle with it all the time. But you need to apply yourself. Turn your knowledge and ability into a set of practical skills."

Tony smiled. Just as he'd thought. *Evan is the guy to help me.* That's what the captain's signal had meant. Time to see if he was game. "Funny you should say that. I came to the same conclusion. I have a plan, and it involves you. If you're willing."

"I'm intrigued. Let's hear it."

Tony admitted he'd been coasting since graduation. He recounted what the chief had said, explained he had three months to save his job, and asked Evan to mentor him.

"I didn't realize things had gone so far. Why didn't you come to me earlier?"

“I should have, but I didn’t think you’d have the time, since you’ve been so busy. We barely see you in the platoon.”

“That’s not going to change until the end of our training season, but…” Evan stood up and walked to the window, where he stood for several minutes, gazing at the field. “All right, here’s what we’ll do,” he said and turned back to Tony. “I’ll get with Captain Schrum and Deputy Chief Martone. I’m sure they’ll go along. But you’re going to have to work your ass off.” As Evan explained what he had in mind, Tony felt a thrilling surge of hope.

NINETEEN

Monday, September 26

Drops splashed to the floor in front of Yellow-224. The hard overnight rain was gone, but the shed roof held water. Frank Barlow ran through a quick check of the fluids and slammed the engine cowling shut. Time for the big event—the stupid winter operations drill that the snow crews had practiced for in August. A three-ring circus; the typical airport shitshow.

At nine-thirty, loudspeakers called the drivers to a meeting up front. Frank ambled over and stood in the back of the idiot parade, where Joe Shinsky, who had the most seniority among the field maintenance supervisors, was acting the big man. Ray Wheatley, the second trick supervisor, and Todd Corlett, who ran the graveyard shift, stood beside him like little kids next to their mommy.

"We better be on our toes today," Shinsky said. "The CEO will be out with the director and the rest of the airport brass. And don't forget about the tower. The ground controllers will be watching our every move." Wheatley and Corlett nodded.

Idiot bobbleheads. Who cared about the CEO, or what the controllers in the tower saw?

"Let's show them how we keep Reynolds International open, no matter how bad a storm we get clobbered with."

Frank wanted to clobber his boss.

"You guys have an hour to finish checking your trucks. Do it right."

Frank huffed.

"At eleven o'clock, Ray and Todd will get the rigs lined up. Listen for your number."

What a couple of pussies. Why did they put up with Shinsky's crap?

"Pizzas will be delivered at noon." The supervisor smiled at the crowd. "I want you in your rigs, engines running, by twelve-forty-five."

Frank shuffled away; he'd heard enough. Buddy had been right about one thing: this hullabaloo was all to make the muckety-mucks look good.

* * *

Allie sat in Ops-2 with her hands clamped to the steering wheel. The trucks were lined up and ready to go, but Sterling Price was droning on while Sharon Lambert and Brian Murray stood behind him on the podium. It was 1:20 p.m., and the exercise was late.

The CEO pointed to the lineup of snow-clearing vehicles. "This airport has never closed for weather." Price finished his oration, took a few questions, and closed the press conference.

Allie mimicked his monotonous voice: "And now, ladies and gentlemen, I'm done pontificating.

"Thank you, Director Lambert," Allie announced to the empty cab. "You know I arranged the timing of this drill with the FAA, don't you?" Oh, what did it matter? Sharon didn't have the chutzpah to tell her boss to cut it short while he performed for the cameras.

The media crews and invited dignitaries climbed aboard a motor coach for the drive to the deicing pad on the east ramp, where they would observe the parade. Allie sent Tyler Connolly, an ops specialist, to escort the bus while she remained with the convoy. To her disgust, the CEO delayed their departure by chatting with a couple of reporters.

Joe Shinsky, in Yellow-41, his Chevy Trailblazer, pulled up to Allie.

"I'm gonna get the boys moving."

"Finally. We're thirty-five minutes late."

Shinsky shrugged and drove to the front of the line. She shouldn't have complained to him. The delay wasn't his fault.

Sun glinted off the bright blue blade of Yellow-246, the fleet's newest Oshkosh snowplow, as it passed through Gate-325, departing the nonsecure maintenance pad for the active ramps to the south. An impressive spectacle, although the last of the four plows, Yellow-224, looked like it had seen better days.

Next came a quartet of Kodiak runway sweeper trucks, led by Yellow-274. Known as brooms, these specialized airport vehicles were among the best weapons in the snow-clearing arsenal. With front-mounted twenty-foot-wide rolls of hard plastic bristles, they were ideal for breaking up deposits of ice embedded into a runway's grooved surface.

Yellow-270 fronted a column of three SnowWolf blowers, their big orange blades projecting menacingly from gaping cowlings. Allie loved sci-fi flicks, and she pictured these giants as alien-eating machines. The blowers eliminated dangerous ridges along the runway and taxiway edges by throwing snow far off the paved surfaces.

Two deicing tankers—Yellow-281 and 283—came next. These vehicles dispensed potassium acetate through rear-mounted sprayers to prevent snow and ice from bonding to the surface. Two dump trucks tailed the parade. Salt was verboten on the airfield because of its corrosive effects on aircraft, so Yellow-290 carried sodium formate ice melting pellets, while Yellow-295 was loaded with sand.

Allie tuned her radio to the exercise frequency and followed the procession through the gate. The action was about to begin and she was in her element: on the airfield, amid a bustle of activity.

"Ground, this is Ops-2. We'd like to begin the snow-clearing exercise on the preapproved route, beginning at taxiway Hotel and finishing on runway eighteen-thirty-six."

"Ops-2, ground. That's copied. We've been waiting for you."

Allie noted the snarkiness in the controller's voice. It was warranted. "Ops-2 and seventeen vehicles are on the east ramp at Oscar. We request Oscar, right on Hotel, permission to cross runway two-four-right and make a U-turn at Hotel-1. We'll recross two-four-right and drive back to Oscar. We'd like to run the route three times." She paused for a second and added, "If air traffic permits." That should cool him off.

"Ops-2 and company, that route is approved. Runways six-left/twenty-four-right and eighteen-thirty-six are closed for the exercise. You do not need permission to cross. We'll advise if traffic requires us to cut it short."

Fair enough. "Roger. Oscar and Hotel to Hotel-1 and back to Oscar. Runways six-left/two-four-right and eighteen-thirty-six are closed for the exercise. Be advised Yellow-41 is the exercise leader."

Allie repeated the clearance to Shinsky, and the field maintenance supervisor commanded his vehicles to move off the ramp and follow him across taxiway Oscar to their positions on Hotel.

Arranged in an offset pattern, the four plows stretched halfway across the hundred-fifty-foot taxiway with a quartet of brooms arrayed behind them in the same staggered formation. The blowers, deicers, and dump trucks brought up the rear. Allie wheeled Ops-2 to the back of the line.

Shinsky gave the go-ahead, and the dry run commenced. The conga line accelerated to fifteen miles per hour for the simulated snow removal. At Hotel-1, the lead plow executed a smart U-turn to begin clearing the other half of the taxiway.

Such an awesome sight. The power and choreography of all that heavy machinery. The only thing missing was snow. In a strange way, Allie loved snowstorms, which presented another challenge to safe airport operations, another opportunity to show her stuff.

Wait. "Where the hell is he going?" Yellow-224 failed to follow the three lead plows and continued across taxiway Hotel to the approach end of runway two-four-left.

Allie snatched the mic. "Yellow-224 from Ops-2. You've deviated from the approved route."

No reply.

Now it was Shinsky's turn. "All vehicles from exercise leader. Stop where you are. Yellow-224, turn around and get back in line on Hotel. Immediately."

Still nothing from the driver. Allie hit the brakes and pulled to the edge of the taxiway. Did she have to chase this idiot?

"Yellow-224, return to Hotel. Now." Shinsky's voice rose. "Yellow-224, do you copy?"

Five seconds passed. Yellow-224 turned and started back for Hotel. Just like nothing had happened.

"FM supe from Yellow-224. I had to pull off. It sounded like the plow was coming loose."

"Oh, no you don't. You're not getting away with that," Allie muttered as she skirted the last truck in line and made for the runway. She screeched to a halt a hundred feet from Yellow-224, jumped out, and crossed her arms over her head, the signal for the errant driver to stop. For a second, it looked like he would try to drive around her. Then he stopped.

Allie's temper flared. She ran up to the cab and shouted at the driver to lower his window. He gave her a *who, me?* glance but complied.

"What the hell are you doing?" She swung a hand toward the taxiway. "How could you miss that turn? You were in a fricking line! And now you're on the runway, for God's sake!" Her heart pounded as the invectives spewed out.

The driver's face flushed.

She blanked on the name before recognizing him. "You're Barlow, aren't you? How dumb can you be?"

"Don't you call me dumb!" He jabbed a finger at her. "The damn runway is closed. I didn't do anything wrong."

"That doesn't matter. If you screw up on a clear day, what are you going to do in a snowstorm? What if you drive onto an active runway? How many years have you been here?"

"Shut the fuck up!"

She stopped, stunned.

"You're not my boss. You're just some bitch from operations. I don't answer to you."

"You answer to *me*!" Shinsky had come up behind Allie. "What the hell are you doing, Frank?"

"Like I said, there's something wrong with the plow."

"Oh yeah? Why didn't you pull off on Hotel? And why didn't you answer the radio?"

"I was trying to. You didn't give me a chance."

"Don't give me that bullshit. Get the fuck back in line and pay attention to what you're doing. It's like follow-the-leader. Even you can do that, can't you?"

Frank glared at his boss, then at Allie. He rolled up the window and drove past them, nearly sideswiping Allie's SUV.

"Sorry, Allie. I'll deal with him later."

"Thanks, Joe. I shouldn't have yelled at your guy. But when I get pissed, I just—"

"Don't sweat it. He's been a pain in my ass for a long time."

Shinsky resumed the drill and Allie drove back to her tail-end position. The tower allowed all three sweeps, and there were no further incidents. At least the fiasco had occurred out of sight of the news crews.

Allie considered reporting Barlow to her director, but her own angry outburst would come to light. It was the second time she'd blown up in Shinsky's presence. Lambert might suspend her or send her to anger management classes. *Nope, Althea, just suck it up and move on.* Her mother had warned her many times to control her temper before it got her into trouble. Why was it so difficult to follow that advice?

TWENTY

Wednesday, September 28

Once again, Tony found himself standing outside a chief's door, but this time it was the office of Deputy Chief Scott Martone. Just back from a familiarization tour of the fuel farm, he'd been thinking about lunch when the LT had escorted him to officers' row. What was this about? Had Martone changed the chief's mind about giving him until the end of the year to improve his performance? His palms were already sweaty.

Captain Schrum let him in and motioned to one of three seats in front of Martone's desk. Too nervous to look around, Tony noticed an antique Gamewell fire alarm box mounted on the back wall, but little else.

Martone removed his glasses and eyed Tony. "First of all, let me put your mind at ease. I see what you're thinking, but we have no bridge for you to jump off."

Tony sat perfectly still.

"Chief Martone was joking," Schrum said.

"An amateurish attempt, I'm afraid," Martone said. "Please, Tony, breathe."

Tony didn't move. The words didn't register.

"Let's cut to the chase before he faints, shall we, Pete? Could you lead off?"

The captain faced Tony. "Bruce Mihalik and Evan O'Brien got together and told us about your desire for improvement, and how you engaged them for advice."

"Yes," Martone said. "And we're impressed."

Astonished, Tony relaxed.

"You're not the first firefighter to get off on the wrong foot, and we'll assist anyone who wants to be helped." Martone eyed him. "The question is, are you sincere?"

Tony didn't hesitate. "I am, Chief. I really am."

"Very well. Evan is one of the finest firefighters we've had on this job, and he sees a lot of raw potential in you, as do the union president and your captain."

Tony smiled at Schrum.

"Evan also presented us with a proposition to take you under his wing."

Tony sat up in his chair and pulled his shoulders back, his dread now curiosity.

"If you agree, you'll spend the next four weeks at the training academy, working with the instructors and the paying customers: firefighters from airports throughout the Northeast. You'll return to your platoon at the end of October."

Tony leaned forward. Evan hadn't mentioned temporary duty at the academy, but this plan was perfect.

"Don't be fooled; it'll be a grind. We're shorthanded, with one of our instructors on military leave and another on workers' comp, and October is chock-full of training programs."

Martone paused and eyed Tony. "You'll bust your butt humping hose, setting up the field, and doing whatever scut work is needed. You'll participate in the classroom sessions and practical evolutions, and maybe even lead a few when you're ready. Part gopher, part student, part instructor. A crash course, if you'll pardon another bad attempt at humor. And you'll get invaluable practice time, every day. Much more than we were able to give you during your training."

Tony waited, but the chief offered nothing else.

The captain broke the silence. "What do you think, Tony?"

"Oh yes," he said, nodding rapidly. "I'll do it gladly."

"All right, then," Martone said. "Starting next Monday, you'll punch in and out at the academy. Evan will evaluate your performance and send me weekly progress reports."

Tony tried to take in his good fortune. "Thank you both. I want to make this work. I *will* make this work."

"Don't thank us. Thank Evan and Bruce," Martone said. "And good luck."

In the hallway, Schrum patted Tony on the back. "You've got your second chance. Make the most of it."

"No worries, Cap. I will."

"Good, and don't forget: you and Stegler have a tour at the control tower this afternoon. Two o'clock sharp."

A lead weight had lifted and Tony felt he could *fly* to the top of that tower.

* * *

"We'll be able to see forever," Robbie said as he and Tony entered the lobby of the air traffic control facility.

"Better than a trip to Disney," Tony replied with a laugh.

As they chatted with the guard, another airport employee arrived. A stumpy man, probably in his fifties. He wore the standard airport authority gray work shirt with his name—Frank—embroidered on the right and *Field Maintenance* on the left. Grease stained his baggy pants, and his scuffed boots looked like they'd been through a dusty infantry march. He wasn't a new employee; that much was obvious. The man's wavy salt-and-pepper hair needed a wash. Tony thought back to the day the members of his platoon had gotten on him for not ironing his uniform. Comparing himself—now properly turned out—with this man from maintenance, he understood.

Frank didn't introduce himself and stood off to one side. Tony tried not to stereotype people, but Frank reminded him of the mill workers who had populated his northwestern Pennsylvania hometown when he was a kid. It wasn't a criticism. Tony's grandfather had once worked at a now-defunct manufacturing firm.

"Good afternoon, gentlemen," a voice from behind called. "Welcome to the tower. I'm Ellen Ming, the operations manager here at the FAA's air traffic control facility." A tall, thin woman in her late thirties or early forties, Ellen had close-cropped hair that was almost completely white. An occupational hazard, no doubt. She made an immediate impression on Tony with her broad smile, alert eyes, and firm handshake as she greeted the little group.

"Your escort called and said she's running late, but we'll get started," Ellen said. The guard handed her a clipboard. "Oh, I see we have a late addition from…field maintenance. Mr. Barlow, welcome."

Tony eyed Frank Barlow, who now came across as angry rather than disinterested. Ellen led them to a conference room off the main lobby, and everyone took seats at a large rectangular table. As she began, Allie Robinson walked in with a young girl in tow.

"Hi, Ellen. So sorry we're late."

"No worries, Allie." Ellen glanced at her clipboard. "And you must be Trista Nicholson."

The girl mumbled an assent and sat down. Allie shot a disapproving look, shook her head, and motioned apologetically to the crowd.

Allie's short, curly hairstyle and youthful complexion made her look midtwenties, in Tony's estimation, although as a shift manager she had to be closer to thirty. Tony watched her complexion harden as Allie caught sight of Frank, who sat alone at the far end of the table. She appeared surprised and not very pleased to see him. And Frank's return stare was nothing short of vitriolic. Whoa; no love lost there.

"Congratulations on your new jobs," Ellen said. "We enjoy meeting airport employees and showing them around." Tony glanced at Frank, who frowned at Ellen's comment.

"We have excellent working relationships with the operations and fire departments, and the maintenance crews as well. It's important for you to tour our facility and meet a few of our people." She paused and glanced at Allie, who confirmed Ellen's statement with a nod.

"We'll be talking to each other often, and airfield safety depends on the accuracy of our communications. It helps us all when we can put a face to the voice on the radio, don't you think?" She smiled and added, "So that's the official FAA introduction. Now let's meet some of our folks and find out what they do."

Ellen led the little group in a quick walk through the first level of the complex: offices, conference rooms, and miscellaneous spaces. The facility was built in a style Tony called early 1980s university concrete.

Ellen introduced them to the air staff manager, the training coordinator, and a few specialists, who spoke briefly about their responsibilities. Even Robbie looked bored until they arrived at the training room, which featured an impressive array of simulators.

Two controllers sat in front of radar scopes while an instructor threw curveballs at them. Tony cringed. Welcome to a world of nonstop stress.

Next, Ellen led them down a flight of stairs. "We're now entering the terminal radar approach control area, or TRACON," she explained. "This is the darkened room you've seen in movies and TV. But unlike those scenes that depict a setting in the tower, TRACON is usually on the ground floor, or on a basement level like this one.

"The people in this room handle the approach and departure of all aircraft originating or terminating at Reynolds International. These folks represent one of two equally important parts of our system, the other being our ground controllers in the tower."

The tour gathered around one of the radar screens, where a controller was vectoring inbound traffic for landing. Tony, a geek at heart, found this sky dance fascinating. Frank stood apart and continued to shoot eye daggers at Allie. The guy had some serious issues.

After a brief question and answer session, Ellen took them to an elevator that whisked them to the top of the complex, climbing 175 feet in less than thirty seconds. Tony's stomach churned. Trista's face went pale.

The elevator stopped one floor below the top, at the prep and break area. From there, a set of spiral stairs led them to the tower cab. Definitely not ADA compliant.

"I know what you're thinking," Ellen said. "The FAA built this complex in the mideighties, when handicap accessibility wasn't a big concern. They have plans to retrofit it with an elevator, but so far the funding hasn't come through."

Tony chuckled. Ellen was one sharp lady.

"Anyway, we keep three controllers on duty during the daylight and afternoon shifts, and two on the eleven-to-seven shift." The controllers, wearing headsets, stood at the windows, engrossed in their duties. "At the moment, we're handling both inbound traffic and departing flights. Take a listen."

"United two-two-seven, taxi via Bravo and Tango to runway six-right."

"Delta forty-four-thirty-five, runway six-left, winds one-five at ten. Turn right heading three-zero-zero. Cleared for takeoff. Contact departure on one-niner-point-three-five. Good day."

"American eight-seventy-five, Reynolds tower, cleared to land."

"Yellow-254, drive Papa and Hotel to Victor. Hold short of runway two-four-right."

"Republic niner-two-seven, Reynolds tower. Stand by."

"Spirit sixteen-eighty, Reynolds ground. Taxi via Foxtrot, Sierra, Quebec to your gate."

"Southwest sixteen-thirty-three, climb and maintain six thousand. Traffic off your right at one mile."

"Ops-4 drive Tango, Bravo, Romeo to the ramp."

"Fascinating, isn't it?" Ellen asked. "While we're waiting, please enjoy the sights. It's the best perk of our job," she said as she motioned the group to the windows, which presented a crystal-clear 360-degree view of the surrounding area.

Trista took a peek and backed away. Her pallor hadn't changed since the elevator ride. Robbie, as usual, looked like a kid in a candy store. Frank ignored the invitation and plopped into an empty seat.

Between the forested slopes of South Mountain at the northern end of the Blue Ridge five miles to the east and the hazy Appalachian Range ten miles to the west, the fertile landscape of the Cumberland Valley lay before them in spectacular detail.

Rolling hills, snaking streams, rocky outcrops, and patches of forest, interspersed with a patchwork of dairy farms and cornfields, presented a bucolic scene. Quite unlike the satellite views he and Lisa had examined before moving to the region. The prominent spires of the region's many churches, along with a few housing developments, schools, and light industrial facilities, dotted the landscape. Tony could almost make out the apple trees, peach orchards, and livestock he'd seen during explorations along the area's winding secondary roads.

"Looks like we have a break in the action," Ellen said. "Let me introduce Jared Beck, Mason Carillo, and Valerie Yeager. All three are controllers, and Valerie is a frontline supervisor, or *tower supe* in airport vernacular. These are the people who do the actual work around here." The trio smiled and said hello.

"We rotate our controllers between the tower and TRACON. They're fully qualified to perform either function."

"And it gets me away from these two for a couple of weeks," Valerie said with a laugh.

Allie's smile was ear to ear. She really got into this stuff, and Tony understood why.

Ellen continued. "The controllers up here keep watch over the runways and taxiways, monitor the weather, and they're the first to know if any runways or taxiways are closed—your best source of information for all things airfield."

"We are," Mason said. "And don't be intimidated. We sound gruff and mean on the radio, but that's because—"

"Because we are," Jared said.

"No, because we have to deal with arrogant pilots all day," Mason said. "They don't listen unless you put some authority into your voice."

The trio laughed, and it was Ellen's turn to roll her eyes. "Anyway, as you heard, these folks direct departing aircraft from the ramp to the appropriate runway by giving them taxiing instructions and granting the pilots clearance to take off. As for arrivals, TRACON transfers inbound aircraft to the tower at five to seven miles out. Controllers up here give them instructions for their final approach and grant them permission to land and taxi to their gates.

"The tower also controls the movement of all ground vehicles on the runways and taxiways. That's when we communicate with ops or the fire department or maintenance, and as Allie can tell you, we do that a lot."

The controllers resumed their aircraft communications as Ellen walked over to a desk-mounted display with the airfield grid overlaid on a blue background. "This is our As-Dee." Puzzled faces dotted the room. "For those of you who aren't familiar, A-S-D-E stands for *airport surface detection equipment*. It's a network of transponders and SMR, the surface movement radar that allows us to monitor aircraft and vehicles on the airfield."

"As you can see, our three runways are outlined with black lines, and the taxiways and ramp areas with gray. The radar antenna is on the roof, right above us. The system continuously updates the map."

Ellen pointed to taxiway Sierra. "There aren't any ground vehicles on the field right now, but we have four aircraft taxiing to and from the ramp. Radar pinpoints their position while transponders send us their identification codes."

Tony moved closer. Small white aircraft icons moved slowly across the screen, each one tagged with a series of letters and numbers.

"The information is real-time and continuously updated," Ellen said. "It's especially helpful at night, or in bad weather."

"How do the controllers keep track of all this when they're busy?" Robbie asked.

"Good question. The As-Dee sounds an audible alarm if it detects potential runway conflicts."

"Nice," Robbie said. "This is like a video game."

"In a way, but it's not a game," Ellen said. "The controllers, the radios, and the As-Dee. The FAA designed the system to prevent runway incursions or collisions between ground vehicles and aircraft." She pointed to the screen. "Nobody wants a fire truck pulling out in front of a 737, and I'm sure none of you want to find yourself lost or in the wrong place."

"What if a runway is closed?" The brusque question came from Frank, who rose and addressed Valerie. "Can you get in trouble for driving on a closed runway without getting clearance?" His tone was accusatory.

The tower supe hesitated. Ellen stepped in. "Well, no, not if the runway is closed, and as long as—"

"I knew it!" Red spots bloomed on Frank's cheeks and neck.

Tony sensed his own face heating up. What was that guy's problem?

With confusion on her face, Ellen tilted her head toward Allie.

"Closed or not, you still need to notify the tower before you enter a runway," Allie said. "You can't just go on an airfield joyride." Her voice ratcheted higher as she spoke.

"Bullshit." Frank jabbed a finger at Allie. "I got put in the jackpot with my boss. Because of you!" Spit flew as he spoke.

Jared and Mason turned toward Frank. Valerie took a protective stance in front of her controllers. Ellen froze.

Tony's anger flared.

Allie held up a hand and walked to Frank. "Not here, Barlow," she said. "If you have a problem with me, we can talk about it later."

Frank balled his fists. The guy was a loose cannon. Tony tensed, ready to intervene. He wouldn't let this asshole hurt anyone.

Allie turned to Ellen and the controllers, who remained stunned. "I'm sorry. This is an internal matter and we have no business airing it here. I think it's time we left."

Ellen nodded and led the group back to the elevator. No one said a word. Frank stood in front, with Tony behind him. When they reached the ground floor, Frank scurried out the door to his pickup. Allie stood in the lobby, staring after him. She apologized to Ellen a second time and assured her Frank's behavior would be reported.

Tony fumed. That guy was a royal ass. Allie seemed like such a pro, such a nice person. She didn't deserve to be embarrassed like that. He and Robbie remained behind, talking to her in the parking lot, trying to assuage her anger. Tony told her about his debacle at the hose and ladder drill, and Allie confessed she'd witnessed it.

"You saw that?" Robbie asked. "Didn't he look like a turtle on its back?"

"Ha ha. Thanks, buddy."

Tension broken, Allie laughed along with them.

Robbie took a phone call and Tony used the opportunity to tell Allie about his voluntary assignment to the academy, and of his plan to get back into good physical shape. "If I fall off any more ladders, I want to be able to run far away."

Allie smiled. "I go for a run every other morning. Why don't you join me before your academy shift sometime? I run a circuit through the woods along the inner perimeter fence. You're free to bring any of the firefighters in your platoon."

Tony didn't know what to say.

"Don't be so surprised," she said. "I've been looking for early-morning running partners."

He considered. "Well, all right, *if* you promise to go easy on me."

"Don't worry; I won't break you."

With that, it was a deal. Although Tony suspected he'd regret it.

He hadn't known Allie long, but he really liked her. She was funny and easy to talk to. And he was grateful that she was going to help him get in shape.

TWENTY-ONE

Sunday, October 2

Mother Nature flipped a switch in dramatic fashion as cool breezes gave way to a flood of heat and humidity. Not the best day for Tony's first run since… who knew when?

Allie was stretching out in the parking lot when Tony arrived at the academy.

"Hey, I didn't think you'd be out of bed this early," he said with a laugh.

"This early? I get here at five-thirty when I'm working the seven-to-three shift. Do you need to warm up, or are you good to go?"

"It's been a while, but I'm ready. Don't kill me now."

"A big tough firefighter like you? Impossible."

"Yeah, that's me all right. Where do we run, on the road?"

"You mean you trained here all summer and never ran on the trail?"

"Our training runs were half-ass laps around the drill field, and even those became voluntary after the first few weeks."

"And you took the *voluntary* aspect to heart, right?" She pointed to the woods. "Follow me."

Two perimeter barriers ringed Reynolds International. An eight-foot chain-link fence formed a first line of defense along the outer reaches of airport property, while a ten-foot high-security fence, topped with barbed wire, protected the area close to the field, known as the air operations area.

Allie followed a well-worn path into the woods and over a small rise to a crushed gravel path that paralleled the inner fence line. Tony regarded her lithe form as she led the way. Decked out in black spandex running shorts and a light blue tank top, she was the picture of an athlete: tall and slim, five foot eight or nine, with seriously toned legs. Such a contrast to Lisa's curvy frame.

"Let's start here," she said. "The trail is just over two miles long. We'll run west to the fuel farm, where the trail ends. Then we'll turn around, head to the eastern end at the edge of the Air National Guard base, and double back. The whole route covers the distance of a 5K race, three-point-one miles."

Running side by side, Tony and Allie made small talk as they covered the gentle upslope to the hangar line. The area was heavily forested and an aroma of fall filled the air, mingled with the smell of wet weeds and grass. He gazed up at the brilliant fall colors as sunlight filtered through scarlet and amber oak leaves. The chirping of insects suggested an ecosystem not yet ready for winter. It reminded him of his childhood in northwestern Pennsylvania.

Allie explained that ops encouraged trail users to look for anomalies along the inner fence line. "Small animals are always burrowing under it, and heavy rains sometimes wash out a portion of it. And since it isn't covered by cameras, the security department asks everyone to be on the lookout for trespassers in the woods between the two fence lines. Hunters used to be the main offenders, but nowadays it's teenagers who scale the outer fence and post their exploits on social media."

Allie kept her pace to a light jog.

"We can speed it up a little," Tony said, even though he was already panting. "I'm not that out of shape." At least he didn't want her to think so.

"Okay. We're doing ten minutes per mile. Let's pick it up a little. This next leg, two miles to the guard base, is the meat of the run."

As they bottomed out and climbed again, a 737, wheels down,

passed low overhead on its final approach to runway six-right. "Not many runners get to experience sights like that," Allie shouted over the clamor of the turbofan engines. "Isn't this amazing?"

Tony, who'd never been a runner unless he counted the obligatory laps during his one year of high school football, could only manage an "uh-huh" between his gasps. Lungs laboring, he couldn't hold the pace much longer and was starting to fall behind Allie as she glided up the slope.

"Keep up your pace. I'll catch up." But he knew he wouldn't. *What was I thinking?* He was in no shape to run with this physically fit young woman. Soon she was around a bend and out of sight.

A side stitch hit him. He stopped and put his hands on his hips to catch his breath. Nearly spent, he tried alternating between bursts of running and walking, but he was nowhere near the Air Guard base yet. When he saw Allie sprinting down the hill toward him, he gave up all pretense and stopped. She paused next to him, running in place.

"Sorry I lost you. I should've stayed back."

"Not your fault," he said as his breathing eased. "I shouldn't have tried to keep up with you. I'm not in your kind of shape."

"Nothing to be ashamed of. This is only your first day. Are you game to do it again?"

"Absolutely! I *am* going to get myself in shape. But can't you find a faster companion?"

"At the airport? This early? Not likely." She paused and crinkled her nose and curled her lips, a mannerism he found mischievous and cute. "Here's what we'll do. Next time, I'll run at your pace for the first leg, like I did today. Then I'll speed up for the long haul. You can try to keep up, but I won't wait."

"That's encouraging."

"Don't worry. Every time we do this, your stamina will improve. Keep it up."

"Is that a command, Ms. Robinson?"

"It is. We can't have our firefighters out of breath before they get ten feet from their trucks." Another sly smile. "What if you have to pull my butt out of trouble someday?"

"Ouch." The comment stung, but she was tough, and Lisa had taught him the value of a strong woman.

"Our schedules won't always mesh, but with you taking a steady gig at the academy for a month, I'm sure we'll figure it out."

"Sounds like you've already got it figured out. What can I do but agree?"

"Nothing. I'm going to finish my run and hit the showers at the academy. We'll see you soon, Moretti."

TWENTY-TWO

Monday, October 31

Tony spent a quiet weekend at home following the end of his monthlong stint at the academy; Lisa worked Saturday and Sunday. Despite the mental and physical grind of the past month, he was fresh and exhilarated, and ready to get back to the platoon.

Upon his return, Captain Schrum pegged him to drive Rescue-10, which Tony took as a show of confidence. He'd practiced crash truck operations ad nauseam during the past four weeks, and this morning he'd reviewed every control in the cab of his assigned rapid intervention vehicle. He invented scenarios and simulated positioning of the truck and the use of its turrets, and double-checked the location, function, and operation of each piece of Rescue-10's portable equipment.

The morning passed quickly, but as the afternoon's training class—a refresher on bleeding control—wrapped up, the Klaxon sounded.

"Airport fire. Mid-State Aviation Services reports a Jet A spill at gate Bravo-27. The leak is coming from a fuel cart attached to an MD-80 charter. The emergency shutoff is inoperative."

Tony hopped into Rescue-10, the RIV, ten seconds ahead of the captain. Apprehension about his first emergency response in weeks was tempered by a new confidence. Free from concerns about the vehicle's operation, he concentrated on the drive to the ramp. The tower stopped a United A319 and a Southwest 737 on Sierra so the crash trucks could pass. Tony slowed the RIV and maneuvered to the left edge of the taxiway to get around the United aircraft and cut diagonally to the right side to pass beside the Airbus. Captain Schrum beefed up the response with Rescue-11 and Rescue-15, and when Tony checked his mirrors, those rigs were closing fast.

"When we arrive, take position outside the spill area," the captain said. "Get us within range of the roof and bumper turrets, but not so close that we compromise safety."

"Understood, Cap. I'll pick a good spot."

"Rescue-10 from airport dispatch. Mid-State reports they've shut the fuel off, but there is a small pool under one wing of the aircraft."

"Rescue-10 copies. Rescues 10, 11, and 15 approaching the scene. I'll have east ramp command."

Tony exited Sierra at Echo and stopped thirty feet behind the MD-80, at a twenty-degree angle to the aircraft's fuselage-mounted number two engine. Rescue-11 took position forty-five degrees off the plane's left side, while Rescue-15 remained behind the two crash trucks. Fed by the underground piping system, jet fuel had flooded the scene.

"Small pool under one wing, my ass," the captain said. "Get your turrets into position and stand by."

Tony moved fast as muscle memory from his academy experience took over. He gripped the roof turret's joystick, aimed it at the spill, and repeated the action for the bumper turret.

Captain Schrum raised his binoculars. "Let's hope we can get this mess cleaned up fast. It's such a hot day for this time of year. That fuel will reach its flash point in no time. I don't want it to find an ignition source."

Tony nodded as the possibilities ran through his mind. Jet A was a combustible liquid, less volatile than gasoline, but almost as dangerous once it reached its ignition temperature of one hundred degrees Fahrenheit. It would be a bear to extinguish.

"Dispatch from command, this spill is approximately one hundred by fifty. It stretches from the base of the terminal to the tail of the aircraft. Some of it has entered the catchment drains, but the main body isn't moving. Tell field maintenance to bring us every sopper they have. And we're going to need absorbent pigs out here for containment."

Schrum continued to scan the scene through the binoculars. "This concrete settled years ago but was never repaired. That's why it's not running into the drains. I don't like this." He toggled the radio control. "Station Bravo, from east ramp command, respond Rescue-13."

"East ramp command from Station Bravo. Deputy-1 is on his way. Rescue-13 will be right behind him."

Schrum looked to his right. "Rescue-11, you're a little close. Reposition twenty feet farther from the aircraft. Rescue-15, deploy your crew. Stretch a preconnect from 11 to the jetway at Gate-29 and protect the terminal."

Tony monitored Rescue-15's handline crew as they scurried into position at the terminal wall. Then he caught movement to his right. "Hey, Cap, look. There's a tug driving into the spill in front of the plane."

"What?" The captain swung around and lifted the binoculars. "Jesus Christ!" He toggled the radio. "15, there's a tug under the plane. Get the driver's attention."

"Too late!" Tony said as he caught sight of flames trailing from the rear of the tug.

"Damn!" Scrum said. "15, knock that fire down and get that guy out of the tug."

The ground team swept their hose stream over the tug, which was now stopped under the nose. A minute later, the scene erupted as flames raced across the surface of the jet fuel.

"11, sweep that fire away from the engine crew," Schrum radioed.

"Should I open up?" Tony asked.

"Not yet. Wait for 11 to push it."

As they watched, thick black smoke billowed above the MD-80 and the attack team disappeared behind Rescue-11's foam spray.

"Here it comes," Schrum said. "High flow. Angle down. Sweep it."

Tony thumbed the switch for water and foam. The Cummins engine revved and the truck rattled as a potent mixture of twelve hundred gallons per minute, proportioned by the pump at ninety-seven parts water to three parts foam concentrate, rocketed from the roof turret into the burning fuel.

"Wide fog! Wide fog! You're plunging it."

Shit. Tony toggled the pattern control. Careful not to push the fire toward the ground crew, he atoned for his mistake by sweeping the stream over the fuel and letting it rain into the flames.

"Good. Very good," Shrum said.

Without waiting for orders, Tony narrowed the pattern and played the joystick left and right to coat the fuselage. A-Triple-F, the self-sealing Aqueous Film-Forming Foam, rolled off the aircraft and spread across the fuel to separate it from its oxygen supply. His maneuver extinguished the bulk of the flames, and with two more sweeps, the job was done and the smoke dissipated into a strong westerly breeze.

"A little more," the captain said.

Tony switched to the bumper turret and reinforced the smothering white blanket. Rescue-11 confirmed their sector was secure, while Rescue-15's hose team reported they'd pulled the tug driver out of danger. Deputy-1 and Rescue-13 called on scene.

"Airport dispatch from east ramp command," Schrum radioed. "This incident is under control."

The fire was out, but foam was reapplied at regular intervals to prevent stray combustible vapors from reigniting. Once the liquid cooled, firefighters hosed the bulk of the fuel into the catchment drains, where it was piped to storage basins. Ramp crews and field maintenance laborers rolled soppers through the remaining product. The MD-80 suffered minimal damage to its landing gear. The tug was a total loss, but the unfortunate operator was uninjured. Smoke entered the jetway but did not penetrate the concourse.

Before departing, DC Martone commended the captain, who sang Tony's praises.

"Well done, Moretti," Martone said as he shook Tony's hand.

Schrum winked. "Nice work, Tony," he said as they stood looking at the scorched aircraft. "I know how much time and effort you've put in lately. Not many guys would have accepted a month of hard labor at the academy. It paid off today."

"Thanks, Cap, but I should have gone to wide fog from the start."

"Nonsense. I'd have made the same mistake. It was a rapidly developing situation. You recovered quickly and used your initiative."

Tony beamed. His skills had improved; he was much more comfortable with the tools of the trade and how to use them. For the first time in two months, his anxiety about his job eased.

TWENTY-THREE

Saturday, November 12

The commute was brutal, as rain and temperatures in the teens transformed the roads into skating rinks and paralyzed traffic on the major arteries. Tony opted for the deserted back routes, and after a few close calls with parked cars and telephone poles, he reached the fire station with three minutes to spare.

At 7:10 a.m., Captain Rodney Hartman of C-platoon called everyone to the dayroom to explain the situation. Wayne, Iggy, Rosie, and Evan were the only other A-platoon members present. Tony spotted three of his partners from the recruit class and had a brief conversation with them before he settled into a recliner and leaned over to Evan. "I guess the older guys are the only ones who know how to drive in the snow."

"What was that?" Captain Hartman asked.

"Ah, nothing, Cap. Just talking about the weather." Tony wanted to dig a hole and jump in.

Hartman stared at Tony and continued. "Yeah, this crappy weather screwed everything up. Only five members of A-platoon have made it in so far. Captain Schrum, Lieutenant Wozniak, and four others are stuck in traffic jams. They'll get here when they get here. Three more gave up and called off sick." The captain narrowed his eyes and raised his voice when he mentioned the latter trio.

"I'll stick around until one of the A-platoon officers arrives. Firefighter Iverson and our three fine C-shift probies will join us. Seems my senior people would rather go skating on icy roads than stay. Not smart, but by contract, there's nothing I can do about it." The narrow eyes again. Hartman didn't have a fraction of the eloquence or leadership presence of Captain Schrum. And he was dissing his own platoon. No wonder they all went home.

"All morning inspections and outside activities are curtailed until further notice. I'm gonna post truck assignments, but if we get a call, I'll deploy you as I see fit." He scanned the crew and shook his head. "Remember, we're at minimum."

"Half of minimum," Shawn Iverson, a B-platoon veteran, said from the back of the room. "We got four rookies here, Cap. We can't count on *them* for anything."

Hartman's face turned red as he glared at Iverson. Tony thought he was going to explode. He wasn't wrong.

The captain threw his clipboard at Iverson, barely missing him as it deflected off the chair in front of him, zipped past his head, and smacked into the back wall. The room fell silent. This guy was nuts.

"Hey, Cap, don't get pissed. I'm just saying what everybody's thinking."

"Shut the fuck up, Shawn."

"But I—"

"Not…one…more…word." The captain spoke through gritted teeth. "If you open your mouth again—"

"Structural call, airport fire." The Klaxon's piercing *ah-ooga* broke the tension.

"Airport fire," the dispatcher began. "Our panel indicates a foam system activation in the FBO hangar. We can't confirm it. No one is answering the phones at South Mountain Aviation, and we're not showing any smoke or heat sensor activations."

"This call will be for the truck only," the captain said.

Iggy picked up the clipboard and passed it forward. Hartman grabbed it. “Let’s see. Roosevelt driving, O’Brien shotgun, Iverson and Moretti in back. It’s probably a hinky alarm. Don’t break your necks getting there.”

Tony dashed for his gear, which was still hanging in the gear room —a sloppy oversight. Rescue-16 was already on the pad by the time he hopped aboard.

“Rookie,” Iverson mumbled.

Evan instructed Rosie to approach from the field instead of the North Ramp, since it was more likely to be free of ice.

“Do you see that?” Rosie asked in an amused voice as he steered off taxiway Alpha.

“I do,” Evan answered in an equally tickled tone.

“Fuck me,” Iverson said.

Tony craned his neck. “Holy shit.”

A sea of foam rolled out of the open hangar door onto the FBO ramp.

Evan set up command and reported the situation. A South Mountain employee ran out to meet him. Foam covered the man and Tony couldn’t stifle a laugh.

“You think it’s funny?” Iverson asked. “We’ll be here all fucking morning.”

Tony ignored him. Must be fun to work on C-platoon.

The agitated employee wiped the foam from his face as the truck crew clustered around him. Casper the Friendly Ghost. Tony feigned a cough.

“I’m Jaspreet, the acting manager. I wasn’t here five minutes before I heard the prealarm. I ran out to the hangar, but there was no smoke or fire. I hit the abort button on the wall but I was too late. The fire pump kicked in and all three generators started dumping foam. I couldn’t shut them down, so I opened the hangar door to let it out. I’ve got a Cessna Citation, a Gulfstream G650, and a Hawker 400 inside.” The guy looked stricken.

“Rosie, go to the pump room with Jaspreet. See if you can shut the main valves,” Evan said. “Shawn, be ready to close the door once the generators are off. Tony, grab the salvage gear, squeegees, and shop vacs. This is going to be a bitch."

After three trips to Rescue-16, Tony joined Iverson outside. The garage hummed as thick aerated foam cascaded from the overhead generators. He caught a glimpse of a vertical stabilizer from one of the business jets before it disappeared into a cloud of white.

Foam continued to push onto the pad. Every few seconds, the southwesterly wind sent huge chunks of the fluffy mixture flying toward taxiway Tango. Evan detailed Iverson to assist Rosie and radioed the situation to ground control and ops. He also requested help from the station. Hartman refused.

Evan shook his head and patted Tony on the back. "Looks like we're on our own."

"Not surprising after what we saw at the briefing."

"Nope. Hartman is a genuine piece of work."

Two minutes later, the hangar fell silent until the radio crackled. Rosie reported he'd closed the valves on the discharge lines and shut down the fire pump.

"That's more like it," Evan said. "Let's get out of the cold." He started for the door, then stopped. "Looks like we have company."

A yellow SUV pulled off the taxiway and stopped. Allie got out and Tony smiled, happy to see his friend.

"What a mess you guys are making of my ramp," Allie said. "And you're getting foam all over the terminal." She broke into a wide grin. "Don't you know you shouldn't play so near the airplanes?" Even Jaspreet laughed.

Evan gathered everyone in the lobby. "There's nothing we can do until the foam drains down, and that'll take a while."

"But I've got three expensive planes in there," Jaspreet protested.

"That shouldn't be a problem," Allie said. "Provided they're all buttoned up."

Tony looked at Jaspreet. The man was sullen.

Evan inclined his head and gave the South Mountain Aviation manager a quizzical look. "They're *not* sealed up, are they?"

Jaspreet shook his head. “The main doors are open in all three. The owners like to keep them aired out.”

“Hmm… okay.” Evan turned to Iverson. “Let’s get that hangar door closed, Shawn.”

“That won’t help me,” Jaspreet said.

“It will if you crank the heat as high as it’ll go. That’ll help dissipate the foam. In the meantime, we’ll wet down the edges to break it down faster.”

Tony unreeled the hose from the standpipe connection on the east side of the hangar and rotated the red handwheel above the outlet. The line stiffened as the fire pump came to life. Using the line’s small brass nozzle, he directed a gentle stream over and around the big white blob. Iverson did the same on the west side. Within five minutes, three tail sections appeared as the foam subsided.

“Not bad, rookie.”

He turned as Allie lobbed a handful of foam into his face.

He wiped his eyes and swung the nozzle toward her. “I’ll get you for that.” She scrambled for cover as he dropped the line and chased her around the white mountain. “You better run, Ms. Robinson.” Allie raised her hands in surrender. They both laughed.

“You’re not even breathing hard,” she said. “Our runs must be working.”

Allie was right. A month and a half after that first meeting, they were running every two or three days, and his stamina was twice what it had been.

“Ah, excuse me, boys and girls.” Evan stood with his hands on his hips. “If you’re done playing in the foam, there’s still some work left.”

It took another twenty-five minutes, but the planes emerged from their snowy blankets. Once the foam sank to the top of the landing gear, the truckies hosed what remained into the floor drains and finished the job with squeegees and shop vacs. Although the aircraft seats and carpets were soaked, no permanent damage had been done to the three private jets. A relieved Jaspreet praised the crew and insisted on having pizza delivered to the fire station.

"Let's saddle up," Evan said. "I'm sure Captain Hartman eagerly anticipates our return."

"Later, boys," Allie said. "I've got an airport to run, you know."

Tony watched her go, pleased that he was making friends and good impressions at last. And he was thankful Captain Hartman was not his platoon commander.

TWENTY-FOUR

Thanksgiving, November 24

"Take it easy," Phil Wozniak said as Tony slid two twenty-five-pound weights onto the bench press bar. "The way you're throwing those plates around, you're going to drop one on your foot."

"Or on someone else's foot," Nikki said. "You hyped up on caffeine today or what?"

"Hey, I'm always careful," Tony said with a laugh. "But yeah, I'm a little wound up. Anxious to get home, I guess."

"Too bad it's your Kelly day," Nikki said. "The LT and I will be racking up another twelve hours of double time while you're at home stuffing your face."

"The money doesn't matter. I can't let Lisa sit alone all night on Thanksgiving."

"Things haven't improved on the home front?" Wozniak asked.

"No. They've gotten worse." Ever since their argument about Tony's job situation, Lisa had slowly withdrawn into her own world. Nikki and the LT were the only ones Tony had confided in, besides Evan.

"You guys have a lot of history," Nikki said. "Give it some time. She'll come around."

"Maybe," Tony said. What he didn't say was that he feared his wife was sinking into depression and he now harbored serious doubts about the continued viability of his marriage.

"Don't look at the divorced guy for advice," Wozniak said with a shrug. "On the positive side, at least you're not such a weakling anymore. How much do you have on that bar, two hundred pounds?"

"Two-twenty," Tony said with just a hint of boastfulness in his voice.

"But who's counting," Nikki said. "Please don't inflate his ego, Phil."

"Look who's talking," Tony said as Nikki began a set of dumbbell squats. "Look at those thighs. You ever thought about the women's pro football league? You'd be a kick-ass running back."

"Asshole," Nikki said.

"So are you guys doing anything this weekend?" Tony asked, eager to change the subject.

"Well, I'm not dating anyone at the moment," the LT said, stealing a quick glance at Nikki while he said it. "I guess I'll take the weekend off and spend it with my folks in Baltimore. I don't get down to see them as much as I should."

"That's nice. How about you, Nik?" Tony asked.

"My mom and dad live in upstate New York, and I've got to work on Sunday, so I'm going to have a couple of nice quiet days at home. I want to finish the afghan I've been working on."

"Afghan?" Tony asked. "I didn't know you were a knitter."

"I don't knit. I crochet. Two needles are used in knitting. Crochet is done with a hook."

"I stand corrected," Tony said. "But I pictured you more as a practitioner of mixed martial arts."

"Oh, she can kick anyone's ass," Wozniak said as he shot her more than a casual glance. Nikki blushed.

Was something going on between these two? Nikki was probably ten years younger than the LT, but so what? *They might just make a great couple.*

Tony punched out at six-thirty, took a shower and changed into his civvies. He popped into the dayroom and wished everyone a happy

Thanksgiving as they watched football and gorged themselves on Manny's turkey dinner, which smelled delicious.

Robbie wasn't among the crowd, but Tony found him in his bunkroom.

"Why aren't you eating pie and watching the game?"

"Oh, you know. I'm not much for football."

"You miss your folks, don't you?"

Robbie frowned. "I guess. It's my first Thanksgiving away from home."

"Why don't you invite them to the station? The captain won't mind. You know your dad loves to go over the crash trucks with you."

"He does, but Mom won't come. She says it's my place of work. Anyway, we're having a big dinner for our volunteers and their families at the fire hall on Saturday. And me and my dad are going to work on his old GTO tomorrow. We're almost done restoring it."

"That's great, but I don't want you pouting in here all night. Get out there and mingle with the crew. You know they all love you like a little brother."

Robbie beamed. "Okay. I hope you have a great Thanksgiving with your wife."

"I'll second that," Tony said.

* * *

When Tony got home, Lisa was in the kitchen, and the smell of roast turkey filled the townhouse.

"Hi, stranger," she said as she emerged with the eight-pound bird they'd purchased. "I prepared a little something for our dinner."

"Wow. That's an understatement." Stuffing, sweet potato casserole, asparagus, whole wheat rolls, and cranberries fought for space at the dining room table. A pumpkin pie sat on the buffet.

"Are we expecting guests? Or are you trying to plump me up?"

"You can afford it, especially after the way you've been riding our stationary bike and running with your buddy Al. Your face already looks thinner."

"You saying I had a fat face?"

Lisa smiled, but it didn't seem genuine. She laid the bird among the rest of the bounty and gave him a peck on the cheek. Not even a hug? Tony's heart sank.

The food was fantastic. Lisa could cook. She could do it all. But they ate in silence. Tears welled up in her eyes as she forked her pie.

"What's the matter, Leese? You seem so unhappy lately."

"Oh, you know. I miss my folks. My brothers and sisters, my nieces and nephews. The whole crazy bunch."

Tony understood. Lisa had a big family, and they gathered en masse each Thanksgiving and Christmas. Laughter, liquor, and unending chatter ruled in the Szabo household during holidays. It wasn't Tony's thing. He preferred the small, quiet gatherings at his parents' home. Lisa, however, thrived in that atmosphere.

"Why don't you call them? They'd love to hear from you."

"I already talked to them. They FaceTimed me a couple of hours ago."

So that's what had triggered her melancholy. A call from a housefull of relatives while she sat here alone.

"I bet they were happy to see you. How is everyone?"

"They're good. Mom and Dad said they miss us." Lisa choked back a sob.

"Hey, come on, Leese. We're going to spend two weeks at home for Christmas."

Lisa had brightened a little, but the polite silence resumed. To get her talking again, Tony mentioned the airport's upcoming mass casualty exercise. At that, she perked up. He explained the airport maintained a medical assistance team composed of doctors and nurses from nearby health care facilities, as well as airport employee volunteers who'd completed first aid training.

She peppered him with questions. "Could I join? Is it too late? Would they want me?"

"I don't see why not. I'll get a hold of Iggy. He's on the organizing committee for the drill."

"No, don't bother him tonight."

Tony waved a hand. “Not a problem. He’s just sitting at the station, sucking up the OT.”

“Well, okay.” Lisa smiled.

The mood at the table lightened, and afterward, when Tony made the call, he learned the team was looking for nurses with trauma experience. Iggy said they’d love to have her take part in the exercise. Lisa was ecstatic. Tony was relieved.

TWENTY-FIVE

Tuesday, November 29

"This is weird," Tony said. "Driving *you* to the airport to work."

"I wouldn't call it work, exactly," Lisa said. "Maybe a little continuing education."

"It's the airport. They'll put you to work."

"I'm looking forward to it. It'll be fun to get back to my roots, even if it's just a simulation. Sometimes I miss those days in the ER."

"Because you're nuts. Remember how stressed and emotional you'd be when you got home at night? I didn't dare say a word until your second glass of wine."

"That's me. I loved it even while I hated it. I'm complicated."

Tony glanced at his wife. *Does she have the same love-hate relationship with me?*

"Anyway, I'm happy you're doing this." And he was. It got her excited about something again, and he hoped it would carry over into their home life.

When they arrived at the landside terminal, Allie met them at the registration table.

"Hey, Tony. I didn't expect to see you here."

"Allie… hi. Weren't you working graveyard this week?"

"Yep. Just doing a little volunteer work for the first responders. We still on for Thursday morning after your shift?"

Tony felt a twinge of guilt and sensed Lisa's eyes on him.

"Ahh, sure. I think so. But I might have to run a few errands."

"At seven-thirty in the morning?"

"Yeah, uh, by the way, I don't think you've met my wife." He turned to Lisa, who shot him a puzzled look. "Lisa, this is Allie, the colleague I told you about. You know, the one I've been running with."

"Oh, so *you're* the *Al* I've heard about. The one whipping Tony into shape. I *see*."

Allie's eyes widened. Tony didn't know where to hide.

"Nah, Tony doesn't need much whipping. He's motivated."

"I'll *bet* he is."

"Anyway, Leese, why don't you get yourself registered? I'm going to make a quick pit stop and I'll be right back to take you to the shuttle. See you guys in a minute." Tony turned on his heel and headed for the men's room.

When he returned, Lisa was holding a visitor's pass and Allie was gone.

"She said she had to go back to her office to get more registration forms. Funny, with that big stack sitting right there on the table."

Tony rubbed the back of his neck. It was wet.

"You've gone quiet." Lisa smiled and raised a finger. "It's not because of *Al*, is it?"

Tony froze. His thoughts turned to mush.

"No need to be embarrassed, hon. I'm only teasing." But the playful smile was gone.

What just happened? He and Allie were friends—nothing more. He should never have referred to her as Al. Not knowing what to say, Tony escorted Lisa through the security door and onto a shuttle that took them to the exercise site at Hangar-6, where three medical tents, marked TRIAGE, MINOR INJURIES, and TRAUMA, stood in the center of the cavernous space.

While Lisa walked to the tents, Tony made for the orientation station, where local art students applied moulage—the special effects makeup that simulated blood, broken bones, amputations, and a host of other injuries—to the volunteer victims.

He spotted Robbie, who sat on a stretcher, transformed into a man near death. He sported a broken leg, burns on his hands, and an avulsed eye that hung from its socket. Fake blood covered his shirt and pants. A sign on his chest read IN SHOCK. At the sight of Tony, he waved a bloody hand.

"Robert, my friend, you're one happy plane crash survivor."

"Hey, Tony. What do you think about my eye? Cool, huh?" He jerked his head back, causing the dangling eye to bob up and down.

"I think you're going to have trouble ducking left hooks from now on."

Robbie laughed. "Hey, are you volunteering too?"

"Me, no. Not this time. I brought Lisa out for the exercise. She's helping the medical team with the critical care patients. Thought I'd stick around and take it all in."

"Cool. Maybe she'll fix me up."

"There's no fix for you, buddy, but have fun." Tony took a long look at Robbie's simulated injuries and returned his friend's grin. Was there anything he *didn't* like about working at the airport?

Tony entered the trauma tent and tucked himself into a back corner. Twelve hospital-style beds shared the space with an impressive array of advanced life support equipment. The medical team set up their equipment, sorted through a stack of supplies, and discussed lifesaving procedures. Lisa didn't notice him. Or was she ignoring him?

A man and woman wearing blue jumpsuits and vests with fluorescent letters reading EXERCISE EVALUATOR entered the tent. They surveyed the setup, compared watches, and addressed the staff. "Stand by," the female evaluator said. "The drill begins…now."

Nothing happened at first, but by the twenty-five-minute mark, volunteer stretcher-bearers had delivered twelve heavily moulaged victims. Three ER docs, five nurses, and two paramedics endeavored to treat each patient in the twenty-by-thirty space.

The lead doctor addressed the evaluators. "We're going to need at least two of these trauma tents if the real thing hits, and better coordination with the triage tent. They've got to hold the excess until we're ready."

Tony watched his wife dart from bed to bed, blonde ponytail swinging. How could this small team treat a whole planeload of victims?

Two volunteer stretcher-bearers appeared at the door. Before they could push their gurney into the tent, Lisa stepped in front of them.

"We can't take any more. We're overloaded."

"But we were told to bring him here."

"I don't care what you were told. Take them to triage. Tell whoever's in charge to treat them as best they can until we get some of these patients transported."

One of the volunteers opened his mouth to say something, but Lisa stopped him with a resolute glance and a shake of her head.

"Go. We can't save anyone like this," she said and rushed to another victim.

It was the first time Tony had seen Lisa in a trauma setting. Pride and awe swept through him. His wife was a dynamo. It was a drill, yet she played it as if it were real, just like Robbie did. Two people who did their work with professionalism and skill. Yet there was more to it; they were *devoted* to their jobs. Tony's skills as a firefighter were improving, but he didn't share the fervor he saw in Lisa and Robbie. *Will I ever feel that way?*

TWENTY-SIX

Thursday, December 1

Frank Barlow rubbed his temples as he shuffled through the rain to the field maintenance building. He was dog-tired and his migraine wouldn't quit. The fight with his brother over their old man's tools had set him off, and in spite of the booze, he was too pissed off to get any sleep. Three years after their father's death and they still couldn't agree on who got what. That's his thanks for looking out for the ungrateful shit after their mom died. Yep, even your own flesh and blood screwed you when they got the chance.

The drive to work didn't help. Fifty-five minutes with the stupid pickup fishtailing all over the road. Shoulda watched the damn weather forecast, not that those clowns were ever right. It was supposed to be sunny last Thursday when he wanted to go to the shooting range, but it rained all day. Typical. Why did he sign up for OT today, anyway? It's not like he needed the money.

He used the head, toweled his face and hair, and reported to Ray Wheatley, who was sitting at his desk in the cluttered supervisor's office. A box sat on the chair in front of the desk, so Frank stood.

"Barlow, glad you could make it," Wheatley said and sneered. "I don't know how they do things on daylight, but this is afternoon shift and we start on time. That means three o'clock, not three twenty-five."

"It was that screwed-up weather report. Didn't think it would take me an hour to get here."

"Funny, the weather guy on Channel 6 predicted exactly what we have today, a wintry mix of rain and snow. Said it would make driving hazardous all day."

"Okay, my fault." Frank didn't try to hide the disgust in his voice. "I'm here now."

"So you are. I was gonna send you out to babysit the construction crew working on the gas lines outside Terminal-A. You could've sat in your nice warm cab all night." Wheatley leaned back in his chair. "But since you weren't here, I sent Collins out on that one."

Frank wanted to slap the smirk off Wheatley's face. He was never gonna get that detail, the fucking liar.

"Head over to the shed. I need someone to prep the old equipment, the out-of-service stuff we're going to sell at next month's auction."

Frank stared at the calendar above Wheatley's head. A hot brunette in a tank top and tiny shorts leaned against the hood of a Mustang convertible while she held a tire iron. He could use one of those right now.

"You got a problem with that, Barlow? Did you think you'd find a nice cozy spot to nap all night?"

Frank didn't answer.

"Anyway, you'll see a plow, three dumps, a blower, a crash truck, and a couple of old pickups. Start by driving the big stuff through the automated wash bay. You know how to work it?"

"Nope, never used it before." The lie came easily.

"Is that so?"

Frank glanced at the brunette. She had a gorgeous set of tits. Probably fake.

"Never mind the wash. Just get over there and start detailing the interiors, especially the pickups. Cleaning supplies are in the storage locker next to the office." Wheatley looked at his roster. "I'll see if I can shake someone loose to give you a hand with the wash bay, maybe Dixon."

"Don't do me any favors."

"Oh, you'll be disappointed to learn we're getting rid of Yellow-224. Shinsky tells me it's your favorite rig."

Frank balled his hands into fists. Pain shot through his palms as his fingernails dug in. The cocksucker was asking for it.

"Just get your ass up there."

"Got it." Frank turned and walked out. The *brr, brr, brr…zum, zum* of a pneumatic impact wrench tortured his aching head.

The duty turned out to be cake; easy time-and-a-half. With no one to bother him, his migraine faded. The first rig he checked was one of the dump trucks. Detail the interior? What a crock. The seat was ripped in a dozen places, oily grime stained the dashboard, and the metal chassis showed through holes in the rubber floor liner. He'd never get this crap in shape. So why try? Who was going to check?

Frank pulled out his cell, leaned back in the driver's seat, and spent the next two hours losing himself in his Spotify playlist: Led Zeppelin, Deep Purple, Uriah Heep, Three Dog Night, and Grand Funk. It was a hell of a lot better than that country crap the other guys played. His mood improved so much, he decided to do a little work.

With "Over the Hills and Far Away" blasting through his AirPods, he hosed the dirt off the blower, the dump trucks, and even old 224. Next he silenced his tunes and took a look under the engine cowling of the crash truck. The Detroit Diesel engine was massive. He'd seen these trucks fly across the taxiways. What a farce. Sit on your ass all day or scoot over to the terminal for an *inspection*. Those firemen had the life. Yeah, to check out the hot college babes and flight attendants. And when they got bored with that, they took joyrides around the airfield.

Frank wasn't a fan of Dire Straits, but one of their songs came to mind. He belted it out to the empty shed, the words about money for nothing. Nope, *he* was the dumbass for putting up with crap all day from a bunch of losers.

By six o'clock, he'd had enough. Time for a break. He bought a can of Coke from the vending machine and snooped around. He spotted a metal exit door in the back wall, behind a tanker. A sign warned:

SECURITY DOOR
KEEP CLOSED AND LOCKED AT ALL TIMES
EMERGENCY EXIT ONLY
ALARM WILL SOUND

Frank examined the door. If it *was* alarmed, why weren't there any wires running to an electrical contact?

Oh, what the hell. He drained the Coke and dropped the crushed can beside the door. Then he shoved the panic bar. It didn't move. He tried again, this time with more force. The door groaned and moved an inch.

Was it blocked? Probably hadn't been opened in years. He took a few steps back, charged forward, and smashed his hip and shoulder into the door. Metal screeched as it came free of its rusted frame.

Frank stood in the frame and listened. No sound, no flashing lights, and no alarm. He pushed the door farther and stepped outside. It was cold, but the rain and snow had stopped. He shoved his hands into his pockets and looked around. A spotty coat of slush covered the twenty feet of rocky ground between the back of the shed and a hillside. The FBO was up there, and the high-pressure sodium lights of its parking lot backlit the scene in a dim orange glow.

He walked to the corner of the building, where a chain-link fence was bolted to the block wall, probably part of the inner fence line. He'd just breached the security perimeter at the north end of the airport and no one knew it.

Frank shivered, went back inside, and pulled on the panic bar. No matter how much force he used, he couldn't get the damn thing shut all the way. He could ram it from the outside, but how would he get back in? Screw it. Who would ever notice?

Leaving the door ajar, he grabbed his coat, climbed back into the crash truck, and dialed up his tunes.

A ringing phone, amplified by a speaker somewhere in the shed's roof trusses, echoed through the garage. Frank sprang up. What the—? He must've fallen asleep. The ringing died but began again. Frank got out of the cab and scampered to a pole-mounted extension behind a rack of plow blades.

"Shed," he answered in an annoyed tone.

"What are you doing over there, Barlow? Weren't you supposed to report your progress to me every two hours?" Ray Wheatley asked.

"I've been busy doing what you told me."

"I want you back here by nine-thirty to help the guys clean up."

"Yeah, okay. I'll finish up and get back." But maybe not by nine-thirty.

The place was still dead. He'd been sitting around, goofing off all night, and not one person had come into the shed. Except for monthly maintenance checks, he doubted anyone ever did.

He could take one of these big babies out for a spin if he wanted to. He smiled at the thought but dismissed it. Even the union wouldn't help him if he did that. But what fun it would be.

TWENTY-SEVEN

Friday, December 9 - Day Shift

7**:15 a.m.** Tony pulled the knit cap over his ears, snugged the collar of his uniform jacket, and massaged his hands vigorously as needles pricked his fingertips. Jesus, it was cold. The frigid temperatures showed no signs of abating and the nasty winds sweeping out of Canada added another layer of misery. Way too early for this, but at least it wasn't snowing.

He'd finished checking Rescue-14's extinguishing systems, hydraulic tools, and medical gear, but the generator needed another five minutes of run time. He unzipped his jacket and stuck his hands into his armpits while he waited.

The beefed-up Ford F-450 carried 500 pounds of dry chemical and 250 gallons of premixed foam and sported a bumper turret that flowed 350 gallons per minute. Stocked with forcible entry tools, rope, and portable extinguishers, it had the versatility to intervene in almost any situation, while its compact size made it the ideal choice for medical responses, construction inspections, and fire prevention details. Manpower permitting, it was assigned a dedicated two-person crew who responded to everything. A-platoon was well staffed today, and with his skills improving fast, Tony looked forward to the challenge.

The only stumbling block was his assigned partner, Dave Jarvis, who was working a twenty-four-hour shift trade with Keith Weston.

Tony tried to talk with him prior to the morning briefing, but Jarvis responded with sarcastic remarks. When he informed his partner that he was heading out to check his truck, Jarvis told him to go for it. Tony hadn't seen him since.

"All firefighters, breakfast is ready," Manny Santos announced at seven-twenty-five. Tony nestled the truck back in its bay and headed for the kitchen. Perfect timing for a hot meal.

"Mmm, nothing like the smell of fried eggs and bacon in the morning," Tony said as he entered the dayroom.

"Doesn't that go against your health-nut religion?" Rosie asked.

"On a day like today, my arteries will forgive me." He poured himself a cup of the strong fire station brew and savored the warmth as he waited for the chow line to thin out. It was the rare full house of platoon's firefighters and officers, with all eighteen on duty. Who wanted to call off on a five-degree day?

"Yeah, Mr. Super-healthy," Dave Jarvis said. "Too bad you're not Mr. Super-firefighter."

Before Tony could reply, the lieutenant's voice came over the intercom. "Rescue-14, construction inspection at the Hangar-2 pipeline site."

"Oops, no breakfast for you boys," Santos said. "But don't worry; I'll keep it warm and make sure these vultures save you some."

Tony parked Rescue-14 on the access road behind Hangar-2.

"This is gonna suck," Jarvis said as the pair walked over to the excavation site, where a big man in a hard hat and a three-day growth of beard came over to them.

"Morning, men. I'm the site supervisor on this job." He stuck out his hand. "Bill Hendershot, but everybody calls me Deke. Sorry to get you guys out so early on this bitch of a day, but we're running behind schedule. The valve for this pipeline should've been here two days ago, but it came in last night and we need to hook it up and bury it. I told your dispatcher everything was copacetic. We monitor our excavations all the time."

"Thanks, but we're required to inspect the site before we can turn it over to you," Tony said. "Airport rules."

The hole was six feet deep and its sides were shored per OSHA, but airport regulations required continuous monitoring of the below-grade atmosphere. The fire department always took the initial readings alongside the construction crew to verify accuracy.

Tony pulled off his gloves, ran a fresh air calibration of the MSA Altair 4X multigas monitor, and attached the instrument's sampling pump and probe.

"Hurry up, Moretti," Jarvis said. "Can't you work any faster, for chrissakes?"

Tony ignored him as he probed the pit and studied the meter display. "I've got twenty point eight percent oxygen, four parts per million hydrogen sulfide, eleven ppm carbon monoxide, and zero LEL on the combustible gas scale." Jarvis stood there looking sullen while Tony did the work.

"We've got the same," Hendershot said, showing Tony the readings on the construction company's meter. "See, five minutes and you're out of here."

"That's what I wanted to hear," Tony said. "Here's your permit." He held a clipboard out to the supervisor. "Just sign here and we'll be out of your hair."

"Yeah, we got a hot breakfast we're missing for this," Jarvis said in his patented snotty tone.

The comments embarrassed Tony. Jarvis was such an ass.

"Must be nice," Hendershot said. "Think about us poor schmucks when you're back in your warm fire station."

Tony was about to jump back in the cab when Hendershot called to them.

"Hey, boys, hate to do this to you, but my guys need to do some grinding on the pipe to make it fit."

"Okay, that means a hot work permit," Tony said. "No prob."

"There's one small thing," Hendershot added. "We don't have our extinguishers with us. We didn't expect to be doing any heat-generating work today."

Jarvis let out a loud sigh. "We're never gonna get out of here."

The contractor eyed the pouting firefighter. Traces of a smile crease the big man's face.

"You have to get them," Tony said, "or we have to stay here with you."

"Can you guys wait? It won't take more than fifteen minutes."

"Absolutely," Tony said. "We'll grab our extinguishers." The contractor's smirk had turned to a grin. *Nice work, Jarvis.*

Fifteen minutes stretched to forty-five as the construction crew worked to connect the pipe to the valve. Tony paced the site; his toes went numb. Blustery wind penetrated his jacket. The workers didn't use the grinder; the delay was payback for the hot breakfast comment. Tony seethed, but he didn't blame the contractor.

When the work was done, Hendershot thanked them and apologized for the delay. "Guess we didn't need to do any hot work after all. Sorry to keep you from your breakfast for nothing. But we *do* appreciate it."

"That was fucked up," Jarvis said as the pair drove back to the station. "Breakfast is gonna be a pile of cold, soggy shit."

"No, *you're* fucked up. We would have had breakfast a long time ago if you'd kept your mouth shut. They didn't do any grinding. They kept us out there on purpose, because of you."

"Go fuck yourself, Moretti. You don't know what the hell you're talkin' about."

Tony held his tongue on the ride back to the station. It was going to be a long day.

* * *

9**:30 a.m.** "You didn't fall in, did you, Moretti?" Kyle Traynor asked with a chuckle.

It was Tony's second visit to the toilet since downing the postponed breakfast two hours before. Why had he eaten such a greasy meal? Eggs, bacon, and home fries heated in the microwave, which made them particularly unpalatable. And hard to digest. But after the cold pipeline ordeal, he had scarfed it all down, and now his cramping stomach was telling him he'd made a bad mistake.

"Structural call, airport fire."

Damn it, not now!

Ah-ooga reverberated through the locker room.

"We have a report of a fire in escalator L-12 on the ticketing level. We see smoke on our cameras."

Tony's belly grumbled as he hurried to his rig. What if the cramps struck again? He donned his bunker pants and tossed his coat and helmet behind the seat. He fired the engine and hit the remote control for the garage door.

Jarvis jumped in beside him. "I work a shift trade and they put me on 14. What a raw deal."

"It won't be so cold this time," Tony said as he pulled onto the ramp.

"Don't be a pussy. You know how many fires I fought in freezing weather?"

Tony didn't hazard a guess. Heat rose in his face. Who gave a shit? He'd had it with his partner's condescending remarks. But he kept quiet. The chief's admonitions about getting along with his colleagues were never far from his mind.

"Airport dispatch, Rescues 14, 15, and 16 responding," Lieutenant Wozniak radioed. "Stand by to open Gate-140."

"Dispatch copies. We'll watch for your approach."

"Reynolds ground, Rescue-15 and company on emergency from Station Bravo to the landside terminal. Request Bravo, Romeo, and Alpha to the north ramp."

"Rescue-15 and company, that's approved. I have an E-170 heading south on Bravo. He'll hold for you."

Tony hung close behind the pumper and ladder truck as they weaved their way around the regional jet.

"Gate-140 coming open," the dispatcher said as the fire apparatus approached the fence separating the airside terminal and the west ramp from the unsecured north ramp. Once through the gate, the rigs shot across the open pavement, maneuvered diagonally under the monorail tracks, and stopped at the rear of the landside building.

"Rescue-15 from dispatch. A police officer on scene reports people evacuating the area."

"15 copies. We're on the scene. I'll have landside command."

Eight firefighters, suited up in full gear and breathing apparatus, emerged from their vehicles and gathered their tools while Tony and Jarvis grabbed their SCBA from the side compartments of Rescue-14.

"Hurry up, Moretti. We're gonna miss the parade. This ain't the academy."

"Don't worry about me." Tony slammed the compartment door but held his retort, focusing instead on donning his breathing apparatus. Through repeated practice over the last two months, his time was down to thirty-five seconds, and he had his harness cinched up and his BA ready to go while his partner fumbled with a pair of twisted shoulder straps.

When Jarvis reached back to open the cylinder handwheel, high-pressure air sent his lung demand valve flying from its belt-mounted holder.

Look at the hotshot, Tony mused as he rushed over to his partner. "Stand still. I've got it." He grabbed and reset the swaying regulator and straightened Jarvis's straps. "Get the TIC and a portable light and meet me at the door." He retrieved a twenty-pound dry chemical extinguisher and, unable to resist the opportunity, said, "Don't worry, Jarvis. I won't let anything happen to you."

Jarvis walked over with a LiteBox and the thermal imaging camera as the teams entered the secure door at the rear on the baggage claim level. He scowled at Tony. "Don't think for a second I needed your help."

"You're quite welcome, Firefighter Jarvis." Tony covered his mouth to hide his glee.

"Nice of you to join us, Jarvis," Lieutenant Wozniak said. "O'Brien and Brooks, stay on this level and check the bottom of the escalator. Everyone else, with me."

The crew lugged hose packs, extinguishers, irons, pike poles, ropes, and a combination ladder through a short hallway and up a wide set of fire escape stairs to the ticketing level.

Smoke greeted the firefighters as the exhaust fans struggled to remove it from the terminal. Tony inhaled a whiff of the eye-stinging black particulate. It reeked of petroleum and reminded him of the refineries he'd visited as a sales rep. He cleared his throat and coughed.

"Aww, all this smoke getting to ya?" Jarvis asked and sneered.

The LT surveyed the scene. "Krigger, hook up to the standpipe in the stairwell, but don't deploy your hose pack unless I tell you to. If there *is* a fire, it's in the grease pan. Iggy and Leach, get that top plate off. Moretti and Jarvis, hit the emergency stop and stand by with a dry chem and the TIC."

Iggy started coughing, then Nikki, then Jarvis. Hah, the bastard was getting his due.

"This shit's bad," Wozniak said. "Go on air."

Loud inhalations signaled the flow of fresh air as the team activated their BAs. Jarvis donned his facepiece, raised the LDV, and hesitated.

"Anytime, Jarvis." The LT's words were sharp and commanding.

Jarvis plugged in, but Tony heard no inhalation and watched as the facepiece's visor sucked in toward his partner's face.

"Here, you stupid fuck," Krigger said. He reached behind Jarvis and cranked the handwheel open. A sharp whistle sounded. "Fifteen-year vet, huh?"

"Let's get moving," the LT commanded.

Nikki used a power driver to loosen the screws securing the top plate, and Iggy lifted the heavy steel with his Halligan bar. Flames spewed from the escalator's inner workings.

Tony pulled the pin on the dry chem and squeezed the handles, sending sodium bicarbonate into the mechanism and extinguishing the fire.

"Nice, Moretti," the LT said. "Jarvis, use the TIC. That grease can relight any second."

Jarvis aimed the thermal imaging camera at the grease pan.

"Lower, Jarvis. We know it's hot at the *top*," the LT said in an irritated voice. "Get your head down there and aim your camera at the guts of the thing."

When Jarvis bent and extended his arm into the opening, fire shot out at him.

Tony pushed the nozzle of the twenty-pounder into the hole and discharged it in a spray of dry chemical. The flames died out.

Jarvis stumbled to his feet and tugged at his facepiece, but his helmet held it fast. He yanked off his gloves, uncinched his chin strap, and whipped the helmet off. It tumbled to the floor and skittered across the tile. He pulled the facepiece off without resetting the LDV, and the regulator again hissed high-pressure air. Krigger reached over, hit the reset lever, and spun the cylinder wheel shut. Everyone stood silent except for Jarvis, who coughed uncontrollably.

"Iggy, get him out of here," the LT said. "Check him out and put him in the back of 16." The crew watched him go without comment.

Despite how Jarvis had ridden him since the academy, Tony sympathized. He'd been in embarrassing situations many times, and now he regretted his venomous thoughts. Jarvis wasn't a bully after all. He was just a guy trying to cover up his shortcomings by projecting them onto someone else.

Once the escalator cooled, the LT turned the scene over to terminal maintenance. Jarvis went home on a sick shift and Kyle Traynor replaced him on Rescue-14.

As Tony reserviced the equipment, he considered what had occurred. And he took a second to congratulate himself on his performance.

* * *

1:10 p.m. "Remember, the rabbit pops his head out of the hole, runs around the tree, and dives back into the hole," Evan said as he held up a three-foot section of rope.

"Except for Tony's rabbit," Robbie said. "It runs smack *into* the tree."

"That *is* interesting," Evan said as he examined Tony's attempt to tie a bowline knot. "What do you call it, the double granny bowline?"

"Maybe he uses it on his wife for sex games," Keith Weston chimed in.

"You should know, Keith," Nikki Leach said. "Don't you let Margie tie you up every Saturday night?"

Keith's face turned beet red.

"I remember when Keith tried to lash a twenty-foot ladder to a jetway railing," Rosie said. "It almost took out the captain when it fell over."

The conference room dissolved into laughter, and Tony joined in. The vitriol that had marked so many of Tony's early encounters with the crew was gone, and he was fast becoming a trusted member of a close-knit team. Yet he was anxious about his new partner. Two months had passed since the confrontation in the dayroom, and although Tony had apologized for his remarks, he wasn't sure if Kyle held a grudge.

"Okay, knot experts," Evan said, "let's head out to the bays. We're going to tie off to Rescue-16's platform and see what kind of trouble we can get ourselves into."

The yelping tones of the crash phone ended the training session abruptly.

"This is the tower with an Alert-2 for a 757 cargo flight. Pilots are reporting a heat sensor in an aft compartment on the main deck. There are three souls on board and thirty-four thousand pounds of fuel. Aircraft to land on runway two-four-right in ten minutes."

Thirteen firefighters tossed their ropes aside as they dashed for the door. An icy blast hit Tony as he sprinted for his rig and within what felt like only a minute, five vehicles lined the edge of the pad, red strobe lights flashing and engines revving.

"Ground, Rescue-10 and company from Station Bravo. Request Bravo and Tango to our Alert-2 positions along runway two-four-left."

"Rescue-10 and company, drive as requested."

"Roger. Bravo and Tango to our positions. Rescue-10 has ARFF command. Have the tower supe meet me on the fire frequency."

Tony steered Rescue-14 to the back of the staggered line for the drive across Tango and pulled next to the captain's RIV as it stopped at Tango-1, the midpoint of the runway.

"Ground from ARFF command," the captain radioed. "All vehicles are in Alert-2 positions. Do you have any updates?"

"Roger, command. All vehicles in position. Stand by. The tower supe will join you with more information in a minute."

"Cargo planes have aluminum containers molded to the shape of the cabin and packed in tight," Kyle said. "Each one has its own sensor and fire suppression hookup, so any fire should be extinguished already. Anyway, we could never get in there."

Tony considered. If there *was* a fire, the containers would have to be off-loaded one at a time.

"ARFF command from tower supe. The pilot has an illuminated heat sensor, with no indication of extinguisher discharge. They think it's a container about midway back on the main deck. The crew wants to exit the aircraft as soon as possible."

"ARFF command copies. Have him stop on the runway and we'll get a ladder to the flight crew," the captain responded as the long, sleek two-engine aircraft came in from the east and touched down smoothly.

"Tower from command. The aircraft landed without incident. We'd like to follow."

"Follow the aircraft. That's approved."

Tony wheeled onto the runway behind Rescue-10 as the plane decelerated.

"We'll stay behind the captain," Kyle said. "Those big turbofans can throw shit at us that'll punch right through our windshield if we get too close."

Kyle seemed to be in teaching mode. Tony didn't mind.

"When you're driving, always remember to maintain a safety cushion between you and the…whoa! I didn't expect him to stop that soon," Kyle said. "Those babies usually roll out past the high-speed turnoffs. The pilots must have *stood* on the brakes."

"Tower supe from ARFF command. The aircraft landed but stopped short. Have him shut down his engines."

"ARFF command from tower supe. The pilots verify engine shutdown. They said they're coming out."

"Tower supe, tell them to wait," Schrum said, urgency in his tone. "Rescue-14 crew, stop behind him and grab the twenty-footer off our roof and ladder R-1."

Tony stopped behind the tail and hit the ground with his partner. "R-1 is coming open."

"Holy shit!" Kyle said as a yellow chute ballooned from the cabin door. "They popped their slide. What the hell's wrong with them?"

"14 from command, forget the ladder. Get up there and keep them inside."

A white-shirted figure jumped onto the slide. "Too late. There goes one," Tony said.

"And another," Kyle said as a second body slid down the chute.

"They better get out of the way fast," Tony said as the last crew member poked his head out the door.

"Oops," Kyle said as number three tumbled into number two, who'd just stood up. The unfortunate crewman fell facefirst onto the concrete. "That *had* to hurt."

Tony took in the comedic scene. "Just like a bowling ball. Spare!"

"14, see if he's okay," Schrum instructed, exasperation in his voice. "11, swing around to the rescue side. 13, take off-rescue. Use your FLIRs on the cabin. Focus on the midpoint of the fuselage."

Tony and Kyle rushed up to the crew while Rescue-11 sped around behind them and took a position perpendicular to the 757.

"Are you guys all right?" Kyle asked.

A tall, overweight fiftyish man was helping his colleague to his feet. His white shirt sported four stripes on its epaulets. "Yeah, we're good. My copilot has a few scratches, but he'll be okay. What about the plane?"

"We're scanning for heat signatures with our infrared camera," Kyle said.

"Do you need help, sir?" Tony asked the injured copilot, a wiry forty-something with blood dripping from his nose and a cut on his forehead. "We can bring EMS out to take a look, clean and bandage those cuts."

The dazed man shook his head. "No need. It's just a minor bump." It looked worse than that; the man's nose might be broken. Tony guessed he was afraid to look weak in front of his boss.

11 and 13 reported all clear on the FLIR, and the flight crew, now seated in Ops-2 with Ellis Kim, one of the three ops managers, refused treatment. The emergency well in hand, Schrum remained on scene in Rescue-10 and returned all other units.

"That plane's going nowhere fast," Kyle said. "It'll take a while for a maintenance team to deflate and remove that escape slide."

"Wonder why they didn't wait for us?" Tony asked.

"Who knows, but they're going to have some explaining to do to their bosses."

The whole situation was amusing. Even highly trained pilots could screw up.

* * *

3**:45 p.m.** The radio crackled as Tony drove south on taxiway Alpha, returning to Station Bravo from a fuel farm inspection.

"Airport fire from dispatch, AED cabinet-17 was just opened in the A-wing of the airside concourse. We're trying to get more information. EMS has been dispatched."

"Hell, we're just a minute away," Kyle said as he grabbed the mic. "Rescue-14 responding to the A-wing."

Tony cut the steering wheel to the left, entered the West Ramp, and beached the rig beside a vacant jetway at gate A-3, trying to remember the procedures for a defibrillator.

"Rescue-14 from airport dispatch, we're receiving multiple calls of a man in cardiac arrest at Gate A-6. We have the scene up on our monitors and there are people huddled over a prone figure."

"Rescue-14 copies. We're out at the A-wing," Kyle reported.

"Be advised, 14, a police officer on scene confirms cardiac arrest with CPR in progress."

Tony bounded up the steps behind Kyle. The pair ran through the jet bridge to the concourse, holding their med bags in front of them to bull through a horde of bystanders. Two airline employees were administering CPR to a middle-aged Black male at Gate A-6. The man's shirt was open and AED pads were attached to his chest.

An airport authority cop met them at the victim's side. "They've given the victim one shock so far, but it didn't do any good."

"He was talking on his cell phone when he collapsed," a woman in the crowd said.

"The guy didn't say anything or grab his chest. He just dropped," said another.

Tony leaned over the agent who was giving compressions. "We'll take it from here."

The agent looked up, wet with sweat. "Okay…we've been trying…but…we…" He struggled for breath.

"It's okay," Tony said and helped the man to his feet. "You did great."

"Pad placement looks good," Kyle said. One AED pad was affixed to the right side of the man's chest and the other to his left side, below the armpit. "I'll check his vitals." He moved into position at the patient's head, placed a finger on the man's carotid artery, and bent low to his mouth and nose. "No respiration, no pulse. Start CPR." He gave the victim two breaths through a one-way rescue mask.

Tony knew what to do. He felt for the bottom of the rib cage, slid the palm of his right hand one-third of the way up the victim's sternum, interlaced his fingers, positioned his shoulders directly above the chest, tipped his hands back, and pushed down. Whoa. The breastbone gave way under his compressions. He'd never done this for real, not on a human being.

"One and two and three and four and five and six and seven and eight and…"

"Deeper," Kyle said. "Two inches."

"Right." Damn it, he knew that. But a human body wasn't a training mannequin.

"…twenty-eight, twenty-nine, thirty." Crunch. Bones gave way under Tony's palm. He recoiled but kept going. Cracked ribs were irrelevant; the guy was technically dead.

Kyle administered two rescue breaths.

Tony launched into another cycle. "One and two and three and…" After two minutes, the AED prompted a pause.

"Analyzing heart rhythm, stay clear of the patient," the robotic voice of the AED instructed as 14's crew scrutinized the fallen man.

"Shock advised. Charging. Stay clear of the patient."

"Everyone clear!" Kyle said as Tony removed his hands.

"Delivering shock."

The victim's body jumped as the defibrillator administered three hundred joules of electrical energy.

"Shock delivered," the mechanical voice reported. "Analyzing heart rhythm. No shock advised. It is safe to touch the patient."

"He's breathing!" Kyle said. "And he's got a pulse."

"I've got his wallet," the officer said. "His name is Malcolm."

"Hey, Malcolm," Tony said as he shook the victim gently. "Wake up, buddy."

Malcolm opened his eyes and coughed.

"All right, Malcolm! You're okay."

Applause broke out. Bystanders inundated Tony and Kyle with congratulatory words and pats on the back.

The team monitored the patient's condition until paramedics arrived and wheeled him away. Spectacle over, the crowd scattered.

Tony exhaled and willed his taut muscles to relax. No longer laser-focused on his work, he took in the surroundings. The smell of bagels, coffee, and cinnamon wafted through the concourse. PA announcements of arriving and departing flights. The subdued roar of a thousand chattering voices.

Travelers wearing tropical shirts and shorts, in stark contrast to the brutally cold night. Businesspeople in smart suits and heavy overcoats scurrying toward their gates. Parents with their kids in tow. Tony hoped they hadn't witnessed the event. People with cell phones held high. Had they filmed the victim's misfortune for social media? Were they filming still?

Tony spotted the two gate agents standing off to the side. One was crying while her partner tried to comfort her. He and Kyle walked over to them. "That man survived because of *you*, not us," Tony said. "We didn't do anything you weren't already doing."

"That's right," Kyle said. "It was your CPR and the way you used the AED that saved him. A damn fine job."

After more clapping and kudos from outbound passengers who overheard the exchange, both gate agents smiled. Tony looked around at the appreciative onlookers, and his own emotions welled up. He had helped save a life. It was a powerful experience, unlike anything he'd felt before.

TWENTY-EIGHT

Friday, December 9 – Night Shift

6**:05 p.m.** Flavor danced across Tony's taste buds. Juicy T-bone steaks; not the typical fire station dinner. He scarfed up every bit of the grilled apple tossed salad and Brussels sprouts. Manny Santos was quite the chef, especially with beef. His filet mignon and potatoes au gratin were legendary. And after a cold breakfast and an apple for lunch, Manny's cuisine was a gourmet meal. The only missing item was a bottle of cabernet.

For dessert, Manny served a selection of cheesecakes from a local bakery. No grocery store products for *him*. Tony tried to resist, but he couldn't refuse the lemon brûlée, one of his favorites.

Tony's willpower had strengthened considerably as his physical condition improved, and he seldom let his guard down. It would be so easy to munch all day; the food was excellent and junk food abounded. For this meal, however, he made an exception, figuring he could burn it off in the weight room later.

Hooked on sci-fi podcasts, Tony moved to the quiet room to listen to a production where aliens in human form tried to subvert world governments. Unoriginal, lacking verisimilitude, and certainly not Kurt Vonnegut, it was entertaining and unintentionally amusing. Captain Schrum interrupted his dip into escapism.

"I'm leaving in a few minutes on my Kelly shift, but I wanted to compliment you on your work today. You've accomplished what you set out to do, and more."

"Thanks, Cap. I'm grateful for the second chance."

Tony had five minutes to reflect on Schrum's words.

"Vehicle accident with entrapment, airport fire." The prealert drew a weary sigh as Tony got up and headed for Rescue-14. At least he'd eaten dinner.

An update followed the blaring Klaxon. "The accident is in the eastbound lanes of Airport Boulevard, near the office park. According to the state police, it's a chain reaction involving a tractor-trailer."

Rescue-14 led the way out of the fire department gate, with Rescue-15 and Rescue-18 in tow.

"Probably some nut speeding and weaving through traffic," Kyle said.

"Yep, it's a free-for-all." Common sense driving had vanished during COVID, and nowadays you took your life in your hands on the highways. The secondary roads weren't much better.

The westbound lanes were stopped dead as Tony approached the entrance to the highway.

"Shit, it's going to be the berm for us," Kyle said. He keyed the mic. "Lieutenant-1 from Rescue-14, we're going to skirt this traffic. You might want to hang back until we try it."

"Lieutenant-1 copies," Wozniak said. "I'll keep 15 and 18 on the boulevard until we hear from you."

Tony made a sharp right and eased his way along the berm.

"Watch it!"

"I see him," Tony said as he braked to avoid a car that was pulling into their path.

Kyle hit the electronic air horn. "Where the hell does he think he's going?"

The car stopped dead in its tracks. Tony veered around it as the driver tried to rejoin the traffic lane. Red and blue lights lit the scene as the accident came into view.

"There's the cops," Kyle said.

Tony stopped next to a state police trooper who waved him to a parking spot behind a tractor-trailer.

"Hey, Officer, we've got two more trucks about a half mile back. Any way we can get them through?"

"Yeah, we'll have one lane open in a few minutes, but it'll be a crawl. You can park behind my cruiser."

"Thanks," Tony said. "What about the accident? Anyone hurt?"

"A couple of minor injuries. The guy who caused it is wedged in tight."

Kyle relayed the info to Wozniak and the trailing vehicles. He and Tony grabbed the portable hydraulic spreaders and cutters and headed for the point of impact. The state trooper held traffic while the pair crossed.

The car, a white Ford Taurus, was caught between the semi and a Subaru Forester. How the hell had he managed that?

A paramedic met them at the front of the tractor-trailer. "He's okay, believe it or not, but we can't get him out. We tried to move him to the passenger side, but he screamed bloody murder. Called us every name in the book." The medic rolled his eyes. "We don't need the roof cut off, but can you pop the door before he has a mental breakdown?"

Tony chuckled at the sarcasm.

"Sure. The damage doesn't look too bad," Kyle said. "Won't take long."

"Great. The sooner we get him out of here, the better."

Tony glimpsed the scraggly-looking twentysomething who was caught against the steering wheel and the seat. Blood oozed from a cut in his forehead, but otherwise the kid looked okay.

"Jesus Christ. What's taking so long? Get me out already! Don't you stupid fucks know what you're doing?"

A medic draped a blanket over the kid's head, muffling his complaints. "This will protect your face from flying glass."

Tony smiled and gave the medic a thumbs-up.

Kyle grabbed the Halligan bar and stuck it into a small gap between the door and the B-post. "Let's get a bight for the spreaders."

With a short, controlled swing of the flat side of his axe, Tony struck the Halligan and drove the twin-duckbill blade into the gap. Kyle nodded and Tony thumped it again. The blade dug in deeper and Kyle pulled back on the bar to widen the space.

"That's good. Put the tips right here," Kyle said.

Tony hoisted the forty-pound Hurst spreaders—the Jaws of Life. Wind lashed his face, but he ignored the cold and focused on the task. Balancing the hydraulic tool against his right hip, he shoved the tips into the gap and triggered the activating lever. He leaned into it as the powerful jaws spread and the sheet metal groaned and bent outward, tearing as the blades slipped out.

"It's okay; I've got this," Tony said as he closed the blades and repositioned the tips deeper into the gap. *Let the tool do the work.* He eased pressure on the spreaders and the jaws bit into the thin steel. A loud pop sounded as the latch broke.

"That's it," Kyle said. "Let's open it up." Kyle pushed and Tony pulled until the damaged door swung three-quarters of the way open.

"Good enough," the medic said. "We'll take it from here."

"It's about time," the driver said. "Get this damn blanket off my head."

The job was wrapped up before 15 and 18 made it through the traffic, and when the LT arrived, he gave them a very public *attaboy*. Tony took it in stride.

On the walk back to their rig, Kyle patted Tony on the shoulder. "Who says you're a fuckup?" he asked.

"Everybody."

"Well, not me. Not anymore. I'll work with you anytime, partner. Let's pack up and get out of this damned cold."

"I'm with you," Tony said. He beamed. He could do this job after all. The dark times were receding.

* * *

9**:50 p.m.** A carbon monoxide alarm at the Mid-State Aviation Services facility on the ground level of the B concourse interrupted Tony's delayed evening workout. He sped through the last few reps of his second set of dumbbell flys and headed for his rig.

In addition to their responsibilities for aircraft fueling, Mid-State was contracted by several airlines to load, unload, and transfer luggage. They occupied space in each wing. The field was clear, and 14's crew reached their objective in under four minutes.

"Rescue-14 from dispatch, be advised, CO levels have surpassed one hundred parts per million on the garage sensor." Twice the OSHA limit for an eight-hour exposure, but not particularly dangerous for brief periods.

"14 copies," Kyle radioed. "We're on scene."

The crew donned their SCBA, conducted a fresh-air calibration of their multigas meter, and entered an unlocked door to a combination lounge and kitchenette.

An old floor lamp stood along the back wall, between a tattered leather sofa and a filthy recliner. Magazines lay in piles on a small coffee table, and food wrappers littered the threadbare carpet. A wall-mounted TV aired a documentary on the Rolling Stones. A grease-covered electric range and a sink full of dishes lined the back wall.

"This place is a dump," Tony said.

"They don't call them *ramp rats* for nothing," Kyle said. "Doesn't look like anybody's home."

Seconds later, the meter sounded its low-level alarm: *beep, beep, beep, beep.* "I've got fifty-seven ppm CO and rising slowly," Tony said.

"Too low; the source isn't in here. What about combustibles?"

"I'm showing zero on the lower explosive limit."

"Well, it won't blow up on us, anyway. Check the garage. I'll prop the door open and get a blower from the rig."

Tony moved into the adjacent garage, where three propane-fueled tugs sat idle in front of the bay door. The alarm continued its low-level warning as CO shot up to 180 on its way to dangerous territory. Levels between 200 and 400 ppm could cause throbbing headaches, nausea, and confusion.

BEEP, BEEP, BEEP, BEEP. The meter leapt into high alarm as readings passed 200. Way too high for a space with no running engines. What was going on?

Tony spotted twin metal doors set into the far wall. He trotted over and opened one. A storage room with a hodgepodge of tools, coveralls, toilet paper, and kitchen supplies.

Toilet paper? The head…where was the head? He tried the other door. His breath caught and he stumbled back. A figure sat on a toilet, eyes open, slumped against the wall.

Tony dropped the screeching meter, grabbed the man's vest, yanked him out, and slammed the door shut. "Kyle, get in here!" he radioed. "I need help."

"What's wrong?" Kyle asked as he entered the garage.

"Get the door up!"

Kyle hit the opener and rushed over to Tony. The door groaned as it clanged up along its tracks. Cold air blew across the floor.

"He was in there," Tony said, pointing to the closed restroom door.

Kyle squeezed the button on his lapel mic. "Dispatch from Rescue-14, we need an EMS response immediately. We have an unconscious victim. Probable CO poisoning."

The man, a beefy twenty-something, was unresponsive. His pants were down around his ankles and his exposed skin was ashen, which was good. Tony remembered what Iggy had taught the recruits during EMS training: *Cherry-red means they're dead.*

Kyle checked the meter. "One-sixty-six and falling fast," he said as the gusting wind cleared the air. A few seconds later, Tony silenced the alarm as the meter dropped below fifty. He knelt, unplugged his regulator, removed his facepiece, and bent down to the victim's nose. "He's breathing. Respirations are shallow, but steady."

"Let's get him outside," Kyle said.

Tony reached under the victim's armpits as Kyle grabbed his legs. They carried him to the concrete pad in front of the garage.

Tony cradled the victim's head and checked his brachial pulse. It was rapid and thready.

Kyle retrieved an oxygen bottle and two blankets from the truck. Tony put the victim on a high flow of O_2 through a non-rebreather mask and rechecked his vitals as Kyle covered the victim with one blanket and rolled the other into a pillow.

Rescue-15 called on the scene. Evan, who had replaced Wozniak as the officer on 15, strode over with Nikki, Keith, and Manny in tow. "The LT heard your call for help and thought we'd better check on you guys," Evan said. "How's the patient?"

"He seems stable, but he needs the ER, and soon."

"Copy that. We'll take over until the medics get here. What's the source of the CO?"

"Whatever it is, it's coming from the head, and I'm going to check it out." Before Evan could protest, Tony grabbed the gas meter, donned his facepiece, and headed inside.

Evan followed. "Watch yourself."

Ear-piercingly high alarm tones sounded as soon as he opened the door. BEEP, BEEP, BEEP, BEEP. CO readings spiked to 850 ppm but plummeted as fresh air blew into the small space.

Tony spotted the culprit. A portable space heater in the corner under the sink. He hadn't noticed it in his haste to remove the victim. He studied it for a second and switched it off.

Nikki joined them in the garage. "EMS is here and the guy's coming to."

Once the ambulance departed, the crew took a last look at the restroom. Tony pictured the kid slumped over on the commode. "I wonder how long he was in there?"

"Who knows," Nikki said. "But it sounds like the cavalry arrived just in time. The medics said he wouldn't have lasted another ten minutes."

Evan examined the heater. "This thing runs on kerosene. Can you believe that? Who could be clueless enough to sit in a four-by-six room with a running kerosene heater?"

"Someone who didn't want to take a crap in the cold," Nikki said. No one laughed. "Sorry; my bad," she offered.

Evan shook his head. "And the guy works at an airport. Amazing."

Tony regarded the tiny restroom. The ramp worker was going to be okay; the second person Rescue-14's crew had saved today. Amazing indeed.

* * *

1:30 a.m. Tony lay in his dark bunkroom, arms folded behind his head, staring at the small red light on the smoke detector. The clock read 1:27, but Tony was too hyped up to sleep. What a day, and how unlike the typical twenty-four-hour shift. The constant action, the varied nature of the emergencies, the weather conditions. Today had challenged his skills and endurance, and for the first time in his life, his labors had made a real difference in people's lives.

When the airport dispatcher announced a structural call and the Klaxon sounded, he didn't budge.

"We have multiple reports of sprinkler activation in baggage claim B. No reported smoke or fire. We're dispatching terminal maintenance. They'll meet you."

Would Rescue-14 respond to this one? He hoped so. Why break the streak now? He slipped his boots on.

Lieutenant Wozniak's voice came over the intercom. "Rescues 14, 15, and 16, respond."

He jumped to his feet. *One more time, Anthony.*

Ten minutes later, Evan led three crews laden with salvage equipment into the landside building, where a deluge of water cascaded onto the baggage carousel and spread across the carpeted floor. But instead of spraying in the familiar umbrella pattern of a sprinkler head, it gushed from multiple points in the ceiling grid.

Evan pointed to a section of sagging ceiling tiles. "That looks like a burst pipe."

Sopping-wet airline personnel scrambled to remove soaked luggage from the carousel. One approached Evan as the firefighters moved in to help.

"I'm Kate, the night supervisor." She wiped strands of dripping hair from her face. "This mess is from a delayed flight. If the plane had gotten in a half hour earlier, these bags would be gone. What luck."

"Seems like the day for it," Evan replied. "Get your people away from the water. We'll take care of the baggage."

"Thanks. I'm here by myself. Everyone else is from other airlines. They all pitched in. Anyway, the passengers will start arriving any minute." She shook her head. "God, are they going to be pissed."

The engine crew cleared the rest of the luggage while the truckies raised a twenty-foot combination ladder.

"It's definitely not the sprinkler," Keith Weston said. "It's coming from above the ceiling."

"There's a crack in the feeder line," a voice from behind them announced. The terminal maintenance supervisor had arrived. "Probably caused by wind pushing cold air into that damn dead space where the baggage carts enter the building. That area was never insulated properly." The man looked worn out and disgusted. "You'd think they built this place for the tropics."

"Can you cut off the flow?" Evan asked.

"I've got two plumbers up there now. If we're lucky, they'll find a valve to isolate this part of the system. If not, we're gonna have to shut down this whole side of baggage claim. We just can't get a break today."

"Tell me about it." As Evan spoke, the cascade of water slowed to a trickle. "Looks like your guys got it."

"Yeah, I'm gonna go upstairs and see what's what." The weary supervisor turned and headed for the stairwell.

Firefighters were moving the last of the luggage out of the wet zone as passengers arrived to retrieve their bags. "Okay, gang," Evan said. "It's time for pike poles, squeegees, shop vacs, and salvage covers. Let's clean this mess up."

The engine and truck crews went to work while Tony and Kyle helped Kate distribute soggy luggage to an unhappy assemblage of inbound travelers. By three o'clock, they'd sopped up most of the water and stacked the damaged ceiling tiles against the back wall. Caution tape barricaded baggage carousels A and B, but C and D were still available for the morning's flights.

"Will you look at this place?"

Tony turned to the familiar voice. It was Allie, bundled up in work boots and an airport authority parka. He'd forgotten she was on midnight shift this week.

"Well, good morning, Ms. Robinson," Evan said. "Must be slow in operations."

"Oh, you know, same as always." She scanned the scene. "I heard you guys were causing a commotion over here. Thought I'd stop and straighten things out."

Evan laughed. "You're just in time. We're out of here."

"Busy day, huh?"

"You could say that."

"The ops center is buzzing about it. They say Rescue-14's crew was in the thick of it all day, maybe saved a couple of lives too."

Evan nodded toward Tony and Kyle. "That was these two."

Allie raised her eyebrows. "No joke? In spite of the rookie?"

"Not in *spite* of him," Kyle said. "*Because* of him."

Allie let out a long whistle and gave Tony the once-over. "Well, then," she said. "Not bad, Firefighter Moretti. Not bad."

They stood chatting until the maintenance supervisor returned and advised repairs would take another two hours. Evan gathered the troops. "Listen up. The sprinkler system won't be back in service anytime soon, so someone is going to have to stay behind and babysit until the plumbers finish their repairs."

Tony jumped in. "I'll stay."

Evan gave him a curious look. "After the day you've had?"

"I'll stay too," Kyle said. "Somebody's got to keep him out of trouble."

"Okay, boys; it's your choice. We'll leave a long pike pole and a couple of water vacs in case you need them. See you at shift change."

Twenty minutes after 15 and 16's crews had departed, Kyle and Tony strapped on the wet vacs to give the carpeting one more pass. Kate thanked them profusely before she left for home.

Baggage claim was atypically quiet. Tony picked up a pike pole and probed a section of ceiling tiles.

"You're asking for trouble," Kyle said. "There's probably more water up there."

Kyle's warning came too late, as an entire section of ceiling grid came loose and crashed onto Tony, knocking him on his backside. The pike pole flew out of his hands and clanged off the carousel.

Tony sat up, stunned, his head poking through one of the rectangular grids. He looked at Kyle and tried to stand, but he slipped and fell again. Kyle cracked up; Tony joined in. Soon they were laughing uncontrollably.

"At least you were smart enough to keep your helmet on," Kyle said through his howls. "We wouldn't want anything to damage that fine Italian brain of yours."

The partners spent the next half hour policing the area and sopping up the water. Kyle ribbed him the entire time. Tony couldn't stop laughing.

Once they'd finished, Tony brushed the debris off his uniform.

"So why did you stay?" he asked Kyle.

"Why did *you*?"

"I wanted to see this ass-kicking shift all the way through to the end."

"And you thought I was going to let you get all the glory?"

Kyle gave Tony a high five. Mutual respect between fellow professionals. Tony couldn't have asked for more. He'd repaired the damage to his relationship with Kyle, and he felt like part of the team at last.

"Come on, rookie. I'll buy you a cup of that great vending machine coffee."

The fire suppression system came back online at four-thirty and Rescue-14 cleared its last call of an eventful shift.

It was too late to get any sleep, so Tony took a hot shower, brewed a pot of coffee, and ate some toast in the empty dayroom. Twenty-four hours of nonstop action, and he felt more alive than he had in years. And it was nice that Allie had witnessed his success. She was a colleague, after all.

TWENTY-NINE

Thursday, December 15

"It's after six-thirty. Don't you have to get home and pack?" Evan asked.

Tony stepped down from Rescue-18's interior compartment. "What about the airbags?"

"You know all about the airbags. Just like you know about the hydraulic tools, and the jacks, and saws, and the ropes, and every other tool on this truck."

Tony held up his hands in surrender. "Okay, I hear you."

"Your dedication is beyond reproach, Anthony, but your Kelly shift is over." Evan clapped Tony on the shoulder. "Go home to your wife."

"Thanks for your help," Tony said and stuck out his hand.

Evan took it. "You're being a little dramatic, aren't you? It's not like we haven't been over this stuff a dozen times."

"No, I mean thanks for *all* of it. Everything you've done for me over the last three months. I dug myself a hole when I got out of the academy, and I acted like an arrogant ass. It's a wonder the platoon didn't give me a blanket party. But because of you, I finally got past my pigheadedness. I'm getting better at my job and the crew is giving me another chance."

"That's because of your hard work, Tony. I didn't do that much."

"Yes, you did." Tony bit his lip. "I came very close to losing this job."

Evan met Tony's eyes and smiled. "It was my pleasure, but you already had what it took—*inside*. Anyone could see that."

"Maybe, but *you* brought it out." Tony's emotions welled up. "And thank you for your friendship. It's meant everything to me." He reached out and gave Evan a bear hug. It felt good.

"Hey now, let's not get emotional. You're out of here, but I've got another twelve hours. I don't want these jerks to see me with red eyes. I have an image to uphold."

Tony wiped the tears from his own cheeks.

"Come on; I'll get you a cup of muddy firehouse coffee for the drive home. You ready for the big vacation?"

"Yep. We're leaving tomorrow morning and not coming back until New Year's Day."

"Man, two weeks off and you've only been on the job seven months." Evan shot him a sly look. "How did you score a job like this?"

"Careful research."

"Bullshit! If you hadn't been on one of your Civil War sojourns, you'd have never heard about this place. You'd be selling insurance." Evan jabbed a finger at him. "Or cars."

Tony laughed. "Cars? Never!" But who knew? Spotting the civil service exam notice in the *Gettysburg Times* had been pure happenstance. Things might be very different otherwise.

"Just remember," Evan said. "Firefighting isn't like other jobs. It's about much more than your proficiency. It's a mindset, a way of living your life."

"A passion?" Tony asked with what he knew was his best skeptical smile.

"A passion," Evan replied.

Tony nodded, but Evan's words didn't register. Passion wasn't part of the equation.

He took stock as he drove home. He'd come so far since that first shift in August. Chief Martone had complimented his performance after the previous Friday's marathon on Rescue-14, a shift the platoon had dubbed *the longest day*. Best of all, he'd satisfied Chief Archer's parameters and his job was secure. He owed much of his success to Evan's mentoring.

Tony's fitness gains paralleled the rise of his work skills. His workout regimen in overdrive, the calluses on his palms from weightlifting got bigger with each passing week as his biceps, triceps and pecs hardened. The muscles in his calves, quads, and hamstrings tightened as he alternated his four-day-a-week cardio routine between the stationary bike and his runs with Allie. Even the department's twenty-somethings marveled at the old man's strength and stamina. He had Allie to thank for that. Like Evan, she was a special person.

Meanwhile his wholehearted effort to fit into A-platoon's culture was bearing fruit; most of his colleagues had come around. Things were trending upward.

The home front, unfortunately, stood in dramatic contrast to Tony's work life. A week after the medical assistance drill, Lisa had resumed her slide into despondency. Assurances that he no longer harbored thoughts of quitting the department fell on deaf ears. A holiday with family and friends might be his last chance to rekindle old feelings. Time would tell.

Part III

THE VAGARIES OF FORTUNE

THIRTY

Sunday, New Year's Day

Tony and Lisa culminated two weeks in western Pennsylvania by treating his parents to a Welcome to the New Year luncheon at the Knights of Columbus in Meadville. After a tearful goodbye, the couple hit the road.

Traffic was sparse, the turnpike was dry, and thick gray clouds traced their drive home. The outside temperature stood at an unseasonable fifty-five degrees, but the atmosphere inside the Cherokee was ice-cold.

They drove in a deafening silence broken only by Lisa's offers to drive and her admonitions to slow down, both of which Tony ignored. He had no desire to rehash the past seventeen days, and apparently Lisa didn't either. His head throbbed and his stomach churned from the beer, wine, and champagne of the night before. In his haste to get away, he shaved twenty minutes off the three-and-a-half-hour drive.

Arriving home just after five, Lisa unpacked and left for the medical center, claiming she had to catch up on paperwork before her morning shift. Tony didn't question her; he didn't say a word. He sat in front of the television, staring at a bowl game he had no interest in. How had his plan to reconnect with Lisa failed so completely? Instead of bringing them closer, the trip home had only magnified the forces pulling them apart.

An hour slipped by, and Tony decided he had to talk to someone. He texted Evan.

* * *

Hartman's Grill, one of the few restaurants open on New Year's Day, was packed with older men and a few childless couples. Tony lucked out and found a quiet corner booth. Evan came in a few minutes later and Tony waved him over.

"Good to see you, buddy," Evan said and slapped Tony on the back.

"You too. Can you believe all the guys in this place? I thought it would be dead."

"Can you blame them? I love Shannon and the kids, but I needed to get out of that house. It's been a long holiday."

The waitress, a middle-aged woman with a look that said she'd rather be anywhere else, took their order. Tony picked a double-patty cheeseburger, fries, and a Heineken, his last indulgence before returning to healthy eating. Citing his own excessive food intake over the holiday, Evan had a Cobb salad and a Diet Coke.

"How was the big trip?"

"Don't ask."

"Uh-oh. Didn't go as planned, huh?"

"Worse than I could've imagined."

"Sorry to hear that. I know you were banking on it." He paused. "Anyway, you didn't come here *not* to tell me about it."

Evan was right; Tony needed to hash it out with a friendly ear. "It started out okay. Pretty good, in fact. We were both looking forward to going back home, seeing the relatives and our old friends. Reconnecting, you know?"

Evan sipped his Diet Coke. "Yeah, but you expected more than that."

"I wanted to fix things, make it better between me and Lisa. I thought if..." He looked away.

"You thought if you returned to where it all began, you'd both find the magic again."

"I don't know. Maybe. But I thought we'd have a great time at least. Something to put us on the path to getting back to normal."

Evan stopped the waitress and ordered Tony another Heineken and switched to a Coors Light for himself. "So what happened?"

"It actually started out pretty well. Or I thought it did. We were okay driving west, talking about getting together with everyone, eating home-cooked meals, and having a good time. But..."

"Yes?"

"I guess even then there was an undertone of something. It didn't seem genuine, like we were forcing it. I don't know."

Evan gave an empathetic nod.

"The plan was to split our time. Eight days at her folks' place in Pittsburgh through Christmas morning. Then we'd head north to my parents' house in Meadville for New Year's Eve."

"Good plan."

"I thought so, and I thought it worked out pretty well the first few days. Lisa's mom and dad were thrilled to see us, her brother and sister stopped by, and we all went skating at the ice rink downtown."

"Nice."

"On Monday, Lisa dropped in at the oncology floor at her old hospital while I had lunch with a couple of friends from my old marketing gig. After that, everything changed."

Evan took a swig of his beer.

"On Tuesday, I connected with an old frat brother and we went out for a few drinks. That ended *my* socializing for the week. But Lisa stopped at the hospital again on Tuesday, and Wednesday, and Thursday. She even attended the little party they held for the patients. She went out every night, sometimes with former coworkers, other times with old friends."

"And what did you do those nights?"

"Not much. Sat with her dad and watched the History Channel."

"Fun."

"I love the guy, but I wanted to be with my wife and I didn't know where she was." Tony shook his head. "Even her parents began to wonder. Her mom asked if everything was okay between us."

"What did you say?"

"What could I? I told her everything was great. Lisa just had a lot more connections in Pittsburgh than I did."

Evan snatched a couple of Tony's fries.

"On Christmas Eve, the house was crammed with her relatives. Lisa was in heaven. I hadn't seen her that happy in years. Everyone stayed up past two o'clock, laughing, talking, eating, and drinking. But we hardly saw each other because she was so wrapped up in the festivities.

"After we exchanged gifts with her folks Christmas morning, her whole demeanor changed. She didn't look at me during brunch and barely said a word on the drive to my parents' house."

"And when you got there?"

"Oh, she was pleasant enough with my folks; charming, in fact. My sister and her family came over and she played with their kids." Tony took a drink. "We had a quiet Christmas dinner. You have to understand, the Morettis aren't the Szabos. We're a pretty reserved bunch."

"I never noticed that about you." Evan smiled.

"By Sunday night, Lisa was fidgety and anxious. I asked, but she said it was nothing, which was pretty much what she said to me the whole vacation. Nothing." Tony looked into his beer. "Tuesday afternoon, she took the car and went back to her parents' place. She didn't explain, didn't try to make some excuse. And I didn't ask.

"We passed a couple of texts. She wanted to catch up with a few more friends." Tony shrugged. "I rounded up the only three hometown buddies who hadn't moved away, and we hit the bars. Lisa finally returned last night, and we had a quiet New Year's celebration. And that was it. The perfect vacation." Tony swallowed hard. "I half expected her to take a Greyhound home."

Evan gave Tony a long, sympathetic look. “Sorry.”

Tony felt a little better as he said goodbye to Evan and headed home. He hadn’t given up on his marriage, but what else could he do to shore it up?

THIRTY-ONE

Monday, January 2

Head pounding and stomach in knots, Tony dragged himself to work. The talk with Evan had helped, but thoughts of a marriage on the brink clouded his mind.

"Happy New Year, buddy," Robbie said as Tony carried his gear bag to his bunk room.

"Same to you." Without another word, he went inside, closed the door, and plopped onto the unmade mattress. He lay there until the intercom summoned all firefighters to the dayroom.

Tony voiced a half-hearted greeting as the crew talked and laughed. At least some people had had pleasant holidays. Tony leaned against the center island at the edge of the kitchen. Robbie ignored him.

Tony noted three fresh faces. Danny Gardner and Neal Rooney had used their high seniority to bid in from C-platoon—refugees fleeing the grips of Captain Hartman, no doubt. Both had reputations as top-notch firefighters. But Dave Jarvis, the third new guy, was *assigned* to A-platoon when no one else selected the spot. Meanwhile, Nathan Sawicki had switched to B-platoon, while Rolphe Hoffman shifted to C. Tony liked Rolphe but never hit it off with Nate; he wasn't sorry to see him go. Wayne Hughes, who'd given Tony some timely advice, retired at the end of the year.

Captain Schrum delivered a brief update and welcomed the new firefighters to the platoon. Aside from vehicle checks and cleanup, a hot work inspection was the sole scheduled activity. The captain wished everyone a happy New Year and followed department tradition by suspending training for the day. The crowd applauded. Tony didn't hang around for breakfast.

Morning stretched into afternoon. Of all days to have an empty slate. Tony wandered the truck bays, poking around in compartments but not paying much attention to the contents. By three o'clock, he'd had it. He needed something to occupy his mind. He cajoled Evan into an impromptu training session. Then he found Robbie, apologized for ignoring him at shift change, and asked if he'd like to join in.

The trio climbed aboard Rescue-11, where Evan embarked upon a lesson in advanced aircraft incident tactics. He focused on modulation, operating the roof or bumper turret while a crash truck was in motion.

"Firefighters from small Index A or B airports don't have much choice. With one or maybe two crash trucks, they use modulation all the time to get three-hundred-sixty-degree coverage."

"We don't have that problem," Robbie said.

"Not usually, but the technique is good to know," Evan said. "Can you think of a scenario where *we* can use it?"

"How about if there's two aircraft, like in a collision on the runway?" Robbie asked.

"Or if one crash truck gets to the scene quickly, but the others get held up by the terrain or debris?" Tony added.

"Right on both counts," Evan said. "Those things *can* happen here. Sometimes we get too comfortable, too complacent. We assume we'll arrive with at least three crash trucks, but to consider ourselves a top-notch ARFF department, we've got to be ready for anything. Modulation is a standard part of the academy's small airport curriculum, but during your rookie class, we hardly mentioned it."

"Yeah, we only got to try it once, and I screwed it up bad," Robbie said.

"No surprise," Evan said. "It takes a lot of practice, and it's more than a driving and turret operations skill. You need to consider what's going on in front of you. Which way is the wind blowing? Are there obstacles in your way? Can you get past them? If you see survivors on the ground, how will you protect them? Should you extinguish the main fire or cut a rescue path?"

Tony had the concepts down cold, but he welcomed the review.

"While we're talking about using all the weapons in our arsenal, don't forget that each crash truck carries five hundred pounds of dry chem. It's another tool we discussed at the academy, and it packs a tremendous punch when combined with foam. You can use it whether you're modulating or stationary, and since our Strikers encase the dry chemical agent within the fire stream, it won't be affected by strong wind. Well, not any more than the stream itself is."

"Dry chem disrupts the fire triangle, right?" Robbie asked.

"It's actually a fire tetrahedron," Tony interjected. "Fuel, heat, oxygen, and chemical chain reaction. The dry chem interrupts that chain reaction, and the foam suppresses and seals off the vapors." As soon as he said it, he felt bad for correcting his enthusiastic friend so abruptly, but he couldn't help himself. The geek in him was fascinated by the theories behind fire suppression, and he enjoyed talking tactics. He'd always been good at thinking on his feet, and firefighting offered a plethora of scenarios to refine his problem-solving skills. In any case, it was better than dwelling on his domestic circumstances, and he enjoyed these tactical discussions.

"Someone's been hitting the books," Evan said. "I'll arrange a few trips to the academy so you guys can practice."

The high-pitched, yelping tones of the crash alarm interrupted the discussion. "This is the tower with an Alert-3 on runway eighteen-thirty-six."

Tony's muscles tensed and the trio went silent as all ten garage doors rolled up on their tracks. Alert-3? An actual plane crash?

"Atlantic Skyways, an A321. The aircraft aborted its takeoff and stopped at the four-thousand-foot point of the runway, between taxiways Sierra and Hotel-2."

An audible sigh arose in the cab.

The controller's voice returned. "The aircraft has seventy-three souls on board and an unknown amount of fuel, and the pilot is reporting hot brake indicators for the right and left main gear."

"Let's go, boys," Evan said as he fired up the engine.

Tony climbed down to grab his gear. Robbie said, "I'm on 13," as he practically jumped over Tony, hit the floor, and sprinted away. Less than a minute later, five pieces of fire apparatus lined the edge of the taxiway.

"Reynolds ground from Rescue-10 at Station Bravo," the captain radioed. We request Bravo and Sierra to the Alert-3 aircraft on runway eighteen-thirty-six."

"Rescue-10 and company, drive as requested. Sierra is clear."

"Rescue-10 copies. Clear to eighteen-thirty-six. I'll have ARFF command."

Evan steered Rescue-11 behind 10 into the sharp turns onto Bravo and Sierra, trying to keep pace with the captain's RIV.

"ARFF command from ground. Pilots report a blown tire on the left side main gear."

"Command copies. Let them know we're almost there."

Calm and alert, Tony was ready.

"They must have leaned on those brakes," Evan said. A column of smoke came into view as he accelerated to top speed, slowing only as they approached taxiway Hotel.

"ARFF command from ground. The flight crew has initiated an evacuation from the right side of the aircraft."

"Command copies. Evac in progress."

The captain's RIV made a hard left onto Hotel as Evan followed, now fifty yards behind. "Airport dispatch, Rescue-10 is on the scene. We have a fully involved fire of the left main gear. Three escape chutes are visible at R-2, R-4, and the overwing hatch. Make your notifications and alert EMS and our second alarm mutual aid."

"Dispatch copies. Be advised the fire chief and both deputies are en route."

"Rescue-11 from command," the captain radioed. "Angle your

truck in front of the left main gear and use your roof turret to knock that fire down. We've got passengers evacuating in front of us and we'll protect their egress path."

"Rescue-11 copies," Tony acknowledged as black smoke billowed from underneath the wing. "Initiate direct attack on the left main gear."

The captain continued. "Rescue-13, position in front of the right main gear assembly and stand by; it's probably just as hot as the left. Rescue-12, take position behind the aircraft and cut off any fire spread."

Tony's information-gathering skills came alive as he digested Schrum's rapid-fire orders and visualized their potential effects. The strategy was sound and the tactics corresponded with the developments in front of them, but there was something…

"That's a lot of smoke for a landing gear fire," Evan said. "Too much."

Tony glimpsed flames through the thickening smoke. He grasped the joystick for the roof turret. No, that was wrong. He switched to the bumper turret and pointed it straight ahead, adjusting the pattern to a narrow stream.

"The captain ordered roof turret," Evan said as he brought the crash truck to a smooth stop, seventy-five feet in front of the airliner and angled toward the burning landing gear.

"We need to get under the wing. Let me hit it with the bumper."

Evan scanned the scene. "Go for it."

Tony squeezed the trigger. The truck rocked backward as five hundred gallons per minute spewed from the bumper turret in a constricted water-foam mixture that ricocheted off the strut and blown tires.

"A little wider, Tony. Thirty degrees."

Tony adjusted the cone. He swept up and down, left and right. The fire darkened and the smoke cleared.

"Reignition!" Evan warned as the flames shot upward again. "Shrapnel must've punched a hole in the wing tank, and it was full for takeoff." He grabbed Tony's shoulder and pointed. "Push it away from the cabin."

Schrum issued new orders as Tony continued working the bumper turret. "Lieutenant-1, deploy Rescue-15's crew. Your teams will be designated as Attack-1 and Search-1. Pull a line from Rescue-13 and protect the evacuating passengers."

"Just under two thousand gallons remaining," Evan said.

Schrum's voice came across the radio. "Shotgun riders, deploy to the ground and pull a line from Rescue-11. Move in and extinguish the fire in the right main gear. You're designated Attack-2. Keep the flames away from the fuselage and wing."

"That's me," Tony said.

"Go," Evan said. "I'll take the bumper."

Tony ditched his headset, affixed his facepiece, pulled up his hood, strapped on his helmet, and climbed out of the cab to join the ground attack. He yanked a stack of inch-and-three-quarter hose from the side compartment as firefighters from Rescues 12 and 13 joined him. He plugged in his LDV and took the number three position in line. Rescue-10's bumper turret rained a protective foam coating over the team as they advanced toward the flames.

"Attack-1, redeploy and support Attack-2 with the left main gear," the captain instructed.

At fifty feet from the landing gear, Attack-2 opened up. Tony humped hose forward as his nozzle operator attempted to knock down the flames.

"Attack teams from command. We're going to open 10's roof turret. Keep your heads down," Schrum radioed.

A foamy mixture streaked past Attack-2. Overspray coated their gear and breathing apparatus.

Attack-1 moved up on Tony's right. Lieutenant Wozniak, backing up Attack-1's nozzleman, waved his arms at Tony. "Moretti, get over here and take our nozzle," he said. "I'll back you."

Tony yanked twenty feet of hose forward for Attack-2 before dropping it and sidestepping to his left, where he assumed the nozzle position for Attack-1. Wozniak, breathing hard, had just moved in behind him when someone called out. "Hang on, LT; we'll back him up."

Tony glanced back as two firefighters heaved the line and dragged it forward. One of them edged up behind him and leaned into the hose, allowing Tony to maneuver the nozzle.

Heat enveloped him as he positioned the nozzle a foot in front of his body, clamped it to his side, and pulled back on the bale. Tony grabbed the rubber stream shaper and twisted it clockwise to tighten the pattern. Sudden pressure forced him backward and he stumbled.

"I got you," the backup man said. Tony recognized the voice—Dave Jarvis.

"Let's move forward and to the right!" the LT called as he stood between the hose teams and motioned with outstretched arms. "Push it away from the plane!"

"We're moving right," Tony shouted. The trio sidled five feet farther from the fuselage. He drew in a deep breath. "Let's move in!"

Heat penetrated Tony's hood as he led Attack-1 forward. Pain stung his ears. He swung the nozzle left and right, working in unison with Attack-2. Flowing fuel stymied his attempts to smother it with a foam blanket. His instincts told him to retreat, but he couldn't do that. He had to concentrate, ignore the pain. Left and right, left and right. His arms became rubber bands as the effort sapped his strength. Left and right.

"Keep it up! It's working," Wozniak said. Tony dug for his last reserves of energy. His boots sloshed through the deepening mixture of liquids as he raked the flames and continued sidestepping to the right.

As the two teams reached the edge of the wing, the fire diminished and the heat subsided. The last of the stubborn flames disappeared under a thick layer of white suds, overwhelmed by three hundred gallons per minute of foam solution.

"That's it. Shut down," the LT shouted. "Command from Lieutenant-1, the fire is out."

It *was* out, but the fuel continued to flow from the damaged wing. A plug kit arrived with Gardner and Rooney, who were staffing Search-1. Covered by the watchful attack teams, they erected an A-frame ladder under the wing. Rooney pounded a black rubber plug into the hole. The leak slowed to a trickle, but it inundated both new platoon members with Jet A.

"Welcome to the team," Wozniak said to the two new A-platooners.

"Dispatch from ARFF command," the captain radioed. "This scene is under control. We're gathering the passengers now and we need transport."

"That's received, command. Be advised, EMS units are on the way and ops is escorting a bus to your location."

Ten minutes later, the captain ordered the attack and search teams to a makeshift rehab station at Rescue-15. Tony spotted Allie and Ryan Parilla, who were trying to corral a scattered group of cold and disoriented passengers. He walked over to her.

"Need any help?"

"Nah, we're good. This is the last of them. I should have known you'd be mixed up in all this."

"When danger calls…"

"You run like hell." She laughed. "Did you accomplish anything or just get wet?"

"I did okay, but I gotta go." He winked. "See you around," he said and started for rehab.

"Hey, Moretti. Wait."

Tony turned.

"This is my last week on three-to-eleven and my mornings are free. Want to start the new year off with a long, cold run?"

"I think I can make room in my schedule. Meet you Wednesday at the academy?"

"You're on, rookie—and welcome back, by the way."

Back at Station Bravo, Tony pitched in to help reservice the crash trucks, took a hot shower, changed into his spare station uniform, and checked his phone. No calls, but a bunch of texts from his friends back home who'd seen the fire on CNN. Only one from Lisa.

Leese: Saw the news. Hope you're okay. Call me when you can.

. . .

That was it? Christ, did she even care anymore?

The captain ordered pizzas and a boisterous crowd in the dayroom enjoyed a well-deserved break while they thrashed out the details of the most extensive aircraft fire anyone had seen in years.

"This was supposed to be an easy day," Nikki said. "I think we've been jinxed by Gardner and Rooney."

"And they smell really bad," Iggy said and held his nose. The two platoon newbies sat at a corner table, staring at their pizza. Repeated showers had failed to rid them of the petroleum odor.

"Hey, Cap, can we send them back to C-line?" Keith Weston asked.

Everyone laughed except Dave Jarvis, who made a quick exit. Tony caught him in the hall and offered his hand. Dave took it.

"Thanks for the backup out there today," Tony said. "You kept me from falling on my ass."

"Not a problem," Jarvis said. "It's the least I could do after the crappy way I've treated you."

The admission floored Tony. Was Jarvis apologizing? "No worries. That's in the past."

"Maybe, but it doesn't make up for me being an asshole. It won't happen again."

Tony nodded.

"I'm not claustrophobic…exactly," Jarvis said without much conviction. "But I get freaked out in real situations sometimes. That's why I left my last job. Thought it wouldn't be a problem at an airport." He looked down and added, "So I rode you at the academy to keep the heat off me."

Tony, who'd had his share of difficulties, felt sorry for Jarvis.

"Anyway, you coulda given me a lot of shit after that escalator fire in December, but you didn't. I won't forget that."

Tony smiled. "How 'bout I grab us some pizza and a couple of Cokes?"

Personally and professionally, it was another good day at work for Tony. At the hot wash, with all three chiefs present, Captain Schrum lauded his work in the crash truck and on the ground. His crewmates congratulated him. Deputy Chief Martone told him it was “one fine performance.” A far cry from those dark August and September shifts. Tony needed the shot in the arm because the situation at home was getting worse.

THIRTY-TWO

Tuesday, January 3

Tony's sat in the steaming water, his knees bent since he was too tall to stretch out in the tub. His muscles ached from yesterday's fire. The forecast predicted clear and cold weather: temperatures in the midteens, intensified by a brisk wind out of the northwest. Tony would have opted for a recovery day had his phone not chirped:

Arob: Hey, I heard about the big fire yesterday. Are we still on, or are you going to sleep all day? You can tell me all about it, and I need a partner who'll let me vent.

That's all it took to convince him. He was tired of rehashing the situation with Lisa. He left the apartment at eight-thirty and picked up a couple of sixteen-ounce coffees. As usual, Allie beat him to the academy.

"Happy New Year, stranger. Hope you didn't get too tubby on Mom's home cooking, 'cause I'm not going to slow down for you."

"Happy New Year to you." He unzipped his jacket and poked his belly. "I guess I *did* put on a few pounds, and I didn't do much exercising, so you'll have to take pity on me." It was true he had eaten too much while he was away, but he'd been out every morning, running the killer hills near his in-laws' house or the rural roads outside his hometown. He'd even dusted off the old weight set in his parents' basement.

Allie wanted to hit the trail, but he convinced her to share a coffee with him first. He turned up the thermostat in the lunchroom and gave her an abridged firsthand account of his experience at the wheel-brake and jet fuel fire. But she'd called him for support and he encouraged her to unload.

Allie expressed her frustrations with Sharon Lambert, who'd rejected one suggestion after another. Tony understood her irritation, but beyond a veneer of anger at her boss, he sensed a deeper unhappiness, perhaps loneliness. He wondered if she was picking up on *his* personal problems as well. Maybe it was time to speak of something besides work. He tested his theory by explaining the state of his marriage and detailing the disastrous Christmas vacation. She listened with empathy, offering support without judgment or comment.

Once Tony finished, Allie revealed the plight of her own personal life. She mentioned her inability to find a partner since moving to the area. "Not a lot of farm boys looking for a skinny Black chick." But that's where she stopped. "Let's get outside before you talk yourself out of it."

Buffeted by frigid gusts, they made good time on the crushed gravel trail. After three months of training, Tony had shaved two minutes off his old time. He'd never match Allie's 7:30 pace, but she eased off a bit and they stayed together for the entirety of their longest run to date.

Allie checked her Garmin. "Five miles in forty-one minutes." She gave him a disbelieving look. "I think someone was fibbing about what he did on vacation. You're faster than ever."

Tony bent over to catch his breath.

"Although your endurance needs some work."

He stood up. "I can't let you run my ass off anymore."

"Uh-huh, gotcha."

When they got back to the academy, the parking lot was full.

"That's weird," Tony said. "I didn't see any classes on the schedule. Damn; I don't want to shower with a bunch of strangers going in and out of the locker room."

"Were you shy after middle school gym class too?" she teased. "Did the bigger boys snap your butt with towels?"

"I *was* one of the bigger boys," he replied, with maybe a little too much bravado. "Damn it, I was going to grab a bite and run a few errands before I got home, but I'm soaked with sweat."

"That's par for the course with you." She crinkled her face in mock aversion. "Hey, why don't you come over to my place? It's fifteen minutes away. You can shower and be on your way."

His look of surprise must have been a doozy because she burst out laughing.

"I can't impose on you like that," he said. "I'll just head home and bag my plans."

"Oh, come on, and don't worry. I won't jump you as soon as we get in the door."

"Okay, but just a quick shower."

"Didn't take much to change your mind."

She was right. It didn't.

* * *

At the apartment, Allie suggested Tony shower while she made coffee. "I could be convinced to make us some breakfast, if you ask nicely."

Tony agreed and emerged fifteen minutes later, wearing a Henley pullover and a pair of tight jeans. Not that she minded the view. She'd have to switch to the trailing position during their runs so she could admire that cute butt of his. She giggled at the thought.

He dropped his bag at the door. "Something funny?"

"Uh, it's that mop of hair. Guess you couldn't find my blow-dryer, or my brush."

"Nope, towel dried and patted down."

"I see. Very improvisational," she said. "Have some coffee while I shower."

After dressing in baggy sweats, she found Tony flipping through *I Know Why the Caged Bird Sings.*

"I didn't know firefighters could read." From their brief acquaintance, he'd shown himself to be a thoughtful and intelligent individual. He had so much going for him for such a troubled soul.

"I'm impressed with your bookshelf. Maya Angelou, Octavia Butler, Toni Morrison, N. K. Jemison, and a whole shelf of classic Black literature. And I thought ops nerds stuck to FAA technical manuals."

"Touché," she said, raising her hands in mock surrender. "Don't laugh. I may not have a big-time master's degree but Kent State had some pretty awesome lit classes. I took a couple during my sophomore year and ever since, I can't get enough."

"I might borrow your copy of *The Warmth of Other Suns*. I've read a little about the Great Migration and found it fascinating."

Allie made bacon, eggs, and toast and the pair made small talk as they ate. Tony commented on the tastefulness of the decor and the organization of her kitchen.

"I think you're a neat freak, Althea."

"OCD—a family trait. Why did I tell you my real name?" But she was okay with it, even liked the way he said it.

They dug into their upbringing, their high school and college days, and compared how two people from the same area had ended up at Reynolds International Airport. It was so easy to talk to this guy.

Allie wanted him to hang around, but she had to get on the road to Youngstown for a weekend with her folks. And she was afraid. Were her feelings for this fascinating man developing into something more than friendship? Maybe, but her past was littered with rash decisions and failed relationships.

After Tony left, she voiced her dilemma. "He's married, Allie. Where's that fact going to leave you?"

THIRTY-THREE

Friday, January 6

After three late-night smoke detector activations, Tony was beat. He was looking forward to a couple of days off to catch up on his sleep and work on his marriage. Lisa was in bed when he got home, and he slipped in without waking her. He woke to the sound of her voice and the smell of cinnamon.

"Hey, sleepyhead," she called. "I'm making lunch, so get your butt out here."

Christ, it was eleven-thirty. He slipped on a pair of sweats and followed the aroma to the dining room table.

"Mmm, French toast casserole. Haven't had that in a while. What's the occasion?"

"Nothing special; just felt like something different."

Her sudden change in temperament was baffling.

"Actually, I feel bad about how I've acted. I'm feeling better today and thought I'd apologize with food."

"The way to a man's heart?"

"Maybe." She flashed her cutest smile. "Come on; let's eat before it gets cold."

Lisa's creation danced across Tony's taste buds, and he asked for seconds. They talked, but neither mentioned the recent Christmas trip, the proverbial elephant in the room. He couldn't remember the last time his wife was so upbeat, but maybe it was best to leave the past in the past. As he helped her clean the table, she broached a different topic.

"I've been looking at some opportunities to kick my career to the next level, and I'd like to know what you think." Her tactfulness gave him pause.

"Sure, Leese. What are you thinking?"

"You know how I've wanted to finish my master's degree?"

Was she laying a guilt trip on him? "Of course I do. You had to drop out because I moved you halfway across the state. It's one of the many things I regret."

"You didn't *move* me. I *chose* to come here with you." She hesitated. "I've found an opportunity to complete my degree and get some practical experience while I'm at it. It'll be fully paid for. I just need to buy the books."

"That's fantastic! Which university? Does Gettysburg College have an MS in nursing?"

"I checked, but no, they don't. Penn State does, and they'll take all fifteen of my credits."

Tony considered. "Oh, right. Penn State's Mont Alto campus. I heard they've got a top-notch nursing department. One of the guys at work is in the part-time program and he raves about it." His words spewed out, *willing* her to select the nearby location. "And it's only a half hour away. An easy drive for you, even in the winter. That's perfect. And your job is going to pay the tuition?"

"It's not Mont Alto."

Tony narrowed his eyes. "Okay. Where is it then?"

"It's the program at Penn State's main campus. They're going to cover my tuition."

"Wow, it sounds great. I'm all for it. But State College? That's two hours away, three if the weather's bad, and up north, it usually is."

As she listened, her face began to redden.

"How many days a week? Two?"

Lisa pursed her lips. "At least three days, sometimes four."

Tony's jaw dropped. Was she crazy?

"Classes meet twice a week, but lab and clinical schedules vary. The curriculum is management heavy, so I'll be working with department supervisors and managers on different shifts."

This was worse than he'd imagined. "Why don't you wait?"

"Wait for what?" Her voice rose. "What's going to change?"

Tony had no answer. His gaze dropped to his coffee cup.

She thumped a fork against her plate. "Can you look at me, please?"

He did.

Lisa continued. "I've subordinated my needs for you again and again." She jabbed a finger at him. "Not this time." Her tone was sharp, her green eyes revealing a steely determination.

"But we're just getting settled."

"You call this settled? When have we *ever* been settled?" She inhaled and exhaled slowly. "Do you have any questions so far?" It came out as a dare.

Tony opened his mouth but paused, forcing his wild thoughts into focus. "Yes, I have two." He leveled his gaze. "First, what's going to happen with your job at the medical center? Second, you've mapped out the travel, but how will you handle such a long commute four days a week, especially in the winter?" Her plan was full of holes.

Lisa clasped her hands on the table. "To answer your first question, I've had preliminary discussions with the director of nursing at the medical center and she'll grant me a one-year sabbatical for graduate school education. In fact, she encourages it. I can return to my old job when I've completed my degree."

"Fine," Tony said. "No problem there."

"As for the drive, it's about a hundred miles. Almost two hours if the weather is good. Commuting every day would be almost impossible, and it would be foolish to try."

Tony had been here before. A bomb was about to explode.

Lisa assumed the compassionate expression she used when explaining something difficult. "I'll have to stay in State College at least three nights a week. I hope that's all, but it might be more sometimes."

His jaw dropped. He couldn't believe what he was hearing.

"I know what you're thinking, but I'm sure I can find a girl to room with. It won't cost much."

"Cost? Who gives a shit about cost? You're going to stay in State College? Three or four nights a week? Why not five or six?" He pounded the table. Coffee flew from his mug. "Hell, why not seven?"

Lisa recoiled. Doubt crossed her face.

"Holy shit, Lisa! What the hell are you thinking?"

"I wanted to be completely honest with you."

"That's great! Lisa Moretti is honest."

She averted her eyes and dabbed at the spilled coffee with her napkin.

"So much for our marriage!" He waved his arms. "Nothing else, then?"

Lisa shook her head as tears spilled down her cheeks.

"Wonderful." He felt the walls closing in on him as he grabbed his coat and stormed out.

THIRTY-FOUR

Tuesday, January 10

Ray Wheatley got right to it. "Listen, Barlow, I know you think three-to-eleven is easy time-and-a-half, but this is a good crew and we work our asses off. I don't want anyone screwing it up."

Frank smirked. Hardworking? A bunch of retirees-in-waiting was more like it.

"I took a look at those trucks you were supposed to detail the last time you were here. Did you do anything to them?"

Frank said nothing.

"I'd keep you off my shift if I could, but I can't."

Wheatley had that right.

"You're going back to the shed, and this time, I want to see results. Start with those two ops SUVs you blew off, and there's a black Ford Trailblazer up there now. Make sure they're spotlesss." Wheatley glared. "I'm gonna be checking on you, so don't go goofing off again."

"No prob, Ray." What an idiot Wheatley was.

"Yeah, yeah. This will be your last cushy assignment. After today, we'll be in full-blown snowstorm mode. It'll be elbows and assholes on afternoons. Think about that before you volunteer for overtime again."

"Uh-huh."

"And do it right this time or you're done working on this shift, union rules or not."

"Got it," Frank said. As if a supervisor could keep him from bidding on any OT shift he wanted. But by the time he'd trudged over to the heavy equipment garage and unzipped his coat, he figured he'd better make it look good.

Cleaning the windows, dashboards, and seats would give him the biggest bang for his buck, so with a bucket of soap and water, a bottle of Windex and some rags, Frank set to work. The Trailblazer was a mess. Papers, potato chip wrappers, coffee spilled all over the passenger seat, gum stuck to the carpet. A take-home toy for some office bigshot who didn't deserve it. How he hated the airport and everyone who worked here. After he got the SUV in shape, he checked the ops rigs; they weren't too bad. He cleaned the windows, wiped the dashboards, and scrubbed the seats.

He found a key to the outer perimeter fence—OPF-23—stuck between the seat and backrest of Ops-7. The morons who worked here couldn't be trusted to take care of shit. He tossed it on the garage floor.

Wheatley paid a visit at six, and he seemed surprised. He didn't compliment Frank, but he didn't give him any crap either. Frank asked for a shop vac to sweep out the interior floors. He got it a half hour later.

Frank poked around the garage for a while, had a bag of chips in the break room, and decided to tackle the big rigs. He wiped the cab and seats of the crash truck and swept out its compartments. Then he cleaned the windows and ran a rag around the cab of the blower. No sense doing much with the interior of the dump trucks; they were too far gone, and he didn't go near Yellow-224. The crushed can of Coke from his last OT shift was still on the floor. He figured no one had been here in at least a month.

Because Wheatley cut him a little slack, Frank scrubbed every rig down. By eight-thirty, he'd done enough to stay out of trouble, and he spent the next two hours draining his coffee thermos, listening to his music, and nodding off. Wheatley never returned. At ten-thirty, he had tossed his stuff into his gear bag and started for the door when a glint caught his eye. It was the key he'd found in the ops rig. He'd planned to turn it in, but now he had another thought. No one knew it was here, so why not just keep it? *Never know when a perimeter key might come in handy.* He stuck it in a pants pocket. The first honest-to-Christ firing offense in his decade-long stint at the airport.

THIRTY-FIVE

Friday, January 13

Allie woke to the strains of Beethoven's Fifth on her cell phone, the ring tone she used for Tony. "Huh?" She'd fallen asleep in front of the TV again. On the screen, Kelly Ripa was bantering with an impossibly attractive male actor. She shook the cobwebs away and snatched the cell from the coffee table. Why was he calling? They didn't have a run scheduled.

"Morning, friend. Hope I didn't wake you. I know you're on graveyard shift this week."

"Hey…Tony. No, I was just sipping coffee and watching the news."

"I wondered if you had some time to talk. I'm in a sort of bad place. There's a coffee shop off Airport Boulevard, and I could really use a good listener right about now."

"Sure." Then, without thinking, she added, "Why don't you come over here? I'll make us a pot of coffee and you can spill your guts."

"I'd hate to impose."

"No imposition. Just give me a half hour to freshen up."

"Great; see you soon."

Allie was still foggy from her nap, and a million thoughts ran through her mind. Had she just asked Tony over? Maybe the coffee shop was a better choice. No, it was okay. He just needed a friendly ear.

Allie met him at the door in bare feet, yoga pants, and a loose-fitting pullover. His appearance alarmed her. Stubble covered his face and his hair was a mass of disordered waves. And the smell. No shower for him this morning. Tony looked as if *he* was the one who'd been up all night. He wore a sullen expression.

"What's wrong?"

"Lisa left me."

"What?" Tony's words floored her. "What happened?"

"We had a big fight, and…" He shook his head slowly. "My world is turning to shit. I don't know what to do."

Allie hesitated. What should she say?

They stood there as her heart quickened and her heat rose. Heedless of the consequences, she placed her hands on his unshaven face and kissed him.

Tony backed away. A look of shock colored his features.

She froze; her mind reeled with the implications. *Oh God, what did I do?*

"Allie, I didn't intend to… I mean, this isn't what I wanted to…"

"I'm so sorry, Tony. I'm such an idiot. I wasn't thinking."

Tony wavered. "Um, I'd better go."

What had she done? "Wait. Don't leave." She held out her hands. "You wanted to talk. Come and sit."

"It's okay," he said. "We can catch up later."

Allie said nothing as he turned and walked out of her apartment. She dropped onto the sofa, pulled up her knees, and stared at the door. The guy needed a friend, not someone who'd make a play for him at the first opportunity. Once again, her impulsive nature had led her down the wrong path. And this time, the damage would not be easy to repair.

THIRTY-SIX

Thursday, January 19

Horns blared as field maintenance vehicles blocked the center and right lanes of the airport entrance drive while a street sweeper crawled along the berm, followed by two laborers in a pickup. Frank steered his dump truck behind the little convoy to protect it from the numbskulls speeding to the terminal.

Snarled traffic stretched twenty cars deep. More stupidity. The work should've been done overnight, but no, the suits wouldn't pay the overtime. So here they were at eight-thirty in the morning, smack in the middle of another airport snafu.

The sweeper stopped behind a pile of broken glass and pieces of a tailpipe while the laborers got out with brooms and shovels. Shinsky radioed Frank to place barricades across all three lanes. No way was that a driver's job, but he doubted the damn union would back him, and he didn't need any more trouble.

He grabbed the canvas bag on the passenger seat and climbed out of the cab. Shinsky held out a flag to stop the cars in the left lane. What a raw deal.

Frank pulled one of the foot-high traffic barriers from the bag and activated its flasher. He laid it along the berm, grabbed another from the bag, and moved toward the divider. More honking. He held up a flasher and waved it at the logjam. “Sucks to be you!”

“Open the road already,” an old guy in a red Honda Accord yelled. Frank scowled and continued to set the barriers.

Someone laid on a horn as Frank laid the last barrier.

He jerked upright. A little blonde in a Yukon glared at him.

“What the fuck, lady?”

She shot him the finger.

Frank’s heart pounded. He wanted to throw the barrier at her. Stupid soccer mom. The little bitch could barely see over the steering wheel.

“Barlow, what are you doing?” Frank turned. It was Shinsky. “Pick up those barricades and get back in your truck. We’re ready to move.”

“I just put the damn things down,” he said but scooped up the barriers and ambled toward his truck.

A shout from a guy in a black BMW. “Why the hell are you doing this now? I’ve got a plane to catch.”

“Take it easy, buddy. It won’t be long,” Frank said as he mounted the truck. Big shot.

“Could you move any slower, you lazy ass?”

Frank spun around. He balled his free hand into a fist and squeezed a flasher with the other. He pulled his shoulders back and strode toward the BMW. The guy raised the window.

“That won’t help you, asshole,” Frank shouted. “Who the fuck do you think you are?”

The driver shrank back. Frank heard the metallic click of the door locks.

“Answer me, you fuck.” He slapped the window with an open hand. “You think you’re something special ’cause you drive a fancy fucking car?”

The man grabbed his phone.

Frank lost awareness of what he was doing.

More horns honked. A bunch of people got out of their cars. Frank saw them, but his mind didn’t register the shitstorm he was getting himself into. He pounded a fist onto the roof of the BMW.

A man's shout: "Get away from that car." Another: "Leave him alone." Frank ignored them.

The BMW driver raised his hands as if to say *Sorry, pal.*

"Go fuck yourself," Frank shouted. He lifted the traffic barricade over his head and smashed it down, spidering the windshield and lighting the driver's face in amber strobes. Bystanders shouted that the police were on their way.

Frank cast an angry look at the crowd. People were pointing their phones at him. He dropped the barricade and bent toward the cringing driver. "Come out here, you little prick." Spit splattered against the windshield. "Come out here!"

Hands grabbed Frank's shoulders and yanked him back. Instinctively, he turned and thrust his arms out, sending the figure sprawling to the pavement. Frank moved in and kicked the guy in the ribs. He broke off. The man lay at his feet, moaning. Shinsky.

A shoulder barreled into Frank's gut, knocking him backward. His head slammed into something. The BMW? The scene went fuzzy as more hands grabbed him. Someone landed on top of him and pinned him to the ground. He flailed his arms; he had to get up. Then his senses returned and he let his body go limp. *What did I do?*

The aftermath wasn't pretty. Airport authority police arrived, cuffed Frank, and carted him off to their landside lockup as his coworkers watched. The cops fingerprinted him, took his belt and shoelaces, and put him in a holding cell.

Shoulders slumped, Frank sat on the bunk and stared at the stained concrete floor. The fight had gone out of him.

An hour later, two cops escorted him to a windowless room where Brian Murray sat on one side of a gray metal table. When he saw the director, the consequences of his actions became clear. Union member or not, he had put himself in the jackpot this time.

One of the officers, a tall, beefy Black guy, pulled out a chair and told Frank to sit. Both cops remained standing, flanking him.

"Well, Frank, it seems like you're famous," Murray said.

Frank dropped his eyes.

"Your little tantrum is all over social media. I'm sure it'll headline tonight's news and tomorrow's paper." He pounded the desk. "Look at me when I'm talking to you!"

Frank continued to stare at the table. Beads of sweat formed on his brow. His thoughts wandered.

The director calmed. "I received a call from the CEO. He wants you fired immediately. Joe Shinsky, *your boss*, is being examined at Med Express. It wouldn't surprise me if he pressed charges." Murray threw him a hateful look. "I hope he does."

Frank didn't care. He was screwed either way.

"I'm sure the guy in the BMW is going to sue the authority for your stupidity. Do you have anything to say for yourself?"

"That asshole was…forget it."

"All right. I won't waste any more time on you. I'll be spending the next week doing damage control. You've always been a troublemaker, but this?" Murray glared.

"Unfortunately, the union contract prevents me from firing you on the spot." The director stood. "Francis Barlow, you are suspended without pay as of this minute, pending further investigation and disciplinary action. The police will escort you to your car. Your personal gear will be collected and stored for the time being. You are not to set foot on airport property until further notice. Do you understand me?"

Frank nodded, and it was over. As the cops followed him away from his workplace of eleven years, he counted the cost of his actions.

THIRTY-SEVEN

Monday, January 23

The monthly ops supervisor meeting came off exactly as Allie had expected. Sitting between Clint Slagle and Ellis Kim, she tapped a foot rapidly as Sharon Lambert read from a set of prepared notes. God forbid she hold a dialogue, an actual exchange of ideas.

Sharon reviewed December's statistics in precise and mind-numbing detail. She began by recounting the number of escorts, inspections, and emergencies ops personnel had responded to. Next she listed bird strikes, animals found within the AOA, trespassers sighted within the outer perimeter fence, and Foreign Object Debris—or FOD—removed from the runways and taxiways. Sharon ended her tedious catalog of facts by relating the specifics of January's only runway incursion: a disoriented airport electrician who crossed the hold short line of eighteen-thirty-six at Sierra while on a taxiway center line inspection.

Allie was barely paying attention. She knew the stats. She'd compiled most of them. Besides, her thoughts were filled with Tony and what she'd done. Was she so desperate for companionship that she'd pursue a married man and violate the values she lived by? But she'd done exactly that, and the thought made her ashamed. What was she going to say to him? Would he even want to talk to her again?

Sharon disclosed the inside scoop, or so she said, on the latest senior management meeting. Several construction projects were still on hold because of budgetary concerns. A new airline announcement was imminent. The board of directors was pleased with the results of November's FAA inspection.

Blah, blah, blah. All fluff. What *wasn't* she telling them? How about the widespread rumors of cutbacks? Sharon didn't address that delicate topic and Allie knew better than to ask. Her boss wrapped up the meeting by going around the room for comments.

When it was her turn, Allie pulled out her notes. "I have a question and a suggestion."

The director looked up at her with unmistakable disdain.

"First, I'd like to ask if you've considered my request to initiate inspections of the inner and outer perimeter fence lines. As I explained in my proposal, we'd add an extra level of security while making us more familiar with the crash roads and the undeveloped acreage." She scanned her colleagues before continuing. Ellis was nodding. Clint, as usual, looked bored.

Sharon frowned. "Allie, you know we don't have the manpower or the time. We already conduct three daily runway and taxiway inspections. Our job is on the *airfield*, in the *movement* area. Not out in the woods."

"Sharon's right," Clint said. "We have too much on our plate already."

Allie shot him a look that would have made her mother proud.

"Let's move on," Sharon said. "What else do you have?"

Allie took a deep breath. Should she even bother? But the next item was important to her because it represented the hard work of a dedicated ops specialist. She pulled a plastic binder from her valise. "This is a proposal from Tyler Connolly."

"Go on," Sharon said, without a hint of enthusiasm.

"Tyler has a plan for us to conduct ride-along driver's training for field maintenance employees. Not for union-designated drivers like the heavy equipment operators. They're already pros. Tyler's proposal targets employees who are *technically* qualified to drive on the movement areas but rarely, if ever, do. The field maintenance contract requires *all* union employees to be badged with airfield driving privileges, but Tyler discovered only about a third of them are on the field regularly. Some have never driven at all."

Sharon's frown returned.

"We all know workers with seniority do most of the driving," Allie said. "And we also know those guys won't let the younger employees into the club. This is a chance to give them some actual experience."

"Wait a minute," Sharon said as she held up her hand. "We are the operations department, not the training department. This is not for us to mandate or conduct."

Undeterred, Allie continued. "Tyler believes, and I agree, that if we worked with the newer guys, we could really enhance airfield safety at night or in bad weather."

"The training staff has the responsibility to make sure they do," Sharon said.

"They do the bare minimum, a PowerPoint presentation and a multiple-choice test before they're sent to us for a half-hour ride-along."

"That's correct," Sharon said. "As required by the FAA."

Allie shook her head vehemently. "We do what's *required*, but it's totally inadequate. The rides are always scheduled for daylight hours, and if the weather is bad, the training department cancels it. What if a maintenance supervisor sends those people out in the dark? What if it's snowing and they can't see the airfield markings or edge lighting?"

The director took another deep breath but remained indifferent.

Allie's pulse quickened. Sharon was infuriating. The airport was a complex system of interrelated parts, fraught with potential hazards where even one mistake could result in disaster. "What happens when the senior drivers call off? The work can't stop, so someone else gets pushed into driving and is expected to know what they're doing, but they wouldn't have a clue.

"Training like that leads to accidents." Allie's voice rose with her passion. She checked herself. She knew better, knew she had to keep her cool. "It's not technically our responsibility, but it's our duty. Our mission is to make sure everyone on the airfield performs their job safely."

The director's impassive gaze disappeared as she narrowed her eyes.

Allie plowed on. "What are we going to say when some inexperienced driver pulls onto an active runway and collides with a departing aircraft?"

Ellis Kim leaned forward. "I think we can all agree—"

"That this meeting is over," Sharon said. Anger tinged her voice.

No one moved or said a word. Allie shoved the binder into her bag, stood up, and walked out of the director's office. As she departed the ops floor, her mother's voice echoed through her mind. *You've done it now, Althea.*

Eschewing the elevator, Allie dashed down the stairs to the transit level. Her temples pounded and her jaw clenched as she weaved her way through a throng of noisy travelers, some heading to their gates to begin their journeys, others awaiting a monorail ride to the landside terminal for the trip home. Wheeled carry-on luggage intensified her headache as hundreds of bags clickety-clacked over the ceramic tile. Who designed a floor like this for an airport?

Allie stopped at a nondescript gray door at the edge of the bustle and swiped her ID into the card reader. An LED flashed orange. After checking behind her, she punched her PIN—19779—into the numeric pad. The light changed to steady green and the magnetic lock buzzed as it disengaged. Allie entered a stairwell and descended into the service tunnel—and solitude.

Twenty feet wide with a concrete floor, walls, and roof, the tunnel stretched a half mile under the north ramp, directly below the monorail tracks. Envisioned as a corridor for an automated baggage system that was never built, the passageway featured escape stairways every two hundred feet and fire protection equipment throughout. Powerful overhead fans kept the subterranean air recirculated and fresh, but calcified water stains on the walls and a lingering musty odor spoke to flaws in the original construction. Two electric carts, one used by authority police and the other by terminal maintenance, stood plugged in and idle at the landside end. The corridor was a convenient alternative for airport employees to use to move between the terminals without driving on the ramp or catching the monorail.

Until 9-11, authority employees, airline personnel, concessionaires, and anyone with a basic airport badge were permitted to traverse the tunnel. These days, it required a red badge, the second-highest level of security clearance, to enter, and traffic was sparse.

That was okay with Allie; she loved the serenity. It was her sanctuary, the perfect place to think or vent out loud. A walk through the tunnel was second only to a fast run for generating ideas. "The ones that get you in trouble," she said.

As usual, Allie was alone. Good. What she'd said to her boss was direct insubordination, but she doubted Sharon would take it any further. She'd look weak in front of the CEO. "I hate you, Sharon Lambert!" echoed through the underground passage. She gritted her teeth and shot the bird at the cobwebs.

Allie quickened her pace and inhaled deeply. The soft whir of the overhead fans soothed her and forced air washed over her. Her tense facial muscles relaxed and clear thinking returned.

She exited the tunnel and headed upstairs, smiling as she climbed.

* * *

Tony had time to kill, so he strode through the concourses, burning off nervous energy. He shouldn't have had so much coffee, but he needed the caffeine to fight the crushing fatigue he felt from not sleeping.

So much had happened in the ten days since he'd seen or talked to Allie, and in that time, his initial anger over her kiss had evolved into guilt. It was true that she'd flirted with him, but hadn't he done the same in return? Had he sent the wrong message, and had she acted on those signals? He couldn't deny his attraction to her, but he was married and wanted to stay that way, even though that scenario seemed less probable every day.

After his fourth loop of the A and B wings, he perused the new paperbacks at Hudson Booksellers, bought a copy of the *Philadelphia Inquirer*, and took a break in the vacant boarding area of Gate A-14. Unable to concentrate, he was back on his feet in five minutes. He took in his surroundings to clear his head.

Travelers filled both wings. Bright-eyed children scampered along as their harried parents tried to corral them. Businesspeople talked on their phones and gestured into the air as they weaved their way through the crowd. Airport carts beeped in monotonous rhythm as their drivers ferried the less mobile to and from their gates. Glossy posters of happy families on the beach advertised exotic warm-weather destinations. McDonalds and Starbucks were packed, as was the newly renovated Landing Zone Restaurant, but empty retail storefronts spoke to the lingering effects of the pandemic. Carry-on luggage trailed behind almost everyone he saw. Did anyone check their bags anymore?

Tony zeroed in on faces to gauge expressions. Everyone seemed oblivious. It reminded him of the psych experiment where students watched a video of basketball players while a man in a gorilla suit walked through their midst. No one noticed the gorilla until the professor pointed it out. The same held true at an airport. Except for an elderly couple who asked directions to their gate, no one gave a second glance to the uniformed firefighter with his badge and dark blue uniform.

Through it all came a constant barrage of announcements from the PA system.

"Unattended bags will be removed from the terminal."

"This is the final boarding call for United flight 358, departing for Phoenix from Gate B-20."

"Reynolds International Airport is a smoke-free facility. Smoking is prohibited in any part of the terminal or concessions."

"Please report suspicious activity to the police by pressing zero on the nearest blue courtesy phone."

He laughed. Good luck with that one.

The announcements merged into the marvelous, controlled chaos of a modern airport. Somehow, it all worked.

Tony spotted her as he neared the Airside Center Plex. Allie waved and hurried to him.

"You made it," she said.

"Didn't think I'd show, huh?"

"Who knows? Maybe you were saving the life of some nubile young flight attendant—or falling off a ladder."

"Ha-ha. I've got twenty minutes until I meet Jason. He's grabbing a burger at McDonald's and probably ogling every woman under fifty."

"Some things never change." She shook her head. "Have you made our reservations?"

"Yes, I have, madam. Table for two at Einstein's."

"Well, then," Allie said as she bowed and swept her arm forward. "Lead on."

Six of the eight tables were open, and they selected a back corner spot. A large coffee and a blueberry scone for Allie, and a half-caf and whole wheat bagel with garlic spread for Tony.

"Ooh, your breath is gonna stink," she said.

"What do you care?" Tony cocked his head and raised an eyebrow. "Are you going to kiss me again?" He regretted the statement as soon as the words left his lips.

She frowned and a long silence ensued. He wished he could read her thoughts.

When she spoke, her voice was soft. "How are you, Tony? I've been worried. I tried to get in touch but I didn't want to pester you."

"Sorry; I meant to call you back." In fact, he'd been desperate to get in touch but stopped himself each time he picked up the phone. "Lisa stayed with a friend—another nurse—for a couple of days after she left. When she got back, I slept in the spare bedroom." He sipped his coffee. "It's amazing, really, how two people can coexist in the same small space and manage to avoid each other completely."

Allie put down her coffee. "And then?"

"And then I tried talking with her, tried to apologize and smooth things over."

"Okay, that's good. How did she respond?"

“Not well. She said she needed space.” Tony’s words caught in his throat. “So I moved out.”

“Oh, Tony, I’m sorry.”

“I slept on Evan’s sofa for a couple of days. What a madhouse that place is with the kids running around. They’re calling me Uncle Tony, if you can believe that.”

“I can. You’re a great guy, but by the looks of those eyes, I doubt you’re getting any sleep.”

“Not much.” He didn’t mention that with each morning glimpse in the mirror, the eyes got redder and the circles grew darker. “Well, anyway, I checked around for some temporary quarters and found a place. A two-room flat on a month-to-month lease. Not great, but it’s temporary.” He raised a finger. “And it’s furnished.” With what, he didn’t say.

Allie shook her head slowly. “If what I did had anything to do with this…”

“It didn’t. Like I told you, she left first. It was coming for a long time.”

“Any chance you can work things out? Try counseling or something?”

“I’d like to think so, but I’m not sure. A year ago, maybe, but now...”

Allie looked into his eyes. “I’m here for you if you need me.”

“Thanks.” What did she mean by that? Was she happy about the breakup? No. Allie had acted impulsively, but he couldn’t believe she wished a divorce on him. And what did *he* want? After they parted, he pondered those questions for the rest of the day.

THIRTY-EIGHT

Thursday, January 26

"Mutual aid request, Hamilton Township." Tony looked up from his paperback as the Klaxon sounded. Probably another automatic alarm. It didn't matter. Anything to save him from his ruminations.

"Airport fire from dispatch... stand by."

That was odd. He set the book on the table and checked his watch: 3:12.

"Airport fire. Hamilton Township reports a working residential structure fire at 1619 Castle Ridge Road. Repeat, working structure fire at 1619 Castle Ridge Road, Hamilton Township."

Structure fire? Tony sprang to his feet. Adrenaline surged as he raced to the truck bay.

Captain Schrum came over the intercom. "Rescue-15 and 16 to respond."

Anticipation mixed with trepidation replaced melancholy. A house fire? He thought through the possibilities as he donned his gear and climbed into Rescue-15's enclosed cab. Lieutenant Wozniak got into the officer's seat in front of him. Jason Krigger took the seat behind the driver, Rosie Ramsey.

"Airport fire. Rescue-15 and 16 responding to 1619 Castle Ridge

Road. Give us Gate-140. Have any Hamilton Township units responded?"

"15, Hamilton Chief-250 just reported in service to the scene, but no apparatus yet."

"15 copies. Switching frequency to County Emergency-One. Our call signs are now Engine-815 and Truck-816." The alternate designations conformed with the countywide nomenclature for station and apparatus numbering.

The LT turned to Tony and Jason. "Castle Ridge is less than a mile away. We'll be first on scene." He scanned the crew. "You guys ready?"

"I'm good," Jason answered.

"Good, LT," Tony said.

Wozniak nodded. "Okay. Don't forget to tag in at the command post," he said and turned his attention to the GPS display on the cab-mounted laptop.

15's siren wailed as Rosie turned left onto Airport Boulevard. Wozniak stomped on the air horn to clear traffic as the pumper gained speed. The sounds jolted Tony: audible warning signals were rarely used on the airport's roadways and, unlike the movie depictions, never on taxiways or runways.

In the number two riding position, Tony's assignments were hydrant hookup and backup on the attack line.

"It's gonna be you and me, and it's real this time," Jason said.

"I know. I'm ready."

"Okay, then," Jason said as he reached over for a fist bump.

Tony checked his gear: bunker coat zipped, BA shoulder and waist straps tight, helmet strap cinched, gloves and Nomex hood ready. But *was* he ready?

Frame houses were nothing like the airport's steel-and-concrete occupancies. The academy had acquainted him with basic structural firefighting theory, and the recruit class had spent a weekend in Lewistown, battling fires in the PA State Fire Academy's burn buildings. But wood pallets and straw had fueled those blazes, with elaborate safety measures in place and a team of instructors ready to intercede in any evolution they deemed unsafe. Could he work without a net?

The LT consulted 15's laptop. "Looks like the plug is on the right side of the road, a few hundred feet before the residence."

The radio frequency crackled as local fire department officers—chiefs, captains, and lieutenants—called in, overlapping each other's transmissions.

"Let's hope this ain't a big clusterfuck," Jason said.

"County, this is Chief-250," an unfamiliar voice reported. "I'm on the scene. We have a working fire in a two-and-a-half-story Victorian-style frame structure. Flames are showing from Division-2 on sides A and B. Neighbors advised me the residents are on vacation and the house is unoccupied. I'll have Castle Ridge command."

A hodgepodge of homes lined the rural roadway: one-story brick ramblers intermixed with big old farmhouses. The fire was on Division-2—the second floor. Fires spread upward, so Tony reasoned the first floor would be clear.

"Castle Ridge command, Engine-815 and Truck-816 approaching the scene," Lieutenant Wozniak reported. "Requesting instructions." The LT's voice conveyed cool-headed self-control.

"Engine 815 from Castle Ridge command. You're the first pumper in. Take the hydrant. It's on the right, about three hundred feet from the structure. You can't miss it. Lay past the house. Make sure you leave enough space for your ladder truck." The chief's voice was a little high-pitched, but he gave explicit instructions. Another pro. Tony relaxed a bit. Calm, competent officers made all the difference.

"Truck-816, from command. Position your rig in front of the structure so your basket can reach the top floor and roof."

"Engine-815 copies," the LT radioed. "We're coming up on the hydrant now. The truck will position on Side-A and await instructions."

Tony spotted dark brown columns of smoke as Rosie brought the pumper to a halt. Although keyed up, he focused his thoughts. He had to be on his game today.

"Go, Moretti," the LT commanded. "Don't charge the line until command tells you he's ready. Got it?"

"Got it, LT."

Tony popped his seat belt, hit the ground, hustled to the back of the rig, and lifted the Storz coupling off its tailboard mount. He tugged the strap on the five-inch supply line and slid a hundred-foot section out of the hose bed. After edging the flat yellow line to the side of the road, he looped it around the hydrant, knelt on the back fold, and waved his arms over his head.

The LT waved back and the pumper rolled toward the house. Yellow hose bucked into the air and played out in a wide S-pattern as five-inch couplings clanged off the asphalt. Rosie was driving much faster than the prescribed ten miles per hour.

Tony took his foot off the line and pulled the hydrant wrench from the attached hookup bag. He spun the cap off the hydrant's steamer fitting and threaded the female coupling onto the steamer's male threads. Hookup complete, he affixed the wrench to the hydrant's top nut, keyed his lapel mic, and reported, "Command, hydrant ready."

Tony spotted flames through the trees as he awaited the signal. Once he checked the security of his turnout gear and breathing apparatus, he reached back, found the cylinder hand wheel, and opened it fully. The alarm whistle let out a chirp and the PASS alarm emitted its electronic warble. Even at three hundred feet, the smell of wood smoke filled his nostrils. God, what a big house.

The wait was interminable. His stomach roiled; his jaw clenched. Like a linebacker awaiting the play. *Come on, come on.*

"Engine-815 hydrant from command, charge the line."

Tony grasped the hydrant wrench and pulled; the valve resisted. He groaned, putting his weight into it until it came free. He spun the wrench clockwise, stopping at five turns to allow the line to fill gradually. Once the hose firmed up, he tromped on a section. Hard as a rock. He opened the hydrant fully. It was time to move.

Tony started out at a trot but slowed to a fast walk, Evan's voice in his head: *Don't run on the fireground; save your energy for the fight.* He huffed a little but it was no big deal.

At the pumper, Jason pulled the first seventy-five-foot stack of inch-and-three-quarter from the crosslay tray and loaded it onto his right shoulder. Tony handed his yellow accountability tag, made from heavy-duty plastic and engraved with his name, to Rosie and hefted the second segment of attack line. Smoke hung low in the cold, humid air. Tony drew it deep into his lungs involuntarily as his physical efforts increased.

Approaching sirens, diesel engines, shouted orders, and clanging metal tools assaulted his ears. *Shut it out. Focus on the job at hand.*

"Let's go on air," the LT said. "We'll enter through the front door."

The trio engaged their LDVs and started forward. Tony waited until Jason was five feet in front of him, and followed. Five-foot flakes of hose played off the nozzleman's shoulder while Tony clamped his own stack in place.

A loud crack came from above. Tony looked up to see smoke belch from an attic dormer. "Watch out," he shouted and ducked forward to cover Jason as shards of glass showered the attack team. Something impacted Tony's helmet; part of the window frame hit the ground.

"Come on," Wozniak said. "Let's get in there."

"All units from command. The fire has extended to the attic. Watch out for falling debris."

"A little late," Jason said. "Thanks for having my back, Moretti."

The crew crouch-walked the last twenty feet to the house. Tony dumped his hose load on the ground and spread it across the front porch steps.

Manny Santos and Nikki Leach joined the crew, carrying axes, Halligan tools, and box lights. Evan O'Brien came up behind them with a thermal imaging camera. Jason knelt beside the front door; Tony moved in behind him. Opposite them, the truck crew bent low. Wozniak stood behind the attack crew and keyed his mic. "Engine-815, charge the attack line."

"Engine-815 received, charging now," Rosie replied. Tony glanced back and saw Rosie standing at the top-mounted pump panel, an ethereal figure silhouetted in flashing red lights and gray smoke.

Figures in unfamiliar gear scurried about the hazy scene; Hamilton Township's responders had arrived. Two firefighters deposited saws, pike poles, and ropes onto a tarp in the front yard. Another pair carried an extension ladder toward the house. At the same time, a distinct revving caught Tony's attention as the airport's aerial tower lifted from its bed, with Bruce Mihalik at the controls.

Once the hose firmed up, Jason discharged a test burst off the porch. Tony tightened his core muscles as he leaned in to support his nozzleman.

Tony forced himself to breathe slowly, keep calm, conserve air. *Inhale through your nose, exhale through your mouth*, he told himself.

"We're gonna hit the second-floor fire," the LT shouted over the din. "Truck crew, search the first floor and then follow us upstairs." He tried the knob. It turned but didn't open. "It's deadbolted," he said to Evan. "Open it up."

The truck crew got to their feet. Tony noticed dry rot at the bottom edge of the old, weathered door.

Evan inserted the adze end of his Halligan bar into a gap just above the deadbolt. Nikki struck the Halligan with the flat head of her axe, driving it farther into the jamb.

"Stay down," Evan said as he worked the bar. Wood groaned. He pulled, drove it deeper, and pulled again. A loud crack. Splinters flew as the door sprang open and smoke poured out, enveloping the airport firefighters in a dense gray-brown haze.

"We're in business," Wozniak shouted before radioing command. "Attack and search teams entering the structure with six firefighters."

"Command copies. We're going to vent the remaining windows on Side-A of Division-2 and we'll get a backup line in behind you as soon as we can."

Tony crouched behind Jason as they advanced ten feet into the front room. The LT's light barely penetrated the dense smoke. Something thumped against Tony's BA cylinder, knocking him sideways. "Sorry," Nikki said as she squeezed past with a water can.

Tony grew disoriented. He reached his left hand out to maintain contact with his partner's cylinder while he gripped the hoseline with his right. The environment was hot but tolerable. Not as steamy as the state fire academy burn building.

Muffled voices, scuttling feet, and the distant revving of fire apparatus were the only sounds.

"Evan, find the stairs," Wozniak said.

"Over here!" A weak glow cut through the smoke. Someone waving a LiteBox.

"Ten feet further and to your right, the stairs are here."

As Tony moved forward, the line jerked in his hand and yanked him to a halt. He pulled; it wouldn't budge. He lost contact with Jason.

"Line, Moretti," Jason called.

He turned, grabbed the hose with both hands, and heaved. It came loose. Hand over hand, he pulled, trying to give Jason enough to maneuver. He fell on his butt, dropped the line, and groped for it in the darkness. Scrambling to his knees, he swept his hands across the floor. It had to be close. His pulse quickened. He wasn't prepared for this otherworldly atmosphere.

"Moretti, over here."

Tony moved toward the voice. His foot bumped…the hose! He grabbed it, squeezed it tight under his armpit, and slithered forward. Back in the game. His breathing slowed.

The line angled upward in his hands and his knee contacted the bottom step. He rose to a crouch and climbed with his feet wide apart on the risers, as he'd been taught. His quad muscles screamed as he ascended. Then he felt it. Through his Nomex hood, along the edges of the facepiece. Hotter with every step.

"Stop there," the LT said. "I'm on the landing. Stay low."

Tony dropped his face to the stairs, making his profile as small as possible, using his helmet to ward off the heat. Like a turtle in its shell.

His earlobes burned. Was his hood still in place? Heat penetrated his gloves and his fingers began to sweat. All he could do was stay low.

"Command from interior attack. We've reached Division-2." Tony focused on Wozniak's transmission. "Conditions up here are bad. We need ventilation."

"Interior attack from command. We're venting now."

"About fucking time," Jason said in a voice thick with pain.

It's not just me. We're all cooking. And the LT's getting the worst of it.

The faint sounds of shattering glass, followed by a whoosh of cool air as the searing heat abated.

"Interior attack from command. All windows on the A and B sides of Division-2 are vented. The fire is concentrated on Side-B. Multiple rooms. We're going to hit the fire on Division-3 with your aerial. Just enough to darken it down."

"Interior attack copies. We're moving to the fire rooms."

"Command copies. Be advised, we've got a second attack line entering now. They'll meet you on Division-2."

Smoke continued to lift from the stairway and the temperature dropped to a tolerable level as the ventilation took effect. Tony lifted his head. His fingers burned from the heat trapped in his gloves.

Evan's voice came across the radio. "Command from search team. Division-1 is clear. We're moving to Division-2."

"Okay, boys. It's up to us," Wozniak said and disappeared around the corner. The hose team moved off the stairs and followed. Right behind them, the truck crew helped by dragging hose as they climbed.

"Hey, LT," Evan shouted. "We'll search everything behind the fire."

Wozniak acknowledged and led the attack team down the hallway. Thick smoke issued from a room on the left, sinking low to the floor as they approached.

Fifteen feet from the end of the hallway, flames erupted above them and raced across the ceiling.

"Rollover!" Wozniak pointed to the ceiling. "Hit it before the whole floor flashes over."

The hoseline jumped in Tony's hand as Jason opened the nozzle. He swept the line across the ceiling. The flames ebbed. The team advanced.

Pain flared in Tony's ears as he neared the fire rooms. He didn't think he could take much more, but he struggled forward with the line.

Wozniak stopped one foot from the involved room, where flames licked the top of the open doorway and began rolling over their heads again. The door of the room on the right was shut, but smoke issued from beneath it.

All three firefighters dropped to their knees. Jason spun the bumper counterclockwise and opened up with a forty-five-degree fog pattern. Thousands of droplets converted to steam and enveloped the crew; heat shot through Tony's ears. Water rolled off his helmet, but it didn't help. He suppressed a scream.

The line jumped as Jason slammed the bale shut. "Ventilated, my ass!" he said as he backed himself and Tony into the hallway. "They missed this fuckin' room. It's sealed up tight."

"Hit it from here," the LT ordered.

"Your turn," Jason said as he shoved the nozzle at Tony. "I'm too damn hot."

Tony took it and Wozniak knelt behind him. "Direct attack."

Tony set the nozzle to straight stream and hit the fire, this time using a Z attack pattern. He swung the nozzle left to right across the upper wall, brought it down diagonally, and swept right, just above the baseboard. He repeated the maneuver twice and was going for a third when the LT put a hand on the nozzle. "That's it." Tony shut the bale. The flames were out, but hot, wet smoke continued to assault the attack team.

"Need some ventilation, LT?" It was Evan. "Nikki, give us a primary search. Manny and I will vent those windows."

The truck crew slid into the room and went to work. The attack team followed. In seconds, glass began breaking.

"We're clear of the windows," Evan shouted.

"Primary search compete," Nikki called.

With the truck crew out of the way, Tony took aim at the window with a narrow cone that covered two-thirds of the frame and drew the cloud of smoke and steam outside. The room cleared in fifteen seconds.

The LT keyed his mic. "Division-2 needs mechanical ventilation. Repeat, we need vent fans now."

"Command copies. We're firing up a PPV on the front porch."

Cool, cleansing air washed over the team as positive pressure ventilation took effect. *Thank God for that,* Tony thought.

Wozniak scanned the room. "Command from attack, the fire in the bedroom at the A-B corner is out. PPV is working. We're moving to Side-B."

"Manny and I will check the attic," Evan said. "Nikki will stay with you guys." He nudged Tony. "How'd you do, rookie?"

"Pretty good, I guess."

"I knew you would. Stay safe." He clapped Tony's shoulder and disappeared.

"All right," the LT said. "Across the hall. Let's move."

"Interior attack from command, the backup team is coming up the steps. They'll take over for you on Side-A."

Wozniak didn't acknowledge. "That's our job. Let's finish it." He moved across the hallway with Tony and Jason in tow. Smoke puffed from under the closed door, but visibility in the hallway was good thanks to the positive pressure blower.

Jason fell back as his low-air alarm began to sound. Nikki took backup.

"Interior attack from command. Did you copy my last?"

"Command, we're hitting the second bedroom now," Wozniak replied. "The truck crew is heading to the attic. Send the backup hose team to them."

The lieutenant had just overridden the IC. He had balls.

"Stay low," Wozniak said.

Tony grabbed the bumper with one hand and the bale with the other. In a vented room, a direct attack using a straight stream worked best. Every muscle tensed as Wozniak pushed the door open with his A-tool.

Flames darted inches from Tony's facepiece. He flinched, rocked back on his heels, and felt a hand grip his shoulder. "Easy, big boy," Nikki said.

He steadied and opened the nozzle. Smoke poured from the room; the hallway went black.

"What the fuck happened to the PPV?" Nikki asked.

"Come on," Tony said as he entered the room on his knees. His hurting ears throbbed as he repeated the Z attack: straight stream across the edge of the ceiling, diagonally down, and back across the lower wall. The fire continued to burn; the room was now fully involved. He tried again. No better. His heads-up display flashed yellow and his low-air alarm issued a double chirp: 2,500 psi remaining.

If he didn't change tactics, they were all screwed. He swapped straight stream for a tight fog pattern, pushed the hose out in front of him, and rotated the nozzle in an exaggerated oval pattern. Once, twice, again. Biceps and triceps strained as he whirled the stiff line around the room.

"It's working," Nikki said. "Keep it up!"

The flames died, but the temperature rose once more. Tony pulled the nozzle close to his chest, narrowed the water spread, and directed it at the window. The stream carried the heat and smoke outside.

Once the room cleared, Tony pushed the bale to its halfway position and hit spot fires on the bedclothes, nightstand, and dresser. The job was done and cool air blew into the room.

"Looks like our PPV is back in action," the LT said over the whistles and warbles. "We can go off air." He scanned the room and keyed his mic. "Command from attack. All fires on Division-2 have been extinguished."

"Command copies. Division-2 fires extinguished. Well done. Relief is on its way."

Tony removed his facepiece, closed the cylinder, and hit the bypass to purge any remaining air. The scene went quiet as his partners did the same.

He was astounded by the devastation to the room and its contents, which reeked of the overpowering stench of burnt wood mixed with the acrid odor of melted plastic. The walls were scorched from floor to ceiling. Steam issued from the mattress, and remnants of the bedclothes lay blackened and shriveled. The bedside lamp lay in pieces on the floor. Curtains hung in darkened shards that flapped in the artificial breeze. A mirror on the smoldering dresser reflected the ruin through a crazed pattern of cracked glass. Four stumpy legs were all that remained of a corner table. A ceiling fan dangled precariously from its wiring, blades spinning from the forced airflow. And—good God—the flames had burned through to the attic and daylight was visible through the roof.

"It's worse than I thought," the LT said. "This room must be the origin of the fire. It spread out and up from here."

The team backed into the hallway, where they were met by three firefighters in black turnout gear and yellow helmets. Their relief from Hamilton Township.

"It's not safe in there," Wozniak told their officer. "Let's move back to the landing."

Tony's knees cracked as he stood fully upright for the first time since entering the house. His left hip ached and he had a cramp in his calf muscle. His ears hurt. Were they burned? If so, how bad? He pushed the thought away. The important thing was that he wasn't winded. Three months ago, they'd have *carried* him out of this house.

Once the crews reached the stairs, the LT radioed his report. "Command from interior attack. We have serious structural damage to Division-2. The Side A-B corner has large holes in the ceiling and is open to the attic. The roof assembly might be compromised." He paused and added, "I recommend you get everyone out of the attic."

"Command copies. Division-3 from command. Status report."

"Command from attic. We copied that transmission. The hose team extinguished all but a couple of spot fires and it's clear up here. We're at the A-B corner now, and we have significant charring to the joists and rafters and structural burn-through in the roof. We're backing out."

A thunderclap. Tony stuck a hand to the wall as the house shuddered. One of the Hamilton firefighters lost his balance, his partner tried to grab him, and both went down. Jason lost his balance and his BA cylinder slammed into Tony. Nikki grabbed the LT as he was about to tumble down the steps.

Three loud beeps came across the radio. "Emergency traffic, emergency traffic. This is command. All firefighters evacuate the structure immediately." The IC continued, extreme urgency in his voice. “We’ve had a partial collapse of the roof at the A-B corner. Everyone get out now!”

An air horn sounded in repeated two-second blasts. Other rigs picked up the evacuation signal with long blasts of their own.

“Move!” Wozniak called as he drove the Hamilton crew down the steps.

The three airport firefighters remained. “What about the guys in the attic?” Jason asked as PASS devices sounded from above.

Tony’s stomach dropped. Evan!

THIRTY-NINE

Thursday, January 26

Tony grabbed the LT's arm. "We can't leave them."

"We're not," Wozniak replied. "I'm heading to the attic, but the rest of you are getting out of this house."

"No way," Nikki said.

"We're going with you," Jason added.

"Interior crews from command. Report PAR."

"Interior attack on Division-2. PAR of four, with one firefighter from the search team," Wozniak radioed.

"Backup attack team. We're out of the house. PAR of three."

Nothing from the attic teams, but multiple PASS alarms continued to emit signals of firefighters in distress.

"On me," the LT said as the radio came to life.

"Mayday, mayday. This is Captain-216 with the Division-3 attack team. We've got PAR, but there are two airport firefighters down in the attic. Repeat, firefighters down. We need RIT up here!" Alarming PASS devices filled the radio waves.

"Command copies. Firefighters down. Sending RIT to you now."

Tony didn't think; he darted for the attic. Wozniak called to him but he ignored the command. Operating on pure adrenaline, he straddled the hoseline and ran up the stairs. Sunlight blinded him as he emerged into an attic bathed in daylight. He raised a hand to shield his eyes while he looked toward the A-B corner. A major portion of the roof was gone. Rafters and a big piece of the ridge board lay in a pancaked heap, surrounded by hundreds of scattered shingles.

Two black-helmeted firefighters were dragging someone clad in airport fire gear out of the collapse zone. Air gushed from the man's dislodged facepiece. It was Manny, and he was conscious.

"Where the hell is Evan?" Tony asked.

"He's…he's…under."

One of the rescuers looked up. "We saw it happen. A rafter glanced off this guy's helmet and knocked him out of the way." He shook his head. "Lucky." He pointed to a figure in a red helmet who knelt at the edge of the fallen roof. "That's our captain. He's got a bead on your other guy. He's pinned, but he's near the edge."

Tony darted forward. "Evan!" Nikki and Jason followed.

"Stop!" Wozniak commanded. "Drop your BAs and take care of Manny. I'll see what we've got."

Jason shut Manny's air cylinder and eased him out of his shoulder straps. Nikki removed the helmet and the dislodged facepiece and conducted a quick primary survey. Blood oozed from the injured firefighter's right cheek.

Manny pushed himself to a sitting position. "I'm okay. We gotta get Evan out of…" His eyes rolled back in their sockets.

Nikki caught him as he fell. "He's dazed," she said as she eased him to the floor. "He might have a concussion and other injuries, maybe internal. We better wait for the medics."

Tony shed his BA and moved furtively to the edge of the destruction, where the LT and the red-helmeted officer shined their lights into the fallen roof structure. Tony knelt beside them. Evan's PASS was muffled but close by.

"You're Matt from Allegiant Hook and Ladder, aren't you?" Wozniak asked.

"Yeah, I thought it was you, Phil." The man glanced at Tony, then back to the LT. CAPTAIN was emblazoned on his helmet shield and ELLIOT was lettered across the brim. "Glad it's you up here. We'll get him out." He pointed his light. "That's his arm, under those two-by-fours."

Tony spotted the sleeve of a turnout coat as light hit the reflective band around the wrist. "Can you turn your lights off for a minute?"

When they did, flashing red strobes from Evan's backplate—a secondary PASS indicator—became visible.

Adrenaline surged through Tony. "Oh, damn it to hell, we've got to help him!"

"Hang on, Tony," the LT said. "RIT has the tools. We'd only make it worse."

Tony's stomach clenched. Evan's arm lay there, unmoving. "We'll get you, buddy."

Behind them came the trudging boots and clanging tools of the rapid intervention team. A lieutenant in red turnout gear Tony didn't recognize joined the trio at the collapse site.

"Arnie Waldron, RIT commander. What's the situation?"

"We were operating up here with the truck crew," Elliot said. Pointing toward the gaps in the roof, he continued, "That entire section came down, starting with the rafters on Side-A. We got one of the airport guys out, but the other is under the edge of the collapse." He shined his light at the debris. "You can see his arm and the flashes from his PASS."

"Is he moving? Communicating with you?"

"No, nothing," the LT said.

"Look!" Tony pointed and got to his feet. "He moved! I saw his fingers move."

The hand stopped moving.

"Come on, Evan!" Tony said. "Show us you can hear us. Move your hand again."

As the team looked on, Evan moved his fingers, then his hand.

"He's moving!" Tony said. "We're coming! We'll get you out." Tears came to his eyes. Evan was alive.

"How sturdy is the floor?" Waldron asked.

"This floor is solid up to the collapse point," Elliot said. "But there's a lot of burn-through in the corner."

"That's right," Wozniak added. "We were in the bedroom below. We saw big holes in the ceiling."

Waldron scanned the scene, then got on the radio. "We need the portable hydraulic spreader and four shoring jacks in the attic, pronto."

"I'd like to brace that floor from below, but we don't have the time." The RIT commander nodded to Wozniak. "We don't know how long that floor will hold, and by the looks of that ridge board, the rest of the roof could collapse any minute."

"Agreed," the LT said. "We need to move fast."

"Okay, we'll use the spreaders to lift the rafters at the edge of the pile. Then we'll stabilize the assembly with the jacks and slide your guy out."

The officers withdrew to the stairs, but Tony remained where he was, keeping Wozniak's LiteBox trained on Evan while shouting encouragement over the relentless PASS alarm.

Three more RIT members arrived with the spreader and jacks. Two paramedics came up behind them with a backboard and medical kit.

Waldron returned to the edge and faced Tony. "We're shorthanded and we need some help."

"You've got it. The name's Moretti."

"Good deal, Moretti. I need you to operate the spreader while I keep watch on the pile and your friend. Can you handle that?"

"No problem."

"All right. Slide the blades under the rafter, but don't operate it until I give the command."

Tony lugged the spreaders to the center of the closest rafter, dropped to his belly, and slid the tips into a two-inch gap between the bottom two-by-four and the floorboards. Two RIT members, holding bright yellow shoring jacks, positioned themselves three feet on either side of him.

Tony could now see part of Evan's chest and lower torso. He wasn't moving. "Evan, can you hear me?" Nothing. Was he breathing? "We're almost there. Hang on."

"Start the lift," Waldron ordered.

Tony triggered the activation lever. Wood groaned as the blades spread out and the rafters moved upward. A loud crack. The floorboards shook.

“Stop,” Waldron said as he held up his hand and scanned the rafters.

Tony released the activation lever. He tuned out the PASS alarm and listened for more cracking. There was none.

“Resume the lift.”

Tony hit the lever again and the frame assembly continued upward. Six inches. A foot. It was working. Just a little more…

Another crack, this one louder than the first, followed by debris falling from the damaged roof assembly.

“Hold it there,” Waldron said. “We don’t dare go any higher. Set the jacks and snug them up.” He duck-walked to Tony. “I think we can reach under there and get him. What do you think?”

“Let’s try.”

Waldron nodded and motioned the paramedics over. Nikki, Jason, and the LT joined them. “We’re going to pull him out before the rest of this roof crushes him or the floor caves in.” The medics agreed.

“We’ll move him as a unit,” Wozniak said. “Jason, grab his legs. Nikki, take his hips and midsection. Tony, you’ve got his head and upper body.”

The trio flattened themselves and crawled forward. Tony stretched his arms under the jacked-up rafters and grasped Evan’s neck and shoulders. If the jacks failed, his arms would be crushed. He didn’t care.

“Here we go. On three,” the LT said. “One… two… three.” They slid Evan’s limp body toward them. “Easy, easy.”

“Wait,” Tony called. “His helmet is hung up.” He unclipped Evan’s chin strap and let the helmet fall away. “It’s free.”

The team resumed pulling. They almost had him.

“He’s out,” Wozniak announced.

Tony grabbed Evan’s chest gauge and deactivated the alarm.

The attic went quiet and the paramedics took over. “He’s breathing,” the lead medic said. “Let’s get him out of here.”

Tony wiped cold sweat from his brow and eyed his friend.

Blood oozed from Evan's nose and mouth. The medics rolled him onto his side, eased him onto the backboard, and pulled him to the stairs. Once they strapped him in, Tony lifted the bottom of the board while Jason gripped the top. Together they slid him down three flights to the porch, lifted him onto a gurney, and wheeled him to a waiting ambulance.

Tony visualized the worst possible outcome as Evan was whisked from the scene. He wasn't especially religious, but he said a silent prayer for the survival of his mentor, his friend.

FORTY

Thursday-Friday, January 26-27

Two hours after working the Hamilton Township fire, REY's firefighters returned to Station Bravo. Chief Archer authorized overtime replacements for those who'd worked the scene and released Lieutenant Wozniak and his seven firefighters from further duty.

Ignoring the LT's admonitions to get his possibly burned ears checked, and without bothering to shower, Tony changed into his civvies and tossed his filthy turnout clothes into the washer-extractor. Someone would hang it to dry later. The gear storage room stank of wood smoke and sweat. He paused in front of Evan's rack, empty except for an extra accountability tag and the Celtic talisman, which hung from a hook. Had he forgotten to wear it? Or had someone picked it up at the scene? Unable to think of anything but his injured friend, Tony jumped in the Cherokee and headed for Chambersburg Hospital. Once Tony hit the interstate, the speedometer never dipped below eighty.

The scene in the hospital's emergency department was chaotic, with Shannon and the two raven-haired children surrounded by family and friends in the crowded waiting area. Evan's parents had already made the trip from their home in Scranton, and Shannon's sister took charge of the frightened kids.

The department's informal communications network spread the word with remarkable speed. Chief Archer, his two deputies, and most of the off-duty officers and firefighters from all three platoons filled the hallways and spilled into the parking lot. Tony also noticed a smattering of responders from the region's EMS and fire service agencies.

He navigated the congestion in a daze, desperate for information. Details were sketchy, but Evan's condition was critical. He'd suffered a concussion, lacerations of the face and neck, and fractures of the clavicle, humerus, and several ribs. Doctors also suspected internal injuries. In and out of consciousness since arrival, he was now in surgery. Solemn faces and hushed tones attested to the touch-and-go nature of his condition.

Visitors came and went throughout the evening, but by midnight only Tony, a few firefighters, and Evan's immediate family remained. Heedless of his throbbing ears and Shannon's urging to get some rest, he refused to leave. Reeking of burnt wood despite his shower, he found a spot in the farthest corner of the waiting room and texted the news to Lisa, who drove to Chambersburg immediately after her three-to-eleven shift. When she saw his blistered ears, she grabbed an ER nurse, who treated him on the spot. None of it helped—not the burn cream and bandages or the ibuprofen—but Tony's only concerns were for Evan.

Lisa maintained vigil with Tony for two hours, and although the estranged couple didn't talk much, her presence comforted him. At two-thirty, the lead surgeon emerged and spoke with the family. Shannon, who'd held it together all night, burst into tears. Tony feared the worst.

Evan's father walked over. He must have read the despair on Tony's face. "He's alive."

Tony let out a breath. "Thank God."

"He's in bad shape, but there is some good news. Exploratory surgery revealed internal bleeding, but the medical team transfused him and sealed the leaking blood vessels. The doctors were worried about spinal cord damage, but they didn't find any signs of paralysis.

They took a CT scan, but it didn't show any evidence of brain swelling. I guess Evan's helmet absorbed the blow. Probably saved his life. A helicopter is going to fly him to the Hershey Medical Center."

Tony thanked Evan's father and returned to his chair, heartened but emotionally drained. Lisa convinced him it was time to leave. She invited him to spend the night in the guest bedroom, and he accepted without argument. He didn't want to be alone.

* * *

Tony hadn't been to the townhouse in two weeks; it felt odd but heartening to be back, especially after the sterility of his furnished rental. Lisa insisted he try to sleep, and the next thing he knew, sunlight was filtering through the curtains. After a moment of morning amnesia, he remembered. *Evan.* He snatched his cell from the nightstand: 9:42 a.m. He'd been asleep five hours. No messages. Thank God for that.

He dropped his head to the pillow and considered the roller-coaster ride that had led him to this moment. What had he done? Ruined his marriage? Failed to protect his friend? Screwed up his life? Had he taken Lisa down the rabbit hole with him? And his doubts about the job were back.

There was a knock at the door and then Lisa peeked in. "Good morning. I thought I heard you stirring. There's no mistaking that creaky old bed."

"Morning." He smiled, remembering the early days of their marriage. How they'd made love on this noisy secondhand bed. The corners of her mouth curled into that cute little smile that made her so irresistible, the one he had fallen for so long ago. Was she sharing the same memories?

"You look better. Any updates on Evan's condition?"

"No, nothing. That's good, isn't it?" He looked at her, hoping for confirmation.

"Well…" She hesitated. "It could be. It's probably too early to tell. But it's definitely not *bad* news."

He sat up. "I guess I'll take that, for now."

"I put a fresh towel and washcloth in the bathroom. Why don't you take a shower and change? You still have some clothes in your old dresser."

His *old* dresser. How quickly everything had changed. "Yeah, I think I do. This bed is going to stink like smoke for a long time. Sorry."

"It's not the bed I'm worried about." She gave him a stern look. "Now get yourself cleaned up. Coffee's on and I'm going to start breakfast."

"No, Leese…Lisa. You don't need to do that."

"When was the last time you ate?"

"I can grab a bite at the hospital."

"But you won't. You didn't last night, and today won't be any different. I know how you operate when you're worried."

"Okay, I'll obey." She knew him so well.

"Shower," she said, "and be careful of those ears."

Tony sat on the edge of the bed, considering. Then he went into their—her—bedroom, retrieved his clothes, and showered. Avoiding his face and ears, he adjusted the water until it almost scalded him. He wanted to scrub the stink away, force it from his pores. Erase all physical traces of the fire that had nearly killed Evan. But how could he purge it from his *mind*?

He emerged in a pair of faded jeans and one of his comfortable old Pitt sweatshirts. Bacon and eggs mingled with the aroma of coffee, as if things had never changed. But they had, of course, and the changes were big. Irreconcilable. Irreversible.

"Smells good," he said.

"So sit," she said as she examined his ears. "Ouch; those burns are going to hurt, and it'll be weeks until you're pretty again."

He smiled. "Thanks." He met her eyes. "I *needed* this."

They talked as they ate. About his job, about her job, about their situation. It was always easy to talk to her, yet it wasn't the same. Defense mechanisms were up as they tiptoed around sensitive issues.

"Where did we go wrong?" he asked. "It was more than my job situation, more than the fight about Penn State, wasn't it?"

She looked down at her plate, considered, and met his gaze. He saw sadness in those lovely eyes.

"The fights about my schooling, your job. They were manifestations of a dying relationship." She hesitated. "You know it as well as I do."

He nodded.

"When I agreed to the move, I had my doubts. I loved you and wanted you to succeed, to find what you never could back home. But as I told you, I made a pact with myself. If things didn't work out, it would be the end." Her breath caught. "The end for us."

Now it was his turn to avert his eyes. He felt his face flush as his shame emerged.

"I couldn't sacrifice for you anymore. I know that sounds cruel, but I had to start looking out for myself. God knows I tried. I just couldn't..."

"I'm such an ass," he said. "I had it all, and I threw it away." He stared at Lisa's hands. Her wedding ring was gone. Tony reached out and touched her cheek. "You did everything you could for me, a lot more than anyone else would have. It was me. It was always me. I took you away from everything. Your family, your friends, your career. You supported me through all my job changes, through all the battles I waged with myself. And still you followed me here. You gave up everything. And you never complained. You deserved much better from me, and I wasn't strong enough to come through for you."

She squeezed his hand. "You're not an ass. You're a good person, the best I've ever known." Her words conveyed compassion and love. "I didn't go into our relationship with my eyes closed. Even in college, I knew you were a complex, restless spirit. A man who might never find satisfaction. It was one of the things that fascinated me, drew me to you. I knew life with you would be a roller-coaster ride, but I was all in. I was excited about our future."

She'd never mentioned these things before; he hadn't known she had doubted him back then.

Lisa bit her lower lip. "As time passed, my needs changed. I wasn't a kid anymore, and I developed a need for stability. I longed for a firm base—a rock—so we could finally settle down, start a family. But we never got there. I knew we were growing apart. You did too. I think that's why we avoided talking about having children. The ride never ended. It was just too much."

"You put up with more than you should have, and I'll be forever grateful for that."

"I still love you, Tony. I always will. But it's not…" Tears came to her eyes.

"I know. It's not the same." At that moment, it hit him. This was the end; the story of Lisa and Tony was over. "I feel that too," he said. Tears filled the corners of his eyes. "Being here, now, with you. It feels like what we used to have, it's…"

"It's gone." Tears streamed down her face. "Everything that's happened since we moved? Just the final act of a long tragedy. So many setbacks, added up over so many years. We've changed, evolved."

Tony sat with Lisa a while longer as finality set in. The marriage was over, and the realization twisted him into knots. "I'd better go."

"Before you do, there's something I need to say. Something you need to hear."

He waited. Was she seeing someone? He couldn't bear that. Not today.

"Being a firefighter. It's right for you."

"Huh?"

"All those jobs you had. You didn't fail because you left them. You failed because you took them."

Where was she going with this?

"You weren't cut out for a career in business—the pursuit of money and status." She smiled. "You're a kind person. You get that from your mom. And a committed person, like your dad. I saw those qualities in you a long time ago. You need to *help* people. Make a *difference* in their lives. You couldn't do that as a marketing manager, or a sales rep, or anything else you tried. I wouldn't have agreed to move here unless I believed firefighting was the *right* fit for you."

Her words stunned him.

"Don't you see? This is what you were meant to do, what destiny intended for you." She took a quick look around and grabbed the pepper mill from the table. Holding it like a hammer, she said, "Do I have to knock some sense into that hard head?"

Tony furrowed his brow. It all sounded good, but…

"What happened to Evan is bad, and I know you're thinking about leaving the department because of it, but don't."

"It's more complicated than that, Leese. How can I go back to work after what's happened?"

Lisa sprang from her chair and shot him a death stare. "For God's sake, Tony Moretti. You've *finally* found what you've been searching for all your life, and you're too stubborn to admit it." She sat. "Sorry."

"Don't be. That feisty, opinionated side of you kept me out of a ton of trouble over the years." And it counteracted that stubbornness she spoke of.

Was she right about his career? He wasn't sure, but now he had something else to consider before he made any decisions about his future.

FORTY-ONE

Monday, February 6

Tony went about his life mechanically, with Evan's condition never far from his mind. When he visited the Hershey Medical Center eleven days after the fire, his friend's life was no longer in danger. Since he was still in the ICU, Evan's father provided the latest update. Doctors predicted a long recovery period as months of treatment and arduous physical therapy lay ahead. No one could predict if Evan would ever return to work.

Tony felt differently. He had little doubt about Evan's capacity to recover. Unable to speak to his friend, he lent encouragement to the family and even offered to babysit Teagan and Mason on his days off, a suggestion that drew a laugh and a hug from Shannon.

* * *

An hour after leaving the hospital, Tony was among the familiar surroundings of the Gettysburg battlefield. Dark gray clouds hung low over the horizon as he parked next to a row of cannons opposite the North Carolina Memorial. The early afternoon was dry, with temperatures in the low twenties.

With no one in sight, Tony slipped into wind pants, pulled a thermal hoodie over his bandaged ears, laced up his Nikes, and donned a pair of running gloves. An icy breeze chilled him as he completed a five-minute warm-up walk along Seminary Ridge. When he reached the Virginia Memorial, he broke into an easy trot.

The fire haunted him. He'd seen the holes in the bedroom ceiling. Could he have warned the attic crew of the danger?

He glanced left to peer at the bronze figures atop the Mississippi memorial and picked up speed as he passed the Alabama monument and neared Warfield Ridge, where a weathered stone tablet marked the Rebel right flank. South Confederate Avenue became Sykes Avenue; he'd reached the federal lines.

The skies darkened farther, but Tony didn't notice as he ran up the long slope to Big Round Top. He was in a zone. His physical conditioning had improved so much that his breathing remained easy as he hit the crest. Passing the hulking observation tower with its steel skeleton, he coasted down the reverse slope.

What would he do without Lisa's love and guidance? She was the one who could handle any situation. At least she would be fine; he was sure of that. And what of his emergent feelings for Allie? Was he going to rush into another relationship? Friends and family had frequently commented on how he and Lisa were so much alike, so perfectly paired. But Allie was so different. Would a relationship with her turn out well? And what did *she* want? Did she have any interest in taking things further? He'd set upon a new path in his personal life, and he didn't know where it would lead.

As he ascended the smaller but more consequential of the two hills —Little Round Top—his thoughts turned to his job situation. In the past, he'd been able to cut his losses and move on. But it was different this time. Under Evan's guidance, Tony had invested months of effort to become good at his job, yet skills development was only part of it. From an occupation he'd stumbled onto by chance, firefighting had morphed into a career from which he drew increasing satisfaction.

He passed the rocky slopes where Colonel Joshua Chamberlain and his 20th Maine Regiment made their valiant stand against determined Confederate assaults on July 2. During tourist season, cars and tour buses crammed the hillside, but today, a few shriveled brown leaves blowing across the road were the only obstacles in his path.

Tony was fast becoming a professional firefighter. Although he still had much to learn, he'd reached a point where confidence replaced uncertainty and initiative supplanted hesitance.

Yet his efforts were now fed by a more compelling need. Something deeper than the ability to throw a ladder, tie a knot, or handle a hose stream. More significant than being competent at running a gas-powered saw or manipulating a hydraulic rescue tool. More important than a proficiency at driving and operating the crash trucks and structural apparatus.

Tony reduced his gait as he bottomed out and turned left into the Devil's Den. He wound his way through the massive boulders where sharpshooters from both sides had plied their deadly trade as the ground changed hands again and again.

Tony sensed a growing affinity with his colleagues, and he finally understood what Chief Archer, Captain Schrum, Bruce Mihalik, and especially Evan had tried to tell him. Firefighting wasn't merely a job with coworkers. It was a vocation, a calling, with brothers and sisters. While he'd been skeptical of such feelings, he had to admit his new profession fulfilled him at a personal level unmatched by his previous occupations.

When he wasn't helping others, he was training to help them, or conducting inspections to prevent harm to them. He even enjoyed the simple act of giving people directions in the terminal. It was what his professors had called the *public service ethos*, a desire to be a positive contributor to society.

Climbing, he followed Sickles Avenue, named for the political general who had moved his corps forward without orders, precipitating vicious struggles in the Wheatfield and the Peach Orchard. Tony noted the haunting bronze monument to the Irish Brigade, with its Celtic cross and prone wolfhound. Its ranks had been filled with recent immigrants who knew little of the politics involved but mounted a furious defense of their new homeland. Did Evan know of this tribute to his heritage?

What had Tony learned in nine and a half months? Had he, as Lisa asserted, found a career that would satisfy him at last? He wasn't sure, but for the first time, he felt a sense of duty to something greater than himself or his immediate circle of friends and family. Not a calling, not for him anyway, but maybe, just maybe…salvation?

He crossed the Emmitsburg Road and jumped onto Trostle Lane, a trail marked by gravel, well-trodden grass, and horse droppings.

Quitting this job was certainly an option. His marriage was over, he had no financial obligations, and he had to account only to himself. But what would come next? Would he find the same satisfaction in some nondescript occupation where his primary contribution would be to the company's bottom line?

Fallen leaves crunched underfoot as he veered into a woodland known as Pitzer's Woods. He took no notice of the mud and manure as his contemplations crystalized.

Evan had shown him what it *really meant* to be a firefighter. Not by the training he provided, but in the zeal and dedication he displayed. Tony had been too focused on his deficient skills to recognize it. One must invest heart and soul, sacrifice oneself, if need be, as the troops who clashed on these fields did. Not a lesson to be taught, but an incipient fire in the belly that had to mushroom, or die out, on its own.

Emerging from the barren tree line, Tony stopped at the Virginia Memorial as flurries began to fall. Was snow predicted? He doffed his ski cap; the flakes felt good on his perspiring scalp. He checked his Fitbit: 7.6 miles in sixty-five minutes. The longest and fastest run of his life. His body and mind thrummed with anticipation and vigor.

He pumped his arms skyward. "Yes!"

Part IV

INTO THE CAULDRON

FORTY-TWO

Friday, February 10

Frank wormed his way from the FBO parking lot as knives stabbed his knees with every step. A wrecked body. That's what he got for all the years he put in. He slipped on an icy rock but managed to keep his feet as his heavy backpack propelled him the last ten feet down the hill. With a painful jolt, he hit bottom and crashed headlong into the inner perimeter fence.

He stuck his gloved hands through the mesh to steady himself and took stock. *Don't get reckless.* A broken leg now and he'd probably die here, not that anyone would give a shit. *Only a hundred yards; one football field. Get moving.*

His boots crunched through the crusty glaze as he traced the broken ground along the fence line, the route illuminated by the FBO's lights. Frank hadn't spotted any cameras. And he didn't think the cops patrolled this area. They'd stay in their cars in this weather.

It took ten hellish minutes to cover the distance. He pulled a palm-sized flashlight from his pocket and examined the door. Still ajar, just as he had left it a month before.

Frank unzipped his coat, pulled a six-inch pry bar from the inner pocket, and tried sliding it between the door and frame, but there was no gap. He tried again, pushing on the blunt end. Still no good. "Fuck!" He should have brought a heavier tool. Disgusted, he scraped away a patch of snow with his boots, dropped to his knees, and started chopping through the ice. There! The bar whacked off a fist-sized rock, and he dug it out.

Using the rock as a hammer, he pounded on the bar; it clanged against the metal frame and echoed into the night. So what? Who'd be around to hear it? Frank swung away until the tip lodged against the doorstop. He grabbed the bar with both hands and pushed. Rusty metal surfaces squealed as the door swung open. As before, no alarm sounded.

Frank took a step inside and peered into the big garage. Night-lights mounted along the walls cast a dim glow across the floor. Everything was quiet. If anyone was inside, they'd have heard the pounding and discovered him by now.

No time to waste. Good. The dump trucks hadn't moved. Not that they were going anywhere until some third-rate construction company bought them at the spring auction. He knew which rig he wanted. Yellow-206, the Mack he'd driven many times. Eleven years old, it was the newest of the lot and mounted good tires with deep treads.

Frank climbed into the cab, flipped the battery switch, and hit the ignition button. Diesel exhaust belched from the vertical stack. *Don't hurry, don't rev it. Let it reach its operating temperature.* He checked the gauge cluster: 40 psi oil pressure, air brakes at 120 psi, gas tank a smidge under half. Satisfied, he guided the truck between two long rows of heavy equipment, got out, and eyed the north ramp. All clear. He raised the overhead door, drove onto the ramp, and shut the door behind him. Okay so far.

He made a left and pulled up to Gate-120, a little-used exit from the maintenance area to the business park. Since he was inside the secure area, there was no card reader on his side of the gate, and there'd be no electronic record of who drove the truck through it. An LED flashed from red to green as he slowed to a stop, and an electronic eye activated the opening mechanism. The gate rolled aside. He pulled through and waited for it to close behind him. *Well, what do you know?* He'd beaten airport security again. Too bad Shinsky wasn't here to see it. *I'm a lot smarter than that prick gives me credit for.*

"Suckers," Frank yelled as he drove Yellow-206 past the FBO. A light was on in the office. Probably a janitor. Nothing to worry about. He exited the business park and headed toward the airport's southern border.

Turing off Airport Boulevard, he veered onto a gravel road a quarter mile south of Gate-390. Frank knew the layout of all the crash roads, and two years ago, he'd spent a week dumping gravel on this very one. Only a downed tree could have stopped him now, but aside from a few scattered limbs, the way was clear.

Frank halted the truck, grabbed his backpack, and got out. A standard heavy-duty airport authority padlock and a simple C-clamp secured the gate to the outer perimeter fence line. No fancy electronic keypads to worry about. A red sign with bold white letters warned:

AIR OPERATIONS AREA
KEEP OUT UNDER PENALTY OF LAW

"Watch me," he said.

Frank took off his gloves, pulled a can of Lock-Ease from his pack, and squirted the deicing liquid into the keyhole. Then he dug into his pockets for the outer perimeter key he'd found in the old ops pickup. Nothing. What the hell? He was sure he'd brought it. Then he remembered. He pulled out his wallet. It was there, folded in a ripped piece of newspaper.

Christ, it was cold, and the wind was picking up.

He dropped the key. Shit! Panic seized him as he whipped his light over the snowy rocks. There! Right next to his fucking boot. He snatched it and steadied himself. Better take it easy or he was gonna make stupid mistakes.

Frank eased the key into the cylinder and hesitated. If someone *had* changed the locks, he'd never be able to get past the hardened C-clamp. And his luck always sucked. But the long shackle sprang free. He let out a sigh, pocketed the key, and shoved the lock into his bag. He swung the clamp up and pulled. The gate creaked open.

After steering the truck through the fence line, he closed the gate, killed the headlights to let his eyes adjust to the darkness, and started forward at five miles an hour. The snow was heavier now, but he knew the road ran straight. *So close; don't get careless.*

A quarter mile farther, he spotted the familiar gully on his right and steered off the crash road. The ground was hard packed with slag; Frank had dumped most of it there himself during the reconstruction of the southern runway. He risked the headlights. Forty feet down, he nudged the truck behind an old dirt mound. Satisfied, he set the parking brake, switched off the engine, and trudged back to the crash road.

A stiff breeze rustled the few remaining leaves in the heavily wooded landscape. He pulled his ski cap down over his ears as the wind bit in. He scanned the terrain. The truck was invisible. What did they call it back in his army days? "Defilade," he announced to any critters in the area. He laughed. "Yep, that truck is in a complete defilade."

Frank figured he'd driven a half mile from Gate-390. In the twilight, he spotted the inner perimeter fence, three hundred yards up the slope, and the roar of an inbound aircraft confirmed his nearness to the runway. Things were going according to plan, but it was time to amscray.

By the time he emerged from the woods, the sky was black. His knees were about to give out and his hip screamed, but he kept walking. Another quarter mile through snowy brush before the little dive bar came into view. His breath came in gasps as he dashed across to the parking lot. It was gonna be a bitch getting back up that hill, but that was a problem for another day.

He downed a Miller Lite at the bar, opened his Uber app, and put in for a ride back to the business park. He was taking a chance by leaving a trail, like in the cop shows. But he figured the risk was small. When he got a text that the driver was close, he took a piss and headed outside.

The temperature was dropping fast; he felt it on his face and in his joints. Something big was brewing.

FORTY-THREE

Monday, February 13 - 9:30 a.m

"Man, it's really coming down," Robbie said as he entered the alarm room.

"Yeah, it's been snowing for an hour," Tony said.

Robbie edged next to him at the front window. "Those snowflakes are huge. I can barely see past the pad."

"Look; here they come," Tony said as a line of headlights and amber strobes emerged from the whiteout.

"That's awesome!"

Four yellow plow trucks, tailed by four brooms, advanced north on Bravo. Snow flew from the plow blades while a whirlwind rose from the brooms as the convoy passed. Ops-2 took up the rear. Tony's pulse quickened. Was that Allie?

"Cool. Those things are powerful," Robbie said as he watched the spectacle unfold on the taxiway. "They're really motoring."

Tony clapped his friend on the shoulder. "I wonder how they keep formation in that cloud of snow they're generating?"

"Lots of practice," Lieutenant Wozniak said as he stood in the doorway. "Looks like the forecast was spot-on for a change." The LT glanced out the window. "The weather service is predicting a major storm, a real nor'easter."

Tony was less impressed. “It doesn’t look so bad, LT. Where I’m from, this is a petty annoyance. You should see what comes down off Lake Erie. Don’t you think the maintenance crews can handle it?”

“Maybe.” Wozniak looked toward the sky. “The front office brags about how we’ve never closed for weather, but this stuff is usually spread out over the winter. We’ll see what happens when it comes down all at once.”

“Back when I was a kid, the blizzard of ’93 shut down most of the region,” Tony said. “It all came down in one day. And I was working downtown when Snowmageddon hit in 2010. It dumped on us for a week. That was the storm that paralyzed everything. But neither one closed the airport.”

“I hear you,” the LT said, “but we’ve never been staffed like Pittsburgh.” He studied the alarm room’s weather radar display. “Anyway, I’m going to announce that the airport is now in weather emergency mode. All scheduled inspections and training activities are canceled. Two guys are going home on their Kellys, so we’ll only have twelve overnight. No one leaves the station without orders. Also, make sure you monitor the ops and maintenance frequencies. Let me or the captain know if they give any status reports.”

“What do you think?” Robbie asked after the lieutenant left.

“Well, Robert, I think it’s going to get interesting.”

FORTY-FOUR

Monday, February 13 - 2:00 p.m

"Damn it!" Rocks dug into Frank's knees as he slipped on the slick gravel and hit the ground; the pain shot all the way to his hips. He got to his feet and continued his march up the hill. If he didn't hurry up, he'd never make it back to the stashed truck.

He cursed himself for underestimating the weather. Who knew it would be this bad already? He tightened the straps on his backpack, raised a hand to shield his face from the gusting snow, and resumed his slog up the snow-covered crash road.

Anger fueled Frank's march. Did that asshole Murray think he'd just go away? And what about Local 1733? What did they do to defend an eleven-year union brother? Not a damn thing. Hell, the business agent wouldn't meet with him, and Connor, that waste of a union steward, didn't even return his calls. Yeah, they all wanted him gone. Shinsky was probably doing cartwheels, counting the days till Frank Barlow got fired. Just wait; he'd show them all.

The ground leveled out as he neared the gully, and he covered the last quarter mile in ten minutes. He eased down the slope, grabbing branches from a line of scraggly trees to keep from falling. He paused halfway. Was he in the right place? The snow was like camouflage. Leaning into a tree to keep his balance, he scanned the area. There it was! A sense of victory as he sighted a sliver of windshield and yellow roof. Ready and waiting.

For the last couple of days, he had debated what to do with the stolen truck. He thought about leaving it in the gully so Shinsky and his buddies would scramble come auction time. But what would that accomplish? No, it had to be something big, a real stunner. When he heard a big snowstorm was on its way, everything clicked into place.

He climbed into the cab of the big dump truck, rotated the master battery switch, and hit the ignition button. Yellow-206 came to life. "Hah. Take that, Shinsky!" Settling in for a long afternoon, he poured a cup of joe from his thermos. The black brew felt good going down. As he waited for the heater to thaw his aching joints, a lyric came to mind. He dialed up his playlist to Thin Lizzy and smiled as they sang about trouble in town. Yep. Trouble at the *airport* tonight.

FORTY-FIVE

Monday, February 13 - 3:00 p.m

"Good afternoon and thank you all for coming," Alan Baxter, the air traffic manager, said. "I'm sure everyone has a full plate today, so we'll make this short. The latest forecast from the National Weather Service predicts ten to fifteen inches of snow by midnight. That's an unprecedented amount for this region, and the story is the same all up and down the Eastern Seaboard."

Allie scanned the officials who filled twenty of the twenty-five seats around the conference table, with their laptops, iPads, cell phones, and even a few old-fashioned notebooks arrayed in front of them. Ellen Ming and three controllers flanked Baxter at the head of the table. Deputy Fire Chief Martone, Captain Schrum, a police sergeant, and Alfred Stein, the director of terminal operations, sat on the right side of the room, with four airline station managers, a TSA supervisor, and two screeners on the left. Allie took a seat at the end of the table, beside the FBO manager and the owner of Mid-State Aviation Services. Behind Baxter, a large wall-mounted display traced the storm's predicted path.

"From *our* perspective," Baxter said, "this event doesn't pose much of a problem."

Brian Murray entered the room and pulled up a chair next to Allie. That was everyone—except for Sharon Lambert, of course.

"Major airlines have already canceled over a thousand originating and departing flights, and we expect that number to double within the next few hours, so it won't be a busy evening for us." The manager turned to the blue-shirted contingent on his right. "Or for our colleagues at the TSA."

"No, but it's going to be a shitstorm for the rest of us," Allie whispered to Murray.

Baxter continued. "That said, there are a couple of items everyone should be aware of. First, if history is a guide, we'll see at least a dozen diversions this evening. The storm is more severe along the coast, and several of those airports can be expected to close."

Allie sighed. Who said government-speak was dead?

"Second, the As-Dee is malfunctioning."

Oh Christ. Allie's hand shot up. "Is it completely out of service? Can it be repaired?"

Baxter furrowed his brow. "It's been going in and out, and unfortunately, the weather has made it impossible to service at present."

Concerned about this untimely development, Allie jotted a note to relay the info to all ops personnel.

"Without the As-Dee, our ground controllers will have to rely on visual scanning of vehicle and aircraft movement on the airfield. Normally, this wouldn't be an issue, since ground controllers prefer visual contact, but in this weather, visibility is going to be greatly reduced."

In fact, it would be nonexistent, Allie thought as her tapping foot thumped off the tile floor. The ground controllers would be running blind.

"Extreme caution will be necessary for anyone operating in the movement area, especially tonight. Does the airport authority have an update on the runway and taxiway situation?"

Brian Murray answered. "Our snow removal crews are doing okay so far. All runways and taxiways are operational. The ramp is also in pretty good shape. We pretreated the surfaces, so ice buildup shouldn't be a problem. But the snow is piling up fast. We've switched to twelve-hour shifts and called out all the part-time plow operators." He nodded at Allie. "But as you said, this is an unprecedented storm. If it gets much worse and we fall behind, we won't be able to keep all three runways open." He focused on Baxter. "The question is, which ones do you prefer?"

Allie smiled. Murray was slick. He didn't give Baxter a chance to protest. He characterized the impending closure as a certainty, switched the discussion to the selection of the runways, and left the decision to ATC.

Baxter eyed Ellen Ming, who huddled with her controllers and replied, "We can work with either of the east–west runways, but we'd like to maintain eighteen-thirty-six in case the wind pattern changes. Is that okay with you, Al?"

Baxter nodded.

"Very well," Murray said. "One east–west and the crosswind runway. We can do that."

Glancing at the white bands crossing the weather display, Allie wasn't so sure.

Fifteen minutes later, she entered a boisterous, jam-packed Airside Center Plex. Flights were already stacking up and lots of people were going to be stranded tonight.

She swiped her ID, punched her code into the security pad, and took the restricted elevator to the ops floor, where she looked down at the throng of bewildered travelers, some already camped out along the walls of vacant gates. Good business for the restaurants, but Alfred Stein and his terminal operations staff better get some of this mob shuttled to the area's hotels before the weather closed in. What a mess.

After a quick check-in at the office to make sure the staff understood their assignments, she grabbed ops specialist Trista Nicholson and the pair headed to the field.

FORTY-SIX

Monday, February 13 - 4:45 p.m

Tony looked up from his shoveling. Strobe lights announced another sweep of Bravo. He'd been outside for almost an hour, clearing the area in front of the garage doors that field maintenance couldn't reach with their plows. He didn't blame them for not getting out with shovels. How could they keep up with the rapidly falling snow?

With all nonessential activities canceled, it had been a mind-numbing day. After waking in the dayroom with a crick in his neck and his paperback on the floor, he had grabbed his coat and headed outside. Physical activity in a brisk wind—the perfect antidote for his lethargy.

He stuck the shovel into a snow mound, walked to the edge of the taxiway, removed his gloves, and pulled out his cell. Snow swirled in front of the lens while he shot a video of snow clearing in action. *This'll make for a cool Facebook post*, he thought. The gang back home would eat it up.

The conga line presented a much more impressive sight than what he'd witnessed during his morning alarm room shift. Plows and brooms were now joined by five snowblowers and two tankers. The plows threw the bulk of the snow off the taxiway while the snowblowers cleared what remained. Close behind, the brooms swept deep into the surface grooves, preparing the way for the tankers to spray their chemical deicing agent.

While the heavy machinery rolled south into a windswept white cloud, a yellow pickup with *Operations-2* marked in bold red letters pulled onto the fire department pad and stopped beside Tony. He couldn't make out the occupants until the driver lowered her window.

"Hi, Firefighter Moretti," Allie said. "Playing in the snow?" Trista Nicholson, riding shotgun, smiled and waved.

"Having a blast," Tony said. "Any break in sight?"

"Nope. Radar shows a solid wall of snow."

"Wow. Do you think the airport will stay open?"

"Six-right/twenty-four-left is closed already, but we're trying to keep six-left/twenty-four-right and eighteen-thirty-six open. It's a struggle."

"I'm sure," he said.

"We're heading out to inspect the runways and taxiways. We've got scheduled flights trying to get out of Dodge, and a bunch of East Coast diversions heading our way."

"Good luck. I wouldn't want to be out on the field today."

"Wait till it gets dark. Then the fun really begins."

Tony's head snapped toward the station as the high-low tones of the crash alarm blasted from roof-mounted speakers.

"This is the tower with an Alert-3." The ground controller's amplified voice pierced the howling wind.

"Later." Tony sprinted for the station as five bay doors rolled up in unison and the controller came back on the line.

"A Choice Jet E190 slid off runway eighteen-thirty-six on landing and is sitting at the intersection of runways eighteen-thirty-six and two-four-right."

Tony reached Rescue-12 amidst a scramble for the rigs. He donned his gear and was sliding his arms into his SCBA straps when Steve Brooks climbed into the driver's seat.

"This is the tower with additional information. The E190 has twenty-one souls on board and an unknown quantity of fuel. It spun partway around and is facing southeast, with its nose off the runway and half of its fuselage in the snow. The pilot reports the nose gear has collapsed. We see no signs of fire at this time."

Forty-five seconds later, five ARFF rigs were on the pad and the captain radioed the tower. "Reynolds ground, Rescue-10. Request Bravo, Sierra, and—"

The controller broke in. "Rescue-10, you're cleared to drive to runway eighteen-thirty-six. Use caution; there's a Southwest 737 on taxiway Sierra. He'll hold for you at Foxtrot."

"Rescue-10 copies. We're cleared to the Alert-3 aircraft. Have the tower supe join me on the fire frequency. I'll have ARFF command."

"Rescue-10, roger. The pilot confirms there is no fire and requests direct communications with you on the airport's discrete frequency, one-two-one decimal six."

"Rescue-10 copies. Switching to one-two-one point six."

The captain's RIV pulled onto Bravo, followed by three Striker-3000s and Rescue-14. Once on Sierra, all four rigs barreled into a squall, Rescue-12 in the rear.

Tony's pulse quickened. Freshly fallen snow was fast erasing the efforts of the crews. "How's the traction?"

"Not bad, but I'm not taking any chances. You know how top-heavy this truck is."

Tony thought the extra weight might actually improve traction but said nothing. 12 quickly fell behind the procession.

* * *

Allie radioed the operations center. "Ops-2 responding with the fire department to the Alert-3."

"Operations center copies." It was Ellis Kim, held over from the day shift because of the worsening weather. "Be advised: Tyler Connolly and Kenny Slater are with me up here and Sadie Green is in Ops-4 with the snow crews on the ramp."

"Ops center from 2. Redirect Ops-4 to cover my position on the field. I'll let you know if I need anyone else." As she wheeled onto Bravo behind the crash trucks, her vehicle spun out, tossing the occupants sideways. Allie's shoulder slammed into the window. She righted the pickup and glanced at Trista. "You okay?" The girl nodded, her eyes wide. "Hang on; this could get tricky."

Trista slunk down and grabbed the armrest with both hands.

* * *

"Airport dispatch from ARFF command. We're on the scene. The aircraft is nose-down in the snow. I'm contacting the pilot now."

"That's good," Steve said.

"Huh?"

"It's stuck. Nothing's on fire; no one is evacuating. There's no emergency." Steve pointed to the plane as he pulled to a stop behind Rescue-11. "They'll bring a bus out to get the passengers. We won't have to leave the cab."

Tony shook his head. What if someone was injured? What if passengers needed assistance to get off the plane? He wanted to get out of the damn truck and do something.

"Rescue-14 from command. Follow us onto eighteen-thirty-six. We'll take angled positions behind the aircraft. Rescue-13, stay on two-four-right and take the nose. 11 and 12, remain on Sierra."

"Even better," Steve said and reached out for a fist bump. "We'll stay nice and warm."

Tony ignored the gesture. Unbelievable. *Why did Steve take this job?*

Tony caught sight of yellow strobes in the side-view mirror. It had to be Allie.

Ops-6 pulled up on the passenger side and Allie lowered the window. Tony did the same. She cupped her hands to her mouth. "Anything from the flight crew yet?"

"No. The captain's on the discrete frequency now."

"Tower supe and airport dispatch from ARFF command. The pilot has shut down his engines and reports everyone is okay. He's requesting the portable air stairs and transportation for the passengers as soon as possible. It'll get cold in there fast. He also wants a tow for the plane. I'm returning Rescue-11 and 12 to Station Bravo."

Tony shot Allie a mock salute. She smiled and drove off. Steve did a U-turn and started for the station.

* * *

Allie parked beside Rescue-10 and climbed aboard with the captain, leaving Trista in the SUV. The two conferred with the pilots, who were sure they could evacuate the passengers through the L-1 door. Allie phoned Ellis Kim to send Connolly and Slater to the scene with the air stairs, and to expedite the buses. In the meantime, Schrum ordered the crew of Rescue-14 to ladder the aircraft and check on the passengers. The weather was getting worse and it would soon be dark.

"That gear is dug in deep," Schrum said. "There's no way that plane's getting towed out of here tonight."

"I agree. We're going to have to keep both runways closed, probably until tomorrow afternoon." She rejoined Trista in Ops-2 and reached for her mic.

"Operations Center from Ops-6," Allie radioed. "Tell Joe Shinsky to move the snow crews to six-right/twenty-four-left ASAP. We've got to get that runway open." She took a deep breath. "Until then, this airport is closed."

FORTY-SEVEN

Monday, February 13 - 6:30 p.m

Ozzy Osbourne's voice thrummed through Frank's ears. He wiggled his toes and flexed his fingers, but it was getting harder to keep the numbness away. The thermos was empty and three trips outside to piss had only made him colder. He shined the flashlight around the interior. Snow blacked out the windshield and ice crept across its edges. He flipped the battery switch and hit the starter button.

The diesel coughed and came to life. Less than an eighth of a tank remained. Why hadn't he stashed a couple jerry cans in the woods before he stole the damned thing? His only big-time screwup, and he was paying for it now. Never mind. It was too late to worry about it, and he'd be back home in a hot shower soon enough.

Since four o'clock, Frank had operated the engine in twenty-minute spurts to heat the cab and listen to the maintenance frequency. At five-thirty, he picked up a lot of excited chatter. Something big must've happened at the intersection of eighteen-thirty-six and two-four-right, but what? He figured it was a collision between a couple of plows or brooms. Probably caused by those idiot seasonal drivers. What did they expect? Served Murray right for pushing the crews too hard when they were spent.

Frank figured it was cleared by now, but when he removed his Air

Pods to take a listen, the crews were only working on six-right, two-four-left. Had they given up on the other runways? The accident must have been worse than he thought, or maybe the snow was too much for them.

Inside the icy cab, Frank hit on something. If the clowns could only keep one runway open, the impact of his scheme would be ten times bigger. Hah! The gods were on his side tonight.

But the situation might change any minute and he couldn't sit here all night. His fuel was almost gone and he was freezing his ass off. He cranked up the heat, chucked the AirPods into his pack, and watched the ice melt off the windshield. Once the cab warmed, he wiggled his toes, reached up to stretch his tight shoulder muscles, and got moving.

Frank backed Yellow-206 out of its hiding spot, shifted to low gear, and hit the gas. The tandem wheels spun before digging through the snow into the rough gravel surface. He eased off the pedal. He could drive anything, in any weather. Chancing the low beams, he crept out of the gully and onto the crash road.

White flakes reflected the headlights into his eyes. He switched to fog beams and shifted to drive. The radio crackled. The conga line was sweeping the southern runway. His goal was about three hundred yards ahead, but he couldn't see beyond the hood. No biggie. Frank knew this road well. Using the road's edge as a guide, he inched forward. Nice and slow; no fuckups now.

After an agonizing five minutes, the squall let up and the inner perimeter fence appeared. "Bingo!" The ten-foot barrier ran east–west along the sloping ground, safely below the crest of the hill. Frank wheeled to a halt in front of Gate-107, the last obstacle in his path.

He sat and congratulated himself on his daring. Who else would have the balls to try what he was doing? Or the brains? He'd outfoxed them all, and nothing could stop him. Shinsky and his buddies were in for a big surprise, one that might get that putz Murray fired, and maybe the CEO, too. Heads were gonna roll, and if he was careful, no one would ever find out who was behind it.

* * *

Allie and Trista, sitting in Ops-2 at the edge of the engine run-up pad, watched as field maintenance struggled to clear two-four-left and its adjacent taxiways as the snow continued to fall. The Herculean effort from a group of exhausted drivers who were nearing the end of their twelve-hour shift was nothing short of amazing. Mother Nature pitched in with an assist at five-thirty, when the blizzard morphed into a light snowfall.

Seven diversions had been inbound when REY became the latest of a list of closures that included Philly, BWI, Reagan, and Dulles. Air traffic control redirected five aircraft to Pittsburgh and one to Cleveland, but the seventh, a Leisure Air flight, was low on fuel and couldn't divert.

"Do you think they can clear it in time?" Trista asked.

"Maybe," Allie said, but she needed the big picture to be sure. "Ground, this is Ops-2 on the run-up pad at Tango and Bravo. I'd like to complete an inspection sweep of the field. Request left on Bravo, right on Sierra, right on Hotel, cross the approach end of runway two-four-right, and take Tango back to the run-up pad."

"Ops-2, that inspection loop is approved. Proceed Bravo, Sierra, Hotel, and Tango. Runway two-four-right is still closed, but proceed with caution. It doesn't look good out there."

She cocked her head at Trista. "Don't we know it."

In a low-tech attempt to test traction, Allie hit the brakes as she traversed Bravo. Not bad. At the approach end of six-left, one of the airport's closed runway markers, known as the illuminated-X, shined its twenty flashing spotlights skyward as a warning to flight crews of approaching aircraft. All three runways were now closed, a first for Reynolds. Sharon Lambert had fumed when Allie had informed her, but she had declined an invitation to come out and see for herself, saying the roads were impassable. She had ordered Allie to refer to the closure as a temporary traffic delay. Allie had hung up on her.

* * *

Frank grabbed his backpack and jumped down from the cab, paying no attention to his aching knees or freezing skin. As expected, a heavy-duty chain and an electronic padlock secured the gate.

He unstrapped the bolt cutters from his pack and eyed the chain. The twenty-four-inch cutters were supposed to handle anything up to a half inch thick. Adrenaline surged through his veins as he clamped the jaws onto the top half of the link nearest the hasp and squeezed the handles.

Frank strained with the effort as hardened steel blades bit in. He stopped, repositioned himself against the fence, and pulled. "Cut, you bastard!" The jaws dug deeper. As his shoulder muscles burned, the link snapped. Icy air filled his lungs as he repeated the cut on the opposite side of the link. The chain jangled to the ground. He lifted the C-clamp and pulled the gate open. That was too easy, and with cutters he had bought for fifty bucks.

Frank drove Yellow-206 through the gate and stopped twenty yards below the crest. The hillside shielded him, but he had to be sure the runway was clear for his final act.

Howling wind blasted his face as he got out and trudged up the slope. He should have remembered his ski mask. He stumbled on a patch of ice and his left knee smashed down onto the hard-packed gravel. This time, there was no pain. He was almost there. His feet flew out from under him and he went sprawling backward into the frozen brush. "Motherfucker!"

Frank rolled sideways against the raised berm and pushed himself up. The snow was getting heavy again. He stayed at the road's edge, made it to the top of the hill, and crouched low as lights washed past him from right to left. Flashing strobes marked the conga line as it swept west across the runway. Was that the last pass? There was no time to find out. He'd have to chance it.

Back in the truck, the radio announced the snow team was exiting the field. The runway would reopen soon. Time to fix that.

Heart thumping, Frank felt dizzy. He inhaled, closed his eyes—just like going over the top in a roller coaster—and hit the accelerator. Yellow-206 surged over the hilltop, its bulk coming to rest on open and level ground. He exhaled and scanned the scene. He figured he was at the halfway point of the runway, the best place to gum up the works.

Mounds of snow, backlit by white runway edge lights, but no strobes. The crews were gone. But the falling flakes were as much his enemy as his ally, shielding him from view but guaranteeing it wouldn't be long until the conga line returned. He didn't have much time.

* * *

Allie dropped her speed to fifteen on Sierra to keep from fishtailing. The taxiway hadn't seen a plow in hours. While she focused on the drive, she instructed Trista to scan the conditions on the ramps to their left.

"I can't see the west ramp, but the south ramp is piled high with snow," Trista said. "And the east ramp isn't much better."

"That's what I was afraid of," Allie said. "Even if the inbound aircraft *can* land, it's not going to be easy for the pilots to taxi to the gate." She turned right at Hotel and stopped in the middle of two-four-right. The E190 was still there, sitting astride two runways, nose-down and buried under a white blanket. It wasn't going anywhere until tomorrow at the earliest, when Choice Jet could send a recovery team.

Once they reached Tango, conditions improved dramatically. The crews had just completed their sweeps of the northern half of the taxiway. Allie stopped at Echo and watched as the lights of the conga line approached from the east: six plows, five blowers, four brooms, and two tankers. A maximum effort.

The line passed in a pulsating amber glow as the plow trucks scraped the bulk of the newly fallen snow, while the blowers threw what remained off the runway and the brooms dug into the grooves of the concrete with their spinning bristles. Tankers brought up the rear, applying potassium acetate to prevent ice from bonding to the cleared surface.

"That's amazing," Trista said.

"No argument here," Allie said. "Murray's boys are earning their overtime tonight."

The radio announced that Ops-6, the pickup that carried specialized friction testing equipment to gauge braking traction, had just completed a runway sweep. Allie keyed her mic. "Ground, Ops-2. Holding short of six-right, twenty-four-left at Echo. I'd like to enter the runway and join Ops-6." The field was closed, but she wanted the controllers to know her position.

"Ops-2, drive on six-twenty-four. Give us an update as soon as you can. Inbound traffic is now seventy-five miles out."

"Ops-2 from snow team lead. We'll have the field ready to reopen in ten minutes."

Allie acknowledged and whistled. "Brian Murray…out here leading the charge. Impressive."

She hit the accelerator and made a hard right on six-twenty-four. The tires held traction. She slammed on the brakes. There was no skid. "That's good." Once they reached Ops-6, Allie shifted to the passenger seat of the friction test vehicle while Trista jumped into the back. Tyler Connolly, one of the three extra bodies who'd been called out to bolster the staff, sat in the driver's seat studying the graph on the display.

"We've got a mu of forty-one," Tyler said, relating the coefficient of friction readings. "RCAM is three-two-three," he added, detailing braking conditions at the touchdown, midpoint, and rollout sections of the runway. "It's marginal, but it's not going to get any better."

Allie examined the readout. "I agree," she said and reached for the mic. "Ground, Ops-6. We have conditions of three-two-three on runway six-right, two-four-left. We recommend reopening. Please advise." An hour after the E190 slid off the runway, the airfield was about to reopen. Not bad.

"Ground copies. Stand by."

A horn sounded. Yellow-40, Director Murray's Trailblazer, pulled up.

"Hey, Brian." Allie had to shout to be heard over the howling wind. "Traction and braking readings are in the acceptable range. The tower has an inbound diversion, and I'm waiting for their decision, but we *are* going to reopen."

"All right. I'll make sure Tango and Bravo are clear, and we're working on the west ramp now, so they'll be able to access the A-Gates."

"Kudos to your people. This was one for the books."

"You know it." Murray looked skyward, then scanned the runway surface. "It's getting heavy again." He paused before driving away. "You'd better get that plane on the ground. I can't promise we'll be open for long."

"Ops-6, ground. We checked your numbers and spoke with the Leisure Air pilot. Let's reopen the airfield. And be advised, the winds have changed. We're directing inbound traffic to the six-right end of the runway."

"Ops-6 copies. Reopen the airfield, with traffic to land on six-right." The change directed the inbound aircraft to approach from the western end of the runway. It meant a circuitous taxi to the A-Gates, but that was a minor inconvenience.

Allie directed Trista to remain in Ops-6 with Tyler while she returned to Ops-2 and scanned for stray vehicles. "Ground, all equipment is off the runway," she radioed.

"Ground copies. All airport vehicles off the runway."

"Ops center from Ops-2. The airfield is open. I'm sending the friction tester back to the garage, but I'm going to stay out here and keep tabs on this snow."

"Will do, Allie," Ellis Kim replied. "Stay warm out there."

Allie drove out of the ILS critical area and parked on the engine run-up pad. Was the worst of the storm over? "Don't bet on it, Althea," she muttered.

FORTY-EIGHT

Monday, February 13 - 7:00 p.m.

Frank gripped the wheel with sweaty palms and stared into the gloom as Yellow-206 sat at the intersection of the crash road and the runway access road. One hundred fifty feet of unpaved ground lay between him and his goal. Final doubts crept up. What the fuck was he doing? Did he really think he'd get away with blocking a runway and maybe shutting down the whole airport? Then he thought of how the bigwigs would twist themselves into knots trying to figure out who did it. He laughed. No one could stop him now.

When he flipped the headlights on, his jaw dropped. Deep snow lined the runway safety area. The panic rose again. How was he gonna get across that? He considered jumping out and hurrying back to his car, but there'd never be another chance like this to stick it to the bastards who had fired him.

Don't be a candy-ass. Park the truck on the runway and hoof it out of there. Escaping wouldn't be easy, but it was downhill, and if he pushed it, he'd be home by the time anyone figured out what had happened. The setup was perfect. He regained his resolve and drew up his nerve.

He shifted to neutral, revved the engine, popped the transmission into gear, and floored the accelerator. Yellow-206 rolled onto the snow-covered safety area at thirty miles per hour. Forward momentum slowed, but he made it halfway across before the truck bogged down.

"Damn it to hell!" Feeling the wheels spin, Frank took his foot off the accelerator. He dared not dig a hole he couldn't get out of.

Fear gripped him and sweat poured off his brow. Then his years of driving big trucks in all kinds of weather paid off. He worked the shift lever between drive and reverse, rocking the truck forward and back. He repeated the move. A couple feet each way, then a few more. "Come on, come on, you fucking pig! Move!"

Yellow-206 lurched backward out of the rut. Frank yanked the steering wheel to the right and slammed the gearshift into low. The truck pitched forward. He was moving again. The runway was now fifty feet away but lined with a five-foot pile of snow.

Frank's lurched as the tires bit into a firm patch of ground. Instinctively, he floored the accelerator and the truck responded with a burst of speed. His neck snapped forward and ricocheted back against the headrest as Yellow-206 barreled into the snow mountain. His vision went fuzzy, but he kept his foot on the gas. A metallic crunch under the wheels. Edge lights! He shook away the cobwebs and looked around. He was smack in the middle of the runway!

* * *

Allie flipped the wipers on as snow inundated Ops-2. This wasn't good; the storm was raging again. The deicers had done their job, but the runway would soon be unfit for air operations. "This airport is going to close." She shook her head. "Oops. I mean, we'll have another temporary traffic delay." The hypocrisy of her boss's semantics dumbfounded her. "Won't be so easy to explain away two closures in the same night, will it? No, ma'am, Director Lambert, it will not."

Mesmerized by the monstrous flakes, she almost missed it: something moving on the runway. "Are those lights?" She squinched her eyes. "Are those…headlights? What the hell? Is that a vehicle?" Allie's senses came fully alert as potential explanations bounded through her brain. Was it a breakdown from the conga line? Was someone lost? "Jesus Christ!"

She grabbed the mic. "Field maintenance supervisor from Ops-2, do you have any equipment on the runway?"

"Ops-2 from field maintenance supervisor, that's negative," Shinsky said. "We're clear of runway six-twenty-four. We're making a sweep of taxiway Bravo now."

"Okay, Joe. I thought I saw lights at the midway point. Can you do a count of your vehicles, just to be sure?"

"Will do. Stand by."

Allie listened as each vehicle checked in. After an interminable wait of thirty seconds, she received her reply.

"Ops-2 from FM supervisor, all vehicles are accounted for and clear of runway six-twenty-four."

"Copy, Joe. Thanks. It must be the snow playing tricks." But was it?

Not satisfied, Allie pulled out the binoculars, but looking through them was futile. They only magnified the flakes, although she could still see twin pinpricks of light. *South* of the runway. On the access road? She slowed her breathing and forced herself to think logically. Who would be out there if not from maintenance?

Wait, the lights were moving. Slowly, almost imperceptibly. Back and forth, back and forth. The realization hit. "Rocking! The lights are rocking!" Someone was stuck and trying to get off the grass. But why were they in the grass? The lights moved north and disappeared. "What the hell?" As she tried to refocus, they burst onto the runway.

Allie keyed the mic. "Vehicle on runway six-twenty-four. Clear the runway immediately. The runway is active!"

Nothing.

"Vehicle on the runway. Get clear. Six-twenty-four is active!"

Allie heard engine noise approaching from the west. "God, no!"

She jumped onto the tower frequency. "Ground, Ops-2, emergency.

Tell the landing aircraft to go around. There's a vehicle on the runway. Repeat: There's a vehicle on the runway!"

If the controller acknowledged or replied, she didn't hear it. The roar of powerful jet engines drowned out all other sounds.

FORTY-NINE

Monday, February 13 - 7:10 p.m

Hyped up from the adrenaline pumping through his system, Frank struggled to catch his breath. He scanned for movement, but there was none. Based on past experience, he figured the runway would open in less than five minutes. There was no time to waste.

He killed the engine, reached under the dash, grabbed a handful of wires, and yanked. The harness came loose and with another tug, he ripped it free. Let Shinsky try to drive this monster off the field. And good luck towing it away in the storm. He laughed.

The radio was dead, but he could imagine the ground controller, or some asshole from ops, announcing they found a truck blocking the runway. They'd have to close the airfield for a good long time. "I did it! Kiss my ass, Reynolds International."

Time for a fast exit down the hill. Maybe he'd stop for a drink at the bar.

As he reached for the door handle, a pair of bright lights caught his eye, approaching from the west. The friction tester? Shinsky? Maybe somebody had spotted him. He needed to go.

When he opened the door, he heard it. Thunder, cutting through the howling wind. He froze. Not thunder. The dark shape before him seemed to hang in the air, motionless.

Yellow-206 shuddered and Frank gave voice to his life's final thought.

"It can't be. This fucking runway is cl—"

* * *

For years, Allie had suffered nightmares about aviation disasters replete with midair collisions, onboard fires, structural failures, loss of engine power, and ocean ditching. She chalked them up to a vivid imagination combined with her chosen profession. The action always proceeded in slow motion, without sounds, smells, or tactile sensations. And she always woke before the ultimate moments. What she witnessed now was meteoric, far more horrifying, and quite real.

The roar of powerful turbofans thundered in her head as the plane crossed the runway threshold. The pungent smell of jet fuel was overpowering. Stunned and at a loss for options, she watched but was slow to process the impending disaster in front of her.

Touchdown occurred at the fifteen-hundred-foot marker. Almost immediately, the nose lifted off the ground and the aircraft banked hard right as the pilots attempted to climb over the obstacle on the runway.

"Go! Pull up!" she screamed. But it was too late.

The right main gear and underbelly impacted the truck as the plane struggled for altitude. Then the fuselage broke apart. The forward section catapulted over the truck and disappeared with a resounding thump, followed by a terrible screech. In her mind, Allie pictured the awful details. Simultaneously, the aft section skidded across the ground and came to rest at a seventy-five-degree angle to the runway.

Allie sat, rejecting the sight of a commercial airliner in pieces. But within seconds, her professionalism kicked in and she regained her wits.

"Ground, Ops-2. The aircraft is down! It collided with a truck and crashed halfway past the approach end of six-right."

The controller acknowledged with uncharacteristic emotion in his voice. "We copy. Aircraft down on six-right. We're alerting ARFF."

Ellis Kim's voice came across the radio. "Ops center copied your transmission, Ops-2. Aircraft down on six-right. We're making our emergency notifications now."

"Recall all our people and notify Sharon," Allie ordered. "Get the conference room ready for a command post."

She dropped the mic, hit the gas, and took off across the runway.

FIFTY

Monday, February 13 - 7:15 p.m

Tony sipped coffee as he sat in the back of the dayroom, skimming the op-ed section of the *New York Times* on his laptop. Because the department was operating under emergency conditions, the captain had asked the crew to refrain from working out, and there was little else to do. He had watched in amusement as his colleagues argued about what to stream on Netflix.

Tony's chair shook. A muffled whump followed.

"What the hell was that? A sonic boom?" Danny Gardner asked.

As everyone looked around, the yelping crash alarm sounded. "This is the tower with an Alert-3! Runway six-right." The ground controller's voice had none of the dispassionate calm which typified his profession. Tony slammed the lid on the laptop as the room fell silent.

"It's the Leisure Air diversion. The aircraft crashed on landing." The controller's voice rose. "It looks bad!"

"Motherfucker" was the only comment uttered as everyone sprang from their seats and ran for their rigs.

"The aircraft is at the midpoint of the runway," the controller added. "Ops-2 reports it collided with a ground vehicle on landing."

Tony dashed across the windswept garage bays as airport dispatch repeated the controller's frantic call. "Airport Fire, the tower is reporting an aircraft down on six-right, at the midpoint of the runway. Repeat, aircraft down midway on runway six-right. They think it collided with a ground vehicle on landing."

Steve Brooks, showing uncharacteristic hustle, was already in the cab with the engine running.

In the bay to their left, Captain Schrum stood on the top of Rescue-10 and called to Lieutenant Wozniak. "Phil, jump on 11. I need you on a crash truck." The captain glanced at Steve and Tony and got into his truck.

"Ground and airport dispatch, Rescue-10, 11, 12, 13, 15 are responding to the Alert-3 on six-right." The captain's voice carried restrained urgency.

"Fuck, fuck, fuck," Steve said. "What a night for this."

Tony grunted as he struggled with his BA straps. A million scenarios raced through his mind as he secured his gear. Was the aircraft on fire? Were people trapped?

"Ground, Rescue-10 and company at Fire Station Bravo," Schrum radioed. "Request clearance to the crash scene."

"Rescue-10, this is the tower supe. You're clear all the way to runway six-right. No further clearances needed. The airfield is closed."

"Rescue-10 copies. The field is closed. Do you have a visual on the site?"

"Rescue-10, ground. We can't see much through this snow, but the aircraft was in the process of landing when it appeared to veer off to the right and hit the ground. Operations has it in sight. They think it might have broken apart."

"Rescue-10 copies. I'm shifting communications to County Emergency Frequency One. Rescue-10 has ARFF command."

"Roger ARFF command, switching to emergency frequency one," the supervisor said in a measured tone. "Be advised the As-Dee is still out of service. We can't help you with vehicle movement." After a momentary pause, she added, "We have no contact with the flight crew."

"No shit," Steve said. "They're dead." Tony gave him a sideways glance. If the aircraft had broken apart, he might be right.

Schrum issued more instructions as the fleet made the right turn onto Bravo. "Operations from ARFF command. Implement the airport emergency plan. Airport dispatch, get our second alarm rolling now and recall all off-duty firefighters."

The fire equipment formed a staggered line behind Rescue-10 and followed the captain's RIV south.

"ARFF Command, this is Ops-2." Tony recognized Allie's voice in his headset.

"I'm on six-right, heading for the scene." Allie was breathing hard into her mic. "I saw the plane go down. I think it collided with a truck."

Tony was stunned. "She saw it? Holy shit."

Steve glanced over. "This is going to be a bear."

"Yeah," Tony agreed. "And we only have twelve firefighters on duty."

* * *

On autopilot, Allie spun the Explorer around, put it into four-wheel drive, and drove diagonally off the run-up pad, across the taxiway, through the snow-packed grass, and onto the runway.

"Damn this weather," she muttered as she steered through the falling snow. The radio was alive with traffic from the tower, the fire department, and ops, but it was all background noise as she raced to the scene.

A hulking silhouette came into view. "Slow down, Althea, or you're going to hit something. Or someone." When one of her tires rolled over a metallic chunk, she hit the brakes and flipped on the roof-mounted spotlight. Multicolored fragments littered the ground. She snatched the mic.

"ARFF command from Ops-2. I'm on six-right. I can see the plane, or part of it."

Allie weaved through a field of jutting, twisted metal and stopped a hundred and fifty feet from the aircraft.

"Oh dear Lord!" The remains of a yellow truck lay crushed and mangled on the buffer strip between six-right and Tango. The rear of the fuselage—minus the wings—looked intact. She couldn't see the tail section, but it looked like it had punched through the high snowbank along the runway safety area.

Allie broke through the chatter on the radio. "Emergency traffic! This is Ops-2 at the western end of the crash site. The aircraft broke apart on impact. I'm parked at the rear section of the fuselage. It's upright and looks intact. I don't see any fire. Repeat, the aft section appears intact and there is no visible fire."

She scanned the scene. "There's a debris field across the runway blocking any further access. I can't get around it. I can't see the forward cabin or wings. ARFF command, be advised, you won't be able to reach both sides of the crash site from six-right, but Tango was plowed a few minutes ago. Advise you use it as an alternate route to the eastern end of the crash site."

"Ops-2, ARFF command copies. Aft of the aircraft intact with no fire visible. Forward section not accessible from six-right."

The captain took her advice at once, as she knew he would. "Rescue 12 and 15 from command. Follow me. We'll access the eastern site from Tango. Rescue-11, continue your approach from six-right."

Allie panned the spotlight to get a better image of the surreal scene. "Debris is scattered all over the site. I'm going to take a closer look."

"Ops-2 from command. Be careful, Allie. We're on our way."

Allie gave a quick "Ops-2," retrieved the LiteBox from its mount, grabbed her portable radio, and sprang from the cab.

FIFTY-ONE

Monday, February 13 - 7:20 p.m

The captain's RIV quickly outpaced Rescue-12 until Tony saw only red strobe lights in the distance.

"Come on, Steve. Can't we go any faster?"

"No. Do you want to get there alive?"

Tony shook his head in disgust. In his headset, he heard Chief Archer and a couple of ops vehicles call in to service amid dozens of transmissions from the neighboring fire departments. Radio traffic was crowding out communications from the responding apparatus. The captain addressed it.

"Airport and county dispatch from ARFF command, move all mutual aid traffic to County Emergency Frequency Two. Until we establish a staging officer on the north ramp, ops will have to coordinate inbound responders." He added, "ARFF command to all units on this frequency. Keep the air clear for operational messages only."

"Good luck with that," Steve said. "Every clown with a radio wants to get his two cents in."

A thousand feet and closing, the scene came into murky view through the swirling snow. Tony spotted two pieces of the aircraft, one along the right side of the runway and the other several hundred feet beyond.

"My God, it *is* broken in half," Tony said. "Look how far the nose slid after impact."

"Yeah, and there's shit all over the taxiway. We're never going to get through that debris field."

Steve was right. Tony toggled the radio switch. "This is Rescue-12. Wreckage is blocking our path on Tango. We're going to drive Delta and six-left to Foxtrot."

"What are you doing?" Steve asked. "We can't do that."

"Rescue-12 from command. Try it, but use extreme caution and watch out for ice, especially on your turns. Six-left isn't plowed."

"Who do you think you are?" Steve asked.

"You heard him; let's try. Delta is coming up on the left."

"Rescue-11," the captain asked, "what's your status on six-right?"

"We've got a clear path," Lieutenant Wozniak said. "I have a visual on the ops vehicle and the aft section of the aircraft. Updates to follow."

Concurrently, Rescue-12 turned onto runway six-left, but Steve refused to drive faster than twenty miles per hour.

"Rescue-12 and 15 from command. What's your status?"

"Rescue-12 is on six-left now," Tony radioed. "There's a foot of snow on the runway. We're slowing down."

Schrum didn't bother with proper radio procedure. "To hell with the snow. Get to that scene now!"

"Damn it, why'd you tell him that?" Steve asked as he sped up. "This is crazy."

The captain added, "All units…umph…we're taking Rescue-10 across the buffer zone. Watch the debris field, and…be careful. There might be vic…victims in the snow."

Tony and Steve shared a stunned glance. Victims.

* * *

A frigid blast whipped across Allie's face as she stepped onto the runway. The scene was lit only by the lights of her SUV. Bending forward and holding a hand in front of her face, she advanced toward the cabin. Senses sharp, she scanned the scene and keyed her portable radio.

"ARFF units from Ops-2. The debris field around the rear fuselage is passable. I'm walking toward it now, and…wait one."

Shadowy figures emerged from the snow cloud and came into focus. Allie was struck by exhilaration mixed with terror. "People! Command, I see passengers exiting the aft section, where it separated from the forward fuselage."

"ARFF command copies. Evacuation in progress."

"Rescue-11 and 13 approaching the scene," Wozniak reported. "We see your lights, Ops-2."

Allie sprinted toward the fleeing passengers. She slipped, lost her balance, and hit the ground on her right hip. She used the LiteBox to break her fall, but her portable radio flew from her grasp. "Damn it!" Struggling to her feet, she heard voices—sobbing, screaming, yelling for help.

Disregarding the dropped radio, she waved her light and called to them. "Over here! Hey, over here! Come this way!" Half trotting, half limping, she rushed to meet them. Their faces were etched with shock and horror.

Allie moved closer as she directed the survivors to safety. The fuselage was canted to starboard, forcing the passengers to angle their way out. A steady stream of dazed figures jumped from the stricken aircraft. Some stumbled and several fell as they hurried away from the plane. She corralled about twenty cold and disoriented survivors.

"Move that way," Allie urged, shouting over the howling wind. "Go toward the headlights! It's safe there. That way, that way," she called, swinging her light in an arc toward Ops-2. "Stay together. Help is on the way." It couldn't arrive soon enough.

FIFTY-TWO

Monday, February 13 - 7:25 p.m

With their detour to six-left, the crew of Rescue-12 lost sight of the scene in the dense snowfall, and Rescue-15 was no longer behind them. Tony scanned for hazards and kept an ear to the developing situation as Steve maneuvered across the unplowed surfaces.

"All units from ARFF command. We have the forward section of the aircraft in sight. The passenger compartment is upright on the runway in the middle of a large, scattered debris field. The left wing has broken off at the root, and the right wing is barely visible at the southern edge of the runway, along the safety area." Captain Schrum was remarkably calm. "We're about two hundred feet from the plane, but the broken wing is blocking our access. We're trying to move around it."

Tony strained to spot the scene but could see nothing.

Schrum filled in more details. "The main fuselage is seventy-five feet beyond the broken wing, with the nose pointed at the woods. The left engine nacelle is crushed under the wing. There's a large pool of jet fuel on the ground, all the way from the wing tip to the fuselage. The wing tanks must have ruptured."

"Man, this is terrible," Steve said.

Schrum again. "We see fire under the wing and stand by."

Tony tensed. He grasped the joystick, moved the bumper turret out of its bedded position, and pointed it forward.

"Yes, we can see flames, and they're spreading," the captain said. "The fire is well away from the main cabin, but once the jet fuel heats up, it's going to move fast."

"Shit. We don't have the manpower to—"

"Quiet, Steve! Listen to the report."

"We can't get any closer, but I'm opening up with our roof turret at long range." Frustration tinged the captain's voice. "We're going to ignore the wing fire and lay a foam blanket in front of the aircraft to protect any survivors inside." Like flipping a switch, Schrum's voice morphed into defiance and determination.

"We've got to get there now!" Tony said.

"Do you see what I'm driving through? *People* might be buried under this snow."

Maybe, but Tony doubted they'd be this far from the plane. "Just speed it up."

Steve accelerated, a little. The aircraft came into view as Rescue-12 turned right on Echo. Flames were visible along the trailing edge of the detached wing.

"Look at that. The cargo hold looks like it's crushed," Steve said.

"Yeah, but the passenger cabin might be okay." The forward section was upright, but it looked like a soda can someone had tried to squeeze.

Debris littered the ground, but it wasn't enough to stop a crash truck. To his right, Tony saw the heavy stream from Rescue-10. The foam-water mixture was breaking apart in the air.

"They can't reach the plane from where they are," Tony said. "Not in this wind."

The radio squawked. "This is ARFF command. Our roof turret is ineffective. Rescue-12, get in there and knock those flames down. We'll cover your approach."

"Rescue-12 copies. Moving in now," Tony replied. "Let's go, Steve! Move this thing!"

"There's debris everywhere. We can hit the fire from here."

"No, we can't! That wind is too strong."

"12 from command. Move in closer to that aircraft."

"Come on, man," Tony implored. "This truck can roll over anything. Who gives a damn what we hit; there are people in there!"

Steve grunted and hit the gas pedal. Tony's head snapped back as the crash truck lurched forward, and he felt jarring vibrations under the floor as the Striker rolled over God only knew what. He prayed it wasn't a body.

Fragments of the aircraft peppered the scene. An entire gear assembly, tires intact, lay on its side and directly in their path. Ragged metallic pieces were strewn to either side.

"We're stuck," Steve said as he slowed to a crawl.

"No, we're not. Pull to the right," Tony said as he pointed to a narrow corridor around the obstacle. "The other stuff is small. We can drive over it."

Steve followed Tony's instructions and as they approached the scene, flames leapt from the spreading jet fuel. The fuselage and the wall of snow at the edge of the runway created a dam, allowing a pool of combustible liquid to accumulate from the wing to the cabin. And the flames were creeping toward the plane.

"Rescue-12 from command. We see you. The cold is keeping the fire in check, but you need to get foam on it, fast."

As the captain spoke, the scene erupted as the wing fire heated the Jet-A to its ignition temperature. In seconds, the flames were lapping at the base of the cabin.

"That's it," Steve said as he stopped the truck. "Hit it from here."

"What the fuck, Steve!" Frustrated but wasting no time, Tony grabbed the roof turret joystick, aimed at the fire, and squeezed the trigger. The engine revved and the truck rocked backward as twelve hundred gallons per minute of foam and water jetted from the nozzle. Particles of foam blew back against the windshield.

"Look at that," Tony shouted. "The stream is breaking up. We're wasting our water. We've got to get closer!"

"Rescue-12 from command. Why did you stop? You're too far

from the aircraft. Protect yourselves as best you can, but move in and sweep that fire away from the fuselage."

"Do you see anybody running out of the plane?" Steve asked. "No one's alive in there. If we keep going, we'll be dead too."

"Move it, for Christ's sake! We don't know what's going on in there. The fire hasn't penetrated the cabin. I'll keep it away from us. Just go!"

"You'd better, or we're toast."

Tony recalled Evan's modulation lesson. Crash trucks could pump and roll. He shut off the flow from the roof turret and toggled the water and foam switches for the bumper turret, sending five hundred gallons per minute into the flames, which were now only fifteen feet in front of them. With a thirty-degree fog pattern, Tony swept the nozzle to the right and left, keeping the flames at bay as Steve closed the distance.

* * *

Wading into the exodus, Allie came upon an elderly couple who had fallen. She called out, "Can anyone help me?"

Two women and a teenage boy approached. "We'll help them," they said and lifted the man and woman to their feet.

Allie repeated her plea, and fresh volunteers pitched in. "Get these people over to that vehicle," she said, again signaling with her light.

And they did: rounding up, directing, and leading their fellow passengers to safety. Adults helped children, young people aided seniors, the strong supported the unsteady. Allie watched with satisfaction. It wasn't a bad verdict on humanity.

Diesel engines caught her attention: two crash trucks, slowing as they approached. The cavalry had arrived.

"Help is here!" she announced to the fleeing survivors. "Stay out of their way and watch out for jagged metal." Adrenaline pumping, she didn't notice the cold. With ARFF on the scene, she moved toward the tail. There were more people to help.

FIFTY-THREE

Monday, February 13 - 7:30 p.m

"It's underneath us! I knew it," Steve said as they drove into the pool of burning jet fuel.

"It's too spread out. I can't hit it fast enough." Tony's frantic foam application wasn't enough to keep the flames at bay. He tasted petroleum as fumes filtered into the cab.

"The bumper turret can't keep it away from us."

"Hang on." Tony hit the rocker switch marked UNDERTRUCKS. Designed as a last-ditch defense for the crew, three nozzles sprayed overlapping umbrellas of foam under the chassis of the crash truck.

"That won't save us for long," Steve said.

"I know." As Tony considered his next move, a torrent of water showered the cab roof and foam rolled down the windshield.

"It's the captain! He's got our backs. Keep going, Steve; we're almost in range."

"Rescue-12 from command. We're covering your approach, but our agent is low."

"We've got this, Cap," Tony replied. Ninety to one hundred twenty seconds, that was the burn-through time for aluminum. Survivors were doomed if he let the fire penetrate the cabin.

"A little further…that's it. Stop here!"

Tony jerked forward into his seat belt as Steve slammed on the brakes.

Fifty feet from the imperiled cabin and in the middle of a fuel fire, Rescue-12's position violated every tactic Tony had learned at the academy. But he had to take the chance; it was his only shot to protect anyone still alive inside the aircraft.

* * *

Allie found two children: a girl no more than ten who cradled a little boy of about six. Huddled together against the rear of the canted fuselage, they looked up at her with terror. The boy sobbed while his sister tried to console him.

"We're waiting for our dad," the girl said. "We don't know where he is. Everyone was pushing and we…" She sniffled. "We can't find him."

Allie took off her parka, bent down, and wrapped it around the shivering children. "Don't worry. We'll find your dad." She began guiding them away when a voice called out.

"Hanna! Ryan!" A man approached from the rear of the cabin.

"Daddy!" The little boy's eyes widened. The girl cried.

"I couldn't find you. Thank God you're okay." Tears rolled down his cheeks as he hoisted his son and grabbed his daughter's hand. "I'm so sorry, sweetie."

"Get them out of here." Allie pointed to the procession of passengers. "Stay alongside the plane and follow those people. Help is on the way."

"Thank you, thank you," he said as he hurried his children toward the crash trucks. Allie's coat went with them, but she didn't protest.

FIFTY-FOUR

Monday, February 13 - 7:40 p.m

Tony scanned the developing situation in front of Rescue-12. Flames reflecting off the shiny aluminum fuselage highlighted a crazy quilt of dents all along its length. He glanced at his partner. Steve stared at the scene, spellbound.

"Take the bumper turret while I get the Snozzle in position," Tony said. The driver continued to stare out the windshield. "Damn it, Steve, get your head out of your ass."

Steve started. "What?"

Not waiting, Tony adjusted the bumper turret's nozzle to a forty-five-degree pattern and set it to oscillate. The stream swept left and right in a wide arc as Steve regained his senses.

"Sorry. What can I do?"

"Bumper turret. Keep the fire away from us."

Moving to the control panel for the H-RET, the rig's high-reach extendable turret, Tony hit the rocker switch for the low-attack position. The onboard computer sent an electronic signal that lifted both articulating sections off the roof, angled the lower arm down, and extended the top arm toward the cabin. Alternative tactics ran through his mind as the Snozzle assembly lowered itself to a preprogrammed position ten feet in front of the cab and two feet off the ground.

Tony set the controls to high flow and medium pattern. The instant the tip leveled itself, he squeezed the trigger. Twelve hundred gallons per minute of foam solution stopped the spreading flames in their tracks; the enormous fire darkened but continued to lap the edges of the cabin.

"What's our water level?" Tony asked.

"Two thousand gallons, two-thirds of a tank."

Extinguishment was taking too long and using too much water. Time for another of Evan's tricks.

He tightened the pattern and toggled the switch for auxiliary agent. Potassium bicarbonate, encased within the foam-and-water stream, shot from the turret. He swept the nozzle over the surface of the jet fuel as a cloud of purple chemicals rose above the conflagration.

"That's it! Knock that fucker down," Steve said. Recovered from his stupor, he flipped the bumper turret to manual, depressed the nozzle, and laid a blanket of foam over the flames threatening the crash truck.

"Nice!" Tony said and focused. He switched off the dry chemical, angled the turret upward, widened the V pattern, and coated the length of the fuselage. Foam rolled down from the roof, over the windows, and onto the ground, creating a vapor barrier that smothered the flames impinging on the cabin. Just like Evan had taught him. "Thanks, buddy," he whispered.

"Seventeen hundred gallons," Steve said.

Tony switched to low flow, reducing water discharge to six hundred gallons per minute. The thickening blanket spread out from the aircraft and merged with the layer from the bumper turret. In less than forty-five seconds, the self-sealing A-Triple-F smothered the remaining flames between Rescue-12 and the airliner.

"You did it!" Steve said, his voice brimming with enthusiasm.

"You too, partner. We both did."

Steve smiled and glanced at the dashboard gauges. "Water level is just under sixteen hundred gallons."

Tony released the trigger. "Cap said Rescue-10 is running low, so we've got the only water left. I'll open up with quick sweeps at twenty-second intervals."

"That'll work," Steve said.

Tony toggled the radio switch. "Command from 12, the fire in front of the aircraft and around the wing has been extinguished. We have half of our tank water remaining." He took a breath, massaged his tight neck muscles, and allowed himself a moment of satisfaction.

"12 from command. Nice knockdown. Any sign of survivors?"

The question brought Tony back from his euphoria. "Negative. We've seen no self-evacuation."

While he listened as the captain fired off instructions, Tony reevaluated the situation. They'd stopped the fire from penetrating the cabin, but was it all for naught? Could anyone survive such a ruinous impact? Like Steve, he had serious doubts.

FIFTY-FIVE

Monday, February 13 - 7:50 p.m

Iggy's voice came across the air. "Command, Rescue-15 is on the scene. We see you, but we can't get through the debris field."

Tony had forgotten all about 15. Without the LT, the pumper had a short crew because only Nikki and Robbie in the cab with Iggy.

"Rescue-15 from command. Form attack and search teams for entry. I'll send firefighter Worton to assist you."

Three minutes later, Iggy met up with Zach Worton and the pair carried portable lights, a twenty-pound fire extinguisher, and a sixteen-foot ladder into the foam-covered muck as Nikki and Robbie prepared to pull a hoseline from Rescue-12.

"Search-1 is moving toward R-1," Tony reported and removed his headset. Time to join his buddies on the ground. He grabbed his facepiece and opened the passenger door. But before he could climb down, Steve sounded an alarm.

"Wait, look there." He pointed at the cabin. "Do you see smoke?"

"Where?" Tony jumped back into his seat and scrutinized the scene. The snow made it difficult to discern anything beyond the fuselage.

"It's coming from the other side of the plane. Hold on." Steve re-aimed the Snozzle-mounted spotlights. "There!"

Tony spotted a column of black smoke rising above the cabin. "Shit; you're right. Jump on the FLIR and check the interior for heat."

Steve activated the roof-mounted infrared camera as Tony radioed a report.

"Command from Rescue-12, smoke is visible at the rear of the plane. There must be a fire back there, but we can't see or access it from our position."

"Command copies. Ground teams, belay my previous orders. I'm going to reposition Rescue-12." Schrum continued. "Attack-1, once they stop, pull a line and take it around the fuselage. Search-1, hold your position."

Tony marveled at how the captain's implicit calm conveyed confidence and total control in the rapidly evolving scenario. But where were they moving to?

"I can't find any high heat signatures in the passenger compartment."

Tony leaned over to study the FLIR display. "Not yet, anyway."

Allie encountered three more passengers exiting the plane and pointed them toward safety. So far, she'd seen no serious injuries among the survivors. Although shivering uncontrollably, she continued aft, working her way between the fuselage and the piled snow. What she saw pushed the frigid conditions out of her mind. The tail section was missing—just gone. She hadn't noticed earlier because of the snowbank.

Large airframes sometimes broke apart into three torn sections after a low-impact crash: the flight deck and forward cabin, the aft cabin, and the tail. But this separation was clean, almost surgical. Where was the tail? Over the hillside? Holy Jesus, was anyone still inside? It was possible, but she had to check the cabin first.

Turning to the open cargo hold, she wedged a foot between a diagonal strut and the aircraft frame and climbed until her head emerged above the floor. Her light caught a cluster of dangling overhead compartments, but otherwise the interior looked intact. This section of the plane must have experienced more of a skid than an impact with the ground. It would explain what had saved the passengers. She called out but got no response. "Oh, Mom, you should be here to see this," she said aloud. "It's an honest-to-goodness miracle."

Satisfied everyone was out and aware that firefighters would arrive any second, she jumped down, shined her LiteBox toward the hillside, and trudged into the deep snow.

* * *

The captain issued new instructions. "Rescue-12, move in close to the aircraft and penetrate the top of the fuselage with your piercing nozzle. Saturate the interior of the cabin with water. We need to protect anyone who's still alive in there and inject some fresh air. Do you copy?"

As Tony acknowledged the captain's transmission, Steve eyed the scene. "The ground team is clear," he said. "I'm moving in."

Tony, his mind whirling with a new set of variables, nodded. "We'll have to get really close for this to work." He hit the rocker for high-attack position, initiating a process that repositioned the Snozzle above the crash truck's roof. Less than a minute later, Steve stopped and set the parking brake as Tony waited for the articulating arms to complete their cycle. The crash truck stood fifteen feet from the aircraft, and Tony was about to put Evan's lessons to the test once more.

"Rescue-12 beginning piercing procedure," Tony reported. At this distance, the snow didn't impede his view through the plane's windows, but he didn't see any movement inside.

Meanwhile, the Snozzle's articulating arms stopped their programmed movements. Tony gauged the distance: five feet above and ten feet short of the cabin roof. Almost there.

* * *

Allie's boots sank into the freshly fallen powder and crunched into a deeper, packed layer. Icy wind braced her as it penetrated the pullover sweater, her only defense against the cold. Once she got past the runway's edge, she spotted a trail of flattened snow. She broke into a sluggish trot as her bruised hip tried to impede her movements. Must've pulled a muscle. Perfect.

At the edge of the safety area, she stopped. Her light reflected off pieces of shiny metal, maybe a spar or strut. A little farther, a twisted lavatory door projected out of the snow, its red *occupied* message upside down but clearly visible. She was heading in the right direction; the tail had to be close. *Find it, take a quick look, and go back for the ARFF guys.*

She edged around a piece of torn metal until the slope leveled out and the path became a series of deep, irregular patches. She resumed her trot.

FIFTY-SIX

Monday, February 13 - 8:00 p.m

Tony manipulated the Snozzle's telescoping upper arm to within a foot and a half of the fuselage. Next, he hit the PIERCE switch and a three-foot shaft with dozens of tiny discharge openings rotated into place. At the same time, the roof turret's nozzle pivoted ninety degrees to the right to get clear of the metal tube.

"Don't get it tangled in the overhead bins," Steve said.

Tuning out all distractions, Tony angled the tube down and extended it another six inches. *I can do this*, he thought. He and Evan had practiced the procedure many times on the academy's mockup. Lower the shaft a little farther, a few inches above the window…and… now! Tony slammed the joystick forward. Metal squealed as the hardened steel tip penetrated the aluminum skin and slid into the cabin.

"You got it!" Steve said.

Tony opened the pre-piped discharge line, sending 250 gallons per minute of cooling water—and fresh air—into the passenger compartment.

"Command from 12. We've penetrated the cabin and we're flowing," Tony said.

"Command copies. Attack-1, get moving. Knock that fire down

before it burns through. Search-1, make entry. Twelve will cover you until we can get a backup hoseline inside."

Tony shut the nozzle after ten seconds.

"Twelve hundred gallons left," Steve said.

"Command from 12," Tony radioed. "We have a third of a tank remaining."

"Command copies. I'm working on water resupply, but it might be a while. Save enough for the attack line."

Tony fired a short burst into the plane. It would have to do.

* * *

Allie spotted beverage carts, coffeepots, a fire extinguisher, and bits of luggage as she continued downhill. Another of the aft lavatories lay on its side, twisted and broken.

"Oh no!" An entire row of seats, twenty feet to her right. She rushed over and found a man, facedown in his upturned seat, one arm splayed across the snow. Her light caught a glimmer from his wristwatch. A crop of black hair stuck out above the seat. Allie dropped to her knees, slid a hand under the man's neck, and probed for the carotid artery, knowing it was futile. The man was ice-cold. Trembling, she tucked her fingers into the sleeves of her sweater and kept going.

* * *

Nikki and Robbie extracted a two-hundred-foot inch-and-three-quarter hoseline from the tray in Rescue-12's pump compartment, shouldering as much as they could before advancing toward the mangled end of the forward fuselage. Small fires broke out as their movements agitated the foam blanket, but were quickly smothered by the sealing action of the A-Triple-F. Tony monitored the team's progress, ready to cover his friends with the bumper turret while he continued to send intermittent bursts into the cabin. Before turning the corner, the pair dropped the hose, snapped their regulators into place, and called for water.

"Attack-1, your line is charging now," Tony said and engaged the switch for the passenger-side preconnect.

Nikki waved an arm in acknowledgment and the team disappeared behind the fuselage.

"It's all yours, Steve," Tony said as he opened his door.

"All right. I'll monitor the water level and continue using the piercing nozzle until you guys make entry."

When Tony acknowledged with a smile and a nod, Steve added, "Don't worry. I'm on it."

* * *

"There it is!" Allie shouted into the wind. The tail section rested on its roof, perched at the bottom of the steepest part of the slope, its path down the hill carved with deep gouges.

Allie reached for her radio. "Damn it, Althea." Where was her phone? She stuck her freezing hands into the pocket of her work pants and realized she'd left it in the parka. Her intuition told her to go back for help, but there might be a survivor down there.

She turned sideways and descended obliquely, digging her boots into the crusty surface with every step. She couldn't feel her face and the LiteBox almost slipped from her numb fingers. Thirty feet from the wreckage, she spotted the tail fin, painted with Leisure Air's distinctive palm tree logo, lying on its side.

Allie played her light over the inverted tail. It seemed to be held in place by one of the horizontal stabilizers. The other had apparently snapped off. There were no signs of life. There was no point in going any farther. She turned to reascend the hill.

Then she heard a voice.

FIFTY-SEVEN

Monday, February 13 - 8:10 p.m

Tony donned his facepiece and descended into four inches of Jet A below a sea of white. Spot fires burned at the edges of the foam blanket and noxious fumes hung low in the air. To his right, the search team carried their ladder to R-1. He moved left, wading through the muck along the attack team's hoseline.

Tony stopped to hump hose around the back of the fuselage, where the violence of the impact greeted him in the form of twisted and mangled aluminum. The plane's skeletal structure—its cords and stringers—was bent inward as if squeezed by giant pliers. Jagged shards projected in all directions. Remnants of seats, metal carts, and other unrecognizable items littered the ground, and luggage lay scattered below the crushed cargo hold. Then he saw the unimaginable; for a second his mind didn't register what it was. A headless torso and bloody arm hanging from the wreckage. The hand was gone. Poor bastard. He hoped it had been a quick and painless death.

Tony's progress wrenched to a halt as the hose caught on a piece of debris. Grunting, he leaned back and used his butt as a counterweight to pull it free. Then he lifted the slimy hose, pinned it under both arms, and backed around the corner.

Two figures crouched near the nose, their water stream ineffective against a fire that blew toward them. Tony recalled an instructor's admonition to attack fuel fires *with* the wind, never into it. Good advice, unless there was no choice.

He advanced the line through ankle-deep fuel that was hemmed in by the fuselage and snowpack. Flames soared twenty feet into the air and overlapped the flight deck. A gust carried pungent smoke into his open facepiece, and he paused to catch his breath. Acrid particles stung his eyes and triggered a coughing fit as he pulled the lung demand valve from his belt and snapped it in place. Cool air wafted across his face, but the coughing wouldn't stop. He'd waited too long to plug in. A stupid rookie mistake. He depressed the bypass valve and a shot of high-pressure air surged into his respiratory tract. Deep breaths—that was better. He hoisted the hose and hurried forward.

"I cleared the line," Tony shouted. "You can move up."

"Good to see you, buddy, but I'm spent," Robbie said, his panting audible through the facepiece.

"I'll take the nozzle," Nikki said.

"I'll back you up," Tony said as Robbie closed the bale halfway and let the line slip back into Nikki's hands. Tony edged in behind her and Robbie stumbled back to the feeding position.

Flames surged across their front and left, pinning the trio against the fuselage and threatening their only escape route. Waves of radiant heat enveloped them, pushing the limits of their turnout gear.

Nikki turned her face from the flames. "Back up! It's too hot."

Tony leaned into her. "No. Sweep left before it gets behind us."

Reflected flames danced across Nikki's facepiece as she glimpsed the looming encirclement. "I can't hit it from here."

"We've got to move away from the plane," Tony said.

Nikki sidestepped to her left and pivoted forty-five degrees toward the encroaching flames. Tony squeezed in behind her with his back pressed against the cabin. He pushed forward on the line to free her of its weight and pressure.

With room to maneuver, Nikki switched to a narrow pattern and attempted to sweep the fire from their left as heat assaulted them from their right and flames licked at the cockpit. Nikki banked the fire stream off the fuselage, letting the foam roll off the nose. Then she began rotating her torso left and right in a rapid ninety-degree arc. Her efforts staved off the envelopment, but in less than half a minute, she called for a switch.

* * *

Allie perked up. The sound came from inside. Could someone be alive? She panned her light across the tail and listened as snow swept across her face. Torn metal jutted out in crazy, sharp angles all around the conical frame, but the section was still in one piece.

She heard it again. "Hel…me. El…me."

"I'm coming! I'll help you!" At the base of the hill, her light caught a reflection and she skidded to a stop. Pieces of jagged aluminum stuck out of the snow, angled at her. Using her light to avoid the hazard and struggling to keep her balance, she picked her way to the tail.

"Oh my Lord." A woman's body, apparently lifeless, was strapped into an upside-down galley jump seat. Long blonde hair hung down from her head.

The voice Allie heard rose. It wasn't coming from the blonde. "Help. Please help me."

Allie directed her light into the galley and spotted a woman—another flight attendant—at the left corner of the upended compartment. She had a nasty gash above one eye. "Help me, please," she said at she tried to raise her head.

"I'm here. I'll help you." Allie tossed a serving cart out of the way and bent beside the woman. "What's your name, dear?"

"Brenda…I'm Brenda."

"Don't worry, Brenda. Everything's going to be okay now," Allie said as she carried out a quick visual assessment of the woman's injuries. Brenda—who looked to be in her late forties—lay with her legs stretched upward against the upside-down cabin door. Her head rested on what had been the galley ceiling. Ripped tights revealed a bloody left knee. Her right foot, bent at an impossible ninety-degree angle, rested against the door's porthole.

Tears mixed with blood from Brenda's head wound. "Monica. Sweet Monica."

Allie stood and shined her light at the awful sight. The blonde woman—Monica—was a young girl, probably in her early twenties. Her face was milky white and her arms dangled as if reaching out for help. Allie grasped a wrist—ice-cold. She checked for a pulse—nothing. She turned her attention back to the survivor. Brenda was very pale.

"Poor Monica. Is she…"

"I'm afraid she is. I'm so sorry."

"She was going to get married in June. It's not fair."

"Brenda, look at me."

"Poor Monica, poor—"

"Brenda!"

The woman returned her gaze to Allie. "Wha—?"

Allie repositioned to block Brenda's view of her dead colleague.

"I'm so cold."

Shock couldn't be far behind, so Allie had to act fast. She scanned the galley. The tip of a blanket stuck out from a broken storage compartment. She grabbed it and dug out three more.

"I'm going to keep you warm." She wrapped one over Brenda's torso, another around her elevated legs, and a third to make a pillow for Brenda's head.

Allie wrapped the last blanket around herself and huddled against Brenda. She didn't dare move the flight attendant. All she could do was try to keep her warm—and wait. Rescuers would find them soon.

FIFTY-EIGHT

Monday, February 13 - 8:20 p.m

Nikki cut the nozzle's flow. "Take it."

Tony grabbed the hose, clamped it into his armpit, and tugged the bale fully open. One hundred pounds of nozzle pressure drove him into his backup.

"Easy, big fella," Robbie said as he leaned forward in support.

Tony attacked with a forty-five-degree fog pattern. No good. The wind blew it back at the hose team.

The radio crackled. "This is ARFF command. Rescue-22 is on the way. I've relocated to Rescue-12 and sent firefighter Brooks to meet them. Attack-1, report your progress."

Nikki, now third in line, answered. "We have fire on two sides of us, but we're keeping it away from the aircraft."

"Command copies. Relief is five minutes out, but you're on your own until then." He added, "Five hundred gallons remain. Make it count."

"Did you hear that?" Robbie asked. "Three minutes till we're out of water."

"I heard."

Tony gripped the bumper and turned it clockwise to thirty degrees. The stream penetrated the flames, but not far enough.

Narrowing the pattern to fifteen degrees—taboo in jet fuel firefighting—he swept the stream across the surface of the fire, careful not to plunge it into the liquid. The flames receded and the searing heat eased, but the stream fell short of the main body.

"There's too much fuel," Robbie shouted. "We've got to pull back."

"We can't!" They were a squad of soldiers about to be overrun. What could he do?

"Mortars!"

"What?"

"Never mind." Tony pulled up on the line. "Push down, Robbie."

"What are you doing?"

"I said push down!"

Robbie pushed and the nozzle pitched up. Tony angled the tip eighty degrees and spun the bumper all the way to the right. A solid core of water and foam arced upward through the superheated air and plunged into the middle of the burning liquid.

By switching to a straight stream, Tony sacrificed the protective cone of a fog pattern. Waves of heat, driven by the relentless wind, assaulted the attack team from two directions. He flipped his helmet's reflective shield down, but his ears, still tender from the house fire, burned as heat penetrated his hood. Steam overwhelmed the insulation of his sodden gloves.

"We can't take much more!" Robbie said.

Tony bit down on his lip and swung the hose in a tight circle. Arms like lead weights, he dropped an elbow to his knee and watched as a foam blanket began to form at the center of the flames.

Schrum's voice came over the air. "Two hundred gallons."

Tony continued the circling, high-arcing attack. *Come on, you bastard. Go out*, he willed. Just a little bit more…

Behind him, two low-air alarms broke into high-pitched warbles. Robbie dug his helmet into Tony's back.

Slowly, the A-Triple-F layer expanded outward, swallowing the flames in its path. The main blaze petered out, but vestiges danced along the farthest edge of the foam blanket in ominous peaks and valleys. He couldn't allow the damn fire to resurrect itself.

Tony's heads-up display flashed yellow. Needles pricked his eyes, making it impossible to focus. He steeled himself, lowered the nozzle, and spun the stream shaper back to forty-five degrees. At once, the air cooled. Random pockets of orange and yellow continued to flicker.

"One hundred gallons."

Back to straight stream, he passed the foam mixture over the remaining flames, overlapping the fuselage as he did so. "Give us a break, for Christ's sake!"

"It's out! You got it!" Robbie said.

Tony shoved the bale forward and pushed the send button on his lapel mic. "Command from Attack-1. The fire is out."

"Command copies. Just in time. The gauge showed you out of water thirty seconds ago."

Tony forced a smile and collapsed onto his ass. Despite the chill, his body radiated with trapped heat and his breath came in gasps. He glanced at his team. Nikki was on her hands and knees; Robbie lay slumped against the fuselage. The fire could reignite at any second, but they had neither the water nor the strength to do anything about it.

Tony winced as a storm of drops rained down on his helmet. A fucking hailstorm? His vision went dark. What the hell?

Robbie called out. "Foam! It's foam!"

Tony wiped his visor. Lights and shadowy figures appeared at the back of the plane. Moving toward them.

Another radio transmission: "Command from Attack-2. We have Attack-1 in sight. They appear to be okay. We don't see any fire. We're reapplying a foam blanket now."

Rescue-22 had arrived and its crew was now coating the scene, the fuselage, and the weary firefighters of Attack-1.

"Command copies. Attack-1, report to me at Rescue-12. Attack-2 will remain in place to prevent reignition."

Tony, Robbie, and Nikki stood up, unplugged their LDVs, and deactivated their BAs. Offers of aid from their fellow firefighters were refused as the trio, heads held high, departed the scene.

FIFTY-NINE

Monday, February 13 - 8:40 p.m

Rescue-22, the reserve Oshkosh T-3000 crash truck that Tony knew well from the academy, sat angled toward the back corner of the fuselage. Attack-2's hoseline snaked from its passenger-side pump compartment into the darkness from which Tony, Nikki, and Robbie had just emerged. A figure in the cab waved. Tony stared in wonder at Steve Brooks, who had somehow managed to switch crash trucks and avoid the weather. He raised a hand to his conniving colleague.

Rescue-12's engine was still running, and its spotlights illuminated the point where the piercing nozzle penetrated the cabin. Beyond it, a firefighter stood on a ladder at the R-1 door.

"They're still trying to get inside," Tony said. "Let's give them a hand."

The trio had started for their colleagues when Captain Schrum climbed down from Rescue-12 and called them over.

"We need some help," he said and scanned their faces. "Tony, you were on the ground last. How much air do you have?"

Tony glanced at the digital readout on his chest gauge. "Nineteen hundred pounds."

"That'll do. Join up with Santos and Worton. They're having trouble getting inside. The door frame must've torqued on impact."

Shrum instructed Robbie to lay a tarp and set up a tool station behind R-1. "And bring up some fresh cylinders." Turning to Nikki, he ordered her to stretch a second hoseline from Rescue-22. "Cover this area from the edge of the foam blanket while Attack-2 monitors the back of the plane." The captain eyed the crew. "Sorry. I know you're all tired, but there's just no one else right now."

"Don't worry, Cap. We've got some life in us," Robbie said. The fatigue in his voice indicated otherwise.

Tony retrieved a Halligan and LiteBox from Rescue-12 and hustled to the search team, where Zach heeled the sixteen-foot ladder for Iggy, who was struggling with the retractable door handle. Captain Schrum moved behind them, a worried look on his face.

The aircraft's nose was bent to the right. No doubt the reason the door wouldn't open.

"Here, Iggy, try this," Tony said and handed the Halligan up.

Iggy took it and brought the adze end down against the handle. Nothing. He raised the tool and struck it again and again. His facepiece pendulumed from the neck strap with every blow.

"It's free!" Iggy said. He dropped the Halligan and spun the lever clockwise. The plug-type door popped open and retracted inward.

Schrum yelled to him, "Watch out; the slide might be armed."

"Got it, Cap." Iggy slid his legs into a ladder-lock, with his knee wrapped around a rung and his instep anchored on the outside rail. He grasped the edge of the door with both hands, heaved it outward, and ducked to his left. The door swung out, but the escape slide didn't deploy. He rotated the door toward the cockpit and shoved it open. "We're in," he said and disappeared into the plane. Zach and Tony followed.

Devastation greeted the search team in a cabin lit only by Rescue-12's spotlights shining through the windows. Carry-on bags, ejected from overhead bins, littered the space. Wires dangled from exposed ceiling panels. Noxious Jet A fumes hung in the air.

Entire rows of seats had broken free of their moorings and hurtled forward at impact. Other seats had fallen astride the aisle. Ten rows sat in a compressed jumble amid a lavatory compartment that looked as though it had imploded. The crew gasped in unison as Iggy panned his light across the destruction.

Tony shuddered, mouth agape. They couldn't all be dead, not after everything…

His partners saw it too. Victims filled the crushed forward seats, only the tops of their heads visible. There was no sound.

"God in heaven," Iggy muttered as he crossed himself and shook his head as if to purge the sight from his brain. "Zach, let's go aft and look for survivors. Tony, check the cockpit. Let's dump our BAs."

Iggy's command broke the spell. Tony shrugged the BA off his shoulders, picked up the Halligan, and eyed the reinforced cockpit door. Knocked partially off its mountings, it stood cockeyed and ajar.

Tony gripped the middle of the bar and drove the flat side into the door at chest height. It came loose from its moorings but remained in place. He mustered his strength, hauled back, and hit it again, this time at knee level. The door fell into the cockpit. Hot air rushed out.

Tony flipped on his light and entered the flight deck. Black soot caked the cracked windshield. Lights continued to glow on the instrument panel. He moved up and winced. The pilot's head hung against his chest, his arms still gripping the yoke. The man had no pulse. Had the poor bastard known he was about to die?

Moving to the copilot, he got the same result. The woman lay slumped over the control console, her hand on the throttle levers as if trying to add thrust. Christ, her eyes were still open. What did she see at the end? Disheartened but not devoid of hope, he didn't ponder long. He found the main circuit breaker, switched it off, and reentered the passenger compartment.

Radiated heat from the now-extinguished fire, in combination with the water injected from the piercing nozzle, left the main deck stifling and steamy. Fumes from jet fuel fouled the air. While his comrades squeezed around and climbed over the maze of seats and luggage, Tony ditched his helmet, coat, and sweat-soaked gloves, shoved the radio into his bunker pants, and clipped the lapel mic to a breast pocket.

Halligan in one hand and LiteBox strapped around his neck, he waded into the disorder. The first three rows were passable, but he had to climb atop ruined seats filled with bodies as he navigated the next six. He climbed over a woman whose neck was bent at an impossible angle. Next to her, a teen boy's lifeless face stared at the cabin ceiling, eyes frozen in disbelief.

Iggy called out, "Someone's alive back here." A moment later he added, "There's more than one."

Tony hit the transmit button. "This is Search-1. We have survivors in the plane. We need medical help in here." With renewed vigor, he picked up his pace.

The middle seats were slick from the piercing nozzle, which sat exactly where Tony had aimed it, six inches into the cabin, just above the window. Water from its tiny orifices dribbled onto the bodies of a middle-aged Asian couple.

Tony's knee slipped and he came down hard on a young woman's shoulder, involuntarily grabbing at the girl's long hair and causing her ashen face to snap up at him. Her slack jaw hung open. He recoiled, let go, and closed his eyes, telling himself to focus. *These people are dead. Get to those I can help.*

Ten rows back, the seats were undamaged and the aisle was clear, but the fumes were overpowering. Hot bile rose in his throat. He swallowed hard and tried not to breathe. It was no good. The heat, fumes, and death were too much. His stomach clenched, and he doubled over and vomited onto an empty seat.

SIXTY

Monday, February 13 - 8:55 p.m

"The pilots are dead," Tony told his colleagues as he reached row 12.

Iggy looked up from the teen girl he was examining. Like Tony, he'd also discarded his bunker coat and helmet. "I figured. Those poor bastards took the brunt of the impact. Didn't have a chance."

"Nobody up front did," Tony said. "Find any more survivors back here?"

"So far, we've found five. Two are semiconscious, but none of them are responsive. This one's alive." Iggy reclined the teenager's seatback. "But it's too late for her father. His neck is broken."

Zach called out, "Everything behind row 19 is crushed like a fucking tin can. We'll never get anyone out through there."

"Okay, Zach," Iggy said. "Work your way forward."

"I've got five DOAs so far, and, Christ, there's people torn to pieces back here. I can't—"

"We hear you!" Iggy looked at Tony and lowered his voice. "Anyone still conscious heard him too."

"What can I do?" Tony asked.

"Any other survivors will be clustered in the rows behind us. Let's work our way back. You take the A-B-C seats while I stay on the D-E-

F side. We've got one bottle of O_2 in our bag and a bunch of pressure dressings. We can make quick, half-ass assessments, clear airways, and try to control bleeding."

"I'm on it," Tony said, thankful that Iggy was nearby. He spotted an elderly woman in 13-D and bent down to her nose and mouth while he pressed two fingers to her wrist. "This one's alive but nonresponsive. Her respirations are shallow and her pulse is weak and thready."

"If she's breathing on her own and her airway is clear, move on."

Tony found a dead man in row 13, but in seat 14-B, a middle-aged female was alive. Her head drooped forward and her breaths were ragged. Tony reclined the seat, tilted the woman's head back, and used a jaw thrust to clear her airway. Still unconscious, her breathing evened out. A man seated next to her in 14-A had no pulse. A couple on holiday? One dead and one alive. The randomness of it was inexplicable.

Tony slid back to row 15 and examined a woman with close-cropped hair who looked to be in her early thirties. Her sightless eyes fixed on the seat back. So very tragic.

"I've got three survivors in row 18," Zach said. "But they're all out of it. Like they're in some kinda group coma."

"It's from the concussion of the impact and the bad air," Iggy said. "They're not going to wake up for us."

But they *were* alive. It hadn't all been for nothing.

The radio chirped. "Search-1 from command. Two medics entering the aircraft."

Tony spotted them as they climbed into the forward cabin. "Hey, back here." He waved his light. "You have to climb over the seats."

"You've got real medical help now," he said to Iggy. "Why don't I get one of these wing hatches open? It'll take forever to evacuate the survivors through R-1."

Iggy nodded. "Do it."

The two exits in rows 14 and 15 on the starboard side were Tony's first choices. He grabbed his Halligan and hustled to row 14, tramping over carry-on baggage in the clogged aisle. Three bodies filled the seats, but the exit row was wide enough to move past them. As he pulled a body in 14-F away from the window, the man's head flopped onto Tony's shoulder. He shuddered but eased the body out of the way. The hatch was a spring-loaded model designed to swing up and out. *Good.* Tony popped the plastic cover and yanked the release lever. It didn't budge. He tried again. It held firm.

He allowed the paramedics to pass and moved to row 15, where he squeezed past an obese lifeless man dressed in a tropical shirt and shorts. Reaching up, he exposed the release mechanism and tried the handle. The lock disengaged but the hatch moved only a few inches. He tried again. It moved a little more. *What else, already?* He lifted the Halligan, drew back, and drove it into the base of the hatch. Metal grated and plastic splinters flew into his face as it sprang out and up. Now they had access.

Tony leaned out and sucked in the fresh, cold air. Where the starboard wing should have been, only a mangled stub remained. He keyed his mic. "Command from Search-1, the wing hatch is open. Direct all further help to this position."

"Tell them we need medical supplies, blankets, and those lightweight plastic stretchers we carry," Iggy said.

"And ventilation," Zach added. "These fumes aren't doing anything for the survivors, or us."

Tony relayed the requests.

"Command copies. Stand by." The voice of Deputy Chief Martone caught Tony by surprise. It certainly had taken a long time for a chief officer to arrive. Or had it? How long was it since the crash? He had no idea.

"We're bringing a ladder up to you," Martone added. "And we'll set up a PPV at R-1. Additional medics are coming on scene now."

Tony looked out across a sea of foamy white and flashing red. Ambulances lined the perimeter. Firefighters and medics scrambled back and forth across the soggy ground. Six feet below, a large green tarp lay unfolded at the base of the fuselage. He spotted Nikki at the edge of the action, holding a hoseline and reapplying foam with gentle side-to-side sweeps.

Robbie strode up and dumped an armload of equipment onto the tarp. Nikki passed the hoseline to a couple of mutual aid firefighters and joined him.

"Good to see you, brother," Robbie called. "We've got people coming up to help you."

Iggy interrupted. "Don't allow anyone else in here unless they're paramedics. There's no room. Just pass the stuff up to us."

"I copied that," Robbie said. "Our guys are setting up the PPV, but it's gonna get cold in there."

"Great; we could use some air-conditioning. What about a ladder? It's a hell of a jump."

"Should be here any second," Nikki said with a thumbs-up. "Looks like you're doing okay, rookie, but don't do anything stupid. We'll be right back with the supplies."

Two firefighters from C-platoon strode through the foam and set up a twelve-foot A-frame ladder. Four medics approached the cabin, passed their bags up to Tony, and climbed aboard.

The coughing of a gas engine signaled the start of a positive pressure ventilation fan. In seconds, a steady flow of fresh air replaced the suffocating odor of jet fuel.

The situation was well in hand. He and Zach were in the way, and with Iggy's approval, they prepared to exit the cabin. Stepping onto the ladder, Tony paused at the sound of a familiar diesel engine. Rescue-16 was on the scene, entering the hot zone through a gap in the ambulance row. The driver maneuvered the aerial truck to a position parallel with the aircraft.

Zach poked his head out of the hatch. "Didn't expect to see that beast tonight."

"Nope," Tony replied. "We might want to hang here for a minute."

SIXTY-ONE

Monday, February 13 - 9:10 p.m

As Tony and Zach watched, a familiar figure emerged from Rescue-16.

"That's Rosie," Tony said. "Didn't he go home on a Kelly?"

"Yeah. Looks like he's alone."

The pair descended the ladder and hustled over to the aerial truck.

"Need a hand?" Tony asked.

"You know it, boys. We better use the outrigger pads. I don't know what's under this muck."

Rosie climbed onto Rescue-16's rear pedestal and extended the outriggers. Tony and Zach retrieved the heavy aluminum base plates from their stowage compartments and dropped them at four points around the truck. The runway surface felt solid, but oily liquid splashed their gear as each plate disappeared under the foam and fuel mix.

Rosie lowered the vertical arms of the outriggers onto the ground pads and, with coordinated ease, simultaneously raised and rotated the three-section tower ladder until it was perpendicular to the fuselage. Then he extended the basket to the open wing hatch.

One by one, medics removed survivors from the plane and loaded them onto the basket. In a series of round trips, Rosie maneuvered the tower from the wing hatch to the ground and back again. Tony and

Zach helped carry the victims to waiting ambulances, where medics fitted cervical collars and wrapped them in blankets.

Satisfaction at saving lives mingled with anguish at the heart-wrenching scenes before them. The few survivors who'd regained semiconsciousness looked at their rescuers with agony, fright, and bewilderment. A man mumbled "Amanda" over and over, while a teen boy called for his mother. Others remained silent. After thirteen circuits between the aircraft and the ground, Rosie parked the basket at the wing hatch. It was clear that only the dead remained inside.

Five minutes later, Captain Schrum appeared and rounded up the crews from 10, 12, and 15. Iggy exited the plane and joined Tony, Steve, Robbie, Zach, and Nikki at the captain's side.

"Both crash scenes are under control and Chief Archer has assumed overall command at the unified command post in ops," Schrum explained. "Deputy Chief Martone is now the operations section chief, and he's appointed me the east division supervisor. Captain Hartman has the west division. Help is arriving from all over the region."

"A half hour too late, but just in time for the Sally Wagon," Nikki said, referring to the Salvation Army volunteers who provided coffee and snacks at the scene of major emergencies.

Schrum smiled, but the strain on his face was telling.

"Come with me. Someone wants to talk to you." Schrum walked them over to a small table where Deputy Chief Martone stood in conference with a group of mutual aid fire chiefs and EMS officials. He glanced over and held up a finger.

Tony imagined the worst. Had he blundered during the attack? He'd violated department procedures and people had died, but was that his fault? Would his crewmates face blame for *his* bad decisions?

Martone ended his discussion, walked over to the ragged A-platoon firefighters, and examined each weary face.

"As you know, we have numerous fatalities at this scene," Martone said as he pointed to the forward section of the aircraft.

Tony's spirit sagged.

"Not all of the details are in yet, but we also know that thirteen passengers have been brought out alive, in addition to those who self-evacuated from the aft section of the plane."

Tony eyed the DC.

"Thirteen souls who owe their lives to all of you. The captain tells me you fought your way through deep snow, a debris field littered with parts of the plane, and an enormous flame front. You knocked the fire down before it could penetrate the cabin. Then when flames erupted behind the plane, and with your water running out, you humped hose through thousands of gallons of jet fuel and did it again."

Tony's apprehension morphed into exhilaration.

"Either fire could have killed everyone on board, but the seven of you wouldn't let that happen.

"I can't imagine how close to the end you were, yet you didn't stop there. Somehow, you mustered the strength to force entry into a crushed fuselage and search for survivors. *Seven of you.* Incredible." The DC studied each face. "This event isn't over. We still have work to do, more lives to save. But you've done enough." He turned to the captain. "Pete, get your teams to rehab. They deserve a rest."

As the captain led them away, Martone pulled Tony aside. "I know what you did on Rescue-12, and on the hoseline. More than anyone, the survivors owe their lives to you."

Tony was cold, wet, tired, and stinking of fuel, but the emotion he felt left him speechless. People were *alive* because of his actions.

An air of solemnity pervaded the shuttle. Lives had been lost and the mood wasn't improved by the probability that the fatalities had occurred *prior* to their arrival, nor by the fact that none would have lived without their intervention.

Despite the mood, Tony took a moment to consider what seven individuals had accomplished under the worst possible conditions. Who would believe it?

His thoughts reached back to other jobs, other occupations. What he'd taken part in tonight as a firefighter was more meaningful than anything he'd done before. Nothing came close.

SIXTY-TWO

Monday, February 13 - 9:20 p.m

"Brenda, where's your cell phone?"

The woman gave Allie a blank look. "Wha?"

"Your cell, where is it?"

"In...my pocket?" She struggled for words. "Don't know."

"It's okay. I'll find it." Allie checked the pockets of Brenda's uniform jacket. The phone wasn't there. She searched the scattered remains of the galley. Nothing. Desperate, she climbed onto the overturned serving cart and reached for Monica's pockets, bumping into the lifeless girl's arms. She shuddered. It was no good; there was no phone to be found. She thought about making a dash up the hill for help, but could she leave Brenda?

She glanced at her watch. It had been an hour since she'd located the tail. It couldn't be much longer. Rescuers were bound to spot the trail and follow it over the hillside. With that hope in mind, she rewrapped the blanket around herself and used her remaining body heat to keep Brenda warm.

* * *

The airport shuttle deposited the exhausted firefighters at the level-2 staging area just outside the designated hot zone of the incident, where they entered a temporary rehab facility in a Greyhound motor coach. Red Cross volunteers wended their way through the aisle with water, hot coffee, and snacks.

Four A-Platoon firefighters from the western crash site were already aboard. Their clothes were dry and clean, without the smell of smoke or jet fuel. Danny Gardner tried to compare experiences, but no one from the eastern site spoke up.

Tony wasn't interested in talking. *I'm useless in here.* Ten minutes and half a cup of coffee later, he gathered his gear and went outside.

He pulled up his collar as he left the warmth of the bus. The snowfall had eased to flurries, but the wind continued to howl. Regional emergency services personnel and equipment from unfamiliar agencies crowded the staging area, awaiting the word to go in. Nikki was right: a half hour too late.

Two of the airport's inflatable medical tents abutted the hot zone. Tony squeezed between two ambulances and entered the one marked TRIAGE.

Six victims accounted for half the capacity of the uncomfortably warm tent. A paramedic holding a clipboard told him all the survivors from the aft section had cycled through already. Miraculously, the medical team counted only three fatalities. Eight others had suffered broken bones and lacerations serious enough to warrant immediate transport. The people currently occupying the beds suffered from cuts and bruises and were shaken up but otherwise uninjured. Tony asked about Allie, but the medic hadn't seen anyone matching her description.

Tony poked his head into the adjacent tent, labeled TREATMENT, but found a solitary EMT unloading medical supplies. The man explained that state police were en route with emergency physicians and nurses to provide prehospital care for the severely injured. Was Lisa responding with that group?

He exited the tent and made his way to the west division command post, where Lieutenant Wozniak intercepted him.

"Hey, Tony, you look like hell," Wozniak said.

"I'm okay, and I want to help."

"Thanks, but there's no one left to help. We assisted a few injured passengers off the plane, but the rest had self-evacuated by the time we got to the scene. Now get your butt to rehab."

Tony nodded and started for the bus, but when Wozniak began a tête-à-tête with a couple of EMS officials, he slipped away and caught his first close-up look at the aft section. Except for the amputation at the bulkhead, the fuselage displayed a remarkable lack of damage.

A line of yellow fire scene tape, set up on portable stanchions, delineated the border of the eastern hot zone. A mutual aid officer sat at the check-in table. The guy was on his phone, and while dozens of responders scurried about, Tony ducked under the flimsy barricade.

Volunteers from the region's many small boroughs and townships dotted the scene in a kaleidoscope of helmets and turnout gear. Tony spotted a group of firefighters from B and C platoons—probably those who lived closest to the airport. None of them had seen Allie.

Nothing could drag Allie away from this scene, but where was she? He recalled her initial radio reports and knew she'd been first to the crash site but in the last hour, no one had seen her.

He caught sight of Tyler Connolly. "Hey, Tyler, have you seen Allie? Did she go back to ops?"

Connolly laughed. "Allie? Are you kidding?"

"Yeah, that's what I thought."

"I've been running around, trying to arrange escorts for the medic wagons," Tyler said. "But Ops-2 is still parked where she left it when she got here. Hang on." He lifted his portable radio and tried to raise Allie, but there was no reply. "That's odd."

"It is," Tony said. "No one I've talked to has seen her."

"It's been pretty crazy, and maybe she's in a spot where she can't hear the radio," Tyler said. "I'll check around for her. Somebody must have seen her. She's probably at the command post."

"Okay, thanks," Tony said, not mentioning he'd just come from there. As he scanned the scene without success, his concern for her whereabouts grew. Where was she? She should be—would be—in the thick of it. He couldn't see any activity along the edge of the runway, at the far end of the cabin. He grabbed a LiteBox from a stand of tools and headed that way.

SIXTY-THREE

Monday, February 13 - 9:30 p.m

Allie waited another ten minutes, but no one came. The cold was numbing. Brenda was very pale and almost nonresponsive. Hypothermia was probably setting in, and maybe frostbite. She needed help now.

"Brenda. Hey, Brenda." The flight attendant's eyes displayed a dull, glassy sheen. "I'm going for help."

Brenda's face tightened into a look of dread. "No, don't leave me. Please. I can't stay here," she whispered. "Not with Monica..."

"Brenda, listen to me. I'll be right back with the medics. We'll get you to the hospital."

Brenda went silent, staring blankly at Allie.

"You'll be safe here. I won't be long." If she lingered, Brenda would die. She tucked her blanket around the flight attendant's upper body, grabbed the LiteBox, and got moving.

* * *

Three banks of spotlights—the type contractors used when doing nighttime airfield construction—lit the site. The smell of diesel fuel from their supplying generators brought Tony back to the horrific scene he'd just left. He shook it away. Light emanated from the fractured cabin's windows, projecting the false impression of an aircraft ready for takeoff. A small utility ladder and a trio of electrical cords stretched into the open fuselage. Maybe Allie was inside.

Knifelike shards of aluminum skin gave Tony pause, and as he climbed aboard the artificially lit cabin, he was struck by the dramatic contrast to the interior of the forward half of the fuselage. Although most of the overhead bins were hanging open, the seats were intact and the aisles were clear of luggage. No victims were visible. Passengers from this part of the plane didn't know how lucky they were.

The only people in the cabin—Rolphe Hoffman, who'd switched to C-platoon in January, and Shawn Iverson from B shift—confirmed that three passengers seated near the bulkhead had perished when the plane split apart. As far as the two firefighters knew, everyone else had self-evacuated.

"Don't move anything," Iverson said. "We're taking photos for the NTSB investigators."

"Got it. What about the tail?"

Iverson shrugged. "Probably down in the gully somewhere."

"No one checked?"

"Not sure. We've been pretty busy with the survivors up here." He shook his head. "If someone ended up down there, they're dead."

"Okay, I'm going to check the hillside." Tony followed the aisle to the open back end and jumped into the snow.

* * *

Threading her way through torn metal that had once connected the tail to the main cabin, Allie tromped up the steepest part of the slope. Once over the drop-off, she broke into a run, veering around the vertical stabilizer and passing a body in the overturned seats. In her peripheral vision, she spotted another figure sprawled on the ground. No time to stop.

The snow deepened as she closed with the runway, and she slowed to a trot and then a stumbling walk as the snowpack and her aching hip tried to keep her from her goal. She thought of Brenda. The flight attendant wouldn't last much longer. She shouted in frustration into the whistling wind. "Come on, Allie! You can do this!"

She called her strides, bringing the sum of her athleticism to bear on reaching the hilltop. "One-two, one-two, one-two…" She gulped air. "One-two, one-two…" The crest drew closer.

Allie reached deep within herself for a last burst of energy. "One-two, one-two, one-two, damn it!" The count became ragged and ceased altogether as she expended her last energy reserves. "Come on, Allie! Be strong!" She stumbled over the crest and fell to her knees.

A light shone from the runway. "Over here." She tried to shout, but her voice went hoarse. She swallowed, took a deep breath, and tried again. "Hey, over here! I need help!"

* * *

Tony trudged into the gap in the snowbank and followed a wide swath of compressed snow to the hillside, where he heard a low, ragged voice call out. His light caught a shape in the darkness. A survivor? The figure stumbled, fell to its knees, and called out again. A woman's voice. Could it be? "Allie!"

SIXTY-FOUR

Monday, February 13 - 9:40 p.m

Hampered by his cumbersome bunker gear, Tony broke into a clumsy sprint. When he reached Allie, she was gasping and struggling to speak.

"Tony, down the hill..." Panting, she pointed her light over the hillside. "Down there...the tail." She fought for breath. "A victim. Alive...down there."

He lifted her to her feet. "The tail?"

"Down there! She'll die." Allie's expression was desperate. "We've got to get her."

More voices. Hoffman and Iverson, standing at the edge of the runway. Tony waved them over. "Allie found the tail. It's over the hill, and there's a survivor in it. I'm going down there."

"I'll call for the medics," Hoffman said. "And we're coming with you."

Tony gave Allie the once-over. She was unhurt but clad only in a sweater and was shivering. He pulled off his bunker coat, eased her ice-cold arms into the sleeves, and zipped it up. "Stay put," he shouted as he, Hoffman and Iverson started for the hillside. Pausing at the crest, he turned and repeated his admonition. "Stay there, Allie. We'll get her."

They started down the hill, half walking, half sliding on the slick surface. A burst of activity came across Hoffman's portable; help was on the way.

"Holy shit. Look at that," Iverson said. The vertical stabilizer lay in the snow. Past it was an overturned row of seats. "I'll check it out."

Tony and Hoffman stopped at the edge of a steep declivity. Iverson came up beside them.

"There's a guy in those seats. He's dead."

Tony panned his light down the slope. It caught the top of the broken tail section.

"The damn thing's upside down," Hoffman said.

"You better wait here for the medics, Rolphe," Iverson said. "Give me your portable."

Tony dug his heels into the snow and grasped Iverson's arms for balance as the pair sidled their way down.

Tony spotted a nest of jagged metal protruding from the snow. "Watch out."

"Whoa," Iverson said. "It's a fucking minefield down there."

No, it was more like one of the booby traps made famous during the Vietnam War, lined with punji sticks.

A macabre scene met them as they picked their way around the razor-sharp projections and reached the tail. The body of a female flight attendant hung upside down from her jump seat in the wreckage of the inverted galley, while another had been wrapped in blankets.

"This one's gone," Iverson said, pulling away from the flight attendant in the jump seat.

Tony knelt beside the survivor. The woman teetered on the edge of unconsciousness, her face drained of color, her eyes glassy and unfocused. She wasn't pinned, but a quick examination revealed a contorted foot.

"We better not try to move her until more help arrives." He continued to survey the woman's injuries while Iverson updated the command post and reiterated the need for medics.

"Let's get her down," Tony said. He stood and positioned himself under the dead flight attendant while Iverson reached up and hit the button on her five-point harness. Sudden weight drove Tony to his knees as the body dropped into his arms. Iverson lifted her legs and the two firefighters moved the lifeless girl outside the tail section and laid her face up in the snow. Tony wished he had something to cover her with.

As they moved back to the survivor, Tony heard Allie's voice.

"Brenda! Her name is Brenda!"

Allie stood atop the drop-off. He wasn't surprised. Too stubborn to stay away.

"Don't try to move her," Allie shouted. "Her foot is broken!"

Tony processed the next seconds as if trapped in a surreal dreamscape. Allie lost her footing, tried to right herself, and plunged down the slope. He saw the surprise on her face, saw the jagged metal in her path, but was helpless to intervene.

* * *

It happened too fast for Allie to register fear. She dug her boot heels into the snow, but it was no use. She pitched forward as something tore into her right inner thigh. Then her head snapped back and slammed into the ground.

She opened her mouth to scream, but nothing came out.

The world spun wildly as she attempted to process the scene. Was she lying in the snow?

Her eyes came into fuzzy focus. She was cold, and yet very warm. She looked down at her legs. Bright red liquid on her pants, on the snow.

Heat shot up her thigh. "Oh no. Oh no. Oh no," she muttered through gritted teeth as agonizing pain swallowed her.

SIXTY-FIVE

Monday, February 13 - 9:50 p.m

Tony dropped to his knees and applied direct pressure as Allie lay face up in snow that was crimson from her leaking wound. He could feel the warped metal below her skin. God, it was deep.

"I'm here, Allie. It's Tony. We're taking care of you." His voice caught. "You're going to be okay."

She looked at him, but her eyes held no recognition.

Iverson cradled Allie's head as Tony struggled to staunch the flow from her lacerated leg.

Within minutes, the isolated scene transformed into a hotbed of activity as Hoffman returned with a squad of firefighters toting ropes, portable lights, and a twenty-four-foot extension ladder, which they anchored against the slope. EMS personnel joined them with a pair of Stokes baskets loaded with equipment.

Three medics replaced Tony at Allie's side, while two others entered the tail. He backed away, wiping his bloody hands on his shirt.

Brenda was strapped into a basket and carried to the hill, where firefighters hoisted the unconscious flight attendant up the ladder.

Tony watched as the medical team worked feverishly to stabilize Allie. They cut her pant leg away, injected her with morphine, and administered an IV.

Allie lay ashen and barely conscious. Her trauma dressings were soaked through with blood. She tried to speak, but Tony couldn't make out a word. His mind pleaded: *Don't you die on me, Allie Robinson.*

The medic in charge stood and caught sight of Tony. "Hey, I remember you." It was Teri, from the construction accident at the hangar. "Where's your coat, buddy? It's freezing."

Numb to the cold, he pointed to Allie, who still wore his bunker coat.

Teri nodded. "Was that you doing direct pressure? You saved her life."

Was her life saved? It didn't look that way.

"We found only one entry wound," Teri said. "But the metal might have pierced the femoral artery."

The femoral artery? Allie was hanging by a thread.

Teri radioed the medical tent, then looked to the medics astride Allie. "Let's apply a tourniquet to her upper thigh, just in case."

Five minutes later, firefighters escorted an emergency response physician down the ladder. After a brief consultation with the medics, she directed them to pull Allie's thigh from the shard, advising it was too dangerous to try to cut the metal and leave it in place for transport.

Tony's thoughts returned to that construction worker impaled on the rebar. *Damn it, Allie. Couldn't you have just waited?*

* * *

Shadows danced before Allie's eyes. Muffled voices, indistinct shouts. Why was everybody rushing around? A girl hovered over her. *Who's that?* A tall figure stood behind the girl. Was that Tony? Why did he have that look on his face?

Fire pricked her arm. A bee sting? People dissolved into hazy, ghostlike figures. She was so cold.

Allie had the sensation of rising from the ground. She had a final thought before blackness closed in. *Am I dying?*

* * *

With a paramedic ready to tighten the tourniquet at the first sign of an arterial bleed, the medical team carefully pulled Allie's body off the bloody aircraft skin. Tony marveled at how easily three inches of metal slid out of her thigh.

The doc examined the wound. "Blood flow hasn't increased. It missed the artery. She's lucky the tip wasn't twisted. Let's get her in the basket."

Allie's eyes were open but unfocused. Tony hoped it was an effect of the morphine.

Medics applied a fresh dressing to the now-open incision. The bandage turned red as they strapped Allie in place and Teri detached the IV. Tony and Iverson carried the Stokes to the base of the ladder and secured it with ropes and carabiners.

"We're ready! Pull her up!" Tony yelled.

Two firefighters at the tip hoisted the basket over the rungs while Tony held it in place between the rails. Teri followed.

As soon as she'd cleared the top rung, Teri reattached the IV and held it high. "Go," she said, and the four firefighters muscled Allie—sled dog style—toward the lights of the airfield.

A field maintenance pickup met them at the runway edge, where a wide opening had been cut through the snowbank. Teri jumped onto the bed while Tony and Zach lifted the Stokes aboard.

"Treatment tent. Go!" Teri told the driver.

Tony fell to one knee and tried to catch his breath; he had to get to her. Iverson caught up and helped him to his feet. Heads turned as he broke into a sloppy run in his bunker pants and boots. His physical training paid its final dividend of the night as he quickened his pace and arrived at the treatment tent as the basket was lifted onto a gurney. He rushed forward and grasped Allie's hand as she was wheeled inside, where they were met by…

"Lisa!"

Her eyes locked on Tony. A look of concern, mixed with understanding, crossed her features.

"I'll take her," Lisa said and wheeled the gurney past two

physicians and a nurse who were attending to a now fully conscious Brenda, the only other occupant of the tent. One of the doctors rushed to Allie's aid, and along with Lisa and Teri, they transferred her to a bed surrounded by surgical tools and monitoring equipment.

Tony stood back as Teri related the details of the laceration and the blow to the head. His heart sank at the sight of Allie under the harsh lights. So pale and unresponsive. "Please stay with us," he whispered.

The medical team evaluated Allie's injuries, administered a blood transfusion, and tried to warm her body. They wasted little time. Because the weather had grounded all medical helicopters, she was loaded into an advanced life support ambulance for the thirty-minute ride to Chambersburg Hospital.

While Tony watched it drive away, Lisa came up behind him and placed a hand on his shoulder. "It'll take a while, but she'll be all right."

Tony turned to the woman with whom he'd shared so much over the past sixteen years.

"Thanks, Leese." He paused. "But what about you?"

Lisa gave him a long, considering gaze. "I'll be fine…and so will you."

Epilogue

Federal and state officials descended on Reynolds International in the days following the crash. State police cordoned off runway six-right, twenty-four-left, while the FBI opened a wide-ranging criminal investigation. Concurrently, National Transportation Safety Board inspectors undertook a detailed analysis of the accident, while the FAA sent a team to interview the air traffic controllers on duty the night of February 13.

The airport's field maintenance crews, on extended overtime and supplemented by seasonal help, cleared the ramps, taxiways, and the two usable runways. With the NTSB's permission, Choice Jet personnel extracted the stuck E190 from the snow and towed it to Hangar-3. The airport reopened at eight p.m. on February 14 with unrestricted operations on two runways: six-left/twenty-four-right, and eighteen-thirty-six.

South central Pennsylvania thawed in early March as a warming trend signaled the coming of spring. Once the NTSB concluded their examination of the three fuselage sections and the debris field, the scattered parts were moved to a vacant Air National Guard hangar for reconstruction and further study. The southern runway remained closed until April 3, when repairs to its surface and adjacent safety area were completed.

* * *

Thirty-five souls perished in the crash, including three who succumbed to their injuries in the following weeks. Seventy-one passengers and crew survived—flight attendant Brenda Morgan included.

Following a coordinated investigation, the FBI, NTSB, and FAA issued a joint statement on April 9 in which they cleared the Leisure Air flight crew and REY's air traffic controllers of culpability or contributory negligence. Citing the friction test readings prior to the crash, the panel also exonerated the operations and field maintenance departments and lauded their efforts to prepare the runway for landing. Contributing factors included poor visibility and the inoperable ASDE system.

The NTSB cited the sturdiness of the airframe as one of two key factors in the high survival figure. Fast and effective action by emergency responders were the other factors.

The FBI ruled out terrorism, listing the primary cause as criminal sabotage committed by Frank Barlow, whose crushed body was discovered under the mangled dump truck. FBI agents concluded Barlow acted alone, his motive listed as revenge for his recent suspension and firing. Since he did not leave a note or discuss his intentions with his brother or coworkers, the question of whether he intended to cause a disaster or merely disrupt air traffic remained unanswered. Conspiracy theorists screamed cover-up as they circulated outlandish and contradictory theories across various social media platforms. Frank's remains, released by the FBI in March, were buried in the family plot, with his brother and a pastor in attendance.

Chief Archer and his ARFF team were commended for exemplary efforts under extreme conditions and with limited manpower. But airport officials did not escape criticism. Management was singled out for inadequate perimeter security and failing to account for airport vehicles.

Since a disgruntled employee had defeated airport security by stealing a truck and driving it through two fences, Sterling Price became a target of withering criticism. Yet in a decision that provoked public outcry, the airport authority board absolved him of responsibility. The flawless performance of airport employees during the emergency helped bolster the case that Mr. Price was an effective leader who'd developed a top-notch team. That, along with a heartfelt mea culpa and a detailed plan to tackle the airport's employee relations and security issues, saved the CEO's job.

Meanwhile, despite the actions of her employees, Sharon Lambert was demoted and reassigned as an operations specialist. She resigned in the face of the indignity, and a nationwide search got underway to find her replacement.

* * *

Tony struggled with his emotions following the disintegration of his marriage. Lisa, recognizing his distress and ever compassionate, invited him to move into the guest room while they planned their next moves. For three weeks, they communicated with one another openly by sharing long suppressed feelings and allowing themselves to come to terms with the end of their relationship. In many ways, they became closer than they'd ever been.

Lisa received her formal acceptance into the Master of Nursing program at Penn State and began a full-time supervisory position at the Mount Nittany Medical Center.

Preparing to part ways, the couple agreed to sublet the townhouse and divide their furniture and savings. On a cold and rainy Saturday in late March, Tony, Robbie, Nikki, and Lieutenant Wozniak loaded the living room and guest bedroom sets into a U-Haul and moved Lisa to a small one-bedroom apartment in State College. In April, she filed for divorce. Tony knew it was coming, but when the petition arrived, he sobbed like he hadn't since his grandfather died.

Evan's condition improved steadily, and after three weeks in the hospital and another four in a rehabilitation center, he returned home. Tony visited the family often, and Shannon teased him over his hapless attempts to amuse her kids. Evan was determined to make a full recovery, and while a long and difficult course of physical therapy lay ahead, Tony knew his indomitable friend would return to work one day.

Allie's injuries challenged her fiery spirit. The laceration healed quickly, but she suffered extensive nerve damage to her right leg, which left her in constant discomfort and forced her to walk with a cane. With therapy, the symptoms of her concussion faded, but her equilibrium was sometimes unpredictable and her vision occasionally blurred.

While Allie convalesced, her mom took up residence in the apartment and immediately hit it off with Tony. They passed the days by playing Monopoly, Scrabble, Trivial Pursuit, and Risk—Mrs. Robinson was a ruthless strategist—and streamed classic movies. Once the weather improved, Tony cajoled a reluctant Allie out for walks to improve her stamina, but they were both haunted by thoughts of the horrific things they'd seen at the crash site.

A retired high school counselor, Allie's mom encouraged the two introspective people to talk about their experiences on that cold February night. Combined with cognitive behavioral therapy for post-traumatic stress, those discussions did much to heal their psychological wounds.

Allie kept her hand in the affairs of the operations department by attending staff meetings via video conference. At the urging of Tony, Ellis Kim, Captain Schrum, and several of the ops specialists, she threw her hat in the ring for her old boss's position. She sailed through the online interview process, and with her exemplary record of leadership and innovation as a supervisor, the accolades she received for her selfless acts on February 13, and the endorsements of her coworkers, she was promoted to director of operations.

Allie started her new position on May 8, her first visit to the airport since the crash. She was greeted by the CEO and his senior management team, the entire ops staff, and authority employees from every department. Tony, Robbie, Captain Schrum, all three chiefs, and a host of firefighters were also there to welcome her back.

* * *

The events of February 13 completed Tony's transition from indifferent employee to fully committed firefighter. For a man who had taken a civil service exam on a whim, he now reveled in his work. Fifteen years after earning his undergraduate degree, Tony had finally found his niche. His professional life had evolved from a series of job-hopping misadventures to a stable career that gave him an immense sense of pride and satisfaction.

On April 10, he and his seven academy classmates became full-fledged firefighters, their probationary period completed. Tony had won the respect of his colleagues.

Would he complete a career at Reynolds International Airport? He doubted it. He was still too restless, and his sights were set on bigger opportunities in the public safety arena. But he was content to concentrate on firefighting and let the future take care of itself. His personal life was not so settled.

On a warm evening in mid-May, with the turmoil behind them, Tony and Allie toasted their success at a Mexican restaurant in Harrisburg. They spoke of the events of the past months and marveled at how their careers and personal situations had evolved so dramatically. Neither of them had yet tried to press their relationship further. They needed time: Tony to process his affection for Lisa, Allie to deal with the effects of her lingering injuries, and both to work through their PTSD from the crash.

After dinner, they strolled along the Susquehanna River. "You know," Tony said as he watched Allie hobble, "there's no way you're going to keep up with me on a trail run, but don't worry; I'll just circle back for you if I get too far ahead."

"You just wait, smart-ass. Once I ditch this cane, I'll be faster than ever, and then we'll see who doubles back."

Tony broke into a wide grin and put his arm around her. "Nothing would make me happier."

Acknowledgments

I wrote *Out of the Fire* to entertain while providing a glimpse into the seldom seen world of airport firefighters and operations personnel. This book is the culmination of two years of planning, plotting, researching, writing, editing, revising, and re-editing. It's been a labor of love, and I've had the help of some amazing people, to whom I am very grateful.

First of all, to my wife Karen, who read my rough drafts, encouraged me, steered me through my doubts, offered invaluable advice, and put up with my up and down "writer's moods." I couldn't have done it without her.

I've worked with many top-notch professionals during my career, and several contributed their time and expertise to make sure I got the details right. These include Tim Holmes, Brad Kaiser, Shawn O'Brien, and Steve Wehrspann. These guys, long-time friends and tremendous fire service leaders, helped me recall what I'd forgotten and kept me abreast of current developments in the field. Jeff Miller, another great friend and a consummate aviation professional, assisted me with the technical aspects of airport operations and double checked the accuracy of my descriptions of FAA procedures.

Finding professional help can be a confusing process for a debut author, and I've been fortunate in this regard. My incredible editor, Susan Helene Gottfried of West of Mars Services, guided me through my first major edit, helped me tighten the manuscript, and elevated the quality of my writing. My cover designer, Jerry Todd of TWL Studios, captured my vision and my promise to the reader, perfectly. I can't wait to work with Susan and Jerry on the next one!

Beta readers can be a great asset to debut authors, *if* they tell you the truth. Special thanks goes to Cheryl Isaac, Tim Holmes, and my friends at Pennwriters, especially Sharon Wenger and Tom Joyce. They volunteered their time to read and comment on a 96,400 word novel. Many of their suggestions have been incorporated into this book.

Finally, I'd like to express my high regard for the dedicated airport professionals everywhere, especially the first responders, operations personnel, and maintenance workers. Without much fanfare, they work tirelessly to keep the traveling public safe and secure at airports around the world. I hope that in some small way, this book brings the story of their seldom seen but invaluable services to light.

Author's Note

In the post 9/11 era, airport security is quite a bit tighter than I've described. This novel is fiction, and for purposes of the story, I allowed the character Frank Barlow to penetrate the security perimeter without much trouble, and with a huge dump truck! Lest anyone get the idea that this is the norm at US airports, think again.

About the Author

B.A. Colella, PhD, is a lifelong resident of Western Pennsylvania. He blends his extensive background in aviation and firefighting to craft *Out of the Fire,* a fast-paced, high-stakes tale of personal and professional adversity and determination in an airport setting.

An avid runner, military history buff, amateur photographer, classic rock fan, and 1970s Chevy Camaro enthusiast, he enjoys visiting Pittsburgh's many parks, coffee shops, libraries, and bookstores with his wife, Karen.

Please note: An in-depth author biography is available at bacolella.com.

www.ingramcontent.com/pod-product-compliance
Lightning Source LLC
Chambersburg PA
CBHW020605310726
48979CB00008B/1359/J
9798987755020